D1433834

# PANDORA

# PANDORA

*Written by*

## SUSAN STOKES-CHAPMAN

*A Novel in* **THREE PARTS**

*LONDON:*

Printed for Harvill Secker:

An Imprint of VINTAGE BOOKS, *One Embassy Gardens*

MM.XXII.

HARVILL
*Secker*

1 3 5 7 9 10 8 6 4 2

Harvill Secker, an imprint of Vintage, is part of the Penguin Random House group of companies whose addresses can be found at global.penguinrandomhouse.com

Penguin
Random House
UK

Copyright © Retter Enterprises Limited 2022

Susan Stokes-Chapman has asserted her right to be identified as the author of this Work in accordance with the Copyright, Designs and Patents Act 1988

First published by Harvill Secker in 2022

A CIP catalogue record for this book is available from the British Library

penguin.co.uk/vintage

ISBN 9781787302884 (hardback)
ISBN 9781787302891 (trade paperback)

Typeset in 11.25/16.5pt Bodoni Std by Jouve (UK), Milton Keynes
Printed and bound in Great Britain by Clays Ltd, Elcograf S.p.A.

The authorised representative in the EEA is Penguin Random House Ireland, Morrison Chambers, 32 Nassau Street, Dublin DO2 YH68

Illustrations: magpie © Bridgeman Images; decoration ©Bridgeman Images; Greek vase © Getty Images

Penguin Random House is committed to a sustainable future for our business, our readers and our planet. This book is made from Forest Stewardship Council® certified paper.

FSC
www.fsc.org

MIX
Paper from
responsible sources
FSC® C018179

But he that once embarks, too surely finds
A sullen Sky, black Storms, and angry Winds.
Cares, Fears, and Anguish, hov'ring on the Coast,
And Wrecks of Wretches by their Folly lost.

SAMUEL GARTH

Dedication to Richard, Earl of Burlington
in translated edition of Ovid's *Art of Love* (1709)

Samson, The Scilly Isles
December 1798

He had not allowed for the weight. The cold he anticipated, the water's sluggish buoyancy, this too he considered. The darkness? The lantern does well enough, and his memory allows for shortfalls in sight. But the weight . . . this is something else altogether.

The lantern itself is manageable. It is bound to his wrist with thick twine, affording movement in both hands, but it pulls down uncomfortably on his arm and the salt water stings where the twine has already rubbed the skin. The ropes looped under each armpit – one for the salvage, one to raise him again – are cumbersome, but they help balance his body as he descends. The sinking weights, too, although bulky, can be endured.

The problem is the harness. Strong tin plate. Domed and airy around his head, further down it constricts his torso like an unforgiving corset. On deck it did not feel so heavy. Below the surface, however, the restrictive leather suit, the iron hoop skeleton that pinches meanly, together with the pressure of water and the winter currents . . . He will demand more money once the job is done.

Luck has been with him so far this night. The sky's inky cradle is starred, the moon full and fat. During the storm he took careful note of his surroundings – the ship finally succumbed on the shoals of two small islands separated by an isthmus, their inlands pitted with stone

1

ruins. In the moonlight these ruins shone white, a beacon for their small sailboat, and despite the December squalls the ship's starboard beam end is still visible above the waves. No, the wreck was not difficult to find.

So why is it he feels he has been led here?

Thankfully the ship rests in the shallows. He has not used this apparatus before and will not venture any deeper than he must. Twenty feet below the surface. No danger there, he tells himself. And he knows exactly where to look. Under careful instruction the object he seeks was safely hidden within the starboard bow, away from the other shipments tightly packed in the hold, but the ship broke apart in the storm; he hopes his luck stays true, that the crate has not strayed too far along the seabed, that no one else has managed to retrieve it.

The icy water needles his legs and arms. Cocooned in the heavy suit he descends further, breathing with effort, tasting the sharp taint of metal. The air pipes leading from the harness to the surface are long, and he imagines them stretching behind him like a hangman's rope. He holds the lantern in front of his body, looks through the eyeglass of the harness dome, relieved to see the shadow of the ship's ribs. Down he goes, then, searching, squinting into the murk. He thinks he hears a sound below him, something low and plaintive. He tilts his head, feels his ears pop, continues on.

His feet land. Beneath them, shifting grit. He angles his head and tries to look down. But carefully. Too sudden a movement, he was warned, and the water will seep through the harness. Slowly, yes, slowly. There. The corner of something. Using the ball of his foot he pushes himself off, back into the current. Then he sinks again, making contact with the seabed, raising the lantern to eye level. Six feet or so from the ship's remains he just makes out the dark corners of a crate. The blood pulses loudly in his ears. This is it, he is sure. He

2

edges slowly forward, puts one leg in front of him, then another, his feet dragging through the water. He jumps as something brushes against his shins, and lowering the lantern he watches seaweed dance around his calves.

The crate balances precariously on a large rock. He inches closer, raises the lantern again. The X he painted on its side when the ship left Palermo is clear, even in this deep aquatic dark. For a moment he marvels at how easy all this has been but then the lantern flickers and dips before flaring once again, and he knows that now is not the time to dawdle.

Releasing the twine from his wrist, he places the lantern between two hunks of wreckage so it will not turn up in the current, then unhooks one of the ropes from his arms and begins the painstaking task of securing the crate. He must be careful – there is no room for error – and the rock is a blessing it seems, for without it he would have struggled to lift the crate from the seabed at all. As he works small fish dash and dart about him. At one point he stops, strains to hear within the tin plates of the harness. Is that singing? No, it is the water sickness, it must be. Was he not told that staying under too long can be deadly?

*But so soon?*

He works fast now, as fast as he is able with the harness weighing him down. He wraps the rope around the crate four times and though his fingers are stiff with cold, he ties knots so tight the rope will need cutting free. When he is satisfied he pulls sharply on it – once, twice – signalling to the surface. The length jumps, slackens, becomes taut. Then, triumphant, he watches the crate ascend in a cloud of billowing sand. He hears the muffled groan of wood, the sluggish surge of stirring water and, so quietly he believes he has imagined it, the soft, haunting, almost-whisper of a woman, sighing.

3

London
January 1799

# PART I.

The mind is its own place, and in itself
Can make a Heaven of Hell, a Hell of Heaven.

JOHN MILTON
*Paradise Lost* (1667)

# CHAPTER ONE

Dora Blake has been hunched over her desk since dawn. The stool she sits on is too tall but she has become accustomed to its awkward height. Every now and then she lays down her pliers, removes her spectacles and pinches the bridge of her nose. Often she kneads the knots in her neck, stretches her back until she feels the pleasant crack of spine.

The attic room is north-facing and offers little light. In frustration Dora has moved her desk and stool beneath the small window for this is intricate work, and her lone candle is not fit for purpose. She shifts uncomfortably on the hard seat, replaces her spectacles and applies herself once more, doing her best to ignore the cold. The window is open at its widest, despite the New Year chill. Any moment she expects Hermes to return with a new treasure, something to crown this latest creation of hers, and she has opened his cage door in readiness, the remains of her stolen breakfast scattered beneath the perch to reward what she hopes will be a fruitful morning's hunt.

She sucks her bottom lip between her teeth, angles the pliers against her thumb.

To replicate cannetille was ambitious of her but Dora is, if anything, an optimist. Some might call this optimism mere wilfulness, but she feels her ambition is justified. She knows – *knows* – she has a talent. She is positively convinced it will be recognised one day, that her designs will be worn all across the city. Perhaps, Dora muses, the corner of her mouth twitching as she eases a particularly tiny wire into place, across Europe. But then she shakes her head, tries to pluck her lofty dreams from the woodwormed beams above her and concentrate. It will not do to be distracted and ruin hours of work at the last hurdle.

Dora cuts another piece of wire from the roll hooked over a nail on the wall.

The beauty of cannetille is that it imitates fine lace. She has seen parure sets on display in Rundell & Bridge and marvelled at their intricate designs; a necklace, earrings, bracelet, brooch and tiara would have been the work of months. Briefly Dora had contemplated creating the matching pair of earrings from her sketch, but grudgingly admitted her time was better spent elsewhere. This necklace is only an example after all, a means to demonstrate her skill.

'There!' she exclaims, snipping the excess wire with a pair of fine-handled clippers. The clasp has been bothering her all morning for it proved damnably fiddly but now it is done, worth the dark early start, the strain of back, the numbness of buttock. She lays down the cutters, blows into her hands and rubs them hard together, just as a flurry of black and white descends from the rooftops with a furtive caw.

Dora sits back and smiles.

'Good morning, my heart.'

The magpie sails through the window, lands softly on the bed. Around the bird's neck swings the small leather pouch she has sewn for him. Hermes' neck is bowed – there is weight to it.

He has found something.

'Come then,' Dora says, closing the window tight against the winter chill. 'Show me what you've scurried up.'

Hermes chirps, dips his head. The pouch strap slackens and the bird patters back, shaking his beak free. The pouch sags and Dora reaches for it, excitedly tips the contents on the worn coverlet.

A broken piece of earthenware, a metal bead, a steel pin. She can use all of these for something or other; Hermes never disappoints. But her attention is drawn to another item on the bed. She picks it up, raises it to the light.

'*Ach nai*,' Dora breathes. 'Yes, Hermes. It is perfect.'

Between her fingers she holds a flat oval pebble, made of glass, the size of a small egg. Against the grey of the city's skyline it shines a pale, almost milky blue. In cannetille designs amethysts are the preferred stone; the rich purple hue glints brightly against the gold, enhancing the intensity of the yellow. But it is aquamarine that Dora likes best. It reminds her of Mediterranean skies, the warmth of childhood. This smooth piece of glass will do just nicely. She closes her hand around it, feels its soft surface cool against her palm. She gestures to the magpie. With a blink of his black eye he hops onto her fist.

'I think that deserves a nice breakfast, don't you?'

Dora guides him into his cage. His beak scrapes against the wooden base as he scrabbles at the crusts of bread she left for him earlier. Gently she strokes his silken feathers, admires their rainbow sheen.

'There, my treasure,' she croons. 'You must be tired. Is that not better?'

Engrossed now in his meal Hermes ignores her, and Dora returns to her desk. She looks down at the necklace, contemplates her handiwork.

She is, she must confess, not entirely satisfied. Her design, so beautifully imagined on paper, is a poor show realised. What should be tendrils of coiled gold is merely dull grey wire twisted into miniature loops. What would have been shining seed pearls are instead roughly hewn shards of broken porcelain.

But Dora never expected it to match her drawing. She lacks the right tools and materials, the correct training. It is, however, a start; proof that there is beauty to her work, for despite the crude materials there is an elegance to the shapes she has wrought. No, Dora is not satisfied, but she is pleased. She hopes it will do. Surely with this pebble as a centrepiece . . .

There is a bang, the jangle of a distant bell.

'Dora!'

The voice that calls up from three storeys below is hard, sharp, impatient. Hermes chirps irritably in his cage.

'Dora,' the voice barks again. 'Come down and manage the shop. I've urgent business at the dock.'

The statement is followed by the dull thud of a door closing, another one, far off. Then, silence.

Dora sighs, covers the necklace with a piece of linen, places her spectacles down alongside it. She will have to add the glass pebble later, when her uncle has retired to bed. With regret Dora props it against the candlestick where it wobbles briefly before falling still.

Hezekiah Blake's Emporium for Exotic Antiquities stands out against the coffee-house and haberdasher's it sits between. Its window is large and bowed, obtrusive to passers-by who often find themselves compelled to stop due to its sheer size. But the street is where many of these passers-by stay – nowadays few linger when they realise the window with its peeling frame has nothing more exotic in it than an armoire from the last century and a landscape painting reminiscent of Gainsborough. Once a booming establishment it now houses only forgeries and dust-furred curiosities that hold no real appeal for the public, let alone a discerning collector. Why her uncle felt the need to call Dora downstairs is beyond her; she may well pass this morning without seeing a single customer.

In her father's day, business was brisk. She might have only been a child during those golden years but she remembers the kind of clientele that Blake's entertained. Viscounts would flock to Ludgate Street to request their Berkeley Square townhouses be decorated in a manner that recalled the beauties of the Grand Tour. Men successful in their trade might commission a centrepiece for their shop. Private collectors would pay handsomely for her father Elijah and his wife to excavate ruins overseas. But now?

Dora closes behind her the door that separates the living quarters from the shop floor. The bell tinkles a cheerful greeting as the door slides back into its casement but she remains tight-lipped in the face of it. If it is not Lottie Norris keeping a beady eye on her then the dratted bell Hezekiah installed does well enough to curtail her comings and goings.

Tucking her shawl tight around her shoulders Dora comes full onto the shop floor. It is crammed with furniture, ugly items arranged haphazardly against one another, and bookcases filled to the brim with volumes that do not look a day over ten years old. Hefty sideboards stand side by side, cluttered with mediocre trinkets spread over their unwaxed surfaces. Yet despite the disorder there is always a wide path that winds its way between the wares, for at the far end of the shop are the large doors that lead down to the basement beneath.

Hezekiah's private sanctuary.

The basement had once been her parents' domain – their office, the place where they mapped excavations and restored broken stock. But when Hezekiah moved from his tiny set of rooms in Soho to take over the living he overhauled it completely, erased all trace of her mother and father until only Dora's fleeting memories of them

13

remained. Nothing in Blake's Emporium is what it once was; the business has dwindled, its reputation along with it.

Dora flips over a new page of the ledger (only two entries yesterday) and scrawls the date in its margin.

They do make sales. Over the course of the month money drips slowly but steadily in, like the water from their leaking roof. But each sale is based on lies, on showmanship. Hezekiah attaches all sorts of fantastical histories to his objects. A wooden chest was the means by which a slaver transported two children from the Americas in 1504 (made only the week before by a Deptford carpenter); a pair of ornate candlesticks belonged at one time to Thomas Culpeper (served up by a blacksmith in Cheapside). Once, Hezekiah sold a brothel keeper a green velvet sopha he claimed was owned by a French count during the Thirty Years' War, salvaged when his 'most glorious' *château* burnt to the ground (the count was in fact a desperate widow who sold it to Hezekiah for three guineas to go toward paying her husband's debts). He even furnished the upper rooms of a molly house with six Japanese screens from the Heian period (painted himself in the basement below). If his customers cared to question the authenticity of these items, Hezekiah would have felt the cold hard floor of the Old Bailey beneath his knees long before now. But they do not question. The calibre of them, their appreciation of fine art and antiquities, is distinctly lacking.

Forgeries, Dora has discovered over the years, are not unheard of in antiquity circles. Indeed, many with money to spare commission copies of items they have seen in the British Museum or have admired abroad. But Hezekiah . . . Hezekiah does not admit to his deceit, and there is where the danger lies. Dora knows what the punishment is for such trickery – a heavy fine, a turn on the pillory, months in prison. Her stomach twists sickly at the thought. She could have reported Hezekiah, of course, but she depends on him – her uncle, the shop, they are all she has – and until she can make her own way in the world Dora must stay, must watch the business sink year by year, watch the Blake name become worthless, forgotten.

Not all of the stock is counterfeit, she concedes. The trinkets Hezekiah has accumulated over the years (and from which she sneaks supplies every now and then) make for a small and steady income – glass buttons, clay pipes, tiny moths suspended in blown glass, toy soldiers, china teacups, painted miniatures . . . Dora looks down once more at the ledger. Yes, they make sales. But the money that comes in is just enough to pay Lottie's wage and feed them all, though where Hezekiah finds the coin to fund his little vanities Dora does not know, and nor does she wish to. It is enough that he has sullied the living her father left behind. It is enough that the building falls to ruin, that there is precious little left to pay for the repairs. If the place belonged to her—Dora shakes the melancholy thought from her head, trails a fingertip along the counter, lip curling when it comes up black. Does Lottie never clean?

As if on cue, the bell tinkles again and Dora turns to find the older woman poking her face through the crack in the door.

'You're up, missum. Are you having breakfast? Or have you already helped yourself?'

Dora eyes Hezekiah's housekeeper – a stocky soft-mouthed woman with small eyes and straw-coloured hair – with scorn. Outwardly she looks as though she would fit the role perfectly, but Lottie Norris is as far from excelling in the domestic realm as Dora's uncle is from mastering athleticism. No indeed, Lottie is in Dora's opinion altogether too lazy, too opinionated and, like tar on a gull's wing, noxious, hard to remove, and wily with it.

'I'm not hungry.'

But Dora *is* hungry. The bread was consumed over three hours ago, yet she knows that if she asks for more Lottie will make a point of mentioning to Hezekiah that she has been stealing from the larder and Dora has no patience for his hypocritical lectures.

The housekeeper steps into the shop, looks at her with eyebrows raised.

'Not hungry? You hardly ate a thing at dinner last night.'

Dora ignores this, instead raises her finger to show the black.

'Shouldn't you be cleaning?'

Lottie frowns. 'In here?'

'Where else do you suppose I mean?'

The housekeeper scoffs, swings a stout arm through the air like a fan. 'It's a shop for antiquities, isn't it? They're meant to be dusty. That's the charm.'

Dora turns her face away, purses her lips at Lottie's tone. Always she has treated Dora like this, as if she were nothing more than a servant herself and not, in fact, the daughter of two reputable antiquarians and the niece of the current proprietor. Behind the counter Dora straightens the ledger, begins to sharpen the pencil to a fine point, biting down the bitter words on her tongue; Lottie Norris is not worth the breath it would take to scold her, nor would it do any good if she did.

'You sure you want nothing?'

'I'm sure,' Dora says shortly.

'Please yourself.'

The door begins to close. Dora lowers the pencil.

'Lottie?' The door stops. 'What was so important at the dock that Uncle had me mind the shop?'

The housekeeper hesitates, scrunches her stub nose. 'How'm I to know?' she says, but as the door swings shut behind her, infernal bell tinkling, Dora thinks Lottie knows very well.

16

# CHAPTER TWO

Creed Lane teems like maggots in an open sore.

The traffic seems to have spilled over from the heaving maw of Ludgate Street, flooding into side streets with the ferocity of a burst riverbank. The smells so unique to the city seem more pungent in such close quarters – soot and rotten vegetables, fish on the turn. He keeps a handkerchief clasped firmly to his mouth and nose. When he finally emerges onto the quieter slope of Puddle Dock Hill, Hezekiah Blake breaks into the fastest walk his corpulent body can manage.

The letter – crumpled now from excessive reading – arrived over two weeks ago, and while he anticipated the time it takes to travel such a distance he expected the Coombes to arrive long before now; Hezekiah's patience wears dangerously thin.

Slowing, he lowers his handkerchief and tries to catch his breath. His inclination to idleness is apparent from his squat build, though at fifty-two he sees this as quite, quite ordinary, for a man so long in trade like himself must surely be expected to enjoy the fruits of his labours. Hezekiah tugs at his wig, tweaks the lip of his newest hat, smooths a hand down the muslin waistcoat stretched tight across his rounded belly. Indeed, he is sorry not to be more at liberty to indulge – the luxuries that could be his! – but soon, he thinks with a smile, soon he will be free to indulge all he likes. He has waited in long sufferance these past twelve years. Very soon, his wait will be over.

As he approaches Puddle Dock, Hezekiah lifts his handkerchief once more. He uses this particular wharf for all his more questionable transactions. Here the stench of filth is at its most pungent. Primarily a laystall for the soils of London's streets, shipments here are unlikely to be monitored. He is thankful that this particular transaction will be conducted in the depths of deepest winter for in the summer months the fumes of shit steam and rise, sinking into everything they touch: nostril hair and eyelashes, the very clothes on his back, shipments large and small. The last thing he wants is for this most precious item to be tainted with the stench. No, he thinks, that would not do at all.

This dock is small and narrow as docks go, enclosed between two towering buildings with boarded-up windows. Hezekiah must press his back to the grimy walls to get past the bustle of dockers, tries unsuccessfully to ignore the night-soil men emptying their carts of excrement, the unappealing slop and smack of brim-filled buckets hitting the cobbles. His heel skids on something slick (Hezekiah refuses to entertain the thought of what it might be) and he barrels into the back of a Chinaman holding a bucket, its filthy contents threatening to spill over at the collide. As he reaches out a hand to steady himself against the wall Hezekiah stares, affronted, but there is no apology, no sign the man has even registered his presence at all and he has moved along before Hezekiah can press the matter. Eyes watering he breathes deeply into cotton, continues unsteadily down the sloping ramp to the river's edge.

The foreman, directing the night slop on the barges to be taken downriver, has his back to Hezekiah, and the older man must call out across the racket to be heard.

'Mr Tibb, if you please! Mr Tibb!'

18

Jonas Tibb half-turns his head to see who calls for him then looks back to the barges, and with a gesticulation toward the river says something Hezekiah cannot hear. The foreman turns fully then, makes his way up the dock steps, onto the sloping bank where Hezekiah impatiently waits.

'Again, Mr Blake?' Tibb hooks filthy thumbs over the waistband of his trousers, glances back across to the river. The weather – while cold – has remained dry and bright; the water is as still as a duck pond, smooth as glass. 'I told you yesterday there had been no sign. That's changed none since the sun has set and risen.'

Hezekiah's shoulders slump. He feels the stirring of annoyance in his belly, the harsh punch of renewed disappointment. Seeing his face Tibb sighs, removes his woollen cap, rubs at his bald head.

'Sir, you already said your men won't be taking the quicker route by road. It's nearly five hundred miles from Samson and with winter tides you can always expect a day or two delay. Why must you keep coming here when I've told you I'll send word?'

Usually Hezekiah would not stand for such talk. He is a reputable tradesman after all and this man would ordinarily be beneath his notice, but Jonas Tibb has never once questioned why Hezekiah wishes to conduct his business in such a way and the foreman's discretion has always been unwavering.

'Hell's teeth, Tibb. You have no notion of its import. I paid good money to claim this shipment.'

Money, he thinks now with unease, he could ill afford.

Tibb lifts his shoulders in what seems to be the beginnings of a shrug before he appears to think better of it. His watery grey eyes crinkle in a half-smile.

'I'm sure the Coombes won't be letting you down. They never have, have they?'

Hezekiah brightens. 'No, no indeed, they have not.'

Tibb nods curtly, replaces his hat, and Hezekiah grunts now, annoyed with himself for displaying weakness in front of a lowborn.

'Well, then,' he says. 'I shall look forward to hearing from you in due course. I expect a note delivered as soon as you see his boat coming in, do you understand?'

'Aye, sir.'

'Very good.'

And so Hezekiah – handkerchief once more *in situ* – makes the distasteful journey back up to Puddle Dock Hill, through the cramped cesspit of Creed Lane and onto the crowded bustle of Ludgate Street, but his mind is all a muddle, his temper most aggrieved, despite the foreman's words.

Where *are* they? Where is his shipment, his most longed-for prize? Perhaps something has happened – an ambush, or perhaps the Coombes have run off with it – or – and here Hezekiah barks a laugh that causes a milkmaid to look at him oddly and tip her yoke – it has *sunk*! No, the thought is too awful, too ironically funny to consider. Quick, he thinks, quick! He must have something to ease his turmoil.

Hezekiah's attention is now drawn to shop windows, eyes darting like billiard balls at the break. A new snuffbox? No, he already has two. Another wig? He touches the fine coil at his ear, the silkiness of carefully chosen human hair. Mayhap not, this one was expensive enough. A cravat pin, perhaps? But then his eyes alight on something else and he smiles, feels the familiar surge of *want*, the satisfaction of knowing an item is meant so perfectly for him. He enters the shop and, credit given, the purchase is done in moments.

Back on the street he pats his chest, palm pressing on the small package which sits comfortably within the inner pocket of his great-coat, and smiling widely Hezekiah adjusts his hat, continues on.

20

# CHAPTER THREE

Dinner is a painful affair. Unlike the rest of the house the small dining room with its rich maroon wallpaper and merry fire is cosy and warm, and would be quite an agreeable little place to sit if she were in different company. But Dora and Hezekiah have never been much for pleasant conversation, especially in recent weeks. Christmas passed without any amusement to be taken from it for Hezekiah's humour was dark and mutinous, which made the experience altogether rather trying. That humour continued – unprecedented, it seemed – into the new year, and Dora has been making every effort to avoid his sharp tongue, the irritation that seems to seep from him like Thames fog. Dora curls her fingers round her napkin. She would much rather pass the evening in her damp and draughty bedroom fixing the glass pebble to her necklace with only Hermes for company. Indeed, she has far more rewarding discussions with him than anyone else, and he only a bird.

Thoughtfully Dora watches her uncle. Hezekiah is distracted, more so than usual, for he is slow to eat and keeps his gaze set on the large map of the world that hangs on the wall behind her, absently stroking his scar, a fine white line that spans the length of his cheek. He coughs and fidgets, taps his wine glass with his thumb, its *clink-clink-clink* a wearisome noise as the evening draws on. Every now and then his other hand strokes the gleaming pocketwatch that hangs from his waistcoat, its chain glinting in the candlelight.

Dora stares at it fixedly after the sixth time he reaches for it, trying to recall if she has seen it before. Did the watch belong to her father? But no, she would remember it. A new acquisition then, Dora decides, but she holds her tongue. The last time she asked how Hezekiah could possibly afford to buy such baubles he went an alarming shade of red and scolded her so loudly that her ears rang until the following morning. When her uncle coughs again, the effort making a large globular piece of mutton wobble dangerously on his fork, Dora decides she cannot stand it any longer.

'Uncle, are you ill?'

Hezekiah jumps, looks directly at her for the first time all day. His eyes betray for a moment a nervousness she has not seen before but he shields it quickly.

'What a notion.' He pops his fork into his mouth, chews open-mouthed like a cow. Dora watches with distaste as the overcooked meat swirls about on his tongue. A speck of gravy lands on his chin. 'I was pondering the future of the shop. I feel . . .'

Dora sits up straight in her seat. Is he *finally* going to discuss the running of the shop with her? For she has ideas, so many wonderful ideas! First, she would remove the dead weight and replenish with good, genuine articles sourced from her father's old contacts. Second, make enough money to hire men to undertake digs overseas, employ artists and engravers to catalogue their finds. They could be listed once more in Christie's directory, provide a retreat for scholars and private collectors, house a small museum, a miniature library. Perhaps – for the more frivolous aspects of the business – cater to the aristocracy's whims of themed soirées. Restore the shop to its former glory. Begin again.

'Yes?'

Hezekiah swallows his food, takes a long swig of wine.

'Now we have begun a new year, I feel it might be time to sell. I tire of trade. There is far more pleasure to be had elsewhere, after all, far better things to invest my money in.'

His voice is offhand, almost cold, and Dora stares at her uncle across the table. 'You would sell Father's shop?'

He sends her a level stare.

'It is not his shop. It passed naturally on to me when he died. Does it say Elijah on the board, or Hezekiah?'

'You can't sell it,' she whispers. 'You just can't.'

He dismisses this with a wave of his arm, as if he were batting away a fly.

'Times change. Antiquities are no longer *à la mode*. The money from the sale would be sufficient to purchase a fine seat in a more reputable part of town. It would be an agreeable change for me.' He wipes the corner of his mouth with a napkin. 'The building would fetch a good price, as would the contents, I'm sure.'

Dora feels entirely numb. *Sell* the shop? Her childhood home?

She takes an unsteady breath.

'For shame, Uncle, you would contemplate such a thing.'

'Come, Dora. The shop is not what it once was—'

'And whose fault is that?'

Hezekiah's nostrils flare, but he ignores this too.

'I should think you would be glad of a change of scene, more, ah, *liberating* surroundings. Is that not what you wish?'

'You know what I wish.'

'Oh, yes,' he sneers. 'Those little sketches of yours. You'd be much better off finding someone to buy you such pieces rather than attempting to fashion them yourself.'

Dora lowers her cutlery. 'And where, Uncle, would I wear them?'

'Well now . . .' Hezekiah hesitates, gives a little laugh that carries on its edge something she cannot quite decipher. 'Who knows where our fortunes might take us? You do not wish to stay here for ever, do you?'

She pushes her plate away, her appetite – never prodigious on Lottie's mediocre cooking – completely lost.

'I prefer, Uncle, to think on more practical endeavours rather than flights of fancy.'

'And is designing jewellery a practical endeavour or a flight of fancy?' Dora looks away. 'I thought as much,' he says, his sneer even more pronounced. 'No goldsmith will accept a female designer – you know that, I've said so often enough but you will not listen. You waste the sketchbooks I buy you. Do you realise how much good paper costs?'

Lottie comes in then to clear the plates. It is just as well, for Dora is on the verge of tears. As the housekeeper slides her master's plate across the tabletop, Dora dips her head. She will be damned to let them see her cry.

'I do not want to work for a goldsmith.'

'What now?'

She spoke too quietly, she knows. Dora steels herself, raises her head to look at him squarely across the table.

'I do not want to work for a goldsmith,' she repeats. 'I want to open my own establishment, to work independently of anyone else.'

Hezekiah stares at her a moment. Lottie stares too, empty plate in hand; a drip of gravy threatens to make its escape onto the floor.

'You mean to make the jewellery yourself?'

Her uncle's voice is laced now with amusement, and his mockery makes Dora colour.

'I wish to become a reputable *artist*, for a jeweller to make up the designs on my behalf. Mother's friend Mr Clements, perhaps.'

There is a beat of silence. Dora had not expected Hezekiah to support the notion – that would be far too much to hope for – but then, as the ridicule spills itself from her uncle's lips in cruel disjointed laughter, joined by the giggled snorts of Lottie Norris, her chest tightens with anger.

'Oh, dear heaven,' Hezekiah cries on a sigh, wiping the corners of his eyes with fat thumbs, 'this is the most amusement I've had in weeks. Come now, Lottie, what a fine joke she tells!'

Dora scrunches the napkin she holds in her fist, directing all her frustration into the starch. 'I assure you, sir,' she says tightly, 'I am perfectly serious.'

'And therein lies the joke,' Hezekiah crows. 'Practical endeavours indeed! You have neither the education nor the capital to carry out such a thing. No one in their right mind would take a peculiar half-foreign orphan like yourself seriously. You would be laughed right out of trade before you'd even started.' He sits back in his seat, expression sobering. 'You have your mother's creative talents, I grant you. But also, like your mother, you think far too highly of them. She was convinced she and your father, my own dear brother, God rest his soul, could make their fortune in antiquities, would be recognised the world over for their more, ah, unique finds. But look where her ambition took them . . .'

Dora is silent. Her uncle's neglect, though painful in those early years, she is used to. His fits of anger, manageable. This cruel contempt, however . . . *this* is new, and simply too much for Dora to entertain. She takes a deep breath that pulls painfully at her lungs, begins to push her chair out from behind her when Hezekiah raises his hand.

'Sit. We are not yet done.'

*But I am.* The words stitch themselves to her tongue, will not unpick themselves as she does as she is told, but Dora glowers deeply at her discarded plate, recites the Greek alphabet internally to calm her:

25

*Alpha, beta, gamma, delta . . .*

'Lottie,' Dora hears Hezekiah say, 'will you bring in the tea?'

The housekeeper is all simpers and curtseys. When the door swings shut behind Lottie Dora senses Hezekiah turn back to her, and he offers up a humourless laugh.

'I can admire your aspiration at least, as lofty and unrealistic as it is. Draw away, if you must. It will keep you amused in the coming months. I will even continue to provide the paper.'

Something in his voice. Dora's brow furrows. She looks up.

'Uncle?'

Hezekiah is lazily stroking his scar.

'You've grown to be quite a picture in the last year. So much like your mother . . .' A log in the fire cracks. 'You're twenty-one now,' he continues, leaning his complete weight onto his elbows. 'A woman. You're far too old to still be sharing my roof.'

Dora is silent a moment as the import of his declaration sinks in. She swallows hard. 'You mean to be rid of me.'

He spreads his hands. 'Don't you also mean to be rid of me?'

She hesitates, cannot dispute the question.

'Where would you have me go?' she asks instead, but Hezekiah merely shrugs. Smiles.

Something hard settles in her stomach and turns itself over. Dora does not understand the meaning of that smile, but she does know her uncle well enough to understand that no good can come from it.

Behind her the door swings open. Dora remembers how to breathe, and Lottie sets the tea tray down on the sideboard, the fine bone china rattling.

'Here we are, sir,' she says, over-bright. 'And I've brought in the sugar plums you ordered, fresh this morning.'

Lottie is brandishing a box shaped like a hexagon.

'Offer one to Dora, Lottie.'

26

The housekeeper hesitates, narrows her eyes, but she does as Hezekiah asks and Dora stares at the box, the treats nestled within. Her gaze moves warily to her uncle who watches, hands clasped beneath his chin.

'What are these?'

Her tone is suspicious. She cannot help it.

'Sugar plums, as Lottie said. A delicious delicacy.'

Lottie wafts the box under Dora's nose. She catches the scent of sugar. Hesitates.

'Go on,' Hezekiah presses. 'Why don't you try one?'

Gingerly she selects a plum from the top and bites into it, teeth sinking into the gelatinous orb, and for a brief moment Dora relishes this fine and unexpected offering. The flavour bursts on her tongue – vanilla, spice, a hint of orange and nut, quite unlike anything she has ever tasted in her life – but then she catches Hezekiah watching her from across the table. He is looking at Dora in a way he never has before.

A cat watching an unsuspecting bird. Hungry, calculating.

# CHAPTER FOUR

From a cramped window seat tucked into a small alcove, Edward Lawrence watches January play out its cruel and bitter game. The morning is as cold as a mortuary slab and the wind has whipped itself into a frenzy, sending flurries of biting ice down the terrace of Somerset House. The sycamore trees that line the formal path bend against the wind, empty bird's nests hang on desperately to their bare branches the way a beggar clings to bread. The water in the fountain is frozen solid, the walkways dangerously slick, and over the balcony the barges rock angrily in the Thames.

How long he has been waiting, Edward cannot say. At the far end of the lengthy corridor – above the large doors behind which his fate is being decided – there is a clock, but it needs winding. His shoulders ache from slouching into such a confined space; the window seat is uncomfortably hard. He has been nibbling a jagged fingernail on and off since he got here, counted the frescos on the ceiling twice. He has recited the Society's motto – *Non extinguetur* – too many times now to count. *Shall not be extinguished*. So. He might have been waiting an hour. He might have been waiting only minutes.

On his lap is a copy of the report he presented to the committee. The binding is simple, the paper the cheapest in stock, but it is his labour of love, his proudest achievement in his twenty-six years and what Edward hopes will be his ticket into the Society of Antiquaries. *A Studie of Shugborough Hall's Shepherd Monument*. It all rests on the election – the Blue Paper – a minimum of five votes.

When the doors eventually open Edward stands, clutches his *Studie* close to his chest. Cornelius Ashmole, his oldest (his only) friend, is making his way toward him, parquet creaking beneath the tread of heel to toe. Edward risks a hopeful smile but he can see from Cornelius' face that the news goes badly. When he reaches him, Cornelius gives a small apologetic shake of the head.

'Only two votes.'

Deflated, Edward sinks back onto the window seat, holds his *Studie* loosely between his knees.

'My third try, Cornelius. I was so thorough . . .'

'You know what Gough's methods are. I did warn you. Something less cryptic, more grounded in antiquarian scholarship.'

'When the facts aren't there, Cornelius, sometimes conjecture is all there is!' Edward raises his papers, brandishes them in his friend's face. 'I thought this would be enough. I truly did. The detail I went into. My drawings . . .'

'"Amateur" is the word they used, I'm afraid,' Cornelius responds with a grimace. 'They've been spoilt by the likes of Stukeley. If it's any consolation, they said you showed great promise. The depth of your descriptions really was extremely impressive.'

'Hmph.'

Cornelius, being so very tall, sinks down on his haunches.

'Many,' he says gently, 'do not gain entrance into the Society until much later. Some only when they are nearly decrepit.'

Edward lances his friend with a look. 'Do you think that makes me feel any better?' Then, '*You* are thirty!'

'*I* experienced the joys of the Grand Tour. I spent my summer desecrating Italian tombs and when I returned could devote all my time to scholastic interests at leisure. Besides, my father is on the board.' Seeing Edward's crestfallen expression he lays a comforting hand on the younger man's shoulder. 'I don't mean to rub my good fortune in your face, but it is a fact that these things made all the difference. Think how much better you will feel having achieved a fellowship on your *own* merit. No shortcuts, pure mettle.'

But Edward is shaking his head. 'How much easier it is for those with money to achieve what those without it cannot.'

'Now you're being melodramatic.'

'Says the man who has always been rich.'

Cornelius has no answer to this and the two share a space of quiet, listen to the wind whipping sharply at the windowpane. After a moment Cornelius nudges Edward's knee with his elbow.

'Do you remember when we were boys and I boasted that I could swim to the folly and back without stopping?'

Edward smiles at the memory. 'You got halfway before you started floundering in the reeds and nearly drowned.'

'And you sat right there in the boat beside me and told me to keep going, not to give up, though we both knew I was a damned fool to try.'

So it had always been with them; one would back the other for no better reason than it pleased him to do so, but the two were as different as wine and water. Cornelius was the wealthy to Edward's poor, the learned to his ignorant, the dark to his fair. Edward was the reticent to Cornelius' brash, the short to his tall, the unlucky to his fortunate. What a pair they made back then, what a pair they make now, and they chuckle at the memory, though Edward's laugh is markedly more subdued. Cornelius' smile wavers, then dies. They lapse into momentary silence once more.

'I truly am sorry, Edward. I don't know what else to say.'

'There's nothing *to* say.'

30

'Except . . . don't give up. Though I suppose such platitudes will only frustrate you at this juncture.'

'You suppose right.'

A pause. 'You *must* persevere. I'll support you where I can, no matter how much it costs, whatever you need. You know I will.'

'Even though I'm a damned fool to try?'

'Even then.'

Edward says nothing; in his embittered state Cornelius' words feel hollow. How much money has Cornelius already paid out to help him? How much time away from the bindery has he already been allowed? The thought frustrates him, shames him, and Edward stands, runs a hand through his hair.

'I must go.'

Cornelius stands too. 'The work can wait, you know.'

'It can't. I just . . .' Edward sighs, shakes his head, feels now the hot rush of humiliation like a brand. 'I need to go.'

Edward turns away, makes a hasty retreat down the hall and through into the anteroom, Cornelius following close behind. At the top of the vast staircase Cornelius ceases his dogged chase and as he descends Edward feels his friend's pitying gaze on his back like daggers. Eager to be free of it he picks up his pace, rushes out through the main doors of Somerset House and into the wind, taking refuge in London's clotted streets, the comforting flow of traffic.

His *Studie* bends back against itself in the wind. Briefly Edward contemplates chucking it into the nearest gutter but his love of the thing gets the better of him and he wraps the papers in his coat, crosses his arms, presses them against his chest like a shield. On he tramps down the Strand, head down, chin crushed into the folds of his scarf. He keeps his mind blank for now, focuses instead on putting one foot in front of the other. When Edward passes through the wide arch of Temple Bar he is glad to put the bustle of the Strand behind him.

31

Tired now as much from the bad news as battling the wind full on, he slips into a coffee-house just off Fleet Street, not because it is the rich aroma of coffee he craves (he would much rather lose himself in a hefty glass of ale) but the warmth; his toes are like icicles and he is genuinely surprised they have not snapped off, that he will not find the fleshy nubs jiggling about at the caps of his boots when he peels them from his feet in the warmth of his lodgings later on.

Edward unwinds the scarf from his neck, finds a cosy corner near the fire, orders a cup. The *Studie* he keeps hidden beneath his coat. He takes a cautious sip of coffee but it is too hot and so he cradles the cup in his hand, contents himself instead with the comforting smell of aromatic spice, stares unseeing into the grate.

All that time, wasted. Again.

His first attempt he had not expected to succeed – a report mapping his thoughts on the list of the publications he had read (borrowed from Cornelius and Cornelius' father); the early studies of Monmouth and Lambarde, Stow and Camden, the later works of Wanley, Stukeley and Gough. His grasp of Latin, while deficient in certain areas, was adequate and his interest in the field obvious, but, no – his education was lacking, he did not have enough knowledge; he had no original ideas of his own. So Edward applied himself to further study, chose to focus his efforts on effigies in London churches since there were so many of the damn things. He had been hopeful about that second attempt. But the answer came back that while it was impressively written, it was clear yet again nothing new had been brought forward, and so Edward chose another tack.

When Edward and Cornelius were boys they often explored the Staffordshire countryside surrounding Sandbourne, the Ashmole country seat. The neighbouring estate Shugborough Hall – not six miles away, three via the river – was often a source of adventure for them. Edward remembered how one day they had trespassed on the

32

grounds and discovered a monument tucked away in the woodland. It was a spectacular thing, a large and imposing arch with two carved heads protruding from the stone like stern sentinels. Set within was a rectangular panel which depicted a relief of four figures, clustered around a crypt. It was a copy of a Poussin painting, Edward would later learn, but with alterations: an extra sarcophagus, an inscription that referred to 'Arcadia'. Yet what had fascinated Edward so completely, even as a child, were the eight letters carved in the blank expanse of stone below the sculpture itself: O U O S V A V V, above and between the letters D and M. On Roman tombs the letters 'D M' commonly stood for *Dis Manibus*, meaning 'Dedicated to the shades'. But this was no Roman tomb. A cipher, then. What a perfect specimen to make a study of; what better way to gain entry to the society he had coveted for years? And so, with a letter of introduction from Cornelius and a hefty allowance weighting his purse, Edward was granted permission to stay at the hall and have access to its grounds at leisure.

He contemplated all manner of theories: a coded love letter to a deceased wife, an acronym of a Latin phrase, or mere carvings added after the monument's construction representing the initials of the current owner – a Mr George Adams – his wife, and their relations (though Mr Adams refused to comment on the matter). Edward even pondered how the letters might refer to the coordinates of buried treasure at sea, based on the naval history of the Shugborough estate.

It took four months for Edward to complete his findings which elucidated these different theories, two more months to compile them. No one except Josiah Wedgwood had bothered to take much note of the thing, and that over ten years before, with few recordings of it to speak of. And despite Edward's accompanying drawings being – as Cornelius had grimly denounced them – 'amateur', his written work

33

far surpassed any study of the monument that came before it. From that alone, Edward had been sure of his success.

But it was not enough. *It was not enough.*

'Come, lad, can't be that bad, can it?'

His reverie interrupted, Edward looks up to see the source. In an armchair across from him sits an old gentleman dressed in faded worsted, his white hair and beard worn unfashionably long. Without quite meaning to Edward gives a bitter laugh and shaking his head he raises his coffee cup. He takes a sip and grimaces. It is cold. How long has he been sitting here in a stupor?

The man raises two fingers in the air, beckons a maid. 'Another pot if you please,' and to Edward: 'Won't you join me?'

'I'm not much fit for company.'

'Nonsense, I insist.'

Edward hesitates, relents. He did not intend to be rude, but disappointment has made him harsh. The gentleman, Edward considers, only means to be kind.

'Thank you, sir.'

The coffee pot is duly brought. The old man pours.

'So then,' he says. 'Why is it you look so crestfallen?'

His voice is strong, belies his age. What is he – seventy? eighty? Edward looks at him, torn. Should he confide in a stranger? But as soon as he thinks it he feels compelled to throw caution to the wind; it hardly matters any more.

'My third and final application to the Society of Antiquaries has been rejected,' he explains. Edward opens his coat, slaps the *Studie* on the table between them. It falls with a heavy *thud*, its papers fluttering. 'There. My latest failure.'

The old man's eyes – a striking shade of blue, Edward notes – trail the curve of copperplate. His eyebrows lift. 'Indeed? A setback perhaps, but not the end of the world, surely? Why is it you say "final"?'

'Because I cannot dedicate myself to a fourth go of it.'

'What prevents you?'

'Money, sir. And time.'

'Ah.'

There is a pause. Edward feels more is required. 'I work as a book-binder. It's a modest living and it does not engage. It does not thrill me.' He shakes his head, hears the self-pity in his voice but he has started now and cannot stop. 'I grew up in the grounds of a manor house, spent my childhood digging the earth, collecting trinkets. My friend and I spent hours excavating the woodlands pretending we were great explorers the likes of Columbus and Raleigh.'

The gentleman nods sagely. 'And what happened?'

'My friend was shipped off to Oxford and I to London and the bindery.'

Edward takes a quick sip of his coffee before the memory has a chance to unfurl. He replaces the cup on its saucer. The gentleman regards him in silence. After a moment Edward says, 'My friend advises I keep going.'

'I would heed him.'

'Charity,' Edward sneers. As grateful to Cornelius as he is he cannot abide it, this reliance on someone else. He feels less of a man, more a green boy, the groom's lad still.

The old man tilts his head, seems to contemplate this bitter rejoinder. 'If he is happy to give it why scorn such an offer? Many would give their soul to the Gods for such a benefactor.'

'I know, it is just—'

'A blow to your pride.'

'Yes.'

Another pause, a sudden quiet. As if the coffee-house has stopped mid-air.

*A blow to your pride.* Edward is conscious of a great sense of relief

35

that the words are out in the open but they make him feel no better. Oh, what a fool he has been, to act like such a petulant child! He must apologise to Cornelius, he must make amends. Such behaviour is hardly befitting a gentleman let alone a fellow of the Society. He hopes Cornelius does not begrudge him his moment of dumbfuddery.

The coffee-house breathes again. The old man watches him as if he has heard Edward's every thought. Edward blushes, forces a shamefaced smile.

'You find me quite disgraced, sir. Forgive me my peevishness. I had just set my hopes so high.'

'Might I make a suggestion?'

'By all means.'

The man takes a sip of his coffee, crinkled lips pursing the rim. He licks his mouth, places the cup down on the table with precise care. Then he leans forward, as if ready to divulge a closely kept secret.

'In Ludgate Street, there is a shop. It belonged to an intrepid couple by the name of Blake. Antiquarians by trade, they made a living excavating tombs in south-eastern Europe, in Greece specifically. I understand the taste for antiquities verges more now on British discoveries but there is money in the ancient world, a curiosity for it still. The couple are long dead, I am sad to say, some twelve or thirteen years now, and the shop . . . it is not what it once was. Elijah's brother, Hezekiah –' and here the old man's mouth twists – 'has quite ruined its fortunes, but you might have some luck conversing with the daughter.'

'The daughter?'

'Pandora Blake. She was only eight when her parents died but she accompanied them on every excavation they went on, has a taste for the field. The uncle – a cartographer originally – cared for the child after their deaths, moved into the shop, kept her on. If she is anything like her parents then she will prove quite exceptional.'

36

'You knew them well, then?'

His companion hesitates. 'I make it my business to know those in the trade.'

'You're a collector, then?'

'Of sorts, yes.'

He says nothing more. There is a beat, a beat in which a customer enters the coffee-house, bringing in with him the sharp cold air of Fleet, and now Edward is unsure how to press the matter further. They both are silent. The old man raises his cup. It has left a wet ring.

'How did they die?' Edward finally asks.

The man takes another sip of his coffee. 'A tragedy. They were unearthing a Grecian ruin. The walls caved in. Buried alive.'

'And Pandora?'

'She was saved, be praised.'

Edward shakes his head. 'Dreadful.'

'Indeed.'

The bells of Temple church chime the hour. His cue, Edward thinks, and he digs into his coat pocket, exchanges his *Studie* for a coin.

'I'm much obliged to you, sir. Your kindness . . .'

The gentleman waves him off. 'Not at all,' he says mildly, as if it truly was nothing and not, as Edward believes, a cannily timed intervention. 'It was my pleasure.'

As Edward stands the old man looks up at him, blue eyes clear and piercing: a world in them. He holds out his hand for him to shake.

'Perhaps we shall see each other again, Mr Lawrence?'

'Yes,' Edward says, clasping it. The skin feels papery, a worn-out glove, but the grip is surprisingly firm. 'Yes, perhaps we shall.'

It only occurs to Edward later that evening – his boots and stockings warming by the fire – that he never asked the old man his name, nor was it offered, and more to the point, Edward never mentioned his own.

# CHAPTER FIVE

Hezekiah has left her in charge again, the arrival of a dirty lad bearing a letter having taken him away with unmitigated haste; her uncle bounded up from his half-eaten breakfast and catapulted from the room like a hare before she could blink. Dora had glanced at the clock – twenty minutes past the hour of eight – and wondered what urgent business Hezekiah could possibly have so early with a boy that stank so overpoweringly of something she did not wish to name.

In the shop Dora perches on a stool (this one no less uncomfortable than the one upstairs), swinging her legs in boredom. While she knows there is plenty to entertain her – if Lottie will not do it, she might as well do the dusting herself – Dora cannot quite bring herself to, for her mind is as peaceful as a stormy sea. Under the counter are her sketchbook and reticule, close at hand so that when Hezekiah does return she can make her escape as quickly as possible.

Today is the day that everything will change.

The cannetille design is finished. All it will take is a 'yes', an acknowledgement that her work is worthy of fashioning into beautiful pieces fit for members of high society to wear. It only need start with one item – *just one* – sold to a woman of quality. A lady, maybe a baroness. A duchess, perhaps. Of course, she thinks, the chances of someone so far up the peerage taking a fancy to her designs is unlikely but with any sale Dora would gain a cut of the value, be commissioned for more. It would go from there. She would gain her independence. She would be free.

*What of the shop?* a little voice whispers inside her head. *What will happen to it without you?*

Dora's legs still. This shop is all she has ever known. It is her home. To leave it would break her heart clean in two. And if Hezekiah *were* to sell, her parents' legacy – what is left of it – would be as dead as they are. Though these walls are woodwormed and their joists have begun to weaken like dried-out leaves, they contain within them the very map of her, the memory of what once was.

She thinks back to one Christmas spent at the shop, the merchants and patrons who joined them to toast the season, to celebrate a year of successful trade. Blake's Emporium had been warm and welcoming back then, the oak floor polished to a rich shine, the beams free of cobwebs, and Dora remembers being fascinated by the shimmering candlelight that reflected off the clean unbroken windowpanes. Her father carried her high on his hip, and though she had no true understanding of them he was keen to include Dora in conversations about expansion, East India shipments, new lots to sell at Christie's. Hezekiah was meant to honour those memories. If he can discard his loyalty that easily, Dora thinks, what then will become of her when the time comes to sell? She thinks back to what he said to her at dinner . . . *You're far too old to still be sharing my roof.*

Dora swallows hard. From the very beginning Hezekiah has treated her like an inconvenience. Beyond arranging for a Sunday school education, her uncle had no interest in continuing the classical education Dora's parents began – when she asked him to teach her about the antiquity trade he laughed, said there was no need to clutter her mind with such things, though he never hesitated to put her to use behind the shop counter. And so everything Dora knows has been built on memory, on keen observation. Where would she go, if not for him?

Though neglectful, Hezekiah has never strictly been unkind to her – Dora's sketchbooks are purchased by him, after all – but there is no love lost between them. She thought, perhaps, when he brought Lottie home with him one evening that things might change between them. Dora thinks on when she first saw the woman standing in the narrow stairwell of their apartments (not six months after her parents' deaths), how Hezekiah announced that Lottie had come to live with them. She assumed this woman – decked head to toe in ill-fitting rouge – was to act as a mother to her, that Hezekiah might then treat Dora with a little more warmth, but she had been sorely disappointed. Dora was promptly moved from her comfortable bedroom on the second floor to the cold and dreary attic. And so, if anything, she had felt even more alone.

Where would she go, indeed. The thought sends a cold tug against Dora's ribs. She has no other family aside from Hezekiah. Her paternal grandparents are long dead, and her mother was raised in an orphanage in Greece. Until Dora can provide for herself she *cannot* leave, she cannot be free of him. Her only options – the poorhouse, the streets, or the brothels – well, they are no options at all.

The brothels.

Uneasily Dora thinks of the way Hezekiah looked at her. *I should think you would be glad of a change of scene. More liberating surroundings.* Surely he did not mean . . . ?

Her macabre thoughts are interrupted by the tinkling of the bell. Dora's gaze shoots to the front of the shop but no, it is no customer, only Lottie who has come from the door behind.

'Missum.'

Dora sniffs, needlessly adjusts the position of the empty ledger in front of her. Lottie folds her arms across her chest and looks at Dora, calculating.

'You're very pale. Why don't you take yourself off for a walk? I can see to things here.' The housekeeper hesitates. 'An hour or two will do.'

Dora looks into Lottie's round face, dubious. 'You?'

Lottie's eyebrows lift. 'Why not?'

Her request is curious. Lottie has never offered to look after the shop floor before, nor has she ever cared about Dora's health. But these brief spells of freedom are precious and so Dora reaches for her sketchbook beneath the counter.

She does not need telling twice.

At St Paul's churchyard, located in the north-western corner, stands Clements & Co., a jeweller and goldsmith of the most eminent reputation. It is accessed by four steep and narrow steps and with her free hand – the other clasps the large leather-bound sketchbook – Dora clutches the iron railings, careful not to step a hole through her skirts as she descends them.

She rings the bell, waits to be admitted by a shiny-faced footman. Inside it is warm, and the pleasant smell of beeswax candles is a welcome scent after the putrid air of the streets.

The walls are trussed up floor to ceiling with glass cabinets decorated with carved and gilded appointments, their contents bright and gleaming, filled to the brim. The cabinets near the entrance house the more everyday ware: sturdy goblets, large serving platters, silver-plated cutlery with ivory handles carved into hunting dogs and wild boar. Nice enough items to be sure, but it is those near the counter that have Dora's heart fluttering.

Necklaces, earrings, bracelets, rings. Rubies, sapphires, emeralds and diamonds. Opaline glass, seed pearls, cut steel, a tray of Wedgwood Jasperware. Butterfly brooches, harlequin jewels. And there, directly in front of her, is a new piece, something altogether too glorious to be kept locked away.

On a deep blue cushion sits a tiara. Filigree patterning, embellished with round and pear-shaped rose-cut diamonds and at its centre a flower, its petals bursting out from its pistil like the rays of the sun. Dora tilts her head, stands on tiptoe, tries to view it from a different angle. Silver-topped, closed back. As she moves, the diamonds glint and dance. They truly are exquisite. Dora presses her face close to the glass. If she looks very carefully, she can see her reflection in all their tiny facets.

'Beautiful,' she whispers.

'Beautiful indeed.'

Mr Clements emerges from the back room carrying a tray of rings. A thin, bespectacled man with a thick mop of grey-streaked brown hair that he keeps tightly contained with a ribbon, he reminds Dora of a studious otter. He always wears colours in earthy shades, ties his cravat too tightly, looks as if he has been shoe-horned into his coat. He is one of the few gentlemen of her parents' friendship circle she has maintained regular contact with, and from whom her passion for jewellery blossomed.

One particular year Dora's mother, Helen, took her to Clements & Co. every week to admire his displays, and over tea and sweetmeats the jeweller would – for the purpose of documenting her finds – explain to Dora's mother the difference between gemstones and paste, the best place to source turquoise, how opals came to be. While he and her mother spoke, Mr Clements would give Dora a tin of beads to play with. It was he who taught her how to tie a clasp and curl a wire, he who gave Dora her own set of pliers and cutters.

All the jewellery her mother owned had been made by Mr

42

Clements. Gently Dora touches the cameo brooch at her neck, the only surviving piece from her mother's collection – the rest Hezekiah sold before Dora even realised they had gone. Mr Clements had made the cameo from a cassis shell Dora found on the beach of Paphos. Simple but elegant, it depicts the regal profile of a woman wearing a wreath of grapes that falls over her shoulder. Her mother always let Dora play with the brooch before she went to bed; she used to turn it over and over in her tiny hands, admiring the etchwork, the coolness of it in her palms. Her mother was wearing it when she died.

'Mr Clements.'

'Miss Blake. How are you, my dear?'

'Well, sir.' She proffers the sketchbook with both hands. 'I have brought more of my designs.'

The jeweller lowers the ring tray. She thinks she sees a look of restraint pass across his face but he has bent beneath the counter, exchanged his ring tray with a square of black velvet, and when he looks at her once more his face is open, affable.

'Let's see them, then.'

Dora sets her sketchbook down onto the glass counter and opens her reticule. Very carefully, one by one, she produces her designs. Three pairs of earrings – one drop, one torpedo, one ball – constructed of wire and seeds, carved wood and a marble, respectively. A bracelet in mock pinchbeck and garnet made from lace and glass beads, two brooches in the style of Vauxhall glass achieved with broken mirror shards, a ribbon-tie necklace of porcelain buttons she has painted to imitate agate.

She saves the cannetille necklace to last. Under the golden light of the candles she sees how well the blue glass pebble looks in its new setting. Two nights she laboured over that pendant, two back-breaking nights on her high and uncomfortable stool, but Dora is inordinately proud of it. With painstaking care she managed to coax the wire to form twenty small spiralled florets, the number of which matched identically on either side. It looks elegant, regal. It is the best work she has ever done.

As Dora produces them the goldsmith turns each piece this way and that, squints at the details over the rims of his spectacles, places them down carefully on the velvet, *hums* and *haws*. She is pleased he seems so fascinated, but she is not yet finished.

'I know,' Dora says as she opens her sketchbook, 'these are crude in comparison to what would be produced in your shop. But you can see by my sketches what I was trying to achieve. Here,' she adds, turning to the cannetille. 'Gold and aquamarine. It would look well in either its pure form or paste, as long as the colour is right . . .' When Mr Clements does not respond she rushes on. 'I am happy to be guided by your expertise, of course. Add embellishments, if you will. Flowers would suit, feathers too perhaps if you were to pare down the—'

'Miss Blake,' he interrupts, the words escaping on a deep sigh.

Dora's stomach tightens. The pages flutter from her fingers.

'You do not like them.'

'It is not that. My dear . . .' He pauses, looks uncomfortable. 'How might I put this delicately? I entertain you for your parents' sakes, God bless their immortal souls. But . . .' Mr Clements tries for a kindly smile. 'Your drawings are, I must confess, quite charming for what they are but charming is all I can attribute to them.'

'But . . .' Dora stops, deflated. Tries again. 'You promised me.'

Mr Clements removes his spectacles, places them with precision on the countertop. 'I promised nothing. I merely said I would *consider* them for my collection.'

Dora stares. Then, very slowly, she puts her hands on the counter and leans in.

'Mr Clements. You suggested that I produce a portfolio of designs and create some of them to demonstrate their viability. You might not have outright said you would take them but if you did not believe my designs to be of any worth, if you considered them only the *charming* fare of mere female accomplishment, then why say such a thing and give me false hope?'

The jeweller holds up his hands in an attempt to placate but Dora's disappointment and frustration cannot be quelled.

'You have wasted my time, Mr Clements. Mine and yours.'

The goldsmith heaves yet another sigh. 'Miss Blake. Dora. I did not mean to offend. These designs –' he gestures to them spread out on the velvet, lingers over the milky blue stone of the cannetille-esque necklace – 'they really are quite char—'

'Mr Clements, if you refer to my work as charming again . . .'

'Lovely, then.'

'Is that not the same?'

He purses his lips. 'You show much skill, that I grant you. What you have done with the crudest of materials really is astonishing. But there is nothing *unique* about them, nothing that defines your work from that of the men already in my employ. Fashions move on as quickly as colds nowadays and these you've given me . . . Well, they just won't do. There is whisper now for Grecian styles but next month it could be those of the Orient. I'm sorry, Miss Blake, but my answer is no.'

Dora blinks. 'Grecian?'

Mr Clements appears to sag as he recognises his mistake. 'Y-e-s.' He drags the word over the three syllables.

'What if I were to produce something in *that* style?'

'Miss Blake . . .'

'Please, sir, let me speak. You know my lineage, you're aware of what my parents specialised in. If I were to sketch some new designs for you to consider, surely there is no harm in that? Only a small selection, and if, after that, you still have no liking for them I shall cease in my efforts. You cannot be so cruel as to rob me of one final chance to prove myself?'

'I . . .' The jeweller looks pained but Dora sees the waver in him and deals her final hand. She touches the cameo at her throat.

'*Se iketévo*. Please. For my mother's sake.'

There is a pause. Dora can feel the blood pulse in her ears. Mr Clements heaves a sigh.

'Miss Blake, you really are most vexing.' The goldsmith's expression softens. He shakes his head in defeat. 'Very well. But I am promising you nothing,' he warns. '*Nothing*, is that clear?'

'It is,' Dora replies, reaching for her sketchbook, closing it with a snap. 'But I promise *you*, sir. You won't be disappointed.'

# CHAPTER SIX

Hezekiah, at that very moment, is bright with fury. The three Coombe brothers (who have until now always been so biddable where money was involved), led by the eldest, will not relinquish his most longed-for prize which sits – so tantalisingly close he could touch it – trussed up on a cart, a horse ready to take it home. Ready, if it were not for Matthew Coombe making trouble.

'You know how much this means to me,' Hezekiah is saying, quite unable to keep the whine from his voice. 'After all this time I shall not be thwarted. I've lost it twice already, will you deprive me again?'

Matthew shifts heavily on his feet, boots squelching into the muddy sand of Puddle Dock, but he does not answer, and Hezekiah's throat becomes hot; he must loosen his cravat. 'You will *not* keep it for yourselves, you will *not*—'

'We don't want it for ourselves,' Samuel cuts in, the youngest of the three.

Hezekiah is incredulous. 'You mean to say you have another buyer?'

How *dare* they betray his trust?

'No, sir, that's not it.'

And now this is altogether too much. He clenches his fists, losing what little restraint he managed to muster.

'*Then what the hell are you playing at?*'

At his outburst the horse snorts, its breath pluming the crisp morning air, and Hezekiah can feel the veins popping at his temples. His face must be quite puce, for only now does Matthew flinch.

'It's cursed.'

Hezekiah stares. This he had not expected. The outlandishness of the statement deflates his anger somewhat. 'What utter nonsense.'

'I'm telling you, there's something off about it. It shouldn't be here.'

Matthew scratches at his wrist. Hezekiah notes with distaste a ruddy stain on his cuff.

'Nonsense,' Hezekiah says again. 'You're addled from lack of sleep, that's all.'

'Lack of sleep would be right. We've not had one wink since we brought it up.'

And the brothers do indeed look tired – their mouths are pinched tight like dried-out pears, their skin looks grey as silt, but of this he does not care for behind him Hezekiah is conscious of an audience. The dock has come to a standstill; Tibb and his workers have gathered in a small semicircle, the night-soil men lean rapt on their steaming shovels. He watches as two of them – one the same China-man as before, Hezekiah is quite certain – exchange a comment, a laugh behind their hands. Bridling with mortification he sidles up to Matthew and clamps his own hand round the man's strong upper arm. He can smell the raw essence of unwashed skin, the salt pungence of fish and seaweed. It mixes with the noxious stink of excrement and Thames rot, and Hezekiah must use all his self-control not to vomit onto his shoes.

'Now look here,' Hezekiah hisses. 'I'll not have you ruin this for me.'

'It won't be us that ruins anything. It'll be this thing.' Matthew nods behind him. 'It ain't right. It ain't.'

'Again, nonsense I say.'

'Sir, what this thing has done . . . Poor Charlie's not said a word for days—'

'Enough, Coombe, else you and your brothers will get nothing.'

'No, Mr Blake,' Matthew counters, his tone unbending now. 'We want more money. The effort it took to retrieve, the journey we've had bringing it here. The danger you put me in to begin with. I reckon that's worth twice what we agreed.'

'You'll get no such thing,' Hezekiah sniffs, but he can tell he is losing his hold on the matter. 'The price I stipulated is more than adequate.'

'Then we'll load it back up, take it out to sea and throw it overboard where the damn thing belongs.'

But as Matthew begins to turn away Hezekiah presses down harder on his arm.

'No! Please, I . . .'

Hezekiah's mouth goes dry, his eyes dart. He cannot lose it now, he cannot. The Coombe brothers stare with sunken eyes. Hezekiah grimaces, releases his hold.

'I shall pay you the agreed fee now, the rest when my own business is complete. I can't pay you any sooner than that.'

A muscle tics in Matthew's jaw. The three brothers share a look, a nod.

'Very well,' Matthew says. He chucks his chin at his siblings; they haul themselves up onto the cart. 'But if we don't have payment by month's end you can expect us pounding at your door.'

Hezekiah bristles. 'You think my word not enough? Have I ever let you down?'

'No,' Matthew concedes, taking the reins of the horse. 'But you've never had nothing the likes of this before.'

49

# CHAPTER SEVEN

Again, she must bide her time. For a little while longer she must suffer under Hezekiah's roof. But Dora is a stubborn creature, and her imagination is already at work.

So, then. Her offerings are not in vogue. No matter, Dora thinks, as she passes the path leading up to St Paul's. In a few years they will be again, and she will ensure her pieces are in commission by the time they are. Still, she is no fool. Dora knows the goldsmith means only to delay her. She knows he will likely dismiss her again. But what better person than she to design such jewellery? Her mother was Greek. Dora spent her childhood immersed in Grecian dig sites. It is in her blood.

*Agáli-agáli gínetai i agourída méli.*

'Slowly, slowly, the sour grape becomes honey,' she mutters under her breath.

It takes time to grow bigger or better.

Every morning after breakfast and before her parents went to dig, Dora was taught her Greek letters, her proverbs, the ancient stories of her mother's homeland. Be patient, the proverb meant. But has she not been patient long enough?

When Dora emerges back onto the stir of Ludgate Street, she crosses to the far right where the pavement is at its widest to avoid the tracks of oncoming carriages, the push-pull of London's suffocating crowds. A frost the night before has deposited thin sheets of black ice on the roads; walking here requires a certain tactility, a skill in placing a foot just so, bending the body to weave between the press of others, and a slippery walkway makes it a treacherous exercise. She is halfway between a stationer's and tailor's when behind her St Paul's strikes its bells eleven and ahead of her there is the most almighty crash. A horse's scream pierces the air.

Dora manages to push her way through the building crowd, intending to keep her head down, for accidents like this happen often and most are horrific things – not worth the nightmares you get from looking – but then she hears the unmistakable shriek of Lottie Norris. Dora's head snaps up in time to see the housekeeper rushing from the shop in a flurry of skirts. Dora picks up her own and risks a run.

In front of the shop a cart has upended. The horse, though on its side, appears unharmed. Underneath its flank, though . . . Hezekiah's leg is trapped and he is making a great show of howling his distress. Standing near him in an ungainly semicircle are three men Dora does not recognise. One of them is wringing a threadbare cap in his hands.

'You see!' he is crying, 'You see? It sends things mad!'

Dora stares at them. Large, muscular men, each sharing the same copper hair, the same pale, red-veined eyes and all sickly, she thinks, assessing their grey faces. As she draws closer she smells on them the briny stench of the sea.

'The damn beast slipped on the ice, nothing more!' Hezekiah is now near spitting. 'It has ruined my prize. Shoot it, someone! The infernal creature will pay for this, mark my words.'

'Now, now,' croons Lottie by his side, her hand clenched in his. 'Perhaps there's no harm done . . .'

'Of course there is,' Hezekiah snaps, trying in vain to extricate his

51

leg from beneath the horse. 'How can there not be? Matthew, tell me how it fares.'

Dora's curiosity piqued, she joins the largest of the men at the back of the wagon. A wheel spins on its axel, the cart itself is in splinters, but its cargo . . . On the cobbles, encased in thick rope, is an extremely large wooden crate. The wood is warped at the corners, its boards patched verdigris. Molluscs stick firmly to its sides. A crude sideways cross has been painted on one of the panels. Slowly, the man circles the crate. At one corner, Dora sees, a section of wood has fallen away leaving a dark jagged gap and the man steps forward, presses his face up close to it. There is a pause, the impatient chatter of onlookers.

'*Well?*' Hezekiah leans his substantial weight on his elbows. 'I'm right, aren't I?' he groans. 'It is smashed, completely ruined. That infernal horse!' He aims a fist for the mare but it shies away from him with a whicker.

In his anger Hezekiah has missed the look that the three men – brothers, Dora decides – shared between them. She, however, has not. That look was not one of shock, of bemusement. No, it was one of resignation, as if they have expected this, as if they have known all along . . .

The one called Matthew clears his throat. 'Intact, sir. I am sure.'

Hezekiah gives a shout of laughter and cups a hand to Lottie's face, planting a wet kiss on her cheek. 'Luck is with me, after all! Now, someone get me free of this animal.'

There is a great effort, a pull, a heave. Hezekiah stands and, wincing, plucks a rusty nail from his thigh. The tip of it glistens red.

'Look at this!' he cries, flinging the nail onto the street where it lands with a tinny *ping*. He leans on Lottie for support and she bends under his weight, though she does not look to mind.

An old man with long white hair steps from the crowd, offers

Hezekiah his arm. 'Come, sir, let me assist you inside. You can walk, I trust?'

'Aye, though it's a wonder! Did you see? My leg could have been broken.'

'Indeed it could have been,' the gentleman murmurs. 'But as you say, luck appears to be with you. It is only a small wound. Shall we?'

Hezekiah takes the proffered arm, and with the old man on one side, Lottie on the other, he limps into the shop. At the threshold he turns his head to address the three red-headed men:

'Bring it to the basement. I'll have Lottie unlock the door.'

From beneath his shirt Hezekiah pulls free a chain from which dangles a small metal key, and now Dora can hold her tongue no longer.

'Can I help?'

Hezekiah starts. The chain swings from his fingers. Clearly he had not noticed she was there.

'Dora.' He slides a look to Lottie, lowering his voice to an under-tone. 'She was meant to be gone.'

Lottie shuffles under his weight. 'She was.'

So *this* is why Lottie wanted rid of her!

'Uncle,' Dora says now, impatience tipped. 'What is this thing? What have you bought?' and she can see Hezekiah's thoughts flipping over themselves like fish in a creel.

'Get inside,' he snaps.

'Why?'

There is panic in his face, but before Dora can press him on the matter the white-haired man intervenes on Hezekiah's behalf.

'Miss Blake, your uncle is in pain and it is cold on the street. Per-haps,' he says, indicating the growing crowd with a small nod of his head, 'it would be best to continue this conversation inside?'

Dora opens her mouth then closes it again, and before she can

53

make a second attempt Hezekiah – who refuses to look at her now – is being manoeuvred into the shop. Behind her there is a groan, a creak of wood. Dora turns to watch the three men haul the crate between them.

She steps aside and lets them pass, her eyes narrowed into slits.

# CHAPTER EIGHT

It is the attention to detail he likes, the concentration it requires. It helps him forget.

The bookbindery is tucked at the far end of Russel Street, right on the corner where the road bends sharply onto Drury Lane, and Edward's private workroom backs onto the alley just behind the shop itself. The pocket-sized window is set high up in the wall which affords him little light for his work, but this way he is not disturbed by people tapping on the glass, strangers rudely looking in. So, when he works, he fills the room with candles. An expense the overseer, Tobias Fingle, deems wholly unnecessary.

And it is, Edward concedes. He could get by with half as many; the patterns he works into leather are not done by the delicacy of his fingers but by mere stamps – all he needs do is press them into the right place.

But Edward does not like the dark.

Fingle understands though. He holds his tongue. He and Edward are the only ones left of the original workers, the only ones who know what it was like before. Before, when there was no time to rest, no room to breathe. No time to heal.

Edward presses the fillet into the calfskin, draws the hot metal disk over the binding, leaves a neat double-edged line across its face. His role is reserved for the last stages of book production. It is his task to stain the covers of the books once the pages have been sewn into them, to mark the leather with delicate patterns and grooves. It is an easy job, requiring only a steady hand, an eye for detail. An 'amateur' artist he may be, but producing beautiful book covers . . . in this respect he could outmatch anyone in the trade. Carrow had seen to it.

Setting his jaw Edward lifts the fillet, lays it aside. He picks up a small pallet from the little stove tucked into the corner and used to warm the tools. He turns the pallet to check the pattern – coiling ivy, filigree spindles – and applies himself now to detailing the borders of the book.

*Concentrate. Forget.*

Thanks to Cornelius, Edward is now free to do what he likes here. He could have left, of course. But what, Edward demanded when Cornelius suggested it, could he possibly do? Where could he go? He – unlike Cornelius who has money to spend and freedom to spare – has to make a living. He is not trained for anything else. And so Edward stayed, doing what he was taught to do best, in comfortable near-silence within a room filled with bright candles that kept the darkness out.

Odd, Edward thinks, that in a place he once feared he now feels entirely safe.

The other workers, of course, have no notion. Cornelius brought them in when he took over the place, new blood from Staffordshire, country stock sent to the city to make their trade, as Edward had been once. But they resent him, Edward knows. They resent what they deem to be his privilege, the protection he receives from Ashmole coffers. They resent his frequent absences, the purpose of which they know nothing about. After his sojourn to Shugborough they could scarce believe it when Edward was reinstated to the back room as if nothing had happened at all.

They also hold their tongues. They are paid too handsomely to say a thing (Cornelius has always been far too generous with his money) and Fingle keeps them quiet, he makes damn sure of that, but Edward cares very little what they think. To him the bindery is a stopping point only, a place to bide his time. Admittance to the Society is all he cares about. It would be his pass to travel the world, to spend time doing what he loves – what a mighty thing, to be *paid* to immerse himself in study, to actually see and touch the things he spent so many years only reading about in book after book after book . . .

There is a knock. Edward lifts the pallet from the leather, looks up at the door. On the other side of the mottled glass panes he sees the distorted shape of a man whom he recognises to be Fingle. He looks down again, turns the book at a quarter angle, presses the pallet into the calfskin.

The door opens. Fingle leans on the handle, squinting into the candlelight.

'We're off to the tavern after we shut for the day. Care to join us?'

Fingle always asks. Edward always answers the same.

'No, thank you,' he says without looking up, but his usual dismissive reply does not succeed in getting rid of the man; Fingle hovers still at the door.

'There's more to life than keeping yourself cooped up behind a desk, you know. I thought perhaps we could see the New Year in, start afresh.'

Edward looks up at this. In the half-light of the doorway Fingle seems to be trying for a kindly smile. Edward forces a smile of his own.

'I'm visiting Mr Ashmole this evening.'

Fingle hesitates, seems to make to say something then thinks better of it. Instead he says, 'Are you sure? The boys were all set to have a meal, too. It would be a shame if you didn't come along.'

Edward resumes his stamps. 'I doubt they'd miss me.'

'I might. For . . .' The man pauses. 'For old time's sake. I think it would be good for you.'

To this Edward does not answer, concentrates instead on his patterning. A tendril of smoke curls upward as the hot metal sinks into the leather. He has always liked the smell of that.

Fingle hovers a moment more before he closes the door, leaving Edward in peace.

Edward works on.

When the distant bells of St Paul's church finally strike five, Edward packs his things away, douses the stove, blows out the candles. As he makes his escape he senses the other men's eyes on him like gnats. He ducks his head, continues by them without a word.

The Ashmole townhouse in Mayfair matches its owner perfectly: bright and warm and altogether ostentatious. Cornelius – even in a loose cravat, half-unbuttoned shirt and stockinged feet – makes a regal picture, and he greets Edward with a tight clasp of his hand, an affectionate look spread across the handsome plane of his face.

'I've been worried about you,' he says as Edward follows his friend into the library. 'I was ready to come to your lodgings last night but somehow I felt you wanted to be alone.'

'I almost came to you, but the weather turned.' Edward is apologetic. 'Cornelius, I—'

Cornelius raises his hand, shoots him a look of mock reprimand. 'Don't. I understand completely.'

'I know you do,' Edward says, shamed, 'but I want to apologise anyway. I was a complete fool and acted like a bad-tempered child. I'm sorry, Cornelius.'

His friend grins, saunters over to the sideboard with a grace that makes Edward feel woefully inadequate.

'Never apologise to me, there is no need.' Cornelius pours Edward a tumbler of brandy which he hands to him along with a small bowl of walnuts. As Edward takes the bowl he looks down at them, is reminded of tiny wrinkled vertebrae. Cornelius throws himself into an armchair, gestures for Edward to take the other opposite him by the fire. 'You're allowed, on occasion, to have your moments of chagrin.'

Edward grimaces as he settles into the rich leather. 'You permit me far too many allowances.'

Cornelius raises his glass from the table beside him, smiles softly over the rim. 'Perhaps. But I certainly don't begrudge you them.'

'There will come a point, you know, when you can't protect me. In fact, I'm pretty sure that moment has come and gone. You've done far more for me already than you should have.' Edward sighs, turns his glass this way and that in his hand, and his friend's eyes narrow; in the firelight his pupils look almost black.

'Don't think on it.'

'But—'

'Look, do not trouble yourself. You'll ruin my surprise.'

'Surprise?'

Cornelius' expression falls once more into a lazy grin, and from the small table next to him he produces a little black box. He leans across the rug – a skinned tiger, magnificent head still intact – and passes it to him. His shirt gapes at the neck, revealing a smooth hard chest. Edward takes the box from Cornelius' fingers.

'What have you done now?'

'Don't question,' Cornelius responds, sitting back again. He plucks a walnut from his own bowl and pops it into his mouth, bites down on it with a show of teeth. 'Just open it.'

And Edward does so with a resigned shake of his head, for

Cornelius often does things like this – if he has not secreted money in his coat then he is sending food parcels from Mrs Howe to his lodgings, or . . .

Edward lets his breath out.

'Cornelius, really.'

In the box, on a bed of cream silk, rests a pair of cufflinks. Circular in shape, made of gold (Edward does not need to ask if his summation is correct, Cornelius would choose nothing else) with a simple emerald set in the middle. The size of a button. Understated but elegant. The jewels glint like tiny eyes.

'You like them?' Cornelius asks softly.

'Well, yes, of course, but—'

'Stop,' he cuts in, tone sharp now. 'I wanted to cheer you.'

Edward wants to scold his friend but Cornelius is not looking at him. Rather, he is examining a walnut between forefinger and thumb. Edward knows from his expression that arguing will do little good, and a 'thank you' will only be waved away like a tiresome infant.

Cornelius. He had once called himself Edward's guardian angel with a wry laugh, but the term would not be far from the truth. If it had not been for him, Edward would not be sitting here today. Charity, Edward thinks again, before he stamps the word down, but it leaves a bitter taste in his mouth. Will he ever be free of it?

'After I left you yesterday I met a gentleman in a coffee-house,' Edward says to change the subject, closing the cufflink box and placing it carefully on the table next to his own chair. 'He suggested something to me.'

Cornelius looks up from his examination of the walnut. 'Oh?'

Edward takes a careful sip of his brandy. The taste is sharp, almost hot, and as it rasps down his throat he gives a little shiver. 'What do you know of the Blake family?'

'Who?'

'The Blakes,' Edward presses, sitting forward. 'Elijah Blake and his wife ran an antiquities business in Ludgate Street twelve or so years ago.'

Cornelius scoffs. 'Oh, Edward, twelve years ago we were . . .' He stops, seems to catch himself, looks away. 'Well, how can I possibly know of someone that far back?'

'But surely you must have heard about them since? They were reputable antiquarians, died tragically, apparently, on a dig. Left behind a shop run by Elijah's brother. Hezekiah, I think the name was.'

Cornelius is frowning into his glass, but he wears an expression Edward knows well. A faint line has formed between his eyebrows and he rubs his lower lip on the rim of the brandy glass. Something has struck a chord.

'They specialised in Greek antiquities,' Edward adds, hopeful.

Cornelius nods slowly. 'Now you say that, it does sound familiar. *Blake* . . . I have heard mention of an artist – Helen, I think her name was – who William Hamilton occasionally employed to sketch his Greek vase collection if Tischbein wasn't available.' Cornelius takes a sip of brandy, swirls it around his mouth before swallowing. 'Perhaps they're one and the same. Why, anyway?'

'Well, now, this is the thing. This gentleman –' here Edward pauses, blushing – 'asked why I was so downcast. I explained what had happened, and he advised me to seek out their daughter, Pandora Blake, at the antiquity shop in Ludgate Street. He intimated I might find what I'm looking for there, something the Society would look favourably on.'

Cornelius stares. 'Oh, for pity's sake, Edward, are you really going to set store by something a complete stranger told you in a coffee-house?'

The fire spits loudly as if matching its master's ire. Edward bristles. He cannot help it.

'I know it sounds mad, but there was something about the man. I can't explain it.'

'You can't rely on the advice of strangers.'

'Cynical as ever.'

'Well, really!'

Cornelius swings his leg over the arm of his chair, angles his stockinged feet toward the fireplace, flexes his big toe. Lounging as he is in his state of half-undress and a black curl falling across his forehead, he reminds Edward of a Renaissance painting, a veritable Michelangelo. Cornelius gestures to Edward with his glass.

'A man you don't know tells you to seek out the advice of a girl, whose dead parents specialised in Grecian pottery. You know the Society has no interest in Mediterranean art any more. Gough has distinctly said that the Society needs to focus its efforts on British history. The ancient world has been overdone.'

'Still, it is not without merit.'

'Of course not,' says Cornelius with a frown, 'but—'

'Consider the recent Roman excavations at Pompeii, after all.'

'Yes, but there have been substantial finds there. The Society is hardly going to overlook such a monumental discovery as *that*.'

'Cornelius,' Edward says patiently, 'I hope this girl might have something of value, something worth studying.'

His friend groans in response. 'Grecian artefacts are not what they want, Edward! If you do this, you're setting yourself up for another fall.'

'That's if I decide to do anything about it. I haven't even spoken to her yet.'

'But you *do* intend to?'

'I feel that now the idea has been put into my head I can't not.'

For perhaps the hundredth time today Edward thinks of his meeting with the old man, how fortuitous it was that he should have happened upon him in the manner he did. How it was he knew Edward's name . . .

Cornelius sighs loudly, swings his legs back round and places them squarely either side of the tiger's head.

'I think it's a mistake,' he warns. 'Your logic is based entirely on a chance encounter. Focus on something else, something concrete, for God's sake.'

Edward places his glass down on the table with a pronounced *clunk*. 'I refuse to believe this was a chance encounter.'

He hears the determined lilt to his voice and for a moment Edward feels guilty, as if he has spoken out of turn – but Cornelius' expression has softened now and he is shaking his head not with frustration but resignation.

'You've always been a dreamer. Heaven forbid I try to stop you.' He takes a long swig of brandy and his Adam's apple bobs sharply against his throat. The look he gives Edward is affectionate, but it is laced with something else Edward cannot place. 'I just don't want you to be disappointed. Not again.'

'I know what I'm doing,' Edward returns mildly, and for one blinding moment he believes it, feels unaccountably sure of himself. But Cornelius cradles the glass in his lap, wets his bottom lip with the tip of his tongue.

'Sometimes, Edward, I'm really not sure you do.'

# CHAPTER NINE

It has begun to snow. Across the rooftops London's skyline is peppered white and the gulls cry their grievance to the clouds. In her attic room Dora is in bed, has cocooned herself within her blankets, knees tucked beneath her. She stretches her fingers against the cold, adjusts the grip on her pencil. As she sketches, Hermes potters up and down the headboard, claws scuttle-tapping the wood. The candle flame bows into the light breeze that wends itself from the window frame that is in dire need of repair, sending shadows dancing over the ceiling. Discarded across the floorboards are the remnants of Dora's previous attempts, paper scrunched into compact balls that fit perfectly the cushion of her fist.

She cannot concentrate.

Her current effort is a series of scribbles set about the page as if they have been drawn by a child. A meandros border, its angular lines cutting through the paper where she has pressed too hard with the pencil. Dainty flabella, their leaves shaped into feathers. Repeating waves. Twisted snakes. Floral mandalas. All echo the Grecian form but none of her drawings quite capture the images in her imagination. Each sketch holds within it her frustration, half-formed memories she should not have forgotten.

Dora sighs. Designing something like this should have come

easily, should have been second nature, but she simply cannot apply herself tonight. Her mind keeps wandering down to the bowels of the basement where Hezekiah's mysterious shipment sits.

The house creaks on its joists with a sigh.

Her uncle was not at dinner. Lottie brought Dora a tureen of watery soup and slipped from the room having not uttered a single word, and Dora has seen neither hide nor hair of either of them all evening.

Why should Lottie of all people be privy to Hezekiah's plans but his own niece be excluded? What is in that crate? Why did Hezekiah look so panicked when Dora questioned him? And who were those men that brought it?

Perhaps she could pick the lock to the basement . . .

Oh, but what use is there in speculating? What good does it do her? Stop it, Dora thinks, you will only drive yourself mad.

She tries to conjure up memories of a dig site in Delos. Dora had been very young then – no more than five, she is sure – but she remembers one particular afternoon when her father spent hours uncovering a mosaic. Dora sat with him as he brushed away the dust, fascinated by the shapes revealed beneath: intricate foliage, curling waves, stepped triangles. She remembers how he showed her – his voice rich and warm in her ear – rosette motifs, swirling palmettes. Was there not a bull's head, surrounded by foliage?

It is no good. Dora rips the sheet away with a groan. All she has managed to conjure in the last five minutes is a rambling grapevine in the corner of the page, and she screws the paper up into a ball, throws it down to join the others littering the floor. Not one of her scribblings lends itself to a necklace, a pair of earrings, or anything a member of high society would wear.

'Oh, Hermes,' she sighs. The magpie chirrups, flutters down onto her lap. She reaches out, strokes his head with the backs of her fingers. He nips at them gently. 'Perhaps I'm a fool. What am I to do?'

Though Dora knows it is impossible for him to understand her, Hermes' head has tilted and his black eyes watch her so intently she is sure he does. But then the magpie stretches his wings, begins to ferret his beak between his feathers, and Dora falls back against the pillows. She taps her pencil to her lips. It is obvious she will get no inspiration trapped up here in her room. Dora tries to remember if there is anything in the shop that might inspire her. Was there not a cabinet tucked far back that held fragments of those old mosaics?

*Two birds . . .*

'Hermes, come,' she says, decided, excavating her legs from the twist of blankets, dislodging the bird from her lap. 'Let us go exploring.'

Dora pulls on some woollen socks, bundles herself into her father's old banyan. She takes the candle, pats her shoulder. With a quiet caw Hermes perches on it; his sharp talons bunch the quilted silk, adding to the holes he has already made in the padding. Dora lifts the latch of the bedroom door, breath held for the squeak. It does not come. She breathes out.

Four flights of stairs call for care. She tiptoes her way down them, has memorised their creaks, their weak spots, the bow of rotten wood. At the bottom Dora bites her lip. The bell. In the dark of the stairwell she ponders how to manage it. Impatient with her lack of movement, Hermes emits a tiny squawk.

'*Isychia!*' Dora presses her forefinger and thumb to his beak. The candle wobbles in its chamberstick. 'Don't let me down now.'

In answer to her whispered plea the magpie shakes his head, ruffles his feathers against her hair. Dora releases him, frowns deeply at the door.

All she can do is try.

Placing her palm flat against the wood Dora ever so slowly pushes it open. The door is heavy; it gives with a dull creak. She winces, tries to gauge the distance between casement and bell. It cannot be much. After a moment she hears the door touch metal, the tinny scrape of clapper on lip, and Dora stops before the bell can make another sound. She looks at the gap she has made.

There is just enough room for her to squeeze through.

Strange, how differently the familiar appears in the dark.

Outside, snow is forming tufty mountains on the windowsill. The muffled sounds of coffee-house merriment filter in through the thin glass. The light from the window only serves to throw the towering cabinets into silhouette and Dora blinks into the semi-darkness, stretches her candle arm in front of her. She can just make out the counterfeit Shang dynasty china bowls on the shelves.

First things first.

The cabinet she thinks of can be found deep within the shop and Dora makes her way there from memory, thankful that Hezekiah ensured a wide path through to the back wall.

Still, she must walk carefully. The candle only offers a weak flame and though her eyes have adjusted to the dark, the cabinets towering either side of her block out the light from the street. She holds a hand out in front of her, counting her steps:

*Énas, dýo, tría, téssera . . .*

The tips of her fingers hit wood. She turns right.

*Októ, ennéa, déka.*

Deeper in now, the light grows denser. It is only when she reaches the cool of whitewash on the fifteenth step that she knows she has reached the basement doors. Right again, she thinks, but Dora hesitates a moment. Is Hezekiah down there? She strains to listen but she cannot hear a thing.

She must stop herself from giving in to temptation and continues carefully to the back of the shop. There it is: a small, squat cabinet with clawed feet tucked into the furthest corner of the room. It barely reaches the tops of her thighs. She remembers playing in front of it while her parents informed their clients with news of recent digs, its panelled doors wide open, its treasures littering the floor. Dora sets down the candle on the cabinet's worn unpolished top. On her shoulder, Hermes bobs.

Dora sinks to her knees. The doors are stiff. She places her palm against the hinge to steady herself and when she tugs the doors open, the candle wobbles dangerously above her. Dora's eyes flick up to it in alarm.

*Do not fall, please, do not fall.*

The candle settles. Hermes chitters. Dora lets out a sigh of relief.

The inside is shallower than she remembers it to be, not much room here at all, and its contents seem to have been shoved unceremoniously in. Dora removes them with care. A dented brass cup, a pocket sundial, a set of pewter spoons, a pipe . . . She raises this closer to her face, squints at the pattern. An embossed heart. No good. She reaches in again, pulls out a snuffbox, a miniature of an old woman wearing a towering wig, two matching candlesticks made of brass. At the very back of the cabinet her fingers skim over something small, cool, hard. Dora reaches for it, brings it out, tilts it in the candle flame.

For a long moment Dora stares. She had completely forgotten it existed.

In her hand is an unusual gold key about the size of her thumb, its cylindrical stem – dull now with age and misuse – detailed with pretty filigree patterns. At its head is a revolving oval jet disc. On the disc, a relief. A bearded face.

She has a vague memory of playing with the key when she was a small child, for no reason at all except that she liked to spin the disc around, over and over. Did she ever find out what it belonged to? She cannot remember. Dora reaches her hand back into the cabinet, wonders if perhaps the key accompanies a trinket box, though she has no recollection of the fact, but there is nothing of the kind hidden in the cabinet's bowels. Dora looks at the key again, bites her lip. Can she use it? It is beautiful to be sure, but the detailing has no bearance on the Grecian designs she seeks. Certainly, she has no use for it now. With a shrug Dora places it aside, then searches through some pouches full of nothing more than unserviceable scraps of leather and satin.

Eventually she sags. No mosaics. No pottery fragments, no coins. Dora was sure there had been a small bust of Athena with her nose and helmet plume chipped. But no, there is nothing. Nothing she can use. Dora bites back her disappointment. Even though the items she remembers were broken or in poor condition they were, at least, genuine. Someone would have wanted them. They must then have been sold.

So. That leaves only one place, her second quarry of the night.

The basement.

Dora has never been down there, never gone any further than the doors, not so much as set one foot on the top stair. She had no need to, not even in her parents' day; as their private space Dora had been taught to respect it. When they died she had been too young to catalogue everything they left behind – Hezekiah did that – and after it was cleared and he claimed it as his own office and workshop, Dora never felt the need to question the fact . . . until today. For tonight a crate is stored there, a shipment he does not want her to see. And if there is a shipment he does not want her to see, what else is he keeping down there? What else does he hide from her?

69

Dora quietly replaces all the items in the cupboard. She picks up the candle, turns around, retraces her steps.

The large basement doors rise before her. On her shoulder Hermes bristles.

Dora stares down at the padlock, tries to assess how easy it would be to pick. But just as she reaches out to touch it, there comes a quiet keening sound. Dora's hand stops in mid-air. Her eyes widen, and Hermes curls his talons into the padding of her banyan. But then there is another sound, a much more familiar one, and in part-relief, part-disappointment, Dora drops her arm.

Strains of Hezekiah's voice find their way up the stairs. She puts her ear to the door. He is muttering to himself, as he so often does when he confines himself to the basement. Dora glances at the padlock again. It is open a little at the catch, the chain looped round only one door handle, not both. Of course he is down there; she should have known he would be. And Lottie too, by the sound of it.

So, then. Her adventure this night is done. Dora makes her retreat and begins her slow creep back upstairs to the attic. Halfway up – disguising a misplaced foot on the stair – Dora hears a snore coming from the housekeeper's room. Her old room. Lottie, then, is abed after all.

Frowning, she continues up. And when she slips into her own bed and pulls the covers to her chin, Dora finds herself wondering how her uncle could have produced a sound that reminded her so much of a woman, weeping.

# CHAPTER TEN

It will not open.

By God he has tried – for hours, it seems, he has tried – but the thing remains firmly shut. He could break it, of course, but then the second part of his plan will have failed and this whole enterprise will have been for naught. The time, the *years* he will have wasted! The money he will have lost! No, he cannot bear it.

This was meant to be his salvation. It was to have solved everything.

Hezekiah frowns deeply. His leg throbs.

He runs a finger over the seal. There must be a mechanism, something dastardly clever that he has not yet discovered. He mutters distractedly, taps the sides with his knuckles, searches for a weakness in its structure, a way to get in . . .

# CHAPTER ELEVEN

Despite Cornelius' misgivings, Edward determines to visit the Blake establishment and at the very least put his curiosity to rest.

Last night's snowfall has already turned to sludge; the snow is stained ochre and has formed wet scores along the road where carriages have come and gone. Still, the air is as sharp as a knife edge and Edward pulls his collar up about his neck, hunches his chin into his scarf. By the time he reaches the top of Ludgate Street his fingers are numb.

It does not take him long to spot the shop – its bowed window protrudes over the pavement – and Edward pauses a moment to take it in. The white paint on the panelled window frames peels in large clumps, there is a crack in one of the glass panes. The sign above the shop is faded, the spacing between the words not quite in keeping with its size. Edward squints. Ah, yes. The word 'Hezekiah' has been squeezed inelegantly between the edge of the board and the word 'Blake'. Beneath, the faint outline of 'Elijah' peeps its way through. The white-haired gentleman was quite right; the shop is clearly not what it used to be.

A sudden push at his shoulder knocks Edward off balance and he must grasp at the windowsill for support. 'Gerroutha'way, will ye?' a gruff voice barks and Edward rubs his shoulder, looks to address the man who has pushed past him.

'I beg pardon . . .' he begins, but he speaks now only to a strange and throbbing crowd, one body very much like any other.

'You have to keep moving in these parts,' another voice says, this one infinitely softer, and Edward spins to find a young woman leaning against the doorframe of the shop. 'Standing still will only get you run down.'

Edward stares.

*This* must be Pandora Blake . . . and she is quite unlike anything he has seen before. Tall – the top of his head would come in line perfectly to her nose – her skin a paler colour of the walnuts he and Cornelius ate the night before. Her dress is plain, a serviceable blue, and – though little acquainted with feminine fashions – looks to Edward to be a number of years out of date. A pair of unflattering spectacles frames eyes of which, in the shadow of the door, he cannot fathom the shade. Her hair is as dark as molasses and piled atop her head; a rose-coloured ribbon keeps a few stray curls in place. Bizarrely, a magpie is perched on her shoulder. It peers at him with beady black eyes that seem to know perfectly what Edward is about and why.

He has stared so long that the woman's wry smile has vanished and she has shifted from one foot to another. The magpie chitters. Edward shakes his head to loosen his tongue.

'Yes, yes, you're right of course –' and he feels his cheeks grow pink. 'I didn't mean to . . .'

'Can I help you, sir?'

Edward tries to compose himself. 'Yes! Yes, indeed.' He gestures at the shop. 'I'm looking for . . .'

But she nods, is already retreating, and blinking foolishly at the empty space she has left behind, all Edward can do is follow.

By the time his eyes have adjusted to the dim confines of the shop, the young woman is standing behind a small counter tucked into a cramped corner, and a portly man in a too-tight waistcoat is limping toward him, beefy hand reaching out to shake his.

'Hezekiah Blake, dear sir,' the man says, pumping Edward's hand with such force he feels a tendon tweak in his wrist. The man's hand is clammy and when he releases it, Edward surreptitiously wipes his on the seat of his trousers. 'Why, your fingers are quite frozen! Dora, send for Lottie won't you, and we shall offer our guest a nice warm broth.'

'Really, sir, there's no need—'

'Nonsense, nonsense,' Mr Blake is saying, guiding him over to a pair of ornate gilt chairs set in green velvet. 'I insist. I like to make sure my customers feel quite at home here. You don't mind if we sit?' He gestures to his right leg. 'A small accident yesterday.'

'Nothing serious?'

There is the tinkle of a bell and a door set behind the counter swings where Pandora – no, Dora, Mr Blake called her – has disappeared through it.

Mr Blake grimaces slightly as he sinks down into the cushion of the chair. 'Only a scratch,' he says, gesturing to his thigh. 'It will heal soon enough. But it aches, you see.'

'Of course.'

The large man stares at him. Edward stares back. A thin scar runs down one cheek, livid white against the rouge of the man's flesh.

'Well, then, Mr . . . ?'

'Lawrence.'

'Lawrence. What is it I can find for you?' At Edward's hesitation Mr Blake spreads his arm, gestures at the shop floor. 'As you can see we have many treasures here. Perhaps you wish to browse?'

Edward, who cannot quite bring himself to be rude, finds himself agreeing.

74

'Excellent, excellent. But you will wait for my niece to return before you do? Yes, yes, sit there. No need to exert yourself.'

There is a pause. Somewhere, clocks tick out of sequence. Edward forces a smile.

'Have you been in business long?'

'Oh,' Mr Blake says, as if this is nothing, straightening his cuff, 'many years.' He repeats it. 'A family establishment, you see. Do you know the trade?'

Edward wonders for the briefest moment whether to be honest, but something about this man makes him feel that safety lies in deception and so he says, 'No, sir, not at all.'

'Ah!' The older man smiles, leans conspiratorially in. Edward catches the faint waft of coffee on the stale edge of his breath. 'My dear departed brother left the shop to me. I have made it my life's work to keep its eminent reputation as high as it was in his day.'

Pompous. A touch of conceit.

'Indeed,' Edward says awkwardly. The pair fall back into silence. The clocks whirr in their casings and Mr Blake watches him intently, like a fox gauging for weakness in its prey. When Miss Blake returns Edward is near turning tail to flee.

Miss Blake hands him a small cup. She glances at him, then away, as if guilty. Edward takes the cup with both hands. It warms his fingers immediately, the blood tingling pleasantly down his veins.

'Thank you.'

Miss Blake nods. The magpie on her shoulder squawks.

'Dora . . .' Mr Blake's voice takes on a tired inflection and he sends Edward a diffident look. 'Must you insist on bringing that filthy bird into the shop? You know I dislike you doing so.'

Edward sees a tic in Miss Blake's jaw and suspects she knows full well. He blows steam from the broth.

'He does no harm, Uncle. But,' she says, as Mr Blake makes to object, 'I shall relegate him to a perch out of harm's way, if you prefer.'

'Well . . .' He seems to force a smile, and she sets the bird on a high bookcase behind the counter where immediately the magpie commences to grooming. Mr Blake eyes the bird with distaste. 'I suppose up there I might be able to pass him off as a stuffed commodity. Perhaps I could sell him! Mr Lawrence, might I persuade you?' and Mr Blake laughs heartily at his misdirected humour, a loud and obtrusive laugh that has Edward shifting uncomfortably in his seat. Miss Blake's eyes narrow. Edward takes a sip of broth.

It is rich. Too much salt.

When his mirth has dissipated the older man turns his attention back to Edward, watches him lick the grease from his lips. 'Is that better?'

'Much, sir,' he lies.

'Well, Mr Lawrence, I shall leave you to your broth and browsing.' He presses a finger to his nose, his bloodshot eyes creasing as he smiles in what Mr Blake must consider to be a jovial way, but to Edward appears almost predatory. 'I shall be watching you keenly, sir, ready to offer my assistance.'

And up he gets, off to the counter he goes, favouring his uninjured leg. As Edward diligently finishes his small cup of broth – it has already started to congeal at the bottom – he tries not to watch the way Miss Blake hunches intently over a piece of paper which she marks with a pencil, the way she seems to lean away from her uncle who hovers far too close at her shoulder. Edward turns his attention instead to the cabinets that tower all the way up to a ceiling patched with damp. He puts the cup on the dusty floor and stands up.

From what the white-haired gentleman told him Edward had not expected to find anything of worth here. Still, this does not prepare him for what he sees. Edward is no green man; his childhood at

Sandbourne – despite his lack of formal education – gave him knowledge enough to understand at a very early age what was a genuine antique and what was not. His self-taught education at the generosity of the Ashmoles gave him the discerning eye of a collector and he can say, without a shadow of doubt, that there is not one item in Hezekiah Blake's Emporium for Exotic Antiquities that can reliably be passed off as authentic.

The first shelving cabinet is filled with Oriental pieces. Edward looks at a plate, notes the mix of Japanese cherry blossom and Chinese dragons that would not be paired together were it legitimate. A small ceramic bowl. He picks it up, turns it over. It pretends to be Ming dynasty, but the reign marks have clearly been made by someone with little or no knowledge of that country's calligraphy. The 'Da' symbol, for instance. It portrays a man standing upright with arms and legs, but the leg should not start above the arm as it does here. Cornelius – whose speciality is in Oriental art – would pale with disgust. From the corner of his eye Edward sees Mr Blake make to move toward him and so quickly he replaces the bowl on the shelf.

Mr Blake resumes his position at the counter.

Edward moves on.

The next cabinet is a concoction of mismatched trinkets and glasswear that could easily be found languishing in the basket of a traveller selling their wares outside of Newgate. He pauses to read a little card label – *Curiosities from the 1500s* – and it is all Edward can do not to snort.

He crosses to the cabinets on the other side, walks slowly up and down and back again, marvelling at the rubbish littering every shelf. Cornelius would barely be able to contain his ire. Indeed, he would not even exert himself to try. If the Society ever required someone to write a report on forgery within the antiquity trade, Edward thinks wryly, all he need do is spend an afternoon here and he would sail through the fellowship entry without a blink of an eye. Finally, Edward stops at a cabinet filled with men's fripperies. He leans closer to view a crude-looking cravat pin displayed front and centre on a silk-backed board.

Clearly unable to curb his impatience any longer, Mr Blake is on him like a rash.

'Ah, a true beauty that! Pearl and brass –' in a rush he removes it from the cabinet, makes to peer at it close – 'from the Stuart period if I remember correctly.' Mr Blake proffers it to Edward like a chalice. 'Ten shillings, for you.'

Edward turns the pin over in his hands, feels the weight of it, the roughness of the pearl. A recent fabrication, likely put together in under an hour.

'I don't think so,' Edward says, making to turn away, but Mr Blake places a heavy hand on Edward's shoulder and squeezes.

'Pearls are particularly fashionable right now. I hear the Prince has a great fondness for them. Please, sir, do consider. Eight shillings, perhaps?'

Edward tries not to squirm under his grip. For a moment he is taken back to a dark room, the cruel unyielding hand of another, and he must blink the painful memory away.

'That is not—' he begins, but Mr Blake wags a finger.

'Bills to pay, you see,' he says, mock-jovial. 'I can't let this pretty little thing go for any less than five shillings. You are robbing me quite blind, sir!'

Edward knows perfectly well that what he looks at is no pearl – dipped glass, if he is not mistaken – and the stick is not even brass but steel painted to disguise it as such. No, the item is nowhere near worth the sum Mr Blake asks for it but his unwanted memory has distracted him, he hesitates too long, and somehow all at once Edward is standing at the counter parting with his day's wages, Mr Blake is counting the coins in his hand, his niece is wrapping the cravat pin very carefully in a square of cloth, and Edward is not altogether sure how it happened.

'I say,' Mr Blake exclaims suddenly. The older man is staring at Edward's wrists. 'What magnificent cufflinks you're wearing. May I ask where you purchased them?'

Miss Blake's delicate hands still. Edward steals a look at her face but her expression is as blank as porcelain.

'I . . .' Edward hesitates, glances down at the new gold and emerald-studded discs. 'They were a present. Purchased from a gold-smith in Soho, I believe.'

'Do you happen to know which one?'

With an almost imperceptible shake of her head Miss Blake resumes her wrapping. Edward lifts his shoulders in a shrug. 'Romilly's, I should imagine.' It is Cornelius' favourite shop.

Mr Blake's upper lip quivers. Despite the chill air of the shop, there is a sheen of sweat beading his Cupid's bow.

'Thank you, Mr Lawrence,' Mr Blake says. He pockets Edward's coins, awards him a smile filled with tombstone-like teeth. 'I'm indebted.' Then, to his niece, 'You won't object to minding the shop, will you, my dear?' He does not wait for her answer, is already stuffing fat arms down his coat sleeves. 'Mr Lawrence, perhaps you might accompany me?'

Edward clears his throat, forces a smile. He will not be chivvied from the shop; he must speak with Pandora Blake, alone.

'I regret I cannot.'

'A pity. No matter.' He reaches for Edward's hand again and Edward tries not to grimace, for the man's hand has grown clammier, if that could even be possible. 'A pleasure doing business with you, sir.'

'Indeed.'

But Edward's reply is lost, for Mr Blake is already limping out the door, coat-tails flapping. He leaves it swinging open and Miss Blake sighs, moves from behind the counter to shut it. When she turns back she links her fingers together – nervously, he thinks – and sends him a tight smile.

'I am sorry, Mr Lawrence.'

'Sorry?'

She returns to her post at the counter. 'I'm afraid you have been duped, like everyone else who ventures through these doors.' Miss Blake hands him the now fully wrapped cravat pin and Edward takes it, holds it loosely in front of him.

'I'm well aware.'

She nods. 'I suspected as much. You looked at everything far too closely.'

'Yes.' When she says nothing else Edwards adds, 'But why trouble yourself to tell me this? You surely wish to gain a profit – isn't it your business too?'

Something flashes in her eyes – the colour of spiced caramel, he sees clearly now – and his stomach gives a little flip.

'I don't know why I told you. Guilt, perhaps. And no. The business is not mine.'

A sharp caw makes them both jump. He had quite forgotten about the magpie high up on its perch. Miss Blake raises her hand on the beat of two softly spoken words – *Éla edó*, he thinks, Greek, perhaps? – and with a flurry of rainbow wing the bird flies to her. With a small smile Miss Blake places him on her shoulder where the magpie proceeds to stare at Edward in the same way it did on the street. Edward's grip tightens on the package. He clears his throat, tries to ignore the bird's insistent eyes.

'I have a confession, Miss Blake.'

'Oh?'

80

'I came here today to see you.'

The fingers that have been stroking the magpie's white breast pause. 'Me?'

Her eyes crease in confusion and Edward holds out a hand, meaning to put her at ease.

The magpie lunges.

The quiet of the shop is shattered by the heavy beat of wings and sharp stuttered caws. The cravat pin drops, Edward cries out and Miss Blake gasps, wraps her hands around the flapping bird.

'Hermes, no! *Stop!*'

Edward retreats to the ornate chair. The empty broth cup is knocked on its side and rolls across the floor. He sucks the fleshy V between forefinger and thumb, tastes the warm metallic of blood on his tongue.

'Oh, Mr Lawrence, I'm so sorry!' Miss Blake is rushing over, a bundle of wrapping cloth in her hands. Edward dares a glance upward, sees the magpie has been relegated back onto the bookcase. She sits on the other seat, takes his hand without asking. Her touch is gentle but firm. Miss Blake peers at his wound, dark head bent over his hand, and while the cut does indeed sting he finds far more interest in the curls on her crown, the heavy rope of dark glossy plait.

'It is just a scratch,' he murmurs.

'It is not,' she retorts, moving her head so he can see.

The 'scratch' resembles far more a small triangular wound and Edward blinks down at it in surprise. The bird has actually gouged out a chunk of skin.

Miss Blake sighs, presses the cloth tight against the wound. 'Does it not hurt?' she asks, and when Edward shakes his head – for, oddly, it really does feel no worse to him than a scratch – she shakes her head. 'It will, in an hour or two. Believe me, I know.' She tilts the hand that holds his. On her wrist is a small half-moon scar. 'I made the

81

mistake of trying to tidy his cage with him still in it.' Miss Blake smiles, wry again. 'Hermes is a very protective creature. If he feels something belongs to him, he will guard it steadfast.'

She releases the pressure, looks again. 'I'll wrap it now, before the bleeding worsens.'

Edward watches as Miss Blake binds his hand tightly with a strip of cloth. 'It is odd,' he says, 'that you should be protected by a bird.'

'It is not so strange.'

Miss Blake finishes up with a knot, releases his hand. For a moment he feels quite bereft.

'I found him on the roof just outside my bedroom window, about four years ago now. Fallen from a nest, I think. I left him there at first, thinking perhaps the parents would claim him but they never did, and, well, I couldn't bear to leave the little thing so helpless. So I took him in, nursed him myself. Magpies are clever. They remember who is kind to them.'

For a moment they both watch the bird which now stands balanced on one talon, cleaning its other claw. Then Miss Blake turns back to him.

'Now, sir,' she says. 'What is it you wished to discuss with me?'

# CHAPTER TWELVE

Dora has listened to Mr Lawrence's plea – for that is what it most undoubtedly is – in silence and not without sympathy. This pale, fair-haired man watches her now with trepidation as he waits for her answer, and Dora's heart goes to him – she understands completely what it means to want something that seems to thwart every step of the way – and so she is saddened to say the words, 'I cannot help you.'

Mr Lawrence's face drops. 'You can't?'

Dora stands, sweeps her arm about her in a gesture that shows clearly her distaste. 'Look, sir, where we are. Look –' and here she gestures to the cravat pin in its cloth wrapper still beached on the floor – 'at the bauble on which you spent your hard-earned coin. You know as well as I that this is a shop of fakes and mere fripperies.'

Mr Lawrence watches her from his seat. 'This I cannot deny. But I believe you must have something here that would serve my purpose. You would not have been recommended to me otherwise.'

'Recommended?'

'I was told to come here. To speak to you.'

'By whom?'

'A gentleman I met in a coffee-house. He seemed to know of you . . .'

'Well,' Dora shrugs, 'my parents were very popular; their reputation surpassed many of those in the trade. But Blake's Emporium has not sold items of historic worth for many years now, and certainly nothing of Mediterranean origin. All the pieces my parents found have gone.' Dora pinches her eyes shut, her frustration and pain new and raw once again. When she opens her eyes she sees Mr Lawrence through a sea of black spots. 'I too have craved something of worth in here. Only last night I tried to seek out some of my father's old wares and I was sorely disappointed.'

'What did you want them for?'

Dora hesitates. 'You must promise not to scorn me.'

Mr Lawrence stands. 'Miss Blake, I could not. I *would* not, after you've heard my own plight.'

Behind the counter, Hermes chirps. Dora sighs, rubs her forehead until the spots behind her eyes have vanished.

'I am a designer of jewellery. That is, I hope to be one.' She pauses to look at him, divining only an open face and earnest eyes. 'These past few months I have been building a portfolio of designs in the hope of opening my own establishment one day. The goldsmith I wanted to take them has refused on the grounds that Grecian styles are now the fashion. I thought . . .'

'You thought you would use your parents' pieces for inspiration.'

'Yes.' Dora spreads her hands. 'But I looked. I couldn't find anything.'

Mr Lawrence steps forward. 'So there truly is nothing? Nothing at all? I was so sure . . .'

'Your gentleman must have been mistaken. As I said, Mr Lawrence, you can see what we are dealing with here, what little worth we have.' She fidgets. 'You saw the manner of man my uncle is and . . . I have only one card left to play.'

'And that is?'

The question gives her pause. She stares at Mr Lawrence a moment, the solemn expression on his clean-shaven face. Should she tell him? Should she say? She does not sense him to be a dishonest sort of man. No, indeed, she sees in him quite the kindred spirit, a fellow dreamer – it is why she felt moved to confess how Hezekiah had hoodwinked him – and so Dora, feeling reckless, points across to the basement.

'Through those doors is my uncle's workshop. I do not know for sure what he keeps in it, but I have come to suspect there is more than I originally believed. There could be something down there.'

'And if there is not?'

Behind her, Hermes chitters on his perch.

'Then I must think again.'

Mr Lawrence peers down the room. 'Those doors are locked,' he says, having observed the padlock. 'You have the key?'

'No. My uncle has the only one. But I have a plan.'

'Oh?'

And now, now she has revealed too much. What is she thinking, confiding in a man she has known barely an hour?

'Mr Lawrence,' Dora says, hardening her voice to steel. 'You have taken far too much of my time already. I am very busy.'

He blinks, not at the change of tone, she knows, but at her bare-faced lie. She watches him look around, at the emptiness of the shop, the dust lining the shelves, and Dora blushes.

'Please, sir. It is best you leave. My uncle . . .'

Mr Lawrence stares at her a moment. The disappointment she sees in his eyes makes her belly jump.

'Very well,' he says finally, 'I shall do as you ask. But . . .' He digs into his waistcoat, brings out a small rectangular card. She looks down at it.

85

ASHMOLE BOOKBINDERY
No 6. Russel Street
off Covent Garden Market

The words are set within a beautiful border of filigree patterns inter-
spersed with finely drawn books. Once, Blake's Emporium possessed
cards such as this.

'If you do find something,' he is saying, 'if you think you might be
able to help, I beg of you to seek me out. I would find a way to repay
you. There must be something I can do to assist you.'

'I doubt it, Mr Lawrence.'

He sends her a small smile. 'What is doubt, but a fact not yet
confirmed?'

Dora cannot respond to that. She curls her hand around the card;
the edges dig into her palm. Their eyes meet. Then he retrieves the
cravat pin from the floor and disappears onto the bustling street, the
bell ringing a tinny farewell.

Later that evening, with Hezekiah wearing new cufflinks that match
perfectly those of Mr Lawrence except that the stones in his are blue
rather than green, Dora begins to lay her trap. Her plan requires only
gin, and two people willing to fall folly to its madness.

At the dinner table she watches her uncle from beneath the fan of
her lashes. He has not mentioned the crate, has even attempted to
pretend nothing is amiss at all, tried to mollify her with ill-aimed
compliments that served only to anger her.

'What pretty patterns,' he murmured into her ear earlier in the
shop while Mr Lawrence assessed the fakery of its shelves and she

sketched laurels onto paper. 'You truly have your mother's talent for drawing.'

Hezekiah knows she is suspicious about the crate. She knows it from the way he studies her when he does not think she is looking. His eyes dart, his tongue wets his lips. It is clear from the way he steps tentatively around her that Hezekiah wonders why she does not enquire about it, but Dora has no patience for games. Too often over the years has she asked him questions only to receive a half-hearted response or obvious falsehoods. Why sell forgeries when her parents had not? How did he know how to make them? And why not spend the money from his sales on repairs for the shop instead of on fripperies for himself? Never has she received a straight answer. No, Dora must discover the truth another way.

The solution came to her easily.

One of her early jewellery designs for a brooch required a duplicate pattern. The first piece she had crudely carved from a small block of wood, but Dora had not the energy to carve a second and so instead she created a mould from wax. The same principle applies here. All she needs is the key that hangs from the chain round Hezekiah's neck.

Getting to it, however, will not be so easy, even with gin . . .

Hezekiah shifts heavily in his seat, knocks his plate with his elbow. Dora watches him stretch his leg out from under the table, rub the fleshy pillow of his thigh.

'It pains you, Uncle?'

'Of course it does,' he snaps. His forehead shines. His wig slips. 'The pain does not let up.'

'But it was only a scratch, surely?' she replies with mock patience. 'Rest will help.'

Hezekiah gives a short laugh, like bellows exhaling air. 'Rest! Dora, I cannot rest.'

His words carry with them the echo of desperation. There is a brief silence between them in which Dora makes a decision. She discards her unseasoned quail (another of Lottie's attempts at fine dining gone awry), and rises from the table. With great effort she forces herself up to his end, sits down on the chair closest to him. He blinks at her in surprise. She rests her hand on the table close to his, an attempt to play the part of dutiful, caring niece.

'Of course you can,' Dora says softly, soothingly. 'Rest, Uncle. Take to your bed a day or two. Are you not master here? I can oversee the shop. Do I not do so often enough?'

Hezekiah's eyes are watery in the candlelight. He hesitates, seems about to say something of import, but then he shifts again in his seat, places a clammy hand on top of hers and awkwardly pats it. It takes all of Dora's effort not to flinch.

'I think, perhaps,' she coaxes, 'some gin would help. Do we have any?'

They do, of that she made sure when Lottie was fetching beans from the coffee-house next door. Three bottles of the stuff, hidden behind a large bag of grain.

'What an excellent plan. Why don't you ring the bell?'

Dora cannot cross the room fast enough.

It does not take Hezekiah long to succumb to the effects of juniper for Lottie, who he insisted join them, has made the exercise far too easy. The housekeeper's continual refilling of his glass means that Dora need hardly do a thing except wait.

'Has the pain eased, Uncle?'

Dora keeps her voice low, an innocent caress. This close she can see the tiny network of red veins monopolising his nose.

'Aye,' he says, 'though I'm sure I would feel far better if Lottie were to administer her healing touch . . .'

Lottie – whose eyelids are already beginning to droop – perks up at this, rests a stockinged foot on Hezekiah's leg and rubs it lightly with her toes. Hezekiah sighs deeply. Then, through her drink-fug, the housekeeper slides Dora a suspicious look. 'Why're you here, missum?'

'Why shouldn't I be?' Dora counters, clenching hard the stem of her glass. 'I'm his niece. I've more right to sit at this table than you do, after all.'

For a moment Lottie looks shocked, hurt, almost, and Dora feels a spark of guilt for what she knows was uncharacteristic meanness. But then Lottie's jaw hardens, a scornful light enters her eye, and Dora's guilt vanishes as quickly as it came.

'Now now, Dora,' Hezekiah says, face rosy, his voice lacking its usual ire. 'There's no need for such talk. You too, Lottie. Can we not enjoy a little drink together in peace?'

Lottie pouts. 'I just want to know what she's about.' Her words come slow. 'She's never drank with us before. Why now?'

Dora lifts her eyebrows. 'Perhaps I wanted to try it?'

'A likely story. You've barely had any.'

'How can I when you've drunk the majority?'

To this Lottie says nothing, unsteadily pours herself another glass of gin. Dora looks to the bottle. A third gone. How much longer must she wait? She hides her frustration by holding out her own glass for a refill.

'Am I not allowed a change of heart and spend a little time with my uncle?'

Lottie snorts but fills Dora's glass. The gin spills over the rim onto Dora's fingers.

'Your heart don't change, Pandora Blake. It's as stuck up as your mother's.'

'How would *you* know?'

'Stop, both of you,' Hezekiah slurs, raises an appeasing arm. He fumbles for his glass, slides it toward the housekeeper. Lottie fills it to the brim and he knocks it back, holds the glass out once more.

At the mention of her mother, Dora feels a dull familiar ache in the pit of her stomach. Dora does not drink – has never had the opportunity – and she is conscious that with only a few sips the gin has already begun to take hold, her bravado has risen, and it is for this reason she asks, 'What was she like, my mother?'

Hezekiah blinks blearily. 'Surely you remember?'

Dora hesitates. It has been so long. She was eight years old when her parents died and now, at one and twenty, the memories she has of her childhood are fragmented, glimpsed as if looking sideways at the shards of a broken mirror. She remembers her time in London – her father's business gatherings at Christmas, those weekly visits to Mr Clements with her mother which had meant so very much. And then in Greece, she remembers learning her Greek alphabet and numbers every morning, remembers bedtime stories when her mother would recount her love of history and Grecian myth. She remembers star-gazing on mountaintops, how both her parents taught her to identify Orion, Centaurus and Lyra, the Ursas Minor and Major.

She swallows. Dora remembers the dig site that fateful day, the man who pulled her from the wreckage, who later returned her mother's cameo to her, its carved edges pitted with dirt. Those, those are the large shards. But the smaller ones . . . those are more fleeting, more difficult to grasp. She remembers al-fresco picnics at dusk, her parents' laughter as they walked along sun-baked plains hand in hand. She remembers the cameo brooch, more recently the key. Her father's face she struggles to picture, but her mother's is more vivid: olive skin, dancing eyes, a quick and easy smile. She smelt, Dora thinks, of orange blossom.

'Some things I remember,' Dora says quietly. 'But I knew her only as my mother, not as a woman. Not as a friend, as she would have one day been.'

She cannot keep the wistfulness from her voice. Lottie huffs into her glass.

Hezekiah breathes a deep, lethargic sigh. 'Your mother was the most enticing woman I have ever known. So fine. So accomplished. She could draw, she could sing. Yet she had no qualms about wearing a pair of breeches and gallivanting around in the dirt when it suited her . . .'

Her uncle's voice falters, trails off. Hezekiah stares a long moment at the large map on the wall and Dora wonders what memory he is picking apart. But then Lottie clears her throat, unlaces the top of her bodice, begins to fan herself with Hezekiah's discarded wig and his attention goes immediately to the plump creamy curves of her breasts pushing up teasingly from their stays.

'Why think of her when *I'm* here,' Lottie murmurs, and she resumes rubbing Hezekiah's calf with her stockinged toes.

The relationship between Lottie Norris and her uncle has never been a secret. It did not take Dora long to understand where Hezekiah had found her – Lottie had barely lived with them a week before it became apparent she was no cook or clean. Those tasks did not come naturally to her. Those tasks she learnt as the years went along. No, Dora knows what profession Lottie held before this, but until now she has never had to witness the proof of it and grimacing, Dora looks away. Sitting so close to him she hears the moment Hezekiah's breath hitches. From the corner of her eye Dora sees Lottie raise the hem of her skirt. Hezekiah reaches for her and Lottie giggles as she is pulled onto his lap.

'You're far too warm,' she whispers in his ear, fingers teasing his cravat. Then Lottie twists, reaches for the gin, fills her and Hezekiah's glasses to the top.

Dora looks again to the bottle. Half left.

Very slowly she edges her seat away. The couple do not notice. Lottie tips her glass, lets the gin drip onto her chest. Hezekiah dips his head. The housekeeper laughs.

If, Dora thinks, she is very quiet and still, they will forget she is here.

Her attention turns to a tall thin cabinet in the corner of the room. Sitting on a shelf behind a glass door is a small globe of the world. Hezekiah brought it with him – along with the map on the wall – when he moved into the apartments, set it at first on an octagonal table in the hallway. Dora had been fascinated by the globe's pitted ochre surface, its intricate detailing that set land and sea apart, and she used to spin it wildly on its axis until Hezekiah caught her and forbade her to ever touch it again. It was relegated then to the cabinet, stored safely out of reach from her 'meddling hands'.

There is a sigh, a groan. Dora closes her eyes, tries her best to ignore what she cannot, focuses on her breathing, counts down from one hundred. Finally, just when she thinks she can bear it no longer, there is the dull *chink* of an empty glass dropping onto the rug. Dora opens her eyes. Hezekiah's have begun to droop. Lottie sleeps, head resting on his breast. Hezekiah unsteadily raises his glass.

'Are you tired yet, Uncle?' Dora says softly and he grunts then, turns his head to look at her, and for a moment he stares at Dora as if he does not know her at all.

'You always were difficult.'

His breath causes one of Lottie's curls to ruffle.

'Difficult?'

He wets his lips. 'Why didn't you listen to me? All you had to do was listen . . .' Then Hezekiah's chin falls onto his chest, and to Dora's relief he begins to snore.

Finally. It is done.

Dora rises unsteadily from the chair. She sways slightly on her feet and, nauseous at what she has just witnessed, reaches for the now near-empty gin bottle, finishes the lot in four hard dregs.

Her eyes water. She coughs into her hand.

To work.

She looks at Lottie's head resting against Hezekiah's chest, wonders how far down the chain goes, if pulling it free will disturb her. Thanks to Lottie his cravat is now loose and, cringing, Dora slips her fingers between silk and skin slick with sweat. She reaches deep within the folds of his neck, pressing her fingers into its fleshy creases. When she feels the coarse thread of hair Dora pinches her eyes closed in disgust. Hezekiah sniffs, turns his face, and for one agonising moment Dora thinks she is trapped, but then she dares move her fingers and feels the rough links of chain beneath her nails. She begins to pull.

The chain comes slowly, but it comes, and the grating of the links against his flesh seems to her far too loud. Lottie stirs, falls still. Then, when Dora has pulled the chain free, she starts the painful process of twisting it round until the key itself is clasped in the palm of her hand. It is a simple key: small, made of brass, stained from Hezekiah's sweat to a patched and grimy dark. Gently Dora rests it on the back of the chair, and the chain swings slow and steady like a pendulum.

From her pocket she brings out a shallow tinderbox. Then, one by one, she takes the candles from their sconces, pours melted wax into her makeshift mould casing until there is enough to make an

93

impression. Dora bites her lip. Already the wax has begun to cool. She must be quick.

Very carefully she presses the key into the wax. She holds it down, counts to twenty. When she releases it, the key pulls free with a *snap*.

Dora slips the key back beneath Hezekiah's shirt, arranges the cravat neatly around his neck. She clutches the box to her chest. Then, as quietly as she can manage, she slips from the room, Hezekiah and Lottie's snores following her up the stairs.

# CHAPTER THIRTEEN

The light is beginning to fade by the time Dora is able to leave the shop. Though it was, she concedes, her own fault – Hezekiah and Lottie did not rise from their gin-addled stupor until the church bells rang twelve – the impatience which gnawed at her insides made the wait all the more trying. She served three customers, dusted the bookshelves, swept the floor and rearranged the curiosity cabinet. Once or twice she wandered to the basement doors, cradled the padlock in her hand, pulled uselessly at the chain. By the time Hezekiah finally limps onto the shop floor near three hours later with his wig askew, Dora is making a beeline for the door, an excuse flying from her lips.

It is two miles to Piccadilly where the locksmith Bramah & Co. is located, but her impatience gives her speed. Another one of her parents' former acquaintances, Joseph Bramah had been the one to install a safe in the basement. Dora vaguely remembers the locksmith and her parents sitting together at the dining room table, sheets of paper littered with fine lines and numbers between them, and how – on seeing the finished product being hauled across the shop floor after one of her weekly visits to Mr Clements – Dora thought what a fuss had been made over something so wholly unremarkable.

Now, as she slips past the towering church of St Mary's off the Strand, she thinks instead of Mr Lawrence.

Handsome, though short, he was neatly dressed, his clothes fashionably cut. He had the look of a gentleman, Dora muses, and yet he did not appear such. Not that he was *un*gentlemanlike, but there was something in his manner that did not quite fit the mould. And his age . . . She comes to the conclusion that there cannot be much difference between him and her, though something in his countenance, something haunted in his eyes, makes him seem much, much older.

Lawrence, she thinks. An English name. But there was an unfamiliar lilt to his voice, a bent to the cockney she cannot place. An emphasis on the Gs in his speaking, something altogether warming.

*You must have something here that would serve my purpose.*

If only she did. And still, perhaps yet she does.

She wonders about this Society of Antiquaries he wishes to join, whether her parents – if not her mother then her father – were members. Dora has no recollection of the fact. Still, she can imagine what a privilege it would be to be admitted to their ranks. It is members such as those who could bring credibility to the shop, if only Hezekiah would treat her parents' legacy with the respect it deserves.

So lost is she in her musings that Dora walks straight past the locksmith's, and it is only when the whinny of a passing horse splits the air that she jumps, blinks into the growing dusk, realises what she has done. Scolding herself under her breath she turns back, ducks her head beneath the shop's low lintel beam and pushes open the door.

Inside the shop is dark and narrow, with only a few small candles glowing in their sconces. At the far end of the room, perched behind a glass counter on a stool very similar to the one she suffers on daily, is a thin man who reminds her of a newt trussed up in parson's clothing.

'I wish to speak with Mr Bramah,' she says, voice over-high.

The man lowers his quill, looks her up and down with a sniff. 'Do you have an appointment?'

'No, I . . .' Dora stops. She had not thought of this.

He sniffs again, resumes his number-tallying. 'Then I'm afraid you must make one,' he says curtly. 'Come back another day.'

'I can't!'

At Dora's desperate tone the man stares at her disapprovingly, quill hovering over his papers. A bulbous black drop of ink threatens to spill from the nib. She tries to compose herself.

'Sir, please. If you would be so kind as to tell Mr Bramah that the daughter of Elijah Blake, the antiquarian, wishes to see him on a matter most urgent.'

'Young lady, you cannot stride into a reputable establishment making demands.'

'My name is Pandora Blake. Please. Mention the name Blake and Mr Bramah is sure to see me. Please.'

She stares at him over the counter. He meets her gaze without flinching. But when it is clear Dora means not to move until she is accommodated the man sighs, places down the quill, and the ink makes fast its escape, blooms onto the paper like a flower unfolding to the sun.

'Oh, very well.'

He slips from the stool, disappears behind a curtain into the back room. She can hear muttering, the whisper-hiss of conference. Dora taps her fingers impatiently on the counter. There is a space of silence, then the approach of footsteps; the dark curtain is pulled full across on its pole, metal rings clattering. A man emerges.

'Miss . . . Blake?'

Mr Bramah is a tall, neatly dressed man (aside from the oil-smeared apron at his waist) with steel-grey hair though it was once, Dora remembers, as dark as the black on Hermes' wings. He blinks owlishly at her in the orange candlelight, seemingly waiting for Dora to speak. The dour assistant resumes his perch, purses his lips at the ink splodge and glares.

'Mr Bramah, sir,' Dora begins, a flush filling her cold cheeks. 'Many years ago my father Elijah Blake commissioned a safe from you. I was only a child then but I remember it clearly. As you specialise in locks I had hoped . . .'

She trails off. She does not know how to put her request articulately into words. Hearing herself fumble over them makes her ashamed, embarrassed.

Mr Bramah's mouth twitches. He seems to take pity on her for he says, 'A small fireproof safe, barely large enough for a grown man to stand in. For papers, ledgers. Standard cylinder lock, with pin and steel sliders in gold plate, self-locking. Yes, I remember the commission well.' He pauses, takes a breath. 'A complex job. Gold-and-black keys. Took a year to complete. The passing of your parents, Miss Blake, was an enormous shock. A great shame. But how may I help you now?'

Dora produces the wax-filled tinderbox. She is dismayed to see her hands are shaking.

'I was hoping you might produce a key for me.' As Mr Bramah frowns down at her offering she rushes on. 'I understand this is very unorthodox but it really is rather urgent. I have only this imprint to work from, but it should serve?'

He takes it, tilts the box this way and that. Next to him his assistant shakes his head as though lamenting the whimsy of women.

'Well,' Mr Bramah says, 'the mould is deep enough. It is a simple key from the looks of it. I cannot guarantee it would be perfect but the lines do seem clean enough . . .' He places the tinderbox on the counter. 'I can have it for you by tomorrow eve—'

'Forgive me, sir, but I need it today, this moment.'

She knows she is being unreasonable. To come to a shop and demand immediate service is arrogant, discourteous, but the thought is in her head now and she wants – no, needs – to know what sits in

98

the basement and so Dora places a fat purse on the counter, tries not to squirm as she thinks of how she took it from her uncle's coat pocket that morning. Dishonesty has never sat well with her. But then she stamps it down where it curdles in her belly. Where did *he* get it, after all?

Mr Bramah stares at Dora a moment before sliding the purse across the glass. He opens the drawstring, peers in. Hesitates.

'Unorthodox is the word, isn't it, Miss Blake? And you've left it very late in the day . . .' Dora can only stare pleadingly back at him. Mr Bramah picks up the box. 'It will take an hour,' he tells her.

She sighs in relief, clasps her hands. 'I will wait.'

Dora sits fully clothed on the bed. Hermes is perched on the window-sill. The light from the moon casts a silhouette of him on the floorboards, and if it were not for the small breeze coming from the rotten frames that ruffle his silken feathers, Dora could almost believe the bird to be a shadow portrait set behind a screen.

She is not sure how long she has waited for Hezekiah and Lottie to retreat to their beds. At dinner she pled a headache and retired to her room, marooned herself on the bed so that the floorboards would not groan beneath her from endless pacing. At her side the sketch-book lies flat and blank, her pencil resting on its sheets. Between her fingers Dora twists the new key over and over – ring to tooth, ring to tooth – a methodical spin of brass that hits her knuckles with dull and painless knocks.

Outside it has started to rain, needle-points at the glass. The sound is a comfort and Dora's impatience – sharp as salt – is dulled somewhat by the patter. Still, she cannot stop thinking about what might be waiting beneath the shop, what her new key might unlock. Items of Grecian origin, she hopes, to inspire her designs. But to know what is inside the crate, what else her uncle might be hiding . . . It is this that haunts her now.

Finally there is the creak of stair, the giggled laughter of Lottie, the low murmur of Hezekiah in the stairwell, the thud of door into casement. Dora half-lifts herself onto her elbows and feels the jitter of excitement in her chest, but when the bedsprings begin their abominable squeak she groans, presses the key hard into her palm. A squeal, a moan, a grunt. In vain she tries to shut her ears to the sounds and closing her eyes Dora turns onto her side, tucks her knees up to her chest, waiting for it to stop.

It goes on longer than she expects it to. There is a pause in their coupling – one of them either begged to rest or perhaps they merely started again – but when they finally cease their fleshy intimacies Dora feels exhausted, nauseous, as if someone has hollowed out her stomach and filled it with reeling worms.

She counts down one minute. Then another, another. After Dora has counted down ten she slips from the bed, pads on tiptoe to the door. On the cramped landing she listens, ears straining in the dark to the floor below. And then she hears it: Lottie's unmistakable snore coming from Hezekiah's bedchamber. When her uncle follows suit not a moment later Dora retreats quickly to her bed, takes up the sketchbook, the stub candle in its chamberstick. Hermes flees from his perch at the window and settles on Dora's shoulder, nips lightly at her ear. His feathers are cold against her cheek.

Dora wastes no time. Careful though she is, her impatience has tipped itself over and it is not in her now to be slow. Down the narrow stairwell she goes, stealing over the weak treads. At the bottom she eases the door open as she did before, props it open this time with a grotesque iron fish Hezekiah picked up from a vendor on the Strand,

and it is only when she is standing in front of the double doors of the basement that Dora realises she is shivering. She places her sketch-book and candle on the floor.

'Well, then,' Dora murmurs to Hermes. 'Shall we see if this works?'

Very carefully she reaches for the padlock, cradles it in her hand. It is cool to the touch, and with her bottom lip pressed between her teeth she slips the key into the lock. Please, she thinks, please let it fit, and she almost cries when the key turns easily without a sound.

The padlock gives with a low click, the chain *chk-chking* through the handles as it begins to fall loose. Dora wraps her hand around it, guides its fall quietly to the floor, puts the padlock down beside it. Hermes tugs at a strand of her hair.

For a long moment Dora stands immobile. Now that it has come to it, now that nothing bars her way, she feels unaccountably frightened at what she might find. And yet . . . The urge to fling open the basement doors is as instinctive as breathing. Very carefully, she pulls them open.

They do not creak; Dora releases the breath she has been holding in a long quiet spell. Retrieving the candle and sketchbook from the floor, she crosses onto the top stair.

She cannot see a thing. It is as if before her there is a vat of ink, fathomless, darker than dark. Instantly the hairs on the back of her neck rise up; she feels a whisper of cold air at her cheek like a sigh. On her shoulder Hermes' talons press sharply through her dress into her skin. Dora winces at the pinch.

'Hermes, stop,' she whispers, and to her surprise the bird hisses in response. 'Hermes, what—'

Suddenly the bird launches himself into the basement, and the sound of his wings makes Dora jump. Instinctively she cups the candle, shields the flame from his beating feathers.

'Hermes,' she calls, quiet, a hiss of her own. 'Where are you?'

But there is no caw in answer, no chirrup. There is instead an odd, low hum.

Dora hovers at the top of the stairs, blinking blindly into the dark. '*Hermes!*'

Still, there is nothing. Nothing bird-like in any case, and with a sigh Dora holds the chamberstick out in front of her, very slowly lowers her foot onto the stair below. It creaks beneath her toes. As she descends her eyes begin to adjust, and she sees with relief the bony fingers of a candelabrum sitting atop a small crate at the bottom of the steps.

Dora rests her sketchbook on the crate, lights the tall pillar candles from the stub of her own. The room brightens a moment, the light flickering in on itself before settling into mellow ochre. As her eyes accustom, Dora stares, open-mouthed.

The basement is larger than she expected it to be. Deep bookcases line one wall, filled with item after item that in the murk she cannot make out. More crates are stacked against the back wall, spilling straw. Behind her, beyond the wooden staircase, the basement goes further back, and Dora wonders what the darkness of it hides. In the corner stands Bramah's safe, its gold-and-black lock glinting in the lowlight. On the other wall hang some more shelves, each containing a large collection of tightly packed scrolls. A desk sits beneath, four large crate sides propped next to it. She squints, notes the verdigris, the molluscs clinging to the mottled wood. On the chair that sits tucked beneath the desk perches Hermes, restless, his eyes beads of jet. And there, there in the middle of the room is a vase, the likes of which she has never seen.

The vase is tall and wide, extremely large, would reach her chest if she stood next to it. It is fluted in shape, a small base that expands in the middle, dipping once more at the neck. It has a domed lid, with two handles fashioned into snakes. In the golden glow of the candles

102

the colour is earthen. And on the sides . . . Even from a distance Dora can see a network of images carved into it. Entranced, she takes a step forward, and the candle flames dip.

*Pandora.*

It is a whisper, a keening sigh. Hermes croaks, flaps his wings. Dora gasps, spinning round, afraid her uncle or Lottie might be standing at the top of the stairs, afraid she has been caught.

But there is nothing. There is no one.

The candles brighten.

Very slowly Dora turns back round, her gaze settling unnervingly on the vase. The air seems to crackle, a high thrum of energy that warms her ears, tickling her collarbone.

Surely not, she thinks. She is tired, that is all.

*Hermes heard it too.*

Dora swallows. It cannot be. Shaking herself, she crosses the basement floor.

She stares down at the vase. Her grip on the candelabrum tightens – but beneath her unease she feels excitement, because carved into the lid are a set of distinctive Grecian figures; almighty Zeus, the traitor Prometheus, crippled Hephaestus, beautiful Athena, and Dora smiles.

She has found her inspiration. Dora reaches out her free hand.

There is a sudden sigh, a hum, a fluttering. It comes not from behind but in front of her, from within the vase, and Dora hears all at once its siren call, its darkling plea. It is the hush of wind, the whisper of waves, the music of grief, and she cannot help it, she cannot resist.

Dora lifts the lid.

# PART II.

With ills untainted, nor with cares anoy'd ;
To them the World was no laborious stage,
Nor fear'd they then the miserys of age ;
But soon the sad reversion they behold,
Alas! they grow in their afflictions old
For in her hand the nymph a casket bears,
Full of diseases, and corroding cares,
Which open'd, they to taint the world begin,
And Hope alone remains entire within.

HESIOD

*Works and Days*

Translated by Thomas Cooke (1743)

# CHAPTER FOURTEEN

There is a hiss of compressed air. Dora gasps and drops the lid, the sound echoing dully across the walls. The smell of stale earth is warm and pungent. She is reminded of dusky tombs, fusted rooms – familiar yet not – her memories of them fragmented as if filtered through a sieve.

But there is no voice. Nothing to explain her whispered name, the other sounds that came before and after. The room now is completely silent.

Dora feels a rush of disappointment. What did she expect? What did she want to happen?

'Stupid,' she mutters, and Hermes utters a low squawk as if in reply, angling his head in agreement.

She raises the candelabrum, balances on tiptoe, peers over the rim of the vase. She means to see if there is something inside but it is too tall, she cannot see, and so instead Dora raises her hand to run it along the inside lip. The vase feels rough to the touch, and in the quiet of the basement the sound of pitted terracotta rasps loudly against the soft cushion of her palm.

On the chair-back, Hermes grows restless. He chitters, ruffles his feathers. Then the bird spreads his wings and flies to the floor, begins

107

to peck at the lid as if foraging for food. Dora watches him, notes with vague interest that the lid has not broken. Not even a crack. But Dora shrugs, turns her attention back to the vase.

The carvings, she notes, are quite spectacular. A series of images running all the way down the vase, each one wrapping itself around it to form a seamless image, separated by the meandros borders and Grecian patterning Dora has tried, without success, to replicate in her sketches. She bends to squint at the topmost scene.

Zeus, King of the Olympian gods, sits majestic on his mighty throne. At his feet a bounty of fruit and wine and honey. Dora begins a slow circle of the vase. A village of men. Some appear prostrate, as if sick or dead. Another male figure – Prometheus, this time – holding a fennel stalk, lit with flame. The village again. This time the men are upright, celebrating around a roaring fire. Back to Zeus. The great god has his fist raised to an unrepentant Prometheus.

Dora has returned now to her original position. She looks to the next scene.

Here are Prometheus and Zeus again, journeying to the foothills of a mountain. Here, Prometheus bound to a rock. And here, two eagles perched on the Titan's chest. The eagles alone now, transformed into vultures. Devouring him, again and again.

The scene below depicts Zeus with another man tending a kiln: the Olympian blacksmith, Hephaestus. She takes another turn around the vase, sees the transformation of unruly clay into the form of a woman, given the breath of life. And then the last scene, that of the goddess Athena blessing this new creation with all the wonderful gifts to be found in the world.

Dora knows the story, of course. Her mother recited the legend many times to her as a child during the warm comfort of bedtime. This vase depicts the creation of her namesake – the first mortal woman – whose curiosity unleashed the sins of mankind into the skies like a plague.

'Pandora's Box.'

She speaks in a whisper, but in the confines of the basement the words seem louder somehow and bounce from the walls, almost as if they have a power of their own, and all of a sudden it appears too much for Hermes; Dora hears the magpie let out a harsh cry, his talons scratch sharply across the stone floor, and she turns just in time to see the bird flee up the stairs and out through the door, his black-and-white feathers a blurred silhouette against the dim light of the shop.

Dora stares after him. Never has Hermes acted so oddly. The attack on Mr Lawrence was his way of protecting her, she knows. This is more difficult to make sense of. She sighs, shakes her head. She will find him in his cage, no doubt, his little head tucked deep into his wing, fast asleep. Dora will check on him later. But first . . .

She sets the candelabrum on the floor, sinks cross-legged in front of the vase. Dora raises its lid, turns it over in her hands. It is a heavy thing with a deep, hollow groove running around the inside rim. The border decoration is an elegant repeating pattern of an ouroboros – a snake swallowing its own tail – the symbol for eternity. Otherwise there is nothing remarkable about it. Nothing, at least, that could have fascinated Hermes for so long.

With a little shrug Dora places the lid face down beside the base of the vase. Then, fingertips tingling, she reaches for her sketchbook and begins to draw.

Later that morning, after the sun has risen and made its speedy retreat behind a sheet of sleet-grey cloud, Dora emerges from her attic room and braves the company of her uncle. Hezekiah is already seated for breakfast, holding aloft a china cup as Lottie pours from a pot of steaming tea. They both look up as Dora makes her entrance, and from the expression of reserve that has shifted, liquid-like, onto their faces, Dora is convinced she has interrupted a conversation she was not meant to hear.

'Late rising today,' Hezekiah notes, reclining into his seat, and Dora – whose heart is knocking furiously against the cage of her chest – says nothing, pulls out her own chair and sits. Lottie ambles to the other side of the table, plunks the teapot down in front of Dora and turns immediately away to the sideboard.

Dora keeps her head down, cannot look at either of them, fearful that if she were to meet their gazes they would perceive her duplicity, somehow know exactly what she has done.

'Are you sick?' her uncle says now.

She avoids looking at him by focusing instead on pouring her tea. 'I did not sleep much last night.'

And this is, after all, the truth. When she did finally return to her bed it was after three in the morning.

Hezekiah grunts. At the sideboard, Lottie uncovers a tureen. Immediately the aroma of salted fish pervades the room and Dora swallows, tries not to feel sick. The housekeeper serves Hezekiah first before setting Dora's plate down unceremoniously in front of her, and Dora stares into the blank unseeing eyes of two herrings, their scales swimming in melted butter. She lifts the tail of one with a prong of her fork before letting it drop; it slaps wetly onto the plate.

'Thank you, Lottie,' she says faintly.

The housekeeper sniffs, holds out a bowl of boiled duck eggs to Hezekiah who reaches in, taking two in one fleshy grab. When Lottie proffers the bowl to Dora, she shakes her head.

'I'll leave you to it, then,' Lottie says, putting the bowl in the middle of the table, and in the stark morning light the eggs look like bleached pebbles. 'Best be getting on.'

Hezekiah looks at her from across his eggs, a curl of peeled shell hanging from one still clasped in his hand. 'You'll remember to change the linen, won't you, Lottie? My best blue coverlet. The damask?'

'Of course, sir,' comes the reply, and Lottie bobs a curtsey before closing the door behind her.

Dora turns her attention to the fish. There is one thing she will admit to, when it comes to Lottie Norris – for Hezekiah, the woman will stop at nothing to please him. The housekeeper may be a mediocre cook, but while the shop floor and Dora's attic room are neglected in Lottie's daily rounds, the apartment is spotless. Even the little nooks and crannies of the staircase look as though Hermes has pecked them clean.

She slices into her herring; the silver flesh gives easily – a little too easily – beneath her knife. Across the table Hezekiah eats noisily, breathing heavily through his nose, and Dora distracts herself by thinking about the vase.

It is genuine, she is sure. It would be worth a lot of money, undoubtedly. So why not display it on the shop floor? What is so special about it that makes it necessary for her uncle to keep it locked away?

*What is he about?*

Before returning to her bedroom Dora had taken a cursory look through the crates on the floor and the ones she also found stacked on the shelves – all of them, she had been both shocked and thrilled to discover – contained pottery of Grecian design. Next she had looked through the desk but found only the shop ledgers. The scrolls in the shelving above it turned out to be nothing more than maps; keepsakes, she supposed, from Hezekiah's years as a cartographer. Finally she had tried the Bramah safe, but was disappointed to find her key did not fit the lock, nor – when it occurred to her to check – did the gold-and-black key she had found previously in the cabinet on the shop floor.

Across the table now Hezekiah makes a noise somewhere between a grunt and a groan. Dora lowers her fork, watches him wince.

'How is your leg, Uncle?'

He hesitates, seems to turn something over in his head.

'Like you,' he grunts, 'I slept poorly. The wound . . . it's turning into a sore.'

Dora blinks. 'Then you must fetch for a doctor.'

'And pay a fortune for him to poke and prod and do little else?'

'An apothecary, then.'

He waves his hand. 'Witches, all of them.'

'Then I can say nothing, Uncle.'

'That would be best, Dora, I dare say.'

His tone is cutting; Dora knows when to let be. They eat then in silence, other than for the occasional sucking sound when Hezekiah is obliged to remove a fish bone from his tongue.

Dora forces herself to finish one herring then reaches for her tea, takes a long sip before swirling the liquid in her mouth to wash away the taste of salt. She has just sliced into the second fish when Hezekiah asks, 'Have you seen my coin purse?'

Dora freezes, fork halfway to her mouth. The congealing butter drips from it, makes a tinny *tap-tap* on her plate.

'No, Uncle. Where did you see it last?'

'Hmph. My coat pocket. The black one with the satin seam? It was there the other day, I'm sure of it.'

Dora is glad she wears a high neck which hides the telltale blush at her throat. She gives a tiny shake of her head that could mean anything at all. Hezekiah worries his inner cheek. Dora completes the trajectory of her fork.

It will not occur to her uncle that she is responsible for the purse's disappearance, Dora thinks, not when she has always left well enough alone in the past. It would be easy to misplace, whether she had a hand in it or not. And he *deserves* to lose it, does he not?

Dora chews thoughtfully, navigates a brittle bone between an incisor and her tongue.

Her sketches of the vase are not finished by any stretch of the imagination. She only got as far as copying the first scene – Zeus and the fire – before her fingers began to ache, her spectacles to pinch. To ensure she has enough inspiration for her jewellery designs Dora knows that she must sneak down into the basement again and more than once, no doubt, in order to finish the copy before Hezekiah catches her – or worse – moves it. Will she have time, too, to explore the rest of the basement, examine in detail those straw-filled crates?

Dora kneads her lower lip with her teeth, taps her fork with her fingernail. Perhaps . . .

'Uncle?'

'Mm?'

'Would you mind if I went out for a few hours?'

'Out?' Her uncle's voice is over-sharp. He rolls the second egg across the table with his left hand and its shell splinters under the pressure. 'Why?'

Dora does not want to be seen to plead, but a taint of the plaintive slips its way in nonetheless.

'To sketch. It is so dark and dreary in here, I should like to escape it for a spell.'

'Wouldn't we all.' Hezekiah stares at her a long moment before resuming work on the egg. 'I suppose I can spare you. Lottie may mind the shop.'

She hears the words he does not speak – *I want you out of the way* – and her fingers tighten on the cutlery. 'Thank you, Uncle.'

Dora is surprised how calm she sounds. Inside her heart is clenching like a fist.

# CHAPTER FIFTEEN

The bindery business card presses deeply into her palm as Dora crosses the muddy cobbles of Russel Street, looking for number six in the gloom. By the time she finds it – right at the far end where the road curves at a sharp angle onto Drury Lane – her skirt hem is thickly spattered with muck.

She stops to assess the building. Despite its location (shops down narrow side streets are invariably of a questionable sort), it is strangely elegant. Dora can see that the paintwork is smooth and relatively fresh – red brick with black fascias, gold lettering that actually fits the board. For a moment she thinks of the Blake shopfront. It too, upon a time, had looked much like this. Cared for. A great deal of money has been spent on this business and its quality seems woefully out of place; its decoration belongs to trades situated on Fleet Street or the Strand, not here in the wastrel roads of Covent Garden where whores and pickpockets are as common as fleas.

Dora tucks the business card back into her reticule, takes a firmer hold of her sketchbook. She did not expect to see him so soon, if at all, but they may well be of use to each other; Mr Lawrence's obvious ability to recognise a forgery shows that he must therefore, in turn, recognise pieces of worth. Her own knowledge is limited to childhood memory but he . . . well, he brings scholarly experience with him. It is this experience she needs.

She pushes the door open. Inside it is lit with a warmth that smells of leather and a subtle hint of honey. The counters gleam mahogany and the same black and gold detailing can be seen throughout. A striking Indian carpet runs the length of the shop. On one wall stands a floor-to-ceiling bookcase filled with beautiful books, their calf-skin spines shining richly in the candlelight. A magnificently spiky plant sits grandly in a pot next to the main counter and beyond it, glass cabinets stand full of prints and intricately detailed frontispieces.

Dora can do nothing else but stare. She has never been inside a bindery before, and she is not sure she has ever seen anything quite so lovely. Mr Clements' shop . . . Well, she will always love the flash of white diamond, the deep forest of emerald, the midnight blue of cut sapphire, but this is a beauty quite apart from it, something opulent, ornate. Dora is still staring wide-eyed when a dark-skinned man she had not noticed steps from behind one of the glass counters, a small stack of books held in his arms.

'Can I help you, miss?'

His voice is smooth, warm, carrying on it the lilt of an accent she cannot place

'Oh, I . . .' Dora trails off, feels now unaccountably embarrassed. 'This shop is so . . .' She smiles shyly. 'It is . . .'

The man – tall, his face heavily lined, wearing a neatly coiled but plain grey wig – dips his head. 'I thank you, miss. We take great pride here at Ashmole's.'

'You are Mr Ashmole?'

He blinks. 'The overseer, Mr Fingle.'

'I see,' Dora says, though she does not.

Mr Fingle asks again, 'May I help you?'

Dora takes a breath, summons some authority into her voice.

'I am here to see Mr Edward Lawrence.' She fetches the trade card from her reticule once more and holds it out. 'A matter of business.' Mr Fingle glances at the card but does not take it from her. Cannot, Dora realises, looking at the books in his arms. Her hand falters. 'Is he here?'

'He's here, miss.' The man pauses, sends her a confused but kindly sort of smile. 'If you head through to the very back – the door with the glass panes – you will find him there.'

'Oh, yes, very well. Thank you.'

Mr Fingle nods, once. She does not sense disapproval. No, he appears altogether far too surprised which in itself is surprising. Perhaps Mr Lawrence does not receive visitors? Dora dips her knee needlessly in a nervous bob, disappears through the arched doorway he indicated with a shunt of his chin.

She finds herself in a narrow corridor. Here is decidedly less sumptuous but it is still warm and clean. On either side are two open doors, and as she goes down the corridor Dora looks through each.

Workshops, both, with long tables set in the middle, but the rooms appear to have a different purpose. One holds sheets of paper (some spread on the tables, others hanging from the ceiling), spools of linen, lots of pots and brushes, hammers and metal tools. At the far end are three large wooden contraptions Dora cannot fathom the purpose of. The other room is filled with rolls of leather, more metal tools, and what Dora thinks is a guillotine. And in both rooms are boys and young men in aprons, all of whom have stopped and are looking at her with an almost comical mixture of shock and curiosity. Feeling herself redden she continues on to the end of the corridor, but there is a shuffling commotion behind her and she knows they have come to the threshold to stare.

Just before she reaches the glass-panelled door, Dora pauses. Off to her left the corridor veers sharply. Blackness, no windows, no candle sconce anywhere near. For a brief spell she wonders at this dark space but then catches herself and softly she raps on the door with her knuckle.

There is no answer. Behind the glass, a bright golden glow. She thinks she sees Mr Lawrence sitting at his desk, but he has not moved. She knocks a little louder but, once again, there is no answer.

Dora frowns. 'Mr Lawrence? It's Dora Blake.'

She hears muttering behind her, furtive giggles. She ignores them for behind the glass there is movement now, a rushing to the door. It is flung open and Mr Lawrence stares at her, almost breathless. His cravat is partially undone, his golden hair has fallen over his forehead. A smudge of brownish-red glistens on his cheek.

'Miss Blake!'

He appears, for one brief moment, joyful. But then he notices the audience behind her. Dora looks over her shoulder. Mr Fingle now stands in front of them, as curious as the rest.

'I'm afraid, Mr Lawrence,' Dora whispers, apologetic, 'I have caused a commotion.'

Mr Lawrence scowls. It does not suit him.

'Please,' he says, taking her elbow gently. 'Do come in.'

He shuts the door behind them and Dora blinks into bright light; the room is completely filled with candles. Mr Lawrence scoots past her, begins to tidy his desk in a rush.

'I was not expecting you. I mean,' he adds, flustered, rubbing at the mark on his cheek, 'I hoped I might see you again but had not thought it would be so soon.'

'Nor I,' says Dora. Then, 'Oh, please, do not tidy on my account.'

Mr Lawrence pauses, two small oddly shaped tools in his hands. She takes that moment to survey the room, but her eyes struggle to adjust to the light.

'So many candles . . .'

'Yes.'

He seems to disappear into himself then, and instinctively Dora regrets her words. She smiles to distract him.

'I wanted to show you my sketchbook. I went down to the basement, you see.'

'You found something?'

Mr Lawrence's voice and expression are hopeful.

'I might have. But I need your help.'

She hears a scuffling noise behind her, accompanied by muffled murmuring. Dora turns her attention to the door, to the distorted shadows behind the panes, the laugh-whisper of voices.

Mr Lawrence clears his throat.

'Let's go for a walk.'

Mr Lawrence guides her through the crowded bustle of Covent Garden Market, keeping her a little too close to his side. There is a liberty to this, but Dora finds it hard to mind. After all, she is not much familiar with this side of London. The market is a torrent of noise and commotion, and Dora would find it hard to get – let alone keep – her bearings alone.

They walk past a fruit seller, his hat covered in flecks of dirt; a fishmonger selling fried eels and ugly jellied things; a baker next, his red, round face blanched with flour, sweating in his apron even on this cold January morning. Then there are the barrow boys, basket women, flower girls, all jostling for space amid the tiny stalls, wheelbarrows and donkey carts. The smell of vegetables mixes with the almost-sweet stench of horse dung and wet straw, and when they reach a meat vendor Dora has to turn her face away, for even though the air is sharp with frost, flies circle a pig's head, one disappearing into an ear that looks like a wet shoe left to dry in the sun. There are hunks of pink flesh gleaming on the table, a tableau of raw sinew and fat. As they walk past, the vendor looks up at them, his cheeks ruddy. There is a slop of blood on his apron. Mr Lawrence shields her, steers her down King Street and then onto New.

'I'm sorry,' he says, offering an arm. 'I should have found a more seemly route.'

'It's no matter.' Dora takes Mr Lawrence's arm, an attempt at nonchalance, though her stomach still twists. 'A revelation, really.' And it is; she has never needed to go to market herself – it has always been left to Lottie – and Dora finds within a small scrap of respect for the housekeeper, despite her dislike of the woman.

They walk quietly side by side. She is half a head taller than Mr Lawrence. Dora sends a surreptitious glance down at him.

'Won't Mr Fingle mind?'

'Mind?'

'You leaving.'

There is a beat of silence. A muscle clenches in his jaw.

'No.'

'I see.' Another beat. This is obviously a sore spot for him. 'Who is Mr Ashmole?' she pushes. 'I thought he was Mr Fingle at first when he greeted me, but . . .'

She trails off and this time Mr Lawrence does not let the silence in.

'Mr Ashmole is my friend. He purchased the bindery a few years ago, when I . . .' He pauses, angling himself around a patch of black ice, guides Dora across it. 'Like your shop, it was not the business it is now though in this case Cornelius generously restored it and kept Fingle on as he knew the runnings of the place and he wasn't . . .' Mr Lawrence seems to be speaking without breath, as if afraid of the words. He bites his lower lip. 'Forgive me.' He looks at her now with a small smile that to Dora appears forced. 'The history of it is unimportant. But I work there now and I may come and go as I please. I'm what they call a finisher. I work on all the books in their final stages of decoration.'

'Is that why you have so many candles?'

He hesitates. 'Yes.' A pause. 'It helps.'

Dora senses there is something unsaid here that dares not be pursued, but this time she leaves the matter alone. They continue on.

'Where are we going?' she asks as they squeeze single file down a small alley.

'Leicester Fields,' he answers, his voice easy now, as it was when they first met. When they are through Mr Lawrence offers his arm once more. 'I often sit there, to gather my thoughts. We'll reach it in a moment.'

Mr Lawrence soon brings them out into a green square, with sectioned lawns and wide paths littered with benches. In the middle stands an impressive statue – George I on horseback – and Mr Lawrence is about to draw her in through the iron gates when Dora pulls away.

'Oh, do wait a moment!'

Mr Lawrence politely stops as Dora darts to a holly bush she has seen peeping through the bars of a private house. She holds out her sketchbook. 'Would you?'

Looking perturbed Mr Lawrence takes it.

'The berries,' Dora blushes, taking a handkerchief from her reticule. 'For Hermes. I like to treat him, when I can.'

'Is human flesh not treat enough?'

'Oh, please don't!' Dora looks at him guiltily but then she sees the wry smile playing around his face and smiles herself. 'He became rather panicked last night,' she explains, plucking the tiny ruby berries from their stems. 'I'm hoping these will mollify him.'

121

'Panicked?' Mr Lawrence asks.

Dora closes the handkerchief, full now, the cotton stained faintly pink. 'Yes. Let us sit down and I shall explain.'

Mr Lawrence guides her to one of the benches in the square. She ties the handkerchief into a parcel, puts it carefully into her reticule. He waits for her to finish but she can sense his impatience in the air between them like the advent of a rainstorm in spring. Taking back her sketchbook, Dora draws a breath.

'As I told you, my uncle possesses the only key for the basement. I had a copy made and used it last night.'

Mr Lawrence sits forward, face brightening. 'And?'

'I found crate upon crate of Grecian pottery. I also found a Greek vase. I suspect they're all genuine. But,' Dora adds, looking at him now, 'I cannot know for sure.'

Mr Lawrence's eyebrows rise. 'You can't?'

'Do not sound so surprised, Mr Lawrence. I know what is a fake in the shop because I know the sort of places my uncle gets the wares from. Often they are of his own creation. But I was only a child when my parents died. I am no antiquarian; I cannot be *certain* the vase is genuine. You, however . . .'

Mr Lawrence's expression twists, the excitement in his face now quite gone. 'Miss Blake, I cannot be considered anything but a book-binder for now.'

'I don't believe that,' she counters. 'You understand the field, certainly better than I. You recognised instantly that the contents of my uncle's shop were not genuine.' Dora takes another breath. 'Mr Lawrence, there are things in that basement I suspect are worth something and if they are, I do not understand why my uncle keeps them hidden. There's no logical reason for it. But you can tell me for sure if what he keeps is authentic or mere tradesmen's tat.'

Mr Lawrence is looking out across the square, his expression pensive. 'Yes,' he sighs, 'perhaps. But, I must confess . . . Miss Blake, I have been a student of antiquities – in a manner of speaking – all my life. You are right, I can recognise a forgery, but my pure knowledge of some things is not all I wish it to be. I cannot *guarantee* the authenticity of a piece. I fear I may disappoint you.'

Hesitant, Dora places her gloved hand on his arm. He flinches, looks down at it as if it were something unnatural. Just as he seems about to soften Dora replaces her hand in her lap.

'You must understand,' she says gently, so he might not suspect how much she is relying on his assent. 'I need to finish my copy of the vase. It's the inspiration for my new designs. Sir, may I speak plainly?'

Mr Lawrence looks at her. His lip twitches. 'Aren't you already?'

His tone has a hint of the playful and Dora stares at him. Mr Lawrence clears his throat as if he believes her patience to be waning, but in reality she is wondering at what a changeable creature he is; reserved and nervous one moment, teasing and excitable the next.

'Of course,' he is saying, voice serious now. 'Please, continue.'

Dora splays her hands flat across the sketchbook. 'Mr Lawrence, my prime objective is to sketch the vase in full detail so I can replicate the designs into jewellery. I do not know how long I shall have access to it – as we speak, my uncle is doing heaven knows what with the thing. For all I know he could have got rid of it already. What I need to do is spend each night – after he and our housekeeper have gone to bed – sketching it. I don't have time to look through the crates too. So, here is what I propose.'

Mr Lawrence has half-turned on the bench. His expression is pensive, but his attention is rapt and Dora knows she has him.

'While I sketch, you are to look through everything my uncle has stored in the basement, tell me if what he hides is something genuine. And of course you may use anything you find down there – including the vase – for your own research.' Dora touches the tip of her tongue

123

to the roof of her mouth. 'I do understand that nothing might come of it for you if the items are worthless, but you asked me for your help. This is all I can offer.'

Mr Lawrence worries his inner cheek.

'If I discover the pieces are fakes, what do you intend to do with the knowledge?'

Dora sighs. A dog barks at a squirrel across the other side of the field, pulling at its owner's leash, and she watches the smaller creature's scampered escape up a tree before answering.

'If the items are forgeries, then that will be that. I will do nothing.'

A pause. 'Forgive me, Miss Blake, but why?'

Dora tries to choke down a bitter laugh. She does not quite succeed, and her companion looks at her in surprise.

'Because, Mr Lawrence, I *can* do nothing. I rely entirely on my uncle's generosity. If I were to report him I risk my own livelihood as well as his, and until I have the means to be free of him then I must keep my silence. Perhaps,' she continues, 'my uncle merely keeps them down there because he is not yet ready to bring them onto the shop floor. At least if you can confirm them to be forgeries I shall know, for my own peace of mind. But . . .' Dora pauses, rubs the bridge of her nose. 'I cannot help thinking there is something more to it than that. He has been acting so strange of late.'

Beside her Mr Lawrence takes a measured breath. 'And what if they are genuine?'

'I . . .'

Dora presses her fingers against the sketchbook. For as long as the shop has been under his jurisdiction, Hezekiah has not sold one legitimate article beyond what was already there when it passed on to him. Certainly, if he has, she has never been aware of the fact. If the vase *is* genuine, why does he have it?

124

Maybe there is an innocent explanation. Indeed, he may intend to *restore* the shop, just as she has always hoped. But no . . . did he not intimate he might sell? Dora is so busy troubling over the matter that when Mr Lawrence speaks again she must ask him to repeat himself.

'What if he is already selling them?'

Dora frowns. 'What do you mean?'

Mr Lawrence shifts, adjusts the scarf he wears. '*If* they are genuine,' he says carefully, as if afraid of saying the words, 'then based on his current behaviour, it is possible that he might be peddling on the black-market.'

For a dreadful moment the words pool between them, and Dora's stomach clenches at the possibility. This, *this*, did not occur to her, and she feels now desperately foolish for her naivety. Forgeries are one thing. Illegal still, yes, though harmless to those who have no inclination to care. But if Hezekiah has been trading in contraband all this time, and from within the shop no less . . . That changes things.

For him.

For her.

Dora's hand goes to her throat. She can almost feel the rope tightening around her neck. She turns to look at Mr Lawrence; he watches her, face pitying.

'Miss Blake. Are you all right?'

She has not the words. She wants to cry out, to tell Mr Lawrence that her uncle would never dare stoop to such a thing – why would he risk so much? – but now that the thought has been placed in her mind Dora finds the notion impossible to deny.

'There may be nothing to worry about,' Mr Lawrence says in a rush. 'I am probably mistaken. But I must see them for myself first to be sure.'

'Then you will come?'

Dora cannot keep the fear from her voice. She came to him with hope, thought only of her jewellery designs, her means to escape. And now . . . now, it seems, her very life may depend on what Mr Lawrence might impart. If Hezekiah is trading in stolen goods and he is caught, then Dora will face the noose with him, for who would ever believe she was not aware of such dealings when she herself has knowingly been selling forgeries on the shop floor for years?

'Yes,' he says gently. 'I will come.'

'You will come tonight?'

'I shall.'

'Thank you.'

He smiles at her. His eyes, Dora notes, are grey.

'May . . . may I see your sketches, Miss Blake?'

'Of course.'

It is a distraction, at least. With shaking fingers Dora opens the sketchbook, turns to her preliminary drawings of the vase.

'Here,' she says, trying for stoicism. 'It is a scenic representation of the Pandora myth. This –' she trails her finger across her sketch of Zeus and Prometheus – 'depicts how man was given the gift of fire.' She points to another sketch a little further down the page. 'And here is a quick outline of the vase itself. It stands to just below my shoulders. Could you date it, do you think?'

Their heads are bent over the sketchbook. Dora can hear his steady breath, smells the rich scent of leather on his clothes.

'Your drawings . . . They are extraordinary.' He raises his head. Their faces are so close now their noses almost touch. 'You have a gift. If you were to see mine . . .' Mr Lawrence's lip twists slightly. 'Well, mine are nothing at all in comparison.'

'Thank you, Mr Lawrence.'

'You're welcome, Miss Blake.'

They say nothing for a moment, only look at each other until Mr Lawrence seems to catch himself and, blushing, Dora looks away. As one they sit back on the bench. The cold air that comes between them is like new breath.

'What of Hermes?' he asks suddenly, and the change in tide makes her blink.

'What of him?'

'You said he had been panicked.'

She hesitates. 'It was extremely peculiar, completely out of character for him. As soon as I put the key in the lock he seemed restless, agitated. And when I began to examine the vase he just . . .' Thinking on it now Dora still cannot fathom the change in the bird. She shakes her head. 'Well, he flew out of the basement as if a cat were after him. But when I returned to my room there he was, sound asleep.'

'How strange.'

'It was, rather.'

'And where is the key now?'

'In my desk.'

'Are you sure it's safe there?'

Dora shakes her head. 'My uncle has not set foot in my room for as long as I can remember.'

'Even so,' Mr Lawrence says, running his thumb over the scab on his hand, Hermes' sharp scissor-kiss. 'I would be on your guard nonetheless.'

# CHAPTER SIXTEEN

Hezekiah often wonders why it is his lot to be subjected to the rot and filth of London's putrefied bowels, why the winds of luck insist on eluding him, always.

He was meant for more than this, more than squeezing his corpulent satin-clad belly down dark, dank alleys that smell of rat piss and the teeming unwashed. He was meant for more than sidestepping between questionable sludge-filled puddles – his poor shoes! – with his nose pinched tightly between finger and thumb. *More, more, more,* yet here he is, forced from his work (if one can call agonising over ancient pottery work) to degrade himself in the company of Matthew bloody Coombe.

What nerve, Hezekiah thinks, the lout's barely legible note scrunched up tightly in his fist. To demand that *he*, Hezekiah Blake, come to *him*, a mere shore-lackey, a no-brain! As he negotiates some abandoned crates spilling mouldy gut-split pears – his sore leg making the movement all the more difficult – he chooses to ignore that the Coombe brothers have a right to their money, that he promised a small fortune (to them, at least) and he is yet to deliver it. He chooses not to think that Matthew's fist is as big as his head and that the man could snap his neck in two like a stick with barely a blink of his milky blue eye. No, Hezekiah thinks, climbing the rotten wooden steps to the Coombes' loft, such thoughts are beneath him. *He* is master here, and there are plenty other ways to skin a cat.

The loft – a room above the docks of Pickle Herring Stairs on the south side of the river – smells strongly of decay. Hezekiah's nose wrinkles as he steps over the threshold and his host leaves the door open, for which Hezekiah cannot decide whether to be grateful. The stench from below or the stench from within; neither makes much difference. Foul air, foulness, all of it. He breathes through his mouth, longs desperately for his bed and one of Lottie's soothing teas.

'You'd best be quick,' Hezekiah says tersely, looking around the room with distaste. He notes the small soot-covered stove in the corner, the ugly battered bureau next to it, and wrinkles his nose. 'I've had to leave the housekeeper in charge of the shop. My niece, she hasn't come home yet.'

He should not have let Dora go, Hezekiah thinks. He does not like her going where he cannot keep an eye on her. This new sense of freedom of hers worries him. But stopping her will arouse her suspicions even more. So he will allow it. For now.

Matthew Coombe lowers himself into one of the three small wooden chairs standing around a crude table made from an upturned crate. He cradles a tin mug in his hand. Hezekiah notes that Matthew's wrist is thickly bound with a bandage. Behind him, a dirty sheet separates one part of the room.

'I don't think you got grounds for such talk,' the younger man says now, sitting back into the chair so it lifts at the front. 'It's already been a week.'

Hezekiah wishes Matthew would offer him a seat. His leg is agony.

'There has been a delay. A . . . complication.'

'I thought perhaps there might be.'

Matthew's voice is hard. Despite his best intentions Hezekiah feels his cheeks burn and to hide his face he turns away, limps over

129

to the small uneven window. Across the water the great Tower of London peeks eerily through the mist.

'The vase . . . It won't open.'

'It won't open?'

'That's what I said, isn't it?'

Matthew clears his throat. Hezekiah turns to him again once he is sure his cheeks have cooled, notes Matthew's own cheeks are pale, clammy looking.

A low, breathy noise comes from behind the sheet.

Matthew examines the mug, turns it slowly in his hands. 'I think it would interest you to know,' he says in a measured tone, 'I've kept a record of every transaction I've carried out on your behalf over the years.' He inclines his head toward the bureau behind him. 'It would be nothing for me to report you to the appropriate authorities.'

Hezekiah's throat goes dry. He did not think Matthew Coombe bright enough to display such foresight. He did not think Matthew Coombe to have much thought in him at all. Hezekiah curls his fingers into his sweating palms.

'Are you threatening me?'

'I am.'

Matthew puts the mug down. Hezekiah stares. When the younger man had asked – no, *told* – him to come here he had not expected to be presented with threats. Rather, he had expected pitiable grovelling which could easily be rebuffed, and for a moment Hezekiah is struck quite speechless.

'If you report me, Coombe, you face the noose yourself.' Hezekiah has injected bravado into his voice, a confidence he does not feel, to disguise the sick twisting in his stomach, but Matthew only sneers in the face of it.

'Do you think you scare me? Do you honestly think, after all I've seen and done, that the noose has any power over me?'

130

There is a wild desolateness that Hezekiah has never seen in Matthew Coombe before. He is reminded of a wolf he once saw in Italy, caught between the metal teeth of a hunter's trap. It had stopped its struggles, it appeared, long before Hezekiah, Elijah and Helen had come across it. He remembers the look on its face before, at Helen's plea, his brother put a bullet in its head – wide-eyed, fierce, yet subdued somehow, as if resigned to its fate. Matthew wears the very same expression.

'Death surely has power over everyone,' Hezekiah whispers, desperate.

Matthew barks out a laugh that is devoid of emotion. He rises from his seat. The chair legs drop back on the floor with a loud clatter. Slowly he begins to unwrap the bandage from his wrist and Hezekiah presses himself into the damp wall.

'Aye, that it does.' Matthew crosses the short space between them in seconds. 'Do you think my death will come quick or slow?'

The bandages loosen. From within, the stench of rot. As the material unravels the colour changes from starch white to yellow, to green, and when the wrapping comes free completely it is all Hezekiah can do not to gag. The smell is a sharp, putrid tang on the tongue. It makes his eyes water. He clamps a hand tight across his nose and mouth.

Matthew's wrist is an open sore, a ribbon of raw pustuled flesh. In the lowlight it shines wetly and just where the ragged wound opens, the flesh is patched purple.

'You remember, don't you, how I told you I'd retrieved your precious shipment? Had to go down with a lantern, kept it secure with twine wrapped round my wrist. A small wound, barely a scratch and yet . . .' Matthew turns his wrist, looks at it almost as if he were examining something wholly disconnected from him. 'Tell me, Mr Blake. Should this not have healed by now?'

Hezekiah cannot look at it. He *cannot*.

131

'Please,' he manages through his hand. He turns his head. 'For God's sake put it away!'

Matthew stares at him a few long seconds. Then he bends to retrieve the bandage, binds the wound, but the smell lingers.

'There,' he sneers. 'You may look.'

With difficulty, Hezekiah uncovers his mouth. He watches the hulking man petulantly, and now that the horrific sight is gone Hezekiah wills some strength back into his voice.

'You must fetch for a doctor,' he says, but then is pulled up short when he remembers Dora's same words from that morning, his own fierce rebuke of them.

Matthew lets out another shout of laugher. 'If I had payment, I might! If I had payment, a doctor might make all the difference,' he says, standing now near the sheet. 'Would you like to see something else?'

Hezekiah does not want to see anything else. He wants to leave this filthy disease-ridden hovel and never return. But Matthew is beckoning, and he finds his feet moving over the creaking floorboards of their own accord, his chest constricting like a vice.

'What is it?' he asks, his voice a whisper again.

Matthew's face twists. He says nothing, only fists the sheet. With a sharp movement of his arm he pulls the patched material aside.

On a bed lies one of the brothers – Samuel, Hezekiah thinks – and he swallows. Samuel's eyes are clouded, his skin is yellowed, slick with sweat. A white crusting substance has gathered at the corners of his mouth. The other brother, Charles, sits on a chair next to the bed, staring, unseeing, at the wall.

'What has happened here?'

'Your vase happened.'

'Don't be absurd!'

'Do not be naive!' Matthew clamps a strong hand down on

132

Hezekiah's arm. 'Sam came down with this fever two days after we delivered the shipment to you. Charlie –' here he gestures to the brother sitting comatose on the chair – 'has not spoken since the moment we brought the crate above surface. You tell me then, *sir*, if it is not your precious vase that has done this?'

The venom in his voice is frightening. Hezekiah stares in disbelief.

'It is a piece of crockery,' he sputters, but Matthew Coombe is having none of it and the hand on his arm tightens. Hezekiah yelps in pain.

'*Look at them!* One is near death, the other struck with madness. You think if Sam dies I shall be lenient with you? You think if I lose my hand I will find easy work? How will I support us? How will I care for Charlie? Your vase did this.'

'It did not do this.'

'It did.'

'You caught something,' Hezekiah tries now. He pulls at his arm. Matthew releases it and Hezekiah takes an unsteady step back into the open space of the room. 'Some sea-borne disease. Or perhaps you caught something at the laystall. Maybe it's hereditary,' he adds with a touch of spite. Now that he is free of Matthew's punishing grip he finds his strength returning, the courage to scorn. 'The Coombe family sickness. Or . . .' Hezekiah flails, desperate now. 'Look at the squalor you live in, after all. It's no wonder you're all unwell.'

Something dark shifts in Matthew's face. Immediately Hezekiah's bravado takes flight. He advances another step toward the open door and Matthew releases the makeshift curtain; it falls back into place, its tattered hem whispering the floorboards.

'How is your leg?'

Hezekiah pales. 'Much better.'

Matthew lets out a caustic laugh. 'You're a liar. I see you limp. It will begin to rot, just like this.' He points first at his wrist, then at Hezekiah. 'You have brought a disease onto us.'

'It is a *vase*! A bit of Greek pottery, nothing more.'

'Then how do you explain all this?'

'Coincidence.'

'There is a fine line between coincidence and fate,' he says, and Hezekiah scoffs. Matthew watches him. 'Why is this thing so important to you?' he asks finally.

Hezekiah looks away.

'It's none of your damn business.'

'I think we've just established it is.'

Hezekiah hesitates. 'It . . . belonged to me. Many years ago. I am reclaiming it, that's all.'

'How much is it worth?' Matthew shoots back.

Hezekiah hesitates again. 'Enough.'

'Then why have you not sold it?'

'I told you,' he says stubbornly. 'It won't open.'

'There's something inside?'

It is exhausting, all this back and forth. Hezekiah does not feel he should be questioned like this, like a *criminal*. But the faster he answers the faster he can leave, and as Hezekiah thinks on the question he realises there is no way to lie.

'Yes,' he answers, short. 'As soon as I have retrieved what I need then I will sell. The usual routes. I don't understand why it does not open,' he finishes bitterly.

'Perhaps it does not want to open.'

'It. Is. A. Vase,' Hezekiah bites out.

'It. Is. Cursed,' Matthew returns.

'And I still say you speak nonsense! It has a lid, it opens. There must be a mechanism, a seal, something I am missing. It was opened before, so it can be opened again now. I know it can.'

There is a space of taut silence. Outside, the river laps at the wharf and the angry slop of water on the muddy banks is somehow, oddly, calming.

'I won't wait, *Hezekiah*,' says Matthew. The lackey has never addressed him by first name before, and the sound of it on his tongue makes Hezekiah bristle. 'I need treatment for my brothers. For me. I won't earn enough in time from small jobs alone. Our welfare is in your hands.'

'I . . .' Hezekiah wipes a palm across his face. 'I will send Lottie, for now. She knows some things. Healing hands, she has. And I'll get you the money. I will.'

'I will go to the authorities if you fall back on your word.'

'I *will* get you the money.' Hezekiah cannot keep the whine from his voice and hates himself for it. 'I just need more time.'

'Time,' Matthew Coombe answers, 'is precisely what we don't have.'

# CHAPTER SEVENTEEN

Cornelius, Edward notes – not without a little distress – is determined to think ill of Pandora Blake.

'I simply do not trust her,' he says, piercing a green bean on his plate with more ferocity than is entirely necessary. 'You're barely acquainted with the girl and yet here you are throwing yourself at her mercy. For all you know she could be a swindler as well as her uncle.'

Edward frowns. 'I rather suspect she is throwing herself on mine. If you had seen her face when I suggested the possibility of black-market trading you'd know she is nothing of the sort. Honestly,' adds Edward as his friend lifts the bean-laden fork to his mouth, 'you have such little faith.'

'Not in you,' Cornelius replies, brandishing the implement at him the way a teacher wields a pointing rod. 'In you I have complete faith. It's everyone else I find deplorable.'

Edward sighs, shakes his head. 'She is offering me the chance to look at a large collection of antiquities. To write a paper using them. And I cannot help but feel that there is something in this. What did you tell me the other day? That you would support me no matter what I chose to do.'

For a moment Cornelius looks nonplussed. He finally raises the fork to his mouth and his expression becomes thoughtful as he chews.

'I will,' he says once he has swallowed. 'Of course I will. But this is such a flimsy notion of yours, to put your fate into the hands of a woman who conceded herself that you might not get anything out of it.'

'But there is a chance.'

'There is also a chance I might get run over by a tandem,' Cornelius replies evenly. 'That doesn't mean it will happen.'

Edward opens his mouth to retort, but finds he has nothing to say. Instead he focuses his attention on the leg of lamb swimming in mint gravy on his plate. Absently he swirls a potato around in it, watches the sauce make greasy rivers in its path.

'Is she attractive?'

Edward looks up.

'What?'

'Is she attractive?' his friend says again, and Edward stares at him without blinking.

'Is she . . . Why?'

Cornelius is watching him across the table. His cutlery has been set down neatly either side of his plate. There is a closed look to his face, one Edward has rarely seen, and it worries him.

'Do you like her?' Cornelius asks now, his tone measured, quiet.

'What's that got to do with anything?'

'A great deal, I should think.'

'Ah. You think my head has been turned.'

'Hasn't it?'

Edward shrugs. 'She is . . .' He trails off, tries to put Pandora Blake into words. He thinks of their conversation, how closely she sat next to him on the bench, how he thought he could smell the faint aroma of lilies and how it made him unsure of himself, nervous, almost giddy. He thinks of her as he first saw her, standing at the door of Blake's Emporium, her outmoded clothes, her dark haphazard hair

137

kept in place by a ribbon, those magnificent eyes hidden behind wire oval spectacles. How she is taller than him and he must look up at her which does nothing for his confidence at all.

'She is quite unlike anything I have ever seen,' Edward says finally.

Cornelius snorts. 'That doesn't answer my question.'

'You believe my head has been turned. I cannot rightly say it has.'

And at that moment Edward believes it. He does not understand the measure of his emotions in regard to Miss Blake. It is his lack of experience with the fairer sex, Edward tells himself, which attributes to his shyness, nothing more. He leans forward in his seat – the mahogany creaks beneath him – and tries to mollify his friend.

'She is not attractive in the typical sense of the word. She is no Sarah Siddons. But there is something about her, I admit. Her eyes . . .'

But Cornelius has turned his attention back to his dinner, is cutting into his leg of lamb with renewed vigour.

'What of them?'

'Like honey syrup.'

'Brown, basically.'

Edward stares. 'Why are you being so pig-headed?'

'I'm not. I'm merely stating facts.'

A beat. 'She has a pet bird,' Edward tries instead, and this at least makes Cornelius pause.

'No,' he says, unbelieving.

'She does.'

'Is it an owl? A living Athena. How European of her.'

'Not an owl. A magpie.'

Cornelius' face creases with disgust. 'Filthy creatures.'

'Very clean, actually,' Edward retorts, remembering how Hermes preened his sleek feathers in the shop. 'But it has a temper. Bit me it did, see?'

Edward raises his hand, angles it so Cornelius can see the scab from across the table, the small bruise that has formed around the cut.

'I wondered at that,' he says. He wipes a drop of gravy from his chin. 'You should have it checked. Teeming with diseases, carrion birds.'

'You're being ridiculous. It barely hurts.'

'I'm not being ridiculous at all. But,' Cornelius adds, throwing his napkin down onto his now empty plate, 'I can see you're becoming defensive. Ridiculous, you say? Well then, if you wish for a serious discussion –' Cornelius pins Edward with an assessing look – 'what do you plan to do if you find that this vase is genuine?'

'Ah,' Edward says, 'we come to the crux of it. And it's exactly what I wanted to discuss with you before you went on your tangent.'

One of Cornelius' eyebrows raises high. 'Oh?'

'I would appreciate it if you could set up a meeting between myself and Gough.'

'Why?'

Edward hesitates. How to phrase it? The very mention of the term 'black-market' in antiquity circles is enough to put even the most stalwart of men on edge. Such a serious matter cannot be taken lightly.

He draws in a breath. 'I would like to ask him his advice, see if it is possible that Hezekiah Blake might be trading in underhand circles.' Across from him, as Edward feared he might, Cornelius sits back stiffly in his seat. 'I know,' he says, looking at his friend's tight countenance, 'but if I understood more about it, if I understood how such a crime is prosecuted, how blame is apportioned, then . . .' Edward sighs, places his own napkin down beside his plate. 'Trading of such a nature is the work of true villainy. Selling forgeries without admitting to the fact is one thing, but this? It seems so unlikely he would risk so much. The vase, the other items, might be genuine articles obtained via genuine means, and in that case there is nothing to

139

worry about. I can write my paper with a clear conscience. But if they aren't, then I need to know what I should do . . . without implicating Miss Blake.'

'Edward.' Cornelius' voice is hard, measured. 'What business is it of yours whether the family are crooks? Take what you need from her and be gone.'

Edward has to fight not to snap at him.

'That's not honourable and you know it.' Cornelius pinches his lips. Edward carries on. 'Even if the vase is merely a worthless forgery it would be the right thing to do, to help her. She is trapped there in that shop. Her drawings, Cornelius . . . Oh, you should see them. Quite spectacular. The level of detail! You would not call *her* an amateur.'

'I never called you an amateur,' he replies softly.

'But my drawings are, nonetheless.'

Cornelius looks away. 'What is your point?'

'I could ask her to be my assistant. You know my own sketches are abysmal – any paper I write would be ruined by their inclusion. Miss Blake, however . . . *she* could still help me through when I've found a new project, if this one turns out not to be viable.'

Edward feels the pulse hammer in his wrist, wants to shake his friend for his obstinacy. He has always been thankful for Cornelius' protection but sometimes, Edward finds, there is a claustrophobic bent to it, as if he is afraid Edward will break into tiny pieces if given too much rein.

Cornelius swears under his breath.

'You're quite determined, aren't you?' he says, looking at Edward now.

'I am.'

He sighs, runs a hand down his chin. When Cornelius tries a smile Edward sags in relief.

140

'What time do you go?'

'We arranged to meet at the shop at midnight. Get in two hours' worth of work. It's all that is safe to spare.'

'You'll be fit for nothing tomorrow,' Cornelius says, some of the warmth returning to his voice.

'Perhaps,' Edward assents. 'But it will be worth it.'

'Are you sure?'

'No. But I have faith it will all come right. Everything happens for a reason.'

Cornelius quirks a brow. 'So, my dear friend, you keep saying.'.

Later, when the grandfather clock in the hall has struck its tinny chime to call in the evening, Cornelius helps Edward on with his coat. When Cornelius' fingers linger at Edward's collar he shoots his friend a look. Cornclius' lip twitches.

'Sorry,' he murmurs. 'Bit of lint.' He lowers his hands, rocks a moment on his heels. 'I don't suppose you will allow me to go with you?'

Edward shakes his head. 'I haven't asked if someone else can come. Besides, I think it might be risky enough under the circumstances. One person sneaking around is bad enough. Two, then three . . .'

'Yes. Yes.'

'I can ask for next time?'

Cornelius reaches past him to open the door and the smell of his cologne – sandalwood – tickles Edward's nose.

'No,' Cornelius says, terse again. 'Don't bother.'

Edward steps out into the dusk. The air is sharp, crisp, the mauve sky clear. He sinks his hands deep into his pockets and breathes out deeply, watches his breath plume white, then turns to look at Cornelius.

'You *will* speak to Gough?'

'I will. But I'd rather wait until you can confirm the state of the wares, either way. No point getting his back up unnecessarily.'

'Very well. Good night, then.'

Cornelius looks at him, says nothing. But when Edward reaches the bottom step, Cornelius calls his name. Edwards turns.

'Yes?'

'Be careful.'

Then the heavy oak door shuts, and a light breeze scalds Edward's cheeks with ice.

# CHAPTER EIGHTEEN

She has worried he might be late, but Mr Lawrence is already waiting outside the shop by the time Dora unlocks the door. He steps over the threshold blowing air loudly into his hands and, furtive, she raises a finger to her lips. He nods, chin disappearing into the folds of his scarf, and Dora carefully closes the door behind him, one hand reached up to cup the bell and mute its chime.

Strains of coffee-house merriment temper the dark quiet, drunken laughter penetrating the walls in a low almost-hum. Behind her on his perch Hermes chirps. Mr Lawrence flinches.

'He will not harm you, Mr Lawrence,' she murmurs, and her companion shoots the bird a wary look.

'Are you quite sure?'

'Quite sure.'

Dora put a hesitant emphasis on the word 'quite' and Mr Lawrence now looks at her sharply. Despite her apprehension of what they might find in the basement below — for their earlier conversation is still branded on her mind — she manages to chuckle under her breath.

'One can never be too sure. Come, we shouldn't linger.'

'No,' he replies quietly, but as she turns to guide him to the back of the shop, Dora frowns.

'Mr Lawrence?' He seems agitated, is looking around the room with something akin – if she is not mistaken – to dread. 'Are you quite well?'

He hesitates, seems to shake himself. 'It is very dark.'

'Oh, I have learnt to make my way around well enough. It's fifteen steps to—'

'Can we not light a candle?'

Dora stares at him in the murk. 'I daren't risk lighting candles yet, not until we're below.'

'Right.' His voice is pinched.

'Here, take my hand. I'll guide you.'

His hand is in hers almost instantly.

He is afraid of the dark, she thinks, as she guides him across the shop floor. But no, that is foolish, she decides, for a grown man to be fearful of such a thing. Perhaps he simply feels apprehensive. They are, after all, risking an awful lot. Hezekiah or Lottie could catch them at any moment.

She releases his hand, passes him her sketchbook, then extracts the custom key from her sleeve. Very carefully she unlocks the padlock, gathers the chain quietly in her hands, places both chain and padlock on the floor. She rises, gestures to the cabinet behind him.

'Would you?'

He looks, takes the candelabrum she indicated from its top. Then Dora steps back, raises her arm. 'Hermes,' she calls softly. '*Éla edó.*' Then, 'Come here.'

For a long moment the magpie does not respond. He cocks his head, bobs on his perch. It seems as if he will disobey but then he flies to Dora, settles down onto her shoulder, talons picking at her dress.

Very slowly, Dora opens the basement doors. A flush of cold, stagnant air.

'Be careful,' she murmurs as Mr Lawrence hands the sketchbook back. 'There are eight steps. Hold tight to the banister. I'd not forgive myself if I were the cause of a broken neck. And if my uncle hears us, then we'll be thwarted before we can even begin.'

But beside her Mr Lawrence is hesitating, staring into the dark.

'Mr Lawrence?' Dora prompts. 'Would you like me to go first?'

'I think I can manage,' he finally says, and takes his first step down.

*Yes. He is afraid of the dark.*

Once he begins his descent, she pulls the doors closed behind her. Dora hears when he reaches the bottom – the scuff of heel to stone – and her hand tightens on the balustrade, the rough wood splintering her palm.

'To your right there is a tinderbox. Atop a crate. Do you—'

'I have it.'

There is a scrape, a spark, and Dora sees the ember-glow between Mr Lawrence's fingers. He lights the first candle just as she reaches the bottom of the stairs. Dora peers into his face, and in the lowlight she fancies he looks very pale.

'Here.' She lets him light the second and takes the first candle from him. 'I'll light the rest.'

Dora busies herself with the sconces, gently deposits Hermes on the back of the chair. The bird ruffles his feathers, patters up and down the wood as if it were a tightrope. When she turns she finds Mr Lawrence bent – hands on knees – studying the vase. He looks up as she approaches and her heart begins to thud dangerously in the cavern of her chest.

'Well?'

Mr Lawrence straightens. 'Well.' He unwinds the scarf from his neck and turns the wool in his hands, again and again, in nervousness or excitement Dora cannot tell. 'It certainly *looks* genuine. I'll probably need an analysis of the material to be sure. I can't accurately age it otherwise, and I'll have to look underneath.'

145

'Why?' Dora asks.

Mr Lawrence smiles a little. The colour has returned to his cheeks.

'Forgers often mark the bottom of pottery. Your Oriental wares,' he says with a nod to the floor above, 'all have signature stamps on them that are invariably incorrect, but forgers insist on doing it because they believe it dupes buyers into thinking the item is the genuine article. Grecian pottery however is rarely marked. A relatively small number of Athenian vases bear the signature of the artist or the potter. The thing is, potter and painter were not always one and the same, but they could be.'

'What do you mean?'

'Only that some potters painted their products, and others sent them elsewhere to be painted. But forgers don't take that into account. They often mark the bottoms with a signature that doesn't make logical sense in terms of location, style and historic timing. And this,' Mr Lawrence adds, gesturing to the vase, 'is a pithos, not a standard vase. They are much, much harder to replicate due to their sheer size. Forgers seldom have the patience.'

Dora frowns, the word ghostly, familiar. 'A pithos?'

Seconds before, Mr Lawrence had appeared quite animated and he stops now, as if caught off guard. 'A pithos,' he says patiently, 'is a very large earthenware jar which the ancient Greeks used for holding and storing large quantities of food such as grain, or liquids like wine and oil. You don't know?'

Dora sighs, crosses the room to replace the candle she has been holding back into the candelabrum.

'As I told you, Mr Lawrence, I'm no expert. What little knowledge I have comes from childhood memory. I am surrounded by forgeries that I only know are such because I've been witness to the way my uncle manages the shop. I wouldn't know what differentiates a vase and a pithos any more than I would a . . .' Dora trails off, partly

146

because she cannot think of an example and partly because Mr Lawrence is watching her with a faintly bemused expression. 'I am sorry to disappoint you, sir,' she finishes, defensive.

But he is shaking his head. 'I am not disappointed,' he says quietly. 'I confess, I only know all this because I have read extensively. I suppose,' he adds with a wry grimace, 'you and I are both amateurs.'

'You already know far more than I can hope to.'

A pause.

'Does that sadden you?'

The question surprises her, not least because she has not thought herself to be so transparent. Dora slowly approaches the vase – the pithos – and rests a hand on its lid.

'Yes,' she admits. 'If my parents had lived they would have taught me. My uncle, who knows the trade, chose to keep me from that knowledge. It was not necessary for me to know it, he said.' Dora feels an angry heat in her throat, presses her hand against the clay. 'I could have done so much with this place if given the chance.'

He stands very close. The scarf in his hands now hangs limp from them. She dares look at him. In the golden glow of candlelight she sees the fine shadow-hair on his angular chin.

'I'm sorry,' says Mr Lawrence quietly, and Dora is just thinking how kind his eyes are when her hand becomes, suddenly, very hot. With a gasp she snatches it away, and Hermes lets out a sharp squawk.

'What is it?'

'My hand! It . . .'

But as quickly as the heat came it has gone. Dora stares first at her hand, then at the pithos.

'The lid. It was as though it were burning.'

Eyebrows knitting, Mr Lawrence taps his fingers on it a couple of times as if to test, but then he shrugs, looks up. 'It feels cool.'

Hesitant, Dora touches it herself. He is quite right. It *is* cool, no heat there at all. But she was so sure . . .

She shakes herself, rubs her fingers wearily across her eyelids. 'I must be imagining things. Tiredness, I expect.'

'Then we should get on,' Mr Lawrence says. 'We have a lot to do.'

He begins with the pithos.

A rudimentary examination, for after all – as Mr Lawrence said – Dora is drawing the thing, and all he needs do is establish evidence. He produces a small glass vial from his waistcoat pocket and a scalpel, and very carefully scrapes some grains of clay from under the rim of the lid. Next he attempts to look underneath the pithos itself, but even with Dora supporting one side, it is impossible.

'Too heavy,' he grunts with disappointment. 'And I daren't try force my hand in case it topples. But perhaps the clay sample will be all that's needed.'

After that he takes notes within a small black book he extracts from his other pocket. Measurements, unique markings, a description of the scenes as Dora explains them to him. Then Mr Lawrence leaves her to sketch while he makes a start on the shelving. She notes how he hesitates a moment before leaving the candelabrum with her, taking a candle instead from one of the sconces near the desk. He moves slowly, for Hermes stares at him with a discerning eye.

'He is deciding whether to trust you,' she says, when Mr Lawrence backs away from the bird with unmitigated wariness. 'Perhaps, after a few more visits, Hermes may let you pet him.'

'I think,' Mr Lawrence says as he moves back to the safety of the shelves, 'I would rather keep him at arm's length if it's all the same to you.'

Dora shakes her head and smiles, resumes her copy of the second scene.

She starts with simple outlines, her pencil whispering softly over the page; an uneven arch for the mountain, gentle swirls for its winding path. She moves slowly around the pithos, ensuring each element of the scene is placed correctly, draws in ovals for the eagles, the vultures, a triangle for the rock. She returns then to her original position on the floor, adjusts her spectacles, eyes narrowing as she begins to flesh out the stick figures of Zeus and Prometheus.

'Hmm.'

Dora glances up. Mr Lawrence has some of the Grecian earthenware set down in a semicircle at his feet, is tapping his pencil against the edge of his teeth.

'There are one or two forgeries here, but there are a number of genuine ones too.' He points at a pair of shallow vases near his right foot. 'Same styling, but the one very clearly a copy. A bad one too.' He looks at Dora. 'Perhaps one of your uncle's failed attempts?'

'Perhaps.' She looks at the collection at his feet. 'Some *are* authentic, then?'

'Yes. Quite a few, actually.'

Her stomach sinks. 'And you can date them?'

'Ahh . . .' Mr Lawrence squats, tapping his pencil again to his teeth. 'I think so. Much easier than the pithos over there.' He holds a small bowl-shaped piece up for her to view. 'The pithos is plain clay, no paintwork at all, just simple carvings. It could be a very early piece or simply unfinished. This one though is what they call "black-figure style". Very obviously, the figures are painted black. These didn't come in until the seventh century BC. That one,' he adds,

149

pointing to a taller piece on his left, 'is described as "white-ground technique". Again, rather obvious in that the images are painted on a white background, and these weren't produced until five hundred BC or thereabouts.' Mr Lawrence places the bowl back on the floor. It meets the flagstone with a dull scrape. 'So. I can give you a general idea, at least.'

Dora rests the sketchbook against her knees. 'Then,' she says, resigned, 'while my uncle peddles forgeries and tat upstairs, he keeps genuine antiquities in a basement to . . .'

She cannot finish the sentence. Not out loud. She lowers the pencil, puts her head in her hand.

It is entirely possible Hezekiah keeps these particular antiquities with the intention of selling them legally, at some point. But Dora knows her uncle well enough to understand that if he can pass forgeries off as genuine pieces without any qualms about the matter, then it's likely he will have no qualms about selling true specimens through more questionable avenues if it brings him greater reward.

Dora knows what 'black-market' means – she learnt enough from conversations overheard between her father and his workers on the archaeological sites, and warnings issued to his clients in the shop, that any wares which passed hands in such a way were stolen goods. Illegal trading. And if Hezekiah were to be caught . . . it is punishable in only one way.

One very final way.

'Miss Blake?'

Dora sighs, lifts her head. 'Can we find out for sure where he acquired them?'

'Only if he keeps records of the fact.'

Mr Lawrence looks over to the desk. Hermes cocks his head at him, black eyes glinting in the candlelight.

'That desk only contains the sale ledgers for the shop,' Dora says in answer to his unspoken question. 'Everything above board. I have already checked.' Mr Lawrence looks at her once more, face grim, but he says nothing and Dora sighs, glances at the pocketwatch attached by a ribbon to her belt. 'You'd best carry on. We only have an hour left.'

They settle to their work. Dora forces herself to push her darkling thoughts from her mind, to continue the copy of the pithos. It is, after all, her only hope of escape now. If she cannot sell her designs, then—

Stop, she tells herself. Do not think of it.

Dora fills in the shading of Prometheus and Zeus, the details of the mountain, stratus clouds, trees of fir and pine, starlings in flight. For the briefest of moments she feels the same chill she felt when she opened the basement doors earlier. She tugs her shawl tighter around her shoulders, prods the end of her pencil to her cheek.

*Concentrate.*

The details of the carvings truly are astonishing. But, Dora contemplates, there are some elements of the pithos that will not translate into jewellery. She turns her attention to the meandros borders, sees now why her earlier attempts failed. The lines are thinner, the patterns more sparsely spaced. In comparison to these, her drawings look like childish scribbles. Methodically, Dora transfers the decorations onto paper.

Mr Lawrence, too, is methodical. He examines every crate on the shelf, makes notes on each item, then carefully replaces them exactly as they were before he disturbed them. He manages to sort through four more before Dora announces the time again.

'Seven minutes to two.'

'Two hours is so very little time in which to get anything done.'

'Yes,' Dora says, closing her sketchbook. 'But it is all we can allow. How much do you have left?'

Mr Lawrence adjusts one of the crates on the shelf, then claims his scarf from the banister where he left it hanging. 'Two more crates on that shelf, two more shelves above it . . .' He turns his head, assessing. 'The shelving opposite, the crates on the floor there. And of course, whatever is hiding behind the stairs.'

They look together. Beyond the staircase, that wide expanse of black.

Mr Lawrence hesitates. 'It really is very dark.'

Dora almost asks him why he fears it so, but something in his face stops her. Instead she says, 'Perhaps it is not as deep as it seems.'

'Perhaps. But the shop floor does stretch that way.'

'We can take the candles over, have a look . . .'

'Another night.'

The words come sharp, too sharp, and Dora stares at him, but Mr Lawrence has already turned away, is winding the scarf around his neck. On the last loop he gestures to the Bramah safe near the desk.

'Do you have the key to that?'

Dora shakes her head. 'My uncle only wears the one key around his neck, and it doesn't fit that lock.'

'If he has any paperwork at all,' Mr Lawrence says, 'it will be in there. He must keep the key somewhere.'

'Yes, he must. But you have no idea what it took for me to get the key to the basement.'

Dora manages to suppress a shudder at the memory, but Mr Lawrence gives her a quizzical look all the same.

'Another night,' she says, and his mouth twitches at his own words thrown back at him.

'Touché, Miss Blake.'

'Touché, indeed.'

# CHAPTER NINETEEN

Today the smell of burnt leather makes Edward's nose itch, the candles sting his eyes, and his feet shuffle restlessly beneath the table. He tries to concentrate on the filigree lining of the finish, the narrow strip of fine ivy tendrils and swirls. He sucks in his breath, clenches his jaw, but when he feels his hand begin to shake he admits defeat and places the pallet tool aside, settling into the hard-backed chair with a groan.

This, Edward thinks, is why Cornelius allows him time away when he begins a paper for the Society. Edward is not – nor ever has been – one for juggling several tasks together. A single venture at a time, that is his rule, especially since his work here at the bindery offers him little pleasure. How can he be expected to excel at a thing if he cannot be completely focused on it?

For the past five nights Edward has sifted through crate upon crate of Grecian pottery in the shop's basement. The Blake collection is beautifully preserved, their calibre of the kind only to be seen in the British Museum. Edward is thankful for the opportunity to handle genuine articles (and at least three quarters of the collection appear to be such), to create a comprehensive list of their markings, their age. The fact that they might be stolen goods . . . This, unfortunately, makes producing a study of them untenable. Edward shakes his head to free the thought. At the present moment he does not wish to think on such matters. While his instincts tell him otherwise, he still holds out hope that the collection has been acquired legally.

He taps the tabletop with the tip of his index finger, thinks now of the pithos. It truly is an exceptional-looking piece of antiquity. The carvings in particular are exquisite. He has never seen anything like it, not even in his research books. Where, Edward wonders, did it come from?

Cornelius has taken the terracotta sample to the Society for analysis, and until he receives word, Edward will find it damnably hard to date. Even a guess will not do. As the pithos is unpainted it could come from any period within the Grecian timeline. The only point he can remember from his readings is that scenes which depict myth – as the pithos does – were typically produced within the Archaic and Classical periods, but Edward knows his knowledge is only rudimentary at best.

When he told Miss Blake he has read widely, he spoke the truth. What he has not told her is that his knowledge was acquired only in recent years, during the long painful weeks he stayed with Cornelius' father. How he had poured himself into antiquarian history! How he used that knowledge to help stamp out the memory of what had come before! Unbidden, the darkness of the Blake basement pops into his mind's eye, and on its tail—

Edward grips the chair arm, closes his eyes against the memory. For a long moment he sits there, head against the back, breathes deeply as he was instructed to do when it all threatened to become a little too much. But then there is a knock on the door, and Edward's stomach drops.

'Mr Lawrence?'

Edward looks dully at Fingle's warped shape through the glass panelling. He sighs heavily, sits straighter in his seat.

'Come in.'

There is a pause, a fumble at the handle, and then the overseer is in, the door shut behind him, and he is peering at Edward across the candlelight.

'I wondered how you'd got on with the Helmsley order.'

'Yes.' Edward points to a stack of books on the small cabinet near the door. 'Finished yesterday.'

'Wonderful,' Fingle says, picking them up one by one, turning them over in his hands as he does. 'These are beautiful.' He hesitates. 'Your skill has improved considerably over the years.'

'Well. I didn't have a choice, did I?'

Fingle meets Edward's hard gaze and immediately looks away again. He clears his throat, rubs his thumb against the bridge of his nose.

'Who was the young lady who visited you a few days ago.'

It is a question but spoken without the upward lilt, and while Dora Blake is not a subject Edward wishes to discuss with Fingle she is better than the alternative, so he tries for a brighter tone, grasps the change of tack. What happened was not, Edward reminds himself, Fingle's fault.

'Her name is Blake. She came to ask my advice on some antiquities in her possession.'

'Oh. I see. I thought that perhaps she was your . . .'

He knows what Fingle means to say, and the unspoken word – *sweetheart* – sends Edward warm at his collar.

'I barely know her.'

'Well, now. It might be good for you. Considering.'

'Considering?'

Fingle fidgets again. 'Well, now,' he repeats, placating. 'We all know how close you and Mr Ashmole are. It would be good for you to spend time with someone different for a change. Someone more . . .

155

Well, you've led such a sheltered life.' Edward stares at him. Fingle clears his throat. 'This came for you a moment ago.'

The overseer takes from his waistcoat a crisp-looking note, and as he passes it over the table Edward feels a tightening in his throat. There, plain to see, is the Society of Antiquaries' seal.

Taking it he snaps the red wax, nervously unfolds the letter, stares down at it in disbelief.

'Anything wrong?' Fingle asks as Edward gets up, wordlessly, and reaches behind the overseer for his coat.

Mr Richard Gough – the director himself – has summoned him.

On his arrival at Somerset House, Edward makes his way at speed toward the director's office, the *tap-tap-tapping* of his heels on the parquet floor attracting the unwanted attention of two bespectacled old men who shoot him looks of annoyance, as if he has no right to be walking with such loud purpose at two o'clock in the afternoon on a cold and dreary Wednesday.

Once he has reached the top of the ornately decorated staircase, Edward passes through a wide arch flanked either side with two monstrous-looking gilded amphorae. He continues right – not straight on which would take him through to the Royal Society that shares the anteroom (much to Gough's chagrin) with the Society of Antiquaries – to find Cornelius waiting for him in the large meeting room.

'What is it?' Edward asks, shrugging out of his coat.

'Do not panic,' his friend warns with half-amusement, half-something else, taking the coat from him and hanging it on a nearby hook. 'We have had the clay sample analysed, that's all.'

Edward stares. 'And?'

'The results are ... interesting,' Cornelius finishes, and at Edward's questioning look, he shows him through into Gough's office.

The room is not as large as Edward expected, but certainly it is as grand. Taking up most of the cramped space is a cavernous leather-top desk; on the desk, a decanter filled with claret-coloured liquid sits between two glasses on a circular silver tray; to the left of the desk, a bookcase crammed full of the Society publications that always gives Edward a thrill when he reads their spines – *Vetusta Monumenta* and *Archaeologia* – and to the right, a small fire crackles beneath a narrow fireplace above which hangs a particularly impressive medieval map in a gold-gilt frame.

Gough himself – an ageing man of squat stature – sits behind the desk, indicates Edward be seated with an incline of his bewigged head.

'Mr Lawrence.'

Edward seats himself in the chair opposite Gough, and as Cornelius takes position in front of the bookcase the director produces from the desk drawer the glass vial of powdered terracotta Edward retrieved from the pithos. Very carefully, Gough places it between them where it looks small and innocuous, stranded on leather the colour of pine.

'Tell me, Mr Lawrence, from where did you get this?'

Edward links his fingers together in his lap. He knows Gough's reputation for directness, his predilection for making even the most confident of men quake in their stockings, and Edward strives for calm.

'From a recent acquaintance, sir.'

A beat. Impatience.

'And this acquaintance's name?'

Edward catches himself. He thinks of Miss Blake, the danger it might put her in if he were to answer. He glances at Cornelius, then away again.

'I would rather not say, sir.'

Beside the director, Cornelius stirs.

'You would rather not say,' Gough echoes.

'That is correct.'

'And why is that?'

Edward's palms begin to sweat. He must choose his next words wisely.

'I would like to keep my dealings with the individual on a purely confidential basis for the time being.' After a moment he adds, 'It is in this person's best interests. Sir.'

Something in Gough's face tics. The older man glances up at Cornelius. Then he steeples his fingers beneath his chin, pins Edward with a level stare.

'You do realise, don't you, Mr Lawrence, that you came to us for help.'

'Of course. But my concern, sir, is for the family involved and it requires a great deal of delicacy.' Edward pauses, licks his lips. Dares. 'I also realise that my future with the Society is in question, and I would prefer to have full discretion on this matter.' He pauses again. 'Mr Ashmole says the clay analysis brought up interesting results?'

There is a shift, it seems, in the air, and Edward's heart flutters against the cage of his chest as he realises what that shift might mean. He thinks of Miss Blake and then, in turn, his misgivings. How cruel it would be, how utterly cruel, for the pithos to be something of consequence, only to discover it has been acquired illegally after all . . .

Gough is staring at Edward, and the silence that has built up between them continues to stretch. Cornelius looks pointedly at the toes of his polished boots. Edward shifts in the chair.

'What did you find, sir?'

Gough clears his throat.

'The object in question. May I at least ask you to describe it to me?'

Though reluctant to divulge Miss Blake's involvement, Edward cannot find any issue in this request.

'It is,' he explains, 'or rather it looks to be, a large Grecian vase that would have carried within it such things as grain or wine or oil, known to the ancient Greeks as a pithos.'

'I am familiar with the terminology, Mr Lawrence,' the director says on an impatient sigh, and Edward feels his cheeks flush.

'Yes, sir. Of course.'

Another beat.

'Well, Mr Lawrence, go on.'

Edward ducks his chin. 'It depicts on its body a carved scenic representation of the creation of the first mortals on earth. More particularly, it shows the story of the legendary Pandora.'

Gough drums his fingers on the desk. 'You mean the *myth*, Pandora's Box.'

'The very same.'

'And what age do you believe it to be?'

'I do not *believe* it to be of any particular age. Aside from the carvings themselves there are no differentiating marks that would confirm its era. There are no traces of paint – not the black of, say, a piece from the seventh century, or the red from the third. The pithos was too heavy for me to lift so I was unable to check for a forger's mark on the base.'

He chances a glance at Cornelius. His friend looks, Edward notes, faintly impressed, and he feels a jump of pride.

'Would you care to hazard a guess?' Gough says now, and Edward returns his gaze to the director.

'I . . .' He shrugs. 'I wouldn't want to attempt it, sir.'

Gough sits forward, the space between his heavy eyebrows creasing.

'Mr Lawrence. The manner in which we have tested the clay is very new, and as such I must stress that the method is still widely experimental. But according to my scientists, the clay in this vial predates history. In fact, it appears to be impossible to date.'

A thin camber of smoke from the fire leans into the room.

Edward blinks. 'Impossible?'

'Indeed.'

'It *pre*dates history?'

'That's what I said, Mr Lawrence.'

'But . . . but that's ridiculous!' Edward cries, looking between Gough and Cornelius as if they were playing some mean trick. 'There's not a mark on it. No cracks, no discolouration. It's in perfect condition.'

'And yet—'

'Are you mocking me, sir?'

'I assure you I am not.'

It is all Edward can do not to storm out. How dare they laugh at him like this? And Cornelius, of all people! The hurt, the dismay, it is debilitating, but as he angrily begins to rise from the chair Cornelius holds up a placating hand.

'Edward. This is not a jest. We were as disbelieving as you are.'

And all Edward can do is stare.

The claret is duly poured. Edward sits slumped in the chair, mentally exhausted, cradling his glass.

'No,' Edward is muttering, again and again, 'no. There must be some mistake. You said yourself that the method is experimental.'

'True. But stratigraphy analysis – the measure of grouping and correlating sediments on pedogenic criteria,' Gough explains at

Edward's unresponsive look, 'is a very exact science, and my scientists were most thorough. They even tested it against more recent pottery samples, of which the dates are already known, with success. My scientists, Mr Lawrence, are trained by the Royal Society directly, are masters in their field. No,' Gough says patiently, 'I believe there is no mistake here. Your *acquaintance*, shall we say, is in possession of an artefact of significant historical importance.'

'But—'

Gough waves him into silence. 'I would grasp this opportunity, Mr Lawrence. As I am sure –' and here he shoots Cornelius a querulous look – 'you have been informed by now, I am disinclined to look further into antiquities that do not originate from our own shores. Too long have we ignored our British treasures in favour of more exotic glamour. But the fact that this –' Gough gestures at the vial – 'is so very old is cause for investigation. Certainly, we have nothing like this on record and I have no recollection of anywhere else documenting something of this age, either. Since you refuse to divulge your sources, I permit you to look into the matter.'

Edward can hardly credit it. And now that the shock has begun to wear off, he feels the first stirrings of excitement, of hope. For the first time in years the Society of Antiquaries is giving him leave to pursue something that seems to have a genuine chance of success. And yet . . .

He thinks again of the pithos, the other items stored in the basement of Blake's Emporium. How can he compose a credible report if the pithos has been secured dishonestly? But no. No. He must, he simply *must* remain optimistic rather than assume the very worst. There is still a chance that Miss Blake's uncle has genuine reasons for keeping the pithos and those smaller pieces in the basement rather than on the shop floor. They could still have been obtained legally. It *is* possible. Edward takes an unsteady sip of his claret. Oh, if only he understood more about underhand trading! Edward presses his fingertips against the cut glass, tries to avoid Cornelius' gaze.

'Mr Gough. Sir. I also wanted to ask you about . . .'

'About?'

'The black-market, sir.'

Gough glances up again at Cornelius who now stands ramrod straight, jaw clenched. The director places his glass on the table, looks to Edward once more.

'The black-market,' he echoes.

'Yes, sir.'

'Indeed. Why?'

'I . . .'

Edward colours. He is in a quandary. To explain why is to admit the pithos might – *might* – be stolen, and to admit that would mean Gough may rescind his permission to write the paper at all. Edward opens his mouth to attempt another answer but Gough is leaning across the table now and asking in a harsh tone, 'Do you mean to tell me our mysterious pithos is of questionable origin?'

A spot of perspiration has formed on Edward's upper lip and quickly he wipes it away. The man misses nothing. Deception seems quite impossible.

'There is a small chance,' Edward says helplessly.

'I see.'

Gough sits back in his chair, retrieves his glass of claret, takes a long slow sip.

Inwardly Edward curses. He should have said nothing. Now he has ruined his chances, ruined them completely. Dejected, he begins to rise from his seat.

'I'm sorry, sir. I should not have bothered you with this. I—'

'Sit down, Mr Lawrence.'

Edward pauses midway in the rise, shoots a wary look at

Cornelius. Cornelius nods. Perturbed, Edward sinks back into the creaking leather seat.

'You say there is a chance the pithos is of questionable origin,' Gough says now. 'I must assume, then, you have no concrete proof?'

Edward hesitates. 'No, sir, only a suspicion. And even then—'

'Is it founded?'

With unease Edward thinks of Miss Blake's uncle, how the man cheated him out of five shillings for something that was worth not even one. Still, Edward hesitates.

'Possibly.'

'Hmm.' The older man watches him, marks Edward's hesitance with interest. 'Then, Mr Lawrence, I would keep a careful watch on the matter.'

'Sir?'

Gough clears his throat, links his fingers together in a fleshy basket.

'As I said, this artefact is of significant historical importance. To ignore it would be an insult to the study of antiquities.'

Edward watches him, confused. 'You still wish me to write the paper, even though the pithos might not be credible?'

'I do.'

'But surely the Society could not accept such a paper?'

The corner of Gough's lip lifts. 'Perhaps, Mr Lawrence, there is another avenue you can explore.'

The conversation is proving to be a drain on his senses and Edward sighs, rubs a hand across his face.

'Please, sir, I beg of you to speak plainly. What is it you propose?'

The director looks at him from beneath his dark brows. 'You are quite correct in thinking that the Society cannot align itself with a paper which has as its subject an item which has been stolen. If, on the other hand, it was acquired by legal means then you have leave to write your study and to submit it to us as part of your membership application.' Here Gough pauses. 'If, however, the pithos was sourced dishonestly and you can find out how, then there is an argument to be made about how the antiquity trade functions within more question-able trade circles. A paper on the subject would be highly valuable to our community, for it is we who suffer so cruelly from the effects of such a damning trade. Certainly, no one has attempted to explore this delicate matter before.' Gough spreads his hands. 'So, Mr Lawrence. *That* is what I propose. I would wager that to submit either one of these papers would guarantee your acceptance into the Society. You gain your admittance, the living to which you have always aspired, and we gain a study that would enrich our library. I cannot make it any plainer than that.'

Edward stares.

He meant only to ask Gough's advice, his thoughts on the trade, to ask – without being explicit – what the consequences might be for Miss Blake as an indirect party. If there is a possibility of her being harmed in any way he has no intention of writing a paper at all. He looks at the older man imploringly across the desk.

'But how am I supposed to write such a paper without implicating the people involved?'

Gough takes no notice of Edward's pained look. 'Ah, yes. The people involved. You said your concern was for the family, that your silence regarding their identities was in their best interests?'

'Yes.'

'Then I must ask why you would wish to protect people who disre-gard the legal and moral obligations of antiquarianism? Such people are not deserving of protection.'

Edward's cravat has started to stick at his throat. Quite unable to contain his despair he looks to Cornelius for help, but his friend is not looking at him, is staring so hard at the floor that the floorboards would set fire if the prospect were at all possible.

'Please, sir. Mr Gough.' Edward takes a deep breath. 'If illegal trade has indeed been carried out – and I'm still not wholly convinced it has been – then I can state without any doubt in my mind that one of the party is an innocent. I must ensure this person's safety. I need to know how the trade operates, to see—'

'Of course you need to know how it operates. You cannot write a paper on the subject without such knowledge.'

'But—'

'What do you say, Mr Lawrence?'

'You don't understand,' Edward begins weakly. 'You see—'

'It is either this, or we cannot encourage you further. You have already submitted three papers to us. I seriously doubt you could find as your subject something more significant in antiquarian history than this pithos. If it's been purchased legally then there is no issue. If it hasn't . . . Well. Whether your acquaintance is innocent or not, I find it decidedly unlikely you will be given another chance at the ballot after this. You either write the paper or you don't. The choice is yours.'

Edward swallows.

There is no choice. There is no choice at all.

'Very well, sir.'

'Very good,' Gough says with triumph. He opens a desk drawer, retrieves an elegant calling card from its depths. 'In answer to your question of how the trade operates I suggest you seek out William Hamilton. He is the authority on Grecian pottery and has some knowledge, I understand, of these more delicate matters. Tell him I have sent you, and he will have no objection to speaking with you. Indeed, any opportunity to talk about Greek artefacts is greeted with unmitigated enthusiasm.'

165

Gough holds out the card. It takes a moment for Edward to propel himself from the seat to take it. The card has a quality finish, is rimmed with a gold embossed border. A Piccadilly address. Carefully Edward tucks it into the inner pocket of his coat.

'Remember that I will not stand for any sentimentalism as with your last paper. Cold hard fact – it is the only thing that holds any recognition here. And tread very carefully, Mr Lawrence,' Gough adds, his tone measured and low. 'Not only have you discovered something of monumental significance to the antiquity trade, but you are also swimming in dangerous waters if the pithos does turn out to have been sourced illegally. Very dangerous waters, you understand?'

It seems, then, the meeting is at its end. Edward rises from his chair.

'I understand.'

'Good. I expect regular reports from you. Mr Ashmole,' Gough finishes, opening another drawer and removing a sheet of paper. 'If you would see Mr Lawrence out.'

Cornelius finally meets Edward's gaze across the desk. 'Yes, sir,' he says tightly.

Dazed, Edward dips forward in a short bow. 'Thank you, Mr Gough, for seeing me.'

But the director is no longer paying him any mind. The last Edward sees of the older man is him dipping his quill into an inkwell with decided care.

They are barely two steps from Gough's door when Cornelius takes a firm hold of his arm. Edward can sense his friend's annoyance in the pressure of his fingertips, simmering beneath the surface like steam.

'What were you *thinking*?' he hisses in Edward's ear as Cornelius walks him back through to the staircase. 'The risk you just took! You know that even whispering the words "black-market" is tantamount to treason in these circles.' Cornelius grips his arm harder. 'I told you I would speak to Gough myself, planned to bring it up in casual conversation in a way he wouldn't suspect was connected with you.'

'I'm sorry,' Edward says miserably as they emerge through the arch and come to a stop at the top of the stairs. 'I meant only to ask for his guidance. I never meant for this!'

Cornelius spits an expletive, releases Edward's arm.

'Do you realise the danger you've put yourself in? This is what I wanted to avoid. Contraband trading, it's a deadly game. And you've gone and put yourself directly in harm's way! If you consort with criminals you may well be implicated yourself.'

'I—'

'I'll tell him you can't do it,' Cornelius cuts in, staunch now. 'I'll appeal to his sense of decency. I'm appalled he suggested such a thing at all.'

'No, Cornelius, please.' Edward looks up at him, notes the look of pained chagrin on his friend's face. 'Consider.'

'Consider what?'

Edward feels ashamed of himself, knows he should not be thinking such selfish thoughts when he knows too what it all might cost Miss Blake, but . . .

'This is my chance, Cornelius. Gough has never shown such faith in me before.'

They stare at each other. Then Cornelius releases his breath in one long sigh, runs a hand through his dark hair.

'Remember your acquaintance with Miss Blake is in very short standing. I do not trust the woman, I've made no secret of that. You may shout her innocence to the skies, but how well do you actually

167

know her? If you admit you're collaborating with the Society to investigate the pithos' origins then she may well become a danger to you. You can't risk that.'

'Miss Blake is trustworthy, I know she is.'

Edward cannot explain why he believes this so keenly. But Edward has always trusted his instincts, and his instincts tell him that Pandora Blake is of a completely different calibre to that of her uncle. She is innocent. He is sure of it.

A muscle clenches tight in Cornelius' jaw. 'All right. Let us suspend reality for one moment and say that your illustrious Miss Blake *is* blameless. If she found out you were writing about her uncle's involvement in illegal trading do you really think she would let you near the shop?'

'I . . .' Edward pinches his eyes shut. 'I would not worry her with such matters.'

The sharp stab of guilt he feels is almost a physical pain.

'*Edward.*'

He opens his eyes to find Cornelius staring down at him, a dark eyebrow quirked.

'I don't know whether to be impressed or worried,' he says, dry. 'Deception is unlike you.'

'I know.'

'What is it you propose?'

Edward is silent a moment.

'I am not yet willing to believe that the pithos is contraband. Miss Blake has already offered me the chance to use the pithos and whatever else I find in my studies, and so I shall continue along that vein until proven otherwise. In that way I have nothing to hide.'

'And how do you intend to find out if it *has* been sourced illegally?'

He hesitates. 'I need to discover how the pithos came to be in her uncle's care in the first place. Beyond that, I do not know. I shall write to Hamilton as Gough advised. I must understand the implications for Miss Blake. If she were to be harmed . . .' He trails off. Something shifts in Cornelius' face. 'I will not allow it. I *must* find a way to keep her name out of this and still write the paper for Gough and not have—'

Edward bites his tongue. He cannot say the rest. But he does not have to.

'Not have Miss Blake find out.'

'Yes.'

A pause. Edward looks up at his friend then to see his leonine features are set into an unforgiving frown.

'Worried, I think,' Cornelius murmurs. 'Deception doesn't suit you at all.' Edward is unable to form a response, feels too choked with guilt to do so, and Cornelius folds his arms. 'What worries me even more is that you are willing to risk so much for a woman you barely know.'

Again, Edward can say nothing. Not because he agrees with Cornelius, but because he does not – he is willing to risk so much, he knows, for his own selfish reasons.

And it is this that has him bowing his head in shame.

# CHAPTER TWENTY

When Mr Lawrence arrives that evening on the skirts of the midnight toll and a fog that has in its essence the onslaught of choking damp, his eyes are uncommonly bright, as if a fever has taken hold of him. When Dora asks, Mr Lawrence presses her hand in his and says, only, 'Wait.'

But waiting is difficult when one knows they are on the cusp of a thing, and by the time the basement is unlocked, the candles lit, and they are both sitting crossed-legged on the floor – the pithos looming before them like a sentinel – Dora is restless with disquiet.

'Please, Mr Lawrence, you are quite worrying me.'

'I do not mean to, Miss Blake. It is just . . .'

'Yes?'

'Forgive me, I fear of alarming you. There has been a development.'

There is something in his manner – why is it he looks so uneasy? – and Dora watches him struggle to form the words on his tongue.

'It is the clay sample,' he says finally. 'I received the results today.'

She links her fingers to still them. 'Is it a forgery, after all?'

Mr Lawrence hesitates. 'It appears that it is quite the opposite. Miss Blake, it . . .' He stops, tries again, gently. 'This pithos. They can't date it. Gough's scientists claim that it predates history entirely.'

There is a beat of silence. A low crackle – as if the air has shifted and split – makes both Dora and Mr Lawrence jump. Movement catches Dora's eye; one of the candles is flickering in its sconce. Nothing more, then, than a draught of air.

She takes a breath, looks to him once more.

'Come now, Mr Lawrence,' she says, 'I sense a tendency for teasing in you, but this does seem a little extreme, don't you think?' And now Dora begins to anger. 'Especially considering my predicament. This is a jest in poor taste, I dare say,' she finishes and immediately he is raising his hands, palms forward, as if fending off a tiger ready to pounce.

'Please, Miss Blake, I understand your disbelief. I did not believe it myself at first. But the Society can be trusted. I assure you, I am not in jest. I almost wish I were.'

For a long moment Dora stares at him, then stares up at the pithos. From his perch on the back of the desk chair, Hermes emits a low chitter.

Can it really be true? Dora reaches out a finger, traces the patterning of the bottom meandros border, the elegant feathers, their staring peacock eyes, with a kind of fearful rapture.

'But,' she whispers, 'how can this be?'

Mr Lawrence shakes his head. 'I do not know.'

Her astonishment at such a discovery is twofold. Alone, its very age is most shocking. But . . . Dora is struck with a deep-seated nausea, as if someone has shaken her so hard her stomach has detached itself. This is not what she had vainly hoped it to be, a simple case of underhand trading, of incompetent salesmanship. It is clear, now, that there is something more sinister at play. Where on earth would her uncle have found an artefact this old? How does he even have the means to secure such a thing – such an obscure, expensive thing – as this? There is only one explanation, and Dora closes her eyes, thinks of her father, her mother, how they would never have allowed it. The Blake name, turned as black and noxious as gutter water.

171

When Dora finally shifts her attention back to Mr Lawrence she sees in his face an expression she cannot read. 'What is it?' she asks.

It takes him a moment to answer, and when he does his tone is careful, considered.

'You said yourself you do not wish to confront your uncle?'

'I can't.'

The words catch in her throat, and it takes all of Dora's effort not to cry.

'But you will still permit me to make a study of it?'

'I . . .'

He draws out a breath. 'Miss Blake, this must surely be one of the only pieces of pottery in the world so old and yet so completely intact. It would be a shame not to catalogue it. The clay sample was aged, but there are other tests that can be done. If you'll permit, we'd need to ascertain where the clay came from, consider what sort of people might have created it. You have no notion, none at all, where your uncle acquired it?'

His words are not registering; she is too overwhelmed, too overcome by the thought of Hezekiah's deceit, the historic importance of the pithos before her. But then she realises that Mr Lawrence waits for her answer and in confusion she shakes her head.

'None whatsoever.' Then, 'No, wait. Three men – brothers, I believe, they brought it. I happened upon them when it arrived.'

'Their names?'

She tries to recall if Hezekiah spoke them but her memory is blank, a bank of fog as thick as the one outside. 'I don't remember.'

'Then we must discover them,' says Mr Lawrence. 'But in the meantime I can only stress the importance of finishing your sketches.'

She feels ragged, her head pounds. 'Why?'

Mr Lawrence sits forward, rests his elbows on his knees. 'I understand why *you* wish to sketch the pithos. But . . . Miss Blake, I have had a notion.' Dora waits. Mr Lawrence takes a breath. 'You offered me the chance to use the pithos and whatever I found down here in my studies. Now, my written works, in the manner of their *literacy* – forgive my arrogance – have never been of issue, though the subject matter has never found much favour.' He cuts off, a hint of bitterness. 'My drawings, on the other hand. Well, I'm afraid my artistic skills leave much to be desired.' When Dora does not respond, Mr Lawrence continues in a rush. 'Your skill is most accomplished and far surpasses anything I could produce myself. I thought that we might be able to help each other.'

'How?'

He hesitates. Very slowly, he reaches out to take her hand. Dora lets him.

'Miss Blake. Dora,' he tries, and when she does not object to it – in fact, she finds the sound of her name on his tongue comforting – he carries on, though there is a hesitance now to the tone of his voice. 'There *is* still a chance your uncle obtained these items legally, that a credible paper can be written. And until we find otherwise, well, if you were to provide the sketches to accompany a report of the pithos, it would make all the difference. I could use the other items in the crates, too. Certainly, they would add value to the report. And –' Mr Lawrence draws out a tentative smile – 'if the study were successful, I would ask you to work as my assistant on all future projects for the Society. My *paid* assistant. You would—'

'Be independent. Free,' Dora finishes.

'Yes.'

'And my jewellery? If I were to find success with that?'

A pause. 'Why could you not do both?'

In the silence that follows, Dora lets herself think on it. It sounds like a dream, as delicate a thing as spun glass.

Independent.

173

Free.

*Safe.*

And yet. What likelihood is there of such success? What if both her jewellery ambition and Mr Lawrence's aspirations of academia were to tumble, like a cliff-face into the sea? She pictures herself thrashing in the icy current, gasping for air, drowning in her own folly, her own misguided make-believe.

'Please, Mr Lawrence,' Dora whispers, 'you must understand. This shop is all I have ever known. It belonged to my parents. I had hoped, one day, it would be mine. But then my uncle ruined its fortunes, its credibility. And now I find . . .' She shakes her head, bites her lip so hard she fears it might bleed. 'Do you know the penalty for black-market trading?' Dora does not need to say it; the answer is writ clearly on his face. 'The likelihood of my uncle owning these objects legally is very slim. So my livelihood – in all ways – relies on my success. If we fail in both our causes what will become of me? What then? *You* have the bindery. You may earn your living, and honourably. But if Hezekiah is found out I will be condemned as his accomplice. They'll hang me.'

His face goes very still. 'Listen,' he says, sitting forward, his expression earnest, urgent. 'I've been advised by the Society director – in point of fact, *told* – to contact an expert to gather further information about the pithos. Do I have your permission?'

'Mr Lawrence, I—'

'Edward. Please.'

'Edward, I . . .' Dora falters, tries again. 'If the pithos is as old as you say it is, then my uncle must mean to make his fortune from it. And if he sells, neither you nor I will benefit. The pithos will be lost to us both.'

'But this is why we must work quickly! Learn everything about it that we can.'

She opens her mouth, closes it again.

'Dora.' Mr Lawrence – no, Edward – squeezes her hand. She had quite forgotten he is holding it. 'I know you are afraid. But please, let me investigate this. There could still be an innocent explanation. Let me try.'

Try. A word full of promise. Of hope. And yet . . . Dora shakes her head, the cog of her mind spinning like a tandem wheel. In an effort to stop it she pulls her hand free, rises unsteadily to her feet.

'You have more faith in my uncle than I do. But very well. I give you leave to continue looking through those crates, to take from them anything you can which will help with your studies, and I shall continue to sketch the pithos, for my jewellery. Once I am finished you may take what I have done and I wish you luck with it, truly. But let us not dwell on fancies that may never come to pass.'

Edward rises too. 'You sound like Cornelius.'

Dora does not answer. She crosses to the desk to retrieve the sketchbook from where she left it upon coming down to the basement. Hermes blinks up at her, spreads his wings in a monochrome stretch. Very gently she strokes his fine head with the backs of her fingers. When she turns Edward is watching her, a troubled expression on his face.

'What is it?'

He opens his mouth, closes it again. Shakes his head.

'Nothing. Nothing,' he says again and he shrugs himself from his coat, unwinds his scarf, proceeds to the shelving, and begins to lift down the crates, one by one.

# CHAPTER
# TWENTY-ONE

*Dear Sir,*

*Please forgive my writing to you without any formal introduction, but I wished to direct a missive to you before appearing on your doorstep.*

*I was advised to seek your assistance by the Director of the Society of Antiquaries himself, Mr Richard Gough, as I have recently come across a most extraordinary item that will undoubtedly be of interest to you – a large pithos, of what appears to be Grecian design. On analysing a sample of clay taken from said pithos, the Royal Society have discovered – quite to my own shock, and, I am sure, to yours – that the pithos cannot be dated. Indeed, it is so old that there appears to be no record of anything like it in our known history.*

*The owner of this item presently wishes to remain anonymous – their situation is a delicate one to which I am extremely sympathetic. It seems possible that the pithos – together with a vast collection of Grecian pottery – might have been acquired illegally. I seek not only your opinion but also your assistance, as an esteemed collector of Greek antiquities yourself.*

*Please do forgive the vagueness of this missive – if you might find yourself in a position to discuss the matter with me, then*

*I hope to be more forthcoming and will divulge further details. I enclose within this letter the business card of the establishment in which I work, and I would greatly appreciate the opportunity to discuss this matter with you at your earliest convenience.*

*With deepest Respect*
*& Gratitude, etc.*
*Edward Lawrence*

# CHAPTER
# TWENTY-TWO

Every day Hezekiah disappears down to the basement for hours on end; each time Dora watches his limping descent and return with a feeling she has never experienced before, and, despite it being warranted, it succeeds in making Dora ashamed of herself for feeling such a thing at all:

Hatred.

Until now Dora has only ever felt a fleeting kind of resentment for her uncle; resentment for his blatant disregard of her parents' reputation, the Blake name. But Hezekiah's forgeries have never actually harmed her. For twelve years he has sold his wares without incident and she herself (Dora is mortified to realise) has grown complacent. She thought she had time. But to discover now that Hezekiah unashamedly risks not only his neck but her own . . . There may be no outright proof of the fact, but in the face of recent events how can his guilt be doubted? *This* is why Hezekiah has no concern for the cleanliness, the reputation of the shop, the living Elijah Blake – his own brother – left behind, for he has no real need for its custom. And so, this hatred she now feels eats away at her heart like a maggot, fat and pulsing, gorging on that resentment so long buried deep.

Dora has directed it as best she can. During Hezekiah's sojourns – when, every now and then, she hears the sounds of his angry pacing below – she has spent her days sketching behind the counter with renewed urgency, her only interruption seven customers, four of whom merely browsed and three of whom purchased, in turn, a Ming vase (one of Hezekiah's latest purchases), an African figurine (carved by the Deptford carpenter) and a pair of hat pins that even Dora had not seen before, scurried up, she imagined, from one of the dusty curiosity baskets at the back of the shop.

In this time Dora has produced five designs: three necklaces, one bracelet, a pair of earrings. There is, Dora deduced, no need for more than that. This time she will not worry herself over a sample, not when the likelihood of Mr Clements refusing her efforts yet again is worryingly high. No, this time Dora has chosen to be discerning and produce designs limited in number but of a standard that far surpasses anything she has drawn before. Behind the counter she concentrates on a last flourish to the sketch of a choker cast in gold – reminiscent of one of the pithos' borders – angling her nib at a sharp slant against her thumb to produce the correct pressure for the final flick.

From below comes a frustrated moan, a dull bang.

Dora rests her pencil. While Mr Lawrence – Edward, she remembers to call him – has been so careful in putting everything back where he previously found it, Dora worried her uncle might notice the basement has been disturbed. But not one word has Hezekiah said to her. No indeed, the only sounds she has heard from him are expletives of frustration and wordless grunts of pain.

Over a week has passed since Dora invited Edward to view the contents of the basement, and in that time her uncle's leg appears to have worsened. He walks now with a pronounced limp – her suggestion that he use a cane was met with fierce rebuttal – and his attitude too, while always unpleasant, has diminished further to a surliness that does not relent. Even Lottie has had to bear the brunt of it. The night before Dora heard raised voices come from Hezekiah's bed-room. The shatter of glass. Lottie, crying.

Dora knows she should be concerned. She knows that a doctor should be called, for the faint putrid smell of pus has begun to taint the air each time Hezekiah limps past.

Yet.

*Let him suffer*, a wicked voice whispers in her ear. *He has brought this on himself*, it says.

Dora's hands close into fists. The maggot writhes and eats its fill.

Another shout from below, another dull bang, as if he has flung something down on the floor in frustration.

Why does Hezekiah spend so much time below stairs? Why is it, each day, he reappears looking more frustrated than he did the day before? What is it, she wonders, that has Hezekiah so annoyed? Is it the pithos itself? For what must be the hundredth time she asks herself why her uncle has not yet sold it. Surely an artefact of such monumental worth would have his corrupt buyers fighting to own it.

'Oh, Father, Mother,' she whispers. Dora leans her elbow on the counter, props her chin in her hand and grimly surveys the dimness of the shop, the splatter of mist-rain on the mottled windowpanes. 'What must I do?'

Dora pictures them, how they once were, when the shop was at its finest. In her mind's eye she sees her father arranging the stock – some new acquirements from Venice or Rome, Naples or Athens – in a magnificent window display that would have passers-by stop and stare. She sees her mother, sketching out designs for the advertise-ments that would entice customers across the threshold, singing under her breath a Grecian folk song in her smooth lilting voice. What were the words? Dora tries to recall, but her memory will not conjure them. Those mirror shards are no more.

180

Behind her on his perch Hermes squawks, and Dora twists round on the stool.

'Well, dear heart, do *you* know what I should do?' The magpie looks down with unblinking black eyes. 'No? How unhelpful.' She picks up the sketch, angles the page up to the bird. 'What about this? Do you like it?'

This time Hermes cocks his head and Dora smiles. *She* certainly likes it, would be thrilled to wear such a thing. But would a lady of quality?

It is a broad choker, one that would suit a thicker neck and sit just above the collarbone. The border Dora chose from the pithos was the peacock design, but embellished in her own styling. A gold base of eighteen carat, the peacock feathers would each be filled with lapis-coloured enamel and separated by a square turquoise stone from which would hang a jet-base cameo, linked together by a fine gold chain. The individual shell reliefs would feature a representation of the talents bestowed on Pandora: painting, needlework, weaving, music, gardening, healing. The design is a seamless repeat – except for the cameos themselves – and Dora has sketched the necklace as it might sit around the neck, together with its finer details. Eight drawings for the one design in all, a most impressive offering that Mr Clements surely, this time, cannot refuse.

Dora's mouth twists as she thinks of Edward's proposition. She fears now that he wastes his time, cataloguing the crates in the vain hope they still might be lawfully obtained. Edward, however, does not know her uncle, does not know what he is capable of, and without the help of the three brothers – without confronting Hezekiah himself – there is no way to prove it. Yet she wants Edward's company. It is a lonely task, sketching in the basement alone. But if he cannot publish his paper, if she fails in convincing Mr Clements again . . .

Her fear of the noose aside, there is still the matter of where she would go if Hezekiah sells the shop. Dora thinks again of his words those nights before, the worrying implication of them. *More liberating surroundings.* But, he has made no further mention of it. Perhaps she was mistaken.

The bell rings.

Lottie bumbles her way through the front door, closes it behind her with a bang that sets the bell shaking loudly on its spring. Hermes squawks sharply in protest, black-and-white feathers ruffling, and Dora closes the sketchbook. Lottie shakes water off the hem of her frilled cape, keeps her attention fixed to the floor. Dora thinks of her crying the night before and studies the woman with unease.

'Lottie,' she asks carefully, 'are you quite well?' and when the housekeeper finally deigns to raise her head, Dora stares at her in shock.

She is very pale, eyes rimmed dark as if she has rubbed them with fingers dusted thick with soot. But it is the split and swollen lip that makes Dora step down from her stool and reach out her hand. No matter how much she dislikes the woman, she does not deserve this.

'Lottie, what did he do to you?'

'Nothing, missum.' Lottie does not meet Dora's eye, refuses the hand she offers. 'I tripped on my way up to bed last night.' She places the basket she is carrying on the floor. Inside Dora spies the edge of a discoloured rag, blotched yellow-pink. 'Has your uncle come up yet?' Lottie asks.

The blunt edge to her voice is unmistakable and Dora wants to challenge Lottie's bare-faced lie, but it is clear from her tone that she will not say another word on the matter.

'No, not yet,' Dora answers.

'Then I suppose I should get on with supper. Do you know if he's eaten anything?'

'Not since breakfast, I imagine.'

'Then I'll take something down.'

With seeming difficulty she retrieves the basket, disappears through the door into the living quarters.

Dora stares at the closed door.

So, her uncle has taken to violence. Hezekiah never seemed the type. Though quick to anger he had always appeared to Dora a man who was all show and no substance, full of threats and nothing more. But now . . . She wonders how much Lottie Norris is privy to, how much her uncle has shared with her. It is clear the housekeeper knows more than Dora for Hezekiah permits her presence in the basement but perhaps, Dora muses, he is keeping secrets from her, too.

Returning to the hard stool, she taps her pencil on the sketchbook and ponders.

Dora waits until St Paul's strikes three before hesitantly asking Lottie to take over, and though she anticipated resistance, the housekeeper does not object at all. In fact, she seems relieved of the opportunity to rest.

The fog has lifted but has left in its place a rain that patterns the air in fine mist; Dora is barely out in it five minutes before her face is wet. A fat bead of water runs, tickling, down her nose. Dora rubs it away and tucks a damp curl back into her bonnet.

Never has she known a winter so dismal.

Dora walks fast, head down, arms tucked across her chest so the shawl that protects her sketchbook cannot blow open in the cold breeze. The snow melted three days ago, the sludge too. Now the streets are slick with rainfall, mud squelching underfoot. When she reaches St Paul's churchyard Dora keeps to the cobbles, avoids the slick grassy banks.

Before the liveried guard will let her into Mr Clements' establishment Dora must vigorously wipe her boots on the reed mat. She waits in the dim candlelight for the jeweller to finish with a customer. When said customer (an elderly gentleman by the name of Finch, Dora overhears) finally steps aside – a case of ivory goblets for which he has paid an obscene amount of money clasped tight to his chest – and Mr Clements notices her, he is too lax at concealing his look of resigned chagrin.

'Miss Blake, I—'

'Did not expect me so soon, I dare say.'

The goldsmith sighs. 'No, I dare say I did not.'

'But I am here nonetheless, as promised.'

Dora has spread her sketchbook open on the counter, has turned to the first page before he can object.

'You advised that Grecian designs were in demand. I have produced five designs for your approval. First, the bracelet.'

A design to echo the meandros, it is an elegant circlet to which Dora could not help adding her own flair.

'The diamond rosettes break up the geometric shapes. Within each rosette, a small amethyst, although an emerald or sapphire would work nicely too. Made of gold,' Dora adds, 'of course.'

Mr Clements adjusts his spectacles on the bridge of his nose. Dora turns the page.

'The earrings are daintier. The Greeks, as I'm sure you know –' and here Dora bows her head in deference to the jeweller – 'often favoured laurel crowns. Here, two laurels form a hoop, from which hang three teardrop pearls. I understand chandelier earrings are very much in favour at the moment?'

Mr Clements hesitates, nods his head. Dora takes this as encouragement.

184

'Now the three necklaces,' she says, the pages of her sketchbook crinkling as they flutter right to left. 'As you can see they are all very different in design, but each in keeping with the Grecian mode.'

The goldsmith exhales in what she thinks is admiration and Dora catches a smile between her teeth, looks at the double spread before them, feels a spark of pride. They really are, she thinks, her most accomplished creations yet, better even than the cannetille.

'For this one, I took my inspiration from the Mediterranean landscape. It can be made up in either gold or silver, though my preference is silver – it will set off the stones beautifully, don't you think?'

It is one of the prettier pieces, and also her favourite. Dora thinks of the pithos scene from which she took her inspiration, the one where Zeus and Prometheus journey to the foothills of a mountain. A delicate, multi-gemstone drop necklace with each coloured stone alternated (yellow topaz for the sun, palest jade for the mountain, blue lace agate for the sky) and separated by a single starling in flight.

The second necklace is more ornate than the first, but not as ostentatious as the peacock choker sketched out on the opposite page. It is made up of a long chain that – if one were to look closely – resembles a set of interlocking snakes, separated by flat oblong links.

'The chain can be made of whatever material would suit. Pinchbeck, I suspect would work best. This necklace takes its imagery from Mount Olympus, the banquet of the gods. Here,' Dora says, pointing at the finer detailing on one of the links, 'an elegant repeat pattern of grapes, you see? These images could either be stamped into the links, or perhaps made up from ivory and painted, or carved.'

Mr Clements gives a small nod. Dora turns to her final offering, the peacock choker. She explains the patterning, what each cameo represents.

The jeweller taps a narrow finger on his chin. 'The materials?'

'Gold, enamel, turquoise. Jet and shell for the cameo pendants, or

185

whatever would achieve the look. Ebony perhaps?' Dora touches her mother's cameo at her neck. 'I am not familiar with the construction of cameos as you are.'

Mr Clements is silent. Very slowly he reaches out, turns the pages back and forth then back again. Dora tries to read his expression but it is inscrutable, and she presses her fingers into the glass counter, tries not to let her need, her wanting, show.

I *shall* be mistress of myself, she thinks.

Finally the goldsmith takes a breath.

'These are . . . Miss Blake, I am astonished. They are beautiful. Truly. Truly they are.'

And there it is, the lilt on his tongue that Dora knows to be the beginnings of rejection, yet again.

'What is the matter *now*, sir? These are exquisite. You know they are.'

Dora tries not to cringe at her conceit, but there can be no denying the skill of her work, the beauty of these designs. She levels him with a stare that Mr Clements seems unable to meet.

'They *are* exquisite. This one, especially,' he says, and his hand hovers over the sketch of the peacock choker. 'But . . . Well, the truth of the matter is I cannot guarantee they would sell.'

'Why? Why, when you are one of the leading goldsmiths in town, who might guarantee the sale of anything in this shop by reputation alone?'

It is flattery, pure and simple, but Dora will not let this go so easily. She knows what is at stake here: her happiness, her freedom. Dora swallows. Her life. She will not let Hezekiah drag her down with him.

'Have you not heard? Surely your uncle will be feeling its effects.'

This brings Dora up short. 'Sir?'

Mr Clements straightens, looks at her now with an expression bordering on pity.

186

'At the beginning of the month Pitt introduced an income tax to help fund our war effort against the French. Many are withholding their pocketbooks now, and credit will not be given as freely as it once was. To make matters worse Napoleon has set up his armies in Egypt which has thwarted our access to India. It is difficult now to even procure materials, let alone sell the resulting product. Perhaps, in a few months . . .'

She cannot help it. Dora's eyes begin to fill. 'A few months? Mr Clements, you don't understand. I—'

But then, the tinkle of the bell. The jeweller looks past her to the door and immediately he pales, his Adam's apple bobbing vigorously beneath his cravat.

'My dear Lady Latimer!' Mr Clements looks at Dora over the half-moons of his spectacles, drops his voice to a whisper-hiss. 'Miss Blake, you must excuse me.' He pushes the sketchbook further down the counter and is frantically spreading velvet display cushions on top of the glass before Dora can say a thing.

'Clements! My design is ready, I trust?'

The voice is all audacious pomp. Dora turns to see who has so rudely interrupted them.

Stares.

Approaching the counter is an elderly woman, trussed up so tightly into a corset that her ample wrinkled bosom near spills from the constraints. On her head (or rather, atop a towering white wig that reminds Dora of a three-tiered cake) is a hat from which protrudes an ostrich feather. A few paces behind her stands a tall effeminate man, decked head to toe in sage green livery, who meets Dora's gaze ever so briefly before turning his attention full forward, adopting the stance of a soldier at orders.

As the lady presents herself at the counter in a flurry of muslin and fur and smelling overwhelmingly of lavender, Dora shunts herself

187

further down the counter – her upset momentarily forgotten – and tries to make herself inconspicuous.

'I hope you are ready to impress me,' Lady Latimer says, and the goldsmith dips his head.

'Of course,' he replies, bringing up from below the counter a red box, evidently prepared in expectation of her visit. As Mr Clements fumbles with the latch, the woman taps her gloved fingers impatiently. 'Here you are,' he says. 'As requested.'

The box opens. There is a hush of quiet. Dora angles her neck.

Within is a parure set – a necklace, earrings, brooch, tiara and necklace. A beautiful collection to be sure, made up of diamonds, emeralds and rubies favouring the French design. One of Mr Clements' own, Dora recognises, and she feels within her chest a stab of satisfaction mixed with jealousy; his designs are nothing to hers, yet it is he who makes a living from them!

'The stones are of highest quality,' he is saying, 'and the filigree detailing is remarkably fine, as you can see. The Duchess of Devonshire herself was much in favour of—'

'Really, Clements. I had expected better.'

The old woman's words fall out bored, flat. The jeweller's face drops.

'Better, ma'am?'

A pause, a shift of heavy skirts.

'Do you know who I am?' she returns, her voice now laden with scorn, but she does not wait for his response. 'I am a woman who desires ostentation, to excite my dearest friends and incite envy in those who are not. I need to be the talk of the town, the belle of the ball. It is what I *live* for!'

Dora tries not to stare; a woman of her vastly superior years could not be further from a belle of any ball than Dora could be a duck. She glances at the old woman's companion but the footman continues to look straight ahead. There is not even a tic to his perfectly smooth cheek.

'But, madam,' Mr Clements is stammering, 'that's not the style! The fashions, my lady, as they stand . . . You wished for exotic and I have created just that, as far as reasonably acceptable, created something the Prince himself would wish to wear.'

'That buffoon?' The lady's fleshy cheeks tremble like jelly. 'I do not wish to wear something the Prince would wear. I wish to wear something *I* would wear.'

His skin has paled so much it has taken on the hue of porcelain. 'But—'

'I am most displeased, Clements. My custom is clearly not appreciated here, nor my good opinion.'

'Lady Latimer,' Mr Clements tries again, but the woman is already retreating. 'Madam, please—'

'Ma'am, if I may?'

She cannot help it. The words are out of her mouth before Dora has even realised. As both Mr Clements and Lady Latimer turn their heads to stare – the goldsmith with ill-concealed vexation, and the lady with mild surprise, clearly having only just noticed her pressed resolutely against the wall – Dora's heart hammers in her throat like a drum.

'And who, pray, are you?'

The woman looks her up and down with unguarded interest. Dora licks her bottom lip.

Is it not how she always said? All it takes is one person of quality. Just one. Dora's salvation is now at the tips of her fingers, but only if she is to say something now . . .

'I wondered,' she says, stilted, unable to hide her nerves, 'perhaps, if you might take a look at one of *my* designs?'

Lady Latimer's eyes narrow. '*Your* designs?'

189

Dora reaches out a shaking hand to move Mr Clements' cushions out the way of her sketchbook, then slides it along the glass counter. With a frown Lady Latimer spreads her fattened fingers across the drawing of the peacock choker.

'Oh, yes,' the old woman breathes after a moment. 'This. I like this.'

Mr Clements, quite unable it seems to contain his upset, draws himself up to full height.

'Madam, this is not suitable—'

Her ladyship pins him with a look. 'It's a necklace, is it not?'

'Yes, but—'

'And quite perfect for my soirée.'

'Madam, I'm afraid that particular design isn't part of my—'

'Clements.' A note of warning creeps into the woman's voice. 'You know I do not like to be disappointed.'

'I . . .' The jeweller stops himself, resigned. 'No, Lady Latimer.'

Lady Latimer turns back to Dora. 'Tell me.' She prods the page.

Dora blinks. 'Tell you, ma'am?'

'What materials are used? What stones?'

From the corner of her eye Dora can observe Mr Clements' piercing gaze and she flushes, pulls the sketchbook back toward her across the counter.

'Well, my lady, it does entirely depend on Mr Clements and his men, but I had imagined . . .'

Dora describes the necklace exactly as she had to the jeweller. During her explanations the old woman *mmms* and sighs, and Dora chances a look into her wrinkled face. She seems completely enthralled. Buoyed by this, Dora turns her attention to the patterning.

'Forgive me if you are already familiar, my lady, but this is what you would call a meandros border. The Greeks used the design in their architecture, in either friezes or street paving, and it was often a feature in their pottery.'

She stops. Bites her lip. Lady Latimer taps a gloved finger. That over-sweet stench of lavender again. She nods once, twice, before looking at Dora as if she were a piece of pottery herself.

'And how, my dear, did you imagine such a beautiful design?'

Dora hesitates. 'I was inspired by a large Grecian vase in my possession, madam.'

'How large?'

'Very large, madam.'

Lady Latimer clucks her tongue. 'What is your name?'

'Dora Blake, my lady.'

'Of?'

Dora blinks. 'Of?'

'Do you have no establishment?'

A hint of impatience. Disbelief.

'Not as such.' Dora pauses, decides to offer up a half-truth. 'I help run my uncle's antiquity business. Blake's Emporium for Exotic Antiquities. It's on Ludgate Street, ma'am.'

'Indeed,' Lady Latimer says. She clears her throat, looks at the goldsmith under the wide sweep of her hat. 'Clements, I want *this* necklace. Made up exactly as Miss Blake described. I want it ready by Saturday, you understand me?'

'Lady Latimer,' he tries, looking as though he has been told to fly. 'That is only four days away.'

'And you have produced many a piece for me on short notice before. Do not pretend otherwise.'

It seems Mr Clements has given up his protests for his shoulders have slumped. 'Yes, Lady Latimer.'

'That's better. You may send me the bill once done. I shall pay

191

whatever it takes, you know I'm good for it. Do not disappoint me. As for you, Miss Blake,' the woman says, turning now to Dora. 'I would be interested to see this vase of yours. I shall drop by tomorrow. Expect me at one o'clock.'

'Yes, madam,' Dora says faintly.

There is no room for argument.

'Good. Horatio,' the old woman adds in a lighter tone, indicating that the conversation is over. 'Come!'

The footman is at her side in an instant, offering his arm with a deep bow. With a wide simpering sort of smile Lady Latimer links her arm through his, and Dora and Mr Clements watch them go, open-mouthed.

# CHAPTER
# TWENTY-THREE

Mr Clements had taken the designs, assured Dora in tones both grudging and apologetic, that she would receive a portion of the money paid out by Lady Latimer.

'Perhaps,' he said as Dora was closing her sketchbook, 'I was too quick to judge. Perhaps . . .' But he had trailed off, blinked owlishly behind his spectacles, thin cheeks dimpling pink, and Dora graciously excused herself, promising to visit the week after next. Mr Clements' humiliation was enough. There was no need to prolong the goldsmith's discomfort any more than necessary – she had got what she wanted. After all, Dora thought, her elation dampening with every step she had taken along the muddy streets toward home, there were other matters with which to concern herself.

Now, Dora looks at one of the carriage clocks propped on top of a shelf, chews on the fleshy bow of her upper lip. A quarter to one.

She has not mentioned Lady Latimer's visit to her uncle. How, she worries, is she to tell him without admitting to the fact that she has also been sneaking into the basement every night for near two weeks? That she knows about the pithos, about everything else. She has never *feared* her uncle, but his anger, always ripe, is a grave concern, especially now – Dora thinks of Lottie – that he has begun to channel it with his fist.

193

She spoke of Lady Latimer's impending visit to Edward the previous night as she was sketching in the details of Hephaestus' kiln and he was noting down the measurements of a red-figured lekythos. After he expressed his pleasure at her news (and she was sure, at first, she saw relief cross his face), Dora confessed to him her apprehension over Hezekiah's reaction in hushed guarded tones.

He paused over his notes, seemed to hesitate before saying, 'You can only tell the truth.'

'That I fed him gin, sneaked the key from his neck, copied it, then left him to his stupor?' Edward said nothing, appeared to lack the words. 'You see my dilemma, yes? I *stole*! I schemed against him.'

Again, Edward hesitated. 'If he confronts you, you're perfectly in your rights to confront *him*.'

'And say what, Edward?'

'This would be the perfect opportunity to ask, once and for all, if his trade is lawful. Remember, Dora, there still might be a good reason behind all this.'

With a sigh Dora shook her head. The hope Edward harboured was fruitless, she knew it.

'He will lie.'

'Then ask him to open the safe and prove it.'

'He will not.' Dora licked her bottom lip. 'You realise, don't you, that once Hezekiah knows I have been down here your visits will be at an end?'

In response Edward smiled, but she saw it held little humour.

'Let us worry about that when we have to. *If* we have to.'

A creak now from the basement steps. Dora looks across the shop floor just as Hezekiah emerges from the wide basement doors. His face is pale, clammy, and with a measure of unquiet Dora watches him limp toward her.

'Dora, I will rest. You will not move from this spot until I tell you to.' He wipes his face with a handkerchief, runs the satin square over the fleshy expanse of neck that squeezes itself up like baked bread from his cravat. Before he puts it back into his waistcoat pocket, Dora notices its patched dampness.

'But, Uncle.' She takes a breath. 'You are due a visitor.'

Hezekiah blinks at her. 'A visitor.'

'Yes, a . . .' And then, perfectly on cue, a black carriage pulls up outside. Dora stands up straight behind the counter. Her palms begin to sweat. 'Here she is now.'

'Who?' he asks, twisting round on his good leg.

They watch as the old woman is helped down by the footman from yesterday and Hezekiah's mouth drops slightly as he notes the crest emblazoned on the carriage door. A crest that denotes, of all Hezekiah's favourite commodities in the world, *money*.

'Dora.' Hezekiah's voice has tightened, seems to stretch over his tongue like a gag. 'What have you done?'

But the door is opening, the bell has jangled on its spring, and Dora has no time to answer.

'Hezekiah Blake's Emporium for Exotic Antiquities,' Lady Latimer announces in a loud portentous voice which belies her age. The footman – Horatio, Dora remembers – shuts the door behind her. Lady Latimer is wearing a green dress of crushed silk; her full skirts skip across the floorboards and Dora winces as they disturb the dust, dirtying the crisp white petticoat hems.

'What a name of grand import! And you,' the woman says haughtily, sharp eyes resting on Hezekiah, 'are Mr Blake, I presume.'

'Y-e-s. Yes!' he says again, recovering.

Not for many years has Blake's Emporium entertained customers of such calibre as this.

'How may I help you, madam?' Hezekiah's voice is all a-simper, that flavoursome fakery Dora abhors. 'I have just had the most delightful Chelsea shepherd come in.' He glances at Horatio, appears to mark the soft rosebud mouth, the almost-feminine build trussed up so beautifully in the fine livery that in hue matches perfectly his mistress' gown. 'He looks very much like your companion here. Very, ah, elegant. A perfect addition to your collection.'

But Lady Latimer raises a gloved hand, pierces Hezekiah with a fierce look.

'How dare you, sir. Do you imply my choice of companion is a frivolity? That I collect him like one of your trinkets here to display for mere pomp?'

Dora looks to Horatio. His beautiful features are unmarked by insult or amusement. He bows his head, as if in assent. Hezekiah clamps his mouth. Lady Latimer tosses her chin; the ostrich feather on her hat quivers.

'I am not interested in shepherds. I am interested in your Greek supply.' Lady Latimer looks to Dora. 'Good afternoon, my dear,' she says in a softer tone, and Hezekiah stares at his niece so keenly Dora is afraid her skin will blister.

'Good afternoon, madam.' Dora forces a smile, but it stretches her cheeks painfully. 'Uncle, this is Lady Latimer. We met yesterday at the shop of Mr Clements, the jeweller. You remember him, don't you? A friend of Mother's? He has acquired one of my jewellery designs. Lady Latimer has purchased it.'

Despite the apprehension fluttering in her chest, the elation she felt yesterday bubbles up inside her again, a balm now to her fraying nerves.

'I see,' Hezekiah replies, his answer measured. He looks at Dora for one more long, penetrating second before turning his attention back to the old woman. 'And what can I do for you, ah, *Lady* Latimer?'

'Your Greek supply, as I said. You have a vase.'

Hezekiah stiffens. 'A vase?'

'Yes, Mr Blake, a vase. A large one.'

Lady Latimer is all mock patience. Dora watches her uncle intently. She dreads, but equally wishes, to see how he will react to this, what he will say. Dora presses her fingers hard into the countertop, feels the sharp grain of unpolished wood pressing into the soft pads of her fingertips.

Hezekiah tries for a laugh that comes out as barely a sound at all. 'I have no Greek vases in my possession.'

Lady Latimer is shaking her head. 'But you do. This young lady said so.'

Her uncle stares. Then, very slowly, his gaze moves from Lady Latimer to Dora again. Dora swallows.

'Did she now?' He watches her, casting for a reaction like a fisherman at sea, but somehow Dora maintains her composure, holds her breath: outwardly her waters are perfectly still.

'She did indeed,' Lady Latimer returns stoutly, 'and I shall not be disappointed, Mr Blake, for I am not accustomed to being denied.' The woman takes a step forward and underneath her tread the dusty floorboards creak. 'On Saturday evening I shall be holding my annual winter soirée. It is one of the *highlights* of London's season, you understand. Each year it is themed, and this year I have chosen the Mysterious Exotic, but I have had a devil of a time finding a centrepiece for my display.' The lady nods to Dora. 'Your niece has quite come to my rescue. She says the design of the necklace I have purchased was inspired by a large vase. I want it.' Hezekiah opens his mouth to respond, but what Lady Latimer says next cuts him off: 'I shall pay you a great deal of money, of course.'

Hezekiah hesitates, scratches his scar. His niece's insubordination, it seems, has been temporarily sidelined. Dora can see his brain turning the idea over, sees how he contemplates figures, banknotes, coins, all the things he could buy with them. But then, as if discovering the secret behind a conjuror's trick, his face clears.

'You're right. I do own a Grecian vase. But I'm afraid what I meant, your ladyship, is that it is not for sale.' Hezekiah clears his throat. 'I will however loan it to you, by all means.'

Dora's heart sinks. She hears the deceit in his voice, sees the dark light that appears in his eyes whenever his tongue offers up a lie. If Hezekiah has not jumped at the chance of a quick sale, it must be because he does not deem it the appropriate kind. And so, Dora was right – Edward's hope has been misguided all along.

'A loan.' The old woman purses her lips; the skin around her mouth puckers like dried fruit. 'Very well,' Lady Latimer sniffs, 'since I only require it for the evening I shall accept. I will offer you one hundred pounds.'

Dora's eyes widen. It is a great amount, for only one night's rental. And yet, still, Hezekiah does not jump at it.

'For that much, madam, I would not loan it for an hour.'

Lady Latimer stops in the process of pulling off one of her gloves. 'I beg your pardon?'

The footman glances surreptitiously at Dora. Dora looks away.

Hezekiah draws himself up as best he can on his healthy leg.

'You must understand, my lady, that this vase is very old indeed. It is extremely precious, very delicate. The cost of transporting it alone would be . . .' He trails off, clucks his tongue in salesman brogue. 'Well, madam, it will be costly. Good hands, trustworthy men must be had in for the job. As for the vase itself, what if during your entertainments it is damaged? I already have a buyer lined up – what, then, would I say to them? No, indeed. One hundred pounds is not near enough.'

'Well, then, Mr Blake. What price would be sufficient?'

Hezekiah lets out a small chuckle, a conman's simper.

'I could not let it go for any less than five hundred pounds.'

Lady Latimer blinks. 'Five hundred?'

Dora watches the exchange with deep-seated disquiet. She is not fooled. She knows Hezekiah has deliberately suggested an extortionate price. Ask, he once told her, for twice what you expect to get, and let the buyer appear to dictate a lower price that is still far above the real value. *Barter, coerce, barter, coerce.*

'Two hundred,' the woman counters.

'Three hundred.'

'Two and fifty.'

Hezekiah frowns. 'Three hundred is my final offer, madam. I could not possibly let it out for any less. It has historic value, you understand.'

Dora watches Lady Latimer. The old woman's lip quirks. Horatio shifts against the frippery cabinet.

'You drive a hard bargain, Mr Blake. But, very well. Three hundred pounds. However, I expect it delivered on Friday. I know that means it sits with me an extra night but I promise it will not be touched beyond adding decoration to it. If you wish, your niece may accompany it, see that it is safely handled. Is that acceptable to you?'

Dora cannot read the look on her uncle's face. There is calculation behind the eyes, yes, but there is also something else, something that altogether unnerves her.

'I agree to your terms, madam.'

'Excellent!' Lady Latimer claps her hands together, releases an earthy chuckle, as if the awkwardness of before was a mere nothing. 'Now, then, I wish to see the vase itself. I am laying out an awful lot of money for a thing that is not to be mine. It's only right I view it now, before an agreement is written up?'

Hezekiah dips his back. 'Of course.'

The footman steps forward, then, and Lady Latimer links his arm, presses him to her, and Hezekiah fishes the key from the chain round his neck. For one brief moment he glances at Dora, as if to remind her of the fact that – according to him, at least – only one key exists.

As Hezekiah unlocks the basement doors and, limping, escorts Lady Latimer and her companion down the narrow steps, a painful beat begins to play out on Dora's ribs.

# CHAPTER
# TWENTY-FOUR

Hezekiah waits until the carriage has trundled out of sight before confronting his niece. He makes a deliberate show of shutting the shop door, lets the echo of the bell die down as he tries not to let his anger and fear take over.

Three hundred pounds. That is the *only* reason he has consented for the vase to be removed from his sight – it will pay off Coombe with ample money to spare. But losing it to the old woman for a night's entertainment and everything that risks is a matter he will concern himself over later. It is Dora he must worry about now.

Slowly, he thinks, slowly.

He turns. Dora has pressed herself against the back wall behind the counter and he wonders at it, this show of cowardice. *Is* it cowardice? It is unlike her, unlike her completely, and so this action of hers makes him wary, unsure. If she knows what he does, if she has discovered the vase's secret, she would not act like this. Perhaps, then, he is safe.

'How did you get in?'

For his own sake as well as hers Hezekiah makes sure he keeps his tone quiet, measured.

'I . . .'

Dora is hesitating. That interests him.

'I picked the lock.'

'With?'

'A hairpin.'

He does not believe her. Then, how? Hezekiah touches the brass key at his chest, takes a step forward, trying not to wince at the sharp pull of his wound, the way the binding pinches at the skin underneath.

'You went behind my back.'

'I . . .'

Another step.

'Why?'

And then something shifts in her face.

'*Why?*' She grips the countertop, and Hezekiah watches the skin of her knuckles turn white. 'Why did you keep it from me? Why did you keep all of them from me?'

Hezekiah stops at this, stares at the implication, is confused now for it seems, perhaps, they speak of two completely different things.

'*All* of them?'

Dora's eyes flash with something he cannot name. 'Yes, Uncle,' she says, 'all of them. I have seen the crates on the shelves, seen what is in them.'

Oh, that defiance. So like Helen. Beautiful, scheming Helen! Hezekiah feels his control slipping and he takes a deep breath, reigns himself in.

'I made no secret of them.'

'You did not tell me of them, and that is just the same,' she shoots back. 'You are storing genuine antiquities down there when you could have been selling them up here all along.'

Hezekiah glowers, shifts painfully on his bad leg. 'That is none of your business.'

'I am a *Blake*!'

And in the tortured turn of her voice he suddenly recognises the emotion behind her eyes. Anger – pure, unadulterated. It shocks him. Scares him.

'It has always been my business as well as yours,' Dora continues. 'Father would be ashamed of what you have done to the shop.'

Hezekiah curls his hands into fists. 'Your father was too soft, Pandora.' He only ever uses her full name – that ridiculous name – when he wishes to exert authority, when he feels he is near to losing it. 'I will run this place however I see fit.'

His niece shakes her head, points to the basement doors, a sharp stab in the air.

'For years the basement was closed to me. I never questioned it before since it was closed to me as a child, but then that crate arrived and you were so desperate to keep me away from it! Now I know why.'

'Do you?' he asks. Wary.

'The black-market.'

Dora says the words in an almost-whisper. There is hatred in her eyes now, but in the face of her words Hezekiah almost laughs in his relief. Is *that* all she thinks? He conceals his relief quickly, strokes the scar on his cheek, turns his voice sickly sweet.

'Do you understand what you're accusing me of, my dear?'

'I do.' Dora lifts her chin. 'You mean to sell the pithos, all the pottery in the crates. Illegally.'

'And why would I do that?'

'Because you have not acquired them by legal means. It is the only explanation. If you had, why would you not sell them up here?'

She makes a good point. Still, she only has half of it. Hezekiah takes another small step forward, breathes heavily through his nose.

'I am restoring them. Nothing more.'

Dora glowers at him. 'You lie. They need no restoration. Certainly the pithos is in perfect condition considering its considerable age.'

'Its *considerable* age?' Hezekiah echoes.

'Yes, Uncle. I know it to be so old it cannot even be dated. It pre-dates all known history.'

Hezekiah tries to conceal his shock. Then he thinks she is teasing him, makes to laugh instead. But there is no amusement on her face, and that gives him pause.

Dora must be mistaken. How could she know, after all? She, who has no knowledge of antiquities beyond the limitations of the shop, limitations he himself has put in place to prevent her meddling? But, he considers, it seems she knows far more than he realised. Still, the how does not wholly concern him. *Predates history . . .*

He knew it was old. Of course he knew – he helped Helen find it, did he not? But he had no notion it was *that* old. Not even Helen thought it was so great an age. Why, what he seeks might not even matter at all!

This reminds him.

'Did you open it?'

'The pithos?'

'Of course the pithos!'

'Yes, I—'

'It opened?'

The cutting question seems to take Dora off guard. Her brows knit. 'Yes.'

'How?'

'I . . . lifted the lid.'

'Just like that?' he asks, dubious.

Dora blinks. 'I don't understand.'

Nor does he. Hezekiah tries to swallow, but his paranoia has returned and his breath is trapped painfully in his chest, as if a stone has lodged itself there.

'Was there anything in it?'

'No.'

She hesitated. *Hesitated!* The look on her face is one of puzzle-ment, but Hezekiah feels the blood drain from his cheeks, resents her clever play. She almost had him fooled, the little witch.

'No?'

He asks this almost gently, watching.

'As I said,' Dora says, slowly, for she watches him, too.

'Nothing?'

'Nothing at all.'

And there it is. There, on her face, so like her mother's (*just* like her mother's): the look of barefaced deceit.

The lid opens easily. Lifts right off, no difficulty at all.

Why? *How?*

He checks for a mechanism, something that might have prevented him from opening it before.

There is nothing.

He turns the lid over, runs a fat finger inside the deep lip-groove. Red dust comes loose on the pad of his finger.

But. Nothing.

He does the same to the lip of the pithos itself, lays the flat of his hand on the neck, runs it round and round and round.

Nothing.

He takes the chair from the desk, stands on it – unsteady – peers within. Cannot see. He returns with a candle, angles it, tries to view the bottom.

Shadows, a flame-dance against terracotta.

And there is nothing. *Nothing!*

There is a hiss. Frowning, Hezekiah blows out the candle. The hiss stops.

Perplexed, he steps down from the chair, leans his weight on its spindly back.

Dora has found it, Hezekiah thinks. She must have found it, and therefore she knows! She *must* know! But if she knows, why does she not say anything?

She is planning something, then. She means to distract him with talk of the black-market, means to scare him. Well, he will not let her. He has come too far, waited too long to be thwarted now.

'Hezekiah?'

Lottie calls hesitantly from the top step. He keeps his back to her, grips the rim of the vase, his anger fully ripe now, his frustration fierce.

'Are you all—'

'Get out, damn you!' he shouts.

'But—'

'*Get out!*'

He listens to her retreat, her awkward shuffle, the bell that separates shop from apartment. Tries to breathe.

# CHAPTER
# TWENTY-FIVE

Hezekiah instructed her to go to her room, to not come down again for the rest of the day, and so to her room Dora has gone. But she has no intention of staying there. No, indeed, she thinks as her heartbeat steadies – she will go to Edward. She must tell him what has happened, how Hezekiah's guilt can no longer be doubted. He denied the matter, yes – restoring them, indeed! – but Dora has lived with her uncle too long now not to recognise when he speaks a lie. She laces her boots, reaches for her shawl on the back of the door, her threadbare bonnet, ties the ribbon under her chin.

The day is bright and clear; the first sun in weeks. Dora lifts the window sash, breathes in cold, crisp city, turns then to the birdcage.

'Hermes, I'll be back late.' She lifts the catch of the door, swinging it wide open. 'Here,' she says, reaching in her pocket for the currant bread she took from the kitchen before escaping to the attic. 'Freshly baked today.'

Dora reaches into the cage but the bird – who has been chittering on his perch – suddenly nips her finger. She cries out, dropping the bread, then brings her finger to her mouth, sucks on it to quell the pain. After a moment she looks at it; Hermes has not broken the skin, but his beak has left a red mark and Dora rubs her thumb over it, frowning. He has not lashed out at her since the first year she took him in.

'Whatever was that for?'

Hermes flops onto the cage floor, looks up at her, cocks his head. She watches him, then looks with distaste at the detritus he stands on. Magpies are collectors, this she has always known, has taken full advantage of. Dora lets him keep some of the beads he has brought home, the ribbons and lace he appeared to take a fancy to himself. She has hung mirrors on thread to dangle from the cage roof which Hermes prods with his beak, seemingly taking pleasure from their dancing lights. But these past two weeks he has collected all sorts of extra things on his excursions – white downy feathers, holly leaves, pine cones, newspaper scraps, all scattered now with his droppings. Sighing, Dora rubs her fingers free of crumbs. She has no time to dwell on it, thinks about Hezekiah downstairs in the basement, the way his face paled to chalk when Dora admitted to opening the pithos.

Why did he act so oddly? Why, when Dora confronted him with her suggestion of illicit trading did he barely bat an eye, but at the mention of the pithos itself . . .

Hezekiah's fearful response – and yes, she thinks, it was fear – threw her completely. Dora shakes her head, slips on her gloves. She needs Edward. He will make sense of it.

'Be good, Hermes.'

As she shuts the door behind her the magpie squawks harshly in reply.

Dora tries the bindery first. Mr Fingle is apologetic, informs her Edward has left early and is like, he says, with a knowing sort of look she does not understand, to be with Mr Ashmole. He gives Dora the address of both his employer's and Edward's lodgings, bows his head, shows her back out onto the narrow street and points her in the direction of Bedford Square.

She must assume this is where Mr Ashmole lives, for a bookbinder could not possibly live in an area so fine, and so Dora decides to try her luck there first. But these are streets she does not know; at first she follows the route through Covent Garden Edward took her that morning she had asked for his help, but when she finds herself lost she stops to get her bearings, recalculates the way. By the time she arrives at the foot of the white stucco steps of an imposing-looking house named Clevendale (having asked directions twice more, from a redcoat who looked her up and down like meat on a skewer and an orange seller with crescent moons of black wedged deep beneath her fingernails), her dress sticks to her back and her petticoats are two inches deep in London muck.

Dora smooths down her skirts, tucks a damp curl behind her ear, and with a deep breath she lifts the ornate lion-headed knocker. She shuffles on her toes, clenches and unclenches her hands. Presently the door is opened by a steel-haired woman with too little chin and too much nose.

'Hawkers round back,' she says tartly, but before the woman can close the door Dora steps forward.

'I am so sorry to disturb you,' she says, tongue tripping over her nerves. 'Are you Mrs Ashmole?'

The woman's thin eyebrows rise. '*I* am Mrs Howe, Mr Ashmole's housekeeper. Is it the master you wish for?'

'I'm looking for Mr Lawrence. I was told he might be here.'

Mrs Howe looks Dora up and down, and Dora knows how she must appear in her dated gown and shabby bonnet with its fraying ribbons. A maid. A beggar, perhaps. A nobody.

With a sniff the housekeeper shows Dora into a small sitting room, tells her to wait, indicates two damask chairs for her to sit on, but

Dora feels too afraid to sit in either of them. She can see even from where she loiters near the door, without having to touch them, that they are silk. Expensive. New.

Dora looks around.

Though small it is a fine room, a pleasant antechamber for waiting visitors. A narrow bookshelf holds within it ornate volumes on philosophy, the natural world, Milton's *Paradise Lost*, even a novel or two – Dora spies Richardson's *Pamela* and wonders at the fancifulness of it.

But it is the rosewood cabinet that attracts. Within – lined from smallest to largest – are a set of antique globes, their spheres made from smoked glass to polished wood to shining marble. She thinks of Hezekiah's globe, thinks how much he would covet these ones for they are far finer than his, and Dora's fingers itch to spin them on their axes.

A large window overlooks the street which gives a grand view of a little park filled with trees that Dora imagines will sprout forth some beautiful foliage in the spring. She smiles wistfully. How lovely, she thinks. What a gift to be able to look at nature at leisure from one's windows, from such sumptuous surroundings as this. She wonders then, absently, if Mr Ashmole is an idle sort and it strikes Dora as odd that Edward should know such a person, when he himself is so industrious.

The door opens. Mrs Howe again.

'You may come through.'

Dora is taken through a wide hall, its floor tiled black and white. At the end Mrs Howe pushes open the door into a large room, a library, decorated much like the antechamber but with a hint more ostentation – richer furnishings, dark jewel colours, a deep-set hearth in which roars a fire. Dora has barely taken in the shock of a skinned tiger on the floor before Edward is rushing to her, guiding her into the room, his hand warm on hers.

210

Mr Ashmole, who has not stood, simply stares. Edward draws up a chair – this one not silk she is pleased to see, but serviceable leather.

'Forgive me,' Dora says now to Mr Ashmole as she settles down into the chair's depths. 'I did not mean to intrude without invitation, but it is imperative I speak with Mr Lawrence immediately.' She looks to Edward. 'I tried the bindery first but Mr Fingle assured me I was more like to find you here.'

'I am glad you have come,' Edward answers in a rush, and it does seem he is pleased. His colour is high and Mr Ashmole appears to notice this too, stares at him hard a moment before turning to address Dora directly.

'Mr Lawrence has spoken much of you, Miss Blake. In fact, you have become quite famous in this house.' His voice is rich, like satin, but holds within it the edge of dislike.

'I . . .' Dora glances at Edward, then back again. 'He has spoken of me?'

'Did I not just say?'

Dora swallows the punch. 'It is a pleasure to make your acquaintance, sir,' she says, though she is yet to find the pleasure in it.

Mr Ashmole watches her. Then: 'Mrs Howe.'

'Yes, sir?'

Dora catches herself – she had not realised the housekeeper still loomed at the door. Dora glances at Edward who sends her a small, comforting smile.

'If you would bring our visitor a glass of wine.' He strikes an eyebrow at Dora. 'Are shop girls accustomed to claret?'

'Cornelius.' Edward's tone is low, a warning.

Mr Ashmole laughs humourlessly. 'Of course. Mrs Howe, if you will?'

Mrs Howe curtseys. The door is closed. Silence engulfs the room.

211

Dora allows it to stretch for only a moment before saying, 'Again, Mr Ashmole, please do forgive my intrusion—'

'It is no intrusion,' Edward cuts in.

Mr Ashmole looks at him blankly. Then he turns to her and says, 'Why are you here, Miss Blake?'

Edward's friend is not what she expected. Dora imagined an elderly benefactor, someone with dove-grey hair, a moustache, perhaps, someone with a cane and kindly smile. This tall, austere man with raven-black hair seems altogether too young to own a bindery, too young to have this much money. And he seems altogether too unpleasant to be friends with Edward. He is, Dora senses, the complete opposite of Edward Lawrence in every way.

'I . . .'

Mrs Howe returns, a circular silver tray in her hands on which stands a beautifully cut crystal glass. Dora takes it, thanks the woman who nods once and retreats fast from the room as if she cannot abide being in their presence.

'Please,' Edward says, sitting forward in his seat, his face kind. 'Do continue.'

Dora takes a breath. She begins to speak, addressing Edward and not Mr Ashmole, for his piercing stare unnerves her to the point of distraction.

'I have come to tell you that the lady who purchased my necklace has managed to convince my uncle to loan her the pithos.'

Edward sits back in his chair, leather creaking. 'I see.'

'I confronted him, as you said I should. And . . . Oh, it is clear my uncle has been trading illicitly, just as I thought.' Dora pauses. 'You know, then, what this means. You cannot possibly write your paper now, and I will not be able to finish my sketch of the pithos.'

She thinks of it then, her unfinished progress with its copy – only one scene left! – and is thankful, at least, that she managed to produce the drawings she has. But Edward has not replied. His gaze is fixed somewhere on the stripes of the tiger lying between them.

Is he angry with her? Dora tries to stem her concern, for she has enjoyed her nights with him, has become – without realising it – quite dependent on his company, and for him to be angry with her would upset her deeply.

'I am so sorry.'

Finally, movement. A look passes between Mr Ashmole and Edward which seems filled with some deeper meaning, something to which she is not privy, but before she can question it Edward leans forward in his seat, smiles, and Dora thinks it forced, awkward.

'There is no need to be sorry,' he assures. 'At the very least you have given me the opportunity to examine a genuine collection of Greek antiquity. I'm most grateful. I can write a paper on something else.' He pauses. 'Your drawings. You still have them?'

'I do.'

Edward appears relieved, and Dora looks between him and Mr Ashmole. Something is amiss, she can sense it, but she has something to ask Edward, something she needs him to agree to and so, on that score, she holds her tongue.

'I'm afraid,' Dora says now, 'telling you this was not my only purpose for wishing to see you. I have a favour to ask.'

'Another?'

Mr Ashmole, this. Dora feels his hostility – it comes off him like kettle-steam – and it confuses her.

Edward clears his throat. She is not sure if it is with annoyance or unease.

'Please, Dora, do not mind him. Anything you wish to say to me can be heard by Cornelius.'

She does mind. But that, she decides, is a discussion for another time.

213

'The woman, Lady Latimer, wants the pithos for a soirée she is holding on Saturday night. Themed. Exotic, she says, which is why she feels the pithos is the perfect centrepiece. She is to pay a great deal of money for it.'

'How much?' Mr Ashmole asks.

Dora hesitates, dislikes his presumption at asking such a thing, but she answers all the same.

'Three hundred pounds.'

Edward whistles. He retrieves a glass from the table beside him, takes a long sip. The liquid is dark brown, a hint of red in it. Brandy, perhaps?

'The pithos will be taken to her on Friday. I am to accompany it at Lady Latimer's request and I had hoped, Edward – Mr Lawrence,' she corrects quickly when she perceives Mr Ashmole send her a sharp look, 'that you would come with me.'

Edward looks pleasantly surprised. 'Of course.'

Dora sighs in relief. 'Thank you, thank you so very much. I confess I do not wish to be alone with my uncle when it is taken. I would feel much safer if you were there.'

Edward smiles and she feels a warmth go through her, a pleasurable feeling that dips and turns in the seat of her belly, only for it to be rudely interrupted by Mr Ashmole clearing his throat. Dora blushes, looks away, finally takes a sip of her wine.

'Tell me,' says Mr Ashmole to Edward, his voice a pointed drawl, 'have you heard back from Hamilton?'

That awkward silence again. Dora blinks across her glass. Edward clasps his between both hands.

'I left a note, as I already told you,' he says carefully, 'but have had no response as yet.'

'Who is Hamilton?' Dora asks.

Edward takes a breath, sends a pointed look to Mr Ashmole which the gentleman greets with a smile and an arrogant cock of his head.

'The expert I mentioned. The one I asked if you would object to my seeking advice regarding the pithos.'

'Oh, yes,' Dora remembers. 'But surely there is no need for him to advise you now?'

Another look passes between the two men. No, something is not right, she is sure of it now. What is amiss here? What part does Mr Ashmole play in her business?

'What exactly did your uncle say when he discovered you had been in the basement?' Edward asks, interrupting the train of her thoughts.

Dora blinks. 'He did not react in the way I expected, did not seem much put out at all by the mention of the black-market.'

'But you are convinced he is involved?'

'Absolutely positive. If you had been there, you would have seen from his manner he was hiding something.'

'Did you ask him about the safe?'

'No. We moved so swiftly on to the pithos that I forgot to ask.'

'And what did he say about that?'

Dora frowns at the memory. 'It was most odd. He asked if I had opened it. He looked almost fearful when I said I had.'

Edward frowns too. 'Fearful?'

'Yes.'

'Because you opened the pithos?'

'Yes.'

'How extraordinary,' says Edward.

They fall silent again. In the hall Mrs Howe hums a baleful tune, painfully off-key.

After a moment Mr Ashmole crosses his booted legs, stretches

215

them out, rests his heels against the tiger's head and he looks at Dora then, and Dora does not like the direct way in which he does it.

'Well,' he says slowly, stretching the word out over his tongue, 'there must be a reason why he was so particular about it. Has it not occurred to you there might have been something inside?'

Disliking his sardonic tone, Dora decides to match it. 'But there was nothing in it, sir.'

'Are you quite sure?'

She gives a short, disbelieving laugh, angry now at his audacity, his arrogance, his assumption that he has any right to question her on the matter at all.

'What is it to you?' she asks sharply.

His eyes widen slightly. For a moment Dora thinks he is impressed at her spark but then she notices Edward, his look of discomfort, of embarrassment, of shame, even, and all of a sudden Dora is weary. It will not do to bring herself down to Mr Ashmole's level. It will not do at all.

'Yes,' she answers, softening her tone, 'of course I am. There was nothing. I'd have noticed, I'm sure.'

'Then,' Edward's friend replies, 'this may for ever remain a mystery.'

From the small table at his side Mr Ashmole raises his drink, smiles into it. The afternoon sun streams like rods through the windows. One of the beams lights upon the liquid in Mr Ashmole's glass, and the crystal patterns amber diamonds against his chin.

# CHAPTER
# TWENTY-SIX

'What is wrong with you?'

The door has barely shut on Dora's skirts before Edward turns on Cornelius. He feels mortified, completely mortified that a woman he so admires can be treated in such a cold, unfeeling manner.

'How could you behave so rudely to Miss Blake?'

Cornelius lounges back in the armchair he did not deign to leave when Edward escorted Dora to the door.

'I was not rude.'

'You were. You know you were.'

'Was it not rude that she turned up at my home unannounced?' Cornelius shoots back, refilling his glass from the decanter at his elbow. 'I have a mind to give Fingle an earful when I see him next. He had no right to divulge my address without my express permission.'

'You'll do no such thing,' Edward says, settling himself into the chair vacated by Dora. It is still warm. That faint perfume of lily. 'It was very good of him to help her – she was clearly in need of me.'

'How flattering for you.'

The comment is posed as a sneer. Edward ignores it.

He hoped, he truly did, that Dora would be proven wrong, that Hezekiah Blake's misdemeanours were limited only to forgeries and nothing more. But, it seems, there can be no denying the fact any longer. Gough, Edward thinks with a grimace, will be thrilled when he tells him. He can be thankful, at least, for Dora's sake, that her own fortunes have turned. It eases his conscience somewhat.

'I cannot tell you how relieved I am that Lady Latimer has taken one of her designs,' Edward says to Cornelius now. 'It is precisely the kind of endorsement Miss Blake needs. I hope more will come from it. But according to what Miss Blake has just told us she will need to secure her future as soon as possible in the event her uncle is exposed.' Edward frowns. 'Allowing the pithos to be displayed so openly where it might be recognised is a bold move on his part. To risk so much . . .'

'Three hundred pounds. Many would risk more for less.'

Edward rubs his thumb thoughtfully against his chin. If Hezekiah is discovered as a result of the soirée, Dora will be in immediate danger.

'I still mean to help her, Cornelius.'

'I'm really not so sure she deserves it.'

That sneer again. Edward sucks in his breath in annoyance.

'I told you my plan. She agreed before to let me use her sketches of the pithos, even if she does not now know in what context I mean to use them.' His stomach twists again with the guilt of it. 'But I am determined to keep the Blake name anonymous. I will not expose her. I *will* help her. And when I gain entrance into the Society she can sketch for me. We can form a partnership, one that will allow her to leave the shop. One that will keep her safe.'

A long pause that prickles. Then, 'I see.'

Edward hears Cornelius' disbelief, his disapproval, and he looks at his friend imploringly.

'Cornelius, if you had been with us . . . it was patent she knew nothing of what her uncle kept in that basement. Nothing at all.'

'Why are you so sure?'

'I just am.'

'That is no answer.'

For a moment Edward stares into the hearth. There comes the memory of desolation, of being lost, of screaming over and over, in a darkness that seemed to breathe . . .

'She is trapped,' he says quietly. 'I understand that better than anyone. I *have* to help her. Just as you helped me.'

At Edward's words Cornelius' face closes. Then he squints his eyes shut, snaps them open again.

'I simply do not trust her, Edward. As far as I'm concerned she is as guilty as her uncle.'

Edward sighs. There is nothing else he can say – there is no use in trying – and so the pair slip into silence. As the fire crackles in the hearth Edward worries his inner cheek with his teeth.

He thinks of his visit to Gough that morning, how he pushed the little black book that outlined his notes on the pithos across the ornate desk, watched the older man read over them.

'Have you heard from Sir William?' the director had asked.

'No, sir. I wrote to him, but have received no response.'

'He will reply in due course. His return from Italy has meant that he's in high demand. There are many affairs, so I understand, that he is busy putting in order. He lost a shipment of antiquities in December when the vessel they were being transported on sank just off the Scilly Isles.'

'That's terrible.'

'Indeed. But I bid you patience. When Greek artefacts are involved Hamilton can't resist. For the time being, I would continue as you are. What are your next steps?'

It was a test, Edward knew instinctively. A measure, he supposed, of his knowledge and sincerity.

'I would like to have the clay sample further examined, to

219

conclude its geographical origin. I do not feel I can go much further with my investigations without it.'

'Very good,' Gough said, 'I shall organise it with our scientists. Have you made any progress in ascertaining how the pithos was obtained?'

Edward hesitated. 'I've been advised of three men who might be able to shed light on where it came from. That is, how it was acquired.'

'Then make haste, Mr Lawrence.' Gough handed Edward's black book back to him. 'In matters such as this, time is of the essence.'

Now Edward gazes into the fire. For so long he has wanted his life to have purpose. For too many years he has suffered under his own shortcomings, has feared his own shadow. Those early years in London . . . they continue to be a taint on him, a pestilence that has followed him like a wraith, that has woken him in the dead of night leaving his skin and bed sheets wet with cold sweat. Dora Blake has given him that purpose. In her lies the key to his success.

Make haste, indeed. It is all now he can do.

# CHAPTER
# TWENTY-SEVEN

The same man who delivered the pithos arrives to take it away. From her position at the shop door Dora watches him and her uncle exchange words in undertones that appear both urgent and threatening. Then Hezekiah turns, brushes past her into the shop without meeting her gaze.

The day is dry but there is a sharp breeze that whistles down Ludgate Street and through its clamour of pedestrians kicking up mud and filth on their heels. The red-headed man waits patiently for a hawker – six filthy urchins trailing behind her – to pass before rounding one side of the wagon. He takes a pile of ropes from the back, gestures to his companions with a grunt.

The two brothers, Dora notes, are not with him. Instead he has brought another man – a Mr Tibb, she heard her uncle call him – and two others who smell, faintly, of excrement.

Dora retreats into the murk of the shop, loiters near the green chair Edward sat on that first day. As he passes, the hulking man greets her with a small duck of his chin, a barely-there nod, and Dora thinks how much older he seems since she last saw him. There is a tightness to his face, a tense, sick sort of expression that disturbs her.

She watches the men as they haul the pithos up the basement

steps using a complicated system of pulleys and the ropes. Dora clasps her hand to her mouth, resists the urge to cry out to them to take care, but Hezekiah has no such qualms.

'Watch what you're doing!' he snaps, as one of the smaller men – dark-skinned, little more than a boy – buckles under the weight.

'Now, now, Mr Blake,' the man named Tibb says, tone mollifying, 'we know what we're doing – we got it on the wagon to begin with, if you remember?'

Hezekiah glances briefly at Dora before straightening his cravat.

'Of course I do! But luck was with us that day.'

'Luck,' the large man mutters, shifting the rope holding part of the weight of the pithos on his shoulder, 'had nothing to do with it.'

Hezekiah rounds on him. 'Have a care,' he warns. 'I'll not have such talk here.'

The man glowers, but Hezekiah is already turning away, limping past Dora into the street. Frowning, she looks up at the large man. His lip twists.

'Best keep out the way, miss, until it's loaded.'

They stare at each other a moment. Then Dora nods, follows her uncle outside.

She decides to stand on the far side of the wagon, watches with interest the pithos' laboured journey onto the back. When it has been loaded and covered with a sheet, Mr Tibb and the two lads join it, and the larger man returns to where Hezekiah waits at the shop door. Dora folds her arms as her uncle takes from his waistcoat three paper bills, which the man swipes with his fist, shoving them unceremoniously into his pocket. The payment Lady Latimer laid out was delivered by a footman this morning – a different but equally pretty man this time – but it interests Dora to see so much of it going to Hezekiah's lackey. What are they about?

'Dora!'

She turns to see Edward rushing toward her from the direction of the Strand. He comes to a stop, out of breath.

'I'm sorry for my tardiness. I had a commission to finish. Got here as quickly as I could.' He takes a gulp of air. His cheeks are red. Edward looks at the set-up dubiously, at the sheet and web of ropes keeping the pithos in place, then shoots Dora a concerned look. 'Will it be safe?'

'Safe is not a word I would use,' the large man says as he pushes roughly past them. Dora turns to him in surprise.

'I beg your pardon?'

'If you're asking if it's secure,' he responds shortly, tightening the ropes with a tug, 'then yes, it is that. It won't be falling off, of that you can be certain. But as for its safety . . .'

'Coombe,' Hezekiah says from the shop doorway. 'Enough.'

His voice is a low warning. Across the horse's back the two stare at each other before the man named Coombe gives the buckle one last pull. He says nothing, instead heaves himself up onto the seat, seizing the reins. It is then that Hezekiah notices Edward.

'Mr . . . Lawrence, was it?' he says, his words freighted equally with surprise and suspicion. 'Pray, sir, what do you do here?'

Hezekiah addresses Edward but he is looking at Dora, and she knows it is she who must answer.

'He is here at my request, Uncle. Mr Lawrence, it transpires, is quite the expert in Greek antiquities.'

Dora feels no shame, no qualm in telling him this. Since they came to blows the other evening Dora has felt empowered, rebellious. But beside her Edward takes a hesitant step back. Hezekiah's sharp gaze shifts between them.

'It appears you have been keeping much from me, Pandora.'

'A family trait, it seems.'

Hezekiah blinks at her answer, in surprise or defiance, she is not sure. But then Mr Coombe coughs.

'We'd best be on our way, miss. You may both ride up here with me.'

Hezekiah sneers, turns away. Edward offers his hand, guides her up. As Mr Coombe reaches down to assist her, Dora cannot help but notice a putrid-yellow stain on his cuff.

The wagon trundles away from Ludgate Street toward the more affluent environs of the city, and Dora finds herself leaning against Edward, pressing her weight into his shoulder. He does not seem to mind, but makes no move to draw her closer.

She cannot help it. It is not because she craves Edward's touch. No, indeed – the smell from Mr Coombe's wrist is almost overpowering; even with the wind at its zenith the rancid stench finds a way to itch her nostrils. She tries not to stare at it but her attention is drawn again and again to the stained bandages, the bruised skin of his hand. They ride in silence to begin with, but Mr Coombe happens to catch her looking when directing the horse down onto High Holborn and he grimaces.

'I'm sorry, miss. I bind it every few hours, but the wound still weeps.'

Dora blushes, ashamed. 'Forgive me. I didn't mean to make you feel uncomfortable.'

The wagon bounces. Edward glances at Mr Coombe, seems to notice the wrist for the first time.

'How did it happen, sir? If I do not presume too much.'

The man snorts, flicks the reigns. The wagon takes a slow turn.

'No need to stand on ceremony with me. Sir! As if I had the honour.' He shakes his head. 'How'd it happen, you ask? That damn cargo happened.'

Dora blinks. 'The pithos?'

'Aye, if that's what you wish to call it. Retrieved it myself I did, my brothers and me, but I wish to God I had never agreed to such a deed.'

Edward leans closer. 'So it was *you* who acquired it?'

From behind them, a cough. 'Coombe,' the man Tibb says, voice raised in warning. 'I would watch yourself.'

'And why should I?' Mr Coombe throws back. 'This girl is Blake's niece, Jonas. She ought to know—'

'Know what?' Dora cuts in, but Mr Tibb has raised himself, one hand on the pithos – the sheet that covers it bunching – the other clamped on Mr Coombe's shoulder. 'You will do best to keep your mouth shut.' Then, to Dora, 'My apologies, Miss Blake, but it is not our place to divulge. You must understand . . . it is nothing against yourself. There are just some things that I'd prefer not to be a party to.'

'Are you not already a party to it?' Dora asks, twisting in her seat.

Mr Tibb inclines his head. 'I am, I suppose. But I'll not be the one to confide in such matters.'

'But—'

Mr Tibb turns his back, resumes his perch on some ship's tackle piled on the floor of the wagon. Dora looks at Mr Coombe; he faces front, attention fixed on the road, his thick jaw tightly set. She exchanges a glance with Edward. His eyebrows raise but he gives a small, ever-so-slight shake of his head, and so Dora sits back, losing herself in troubled thoughts.

Lady Latimer's townhouse – nothing short of a villa – overlooks a wide berth of water, and is approached via a cobbled crescent surrounding a green of immaculately cut lawn in which a large ornate fountain sits bubbling away in the middle. If Dora thought Cornelius Ashmole's Clevendale were grand, then this is altogether a palace. Reached by a pair of iron gates the house looms before them, a splendour of blinding white. Large Roman columns flag the vast double doors which are opened almost instantly by two liveried footmen.

As Edward helps Dora down from the wagon, she notes the beauty of them. Tall young men, pretty men, almost doll-like, dressed exactly as Horatio and this morning's footman had been, top to tail in sage green. Lady Latimer, it seems, delights in ornamenting herself with more than just fine gowns and jewels.

Horatio himself emerges from the open doorway, a silver platter balanced perfectly on his fingers. He proffers a small bow.

'Miss Blake, welcome. My esteemed ladyship wishes you to read this letter, and to give your answer before you leave.'

This is the first time Dora has heard Horatio speak, and as she takes the note from the platter she blinks into his perfectly smooth, handsome features.

'You and your companion are to come inside while the shipment is safely transported to the ballroom.'

Horatio's over-formality, his lilting-soft voice – so poised and cultured – has quite distracted her. Dazed, she turns to address Edward but finds he is not at her side. She looks behind her to see him deep in conversation with Mr Coombe.

'Edward?'

He looks up. His face flushes. Then he is tucking his black notebook and a pencil away, hurrying to join her.

'My apologies,' Edward says. He smiles, but to Dora's mind it seems uncharacteristically tight. 'Is everything all right?'

226

'Yes,' Dora answers. She shall question him later, she decides. 'We have been invited to wait inside.'

Horatio inclines his fine head. 'If you will both follow me.'

They are escorted into a grand entrance hall, tiled in white marble, polished to such a shine Dora can see her reflection. She chances a glance at Edward but he seems entirely indifferent, as if such riches were a commonplace thing. The footman reaches a pair of glass doors, flings them open with a flourish.

'The adornment is to go there,' Horatio says, gesturing into the cavernous room. In the middle of it Dora spies a large circular plinth set low to the ground, covered with a sheet of midnight-blue velvet. 'Her ladyship has grand plans for your cargo – it will be decorated to delightful perfection. But come,' he adds, gesturing now to a pair of mahogany high-backed chairs. 'If you wait here, I shall furnish you with some refreshment.'

Dora sits, mute, watching his retreat. Horatio fascinates her. What command of language! She is used to the commonplace brogue of London's trade, not flowery words delivered in a sugared tongue. Beside her Edward stares into his lap, a deep frown on his face.

'You don't seem as awed as I do by such grand surroundings.'

Edward starts, and Dora knows she has disturbed the trajectory of his thoughts.

'Oh,' he says, looking about him without interest. 'It isn't that I have no appreciation for it. But Cornelius, you see . . . he and I grew up together in a place very much like this. In Staffordshire.'

The knowledge surprises. 'Oh.' In the entrance hall, Mr Coombe, Mr Tibb and their companions are guiding the pithos across the floor. 'How so?'

Edward shifts on the satin. 'I was the son of old Mr Ashmole's groom. Mr Ashmole was often away and so Cornelius used to invite me into the house. I would spend many a happy hour there. Nights

227

too, sometimes.' He trails off, takes a small breath. Dora watches the play of emotion pattern his face, like sunshine through a lattice. 'As you have already observed, Cornelius and I are very close. He is like a brother to me. But I always felt so . . . mediocre, compared to him.' Edward frowns again. 'It isn't that I resented his good fortune – he has always been very generous – but I often felt like a child playing make-believe. I wasn't comfortable in such affluent surroundings. An outsider. I never felt truly my own man, if that makes any sense. Does it?'

'I think so,' Dora says. Edward has turned to look at her. His grey eyes are shadowed, as if the weight of his memories has dampened them. 'I understand what it is to feel trapped by circumstance, certainly.'

'Yes.'

'Lemonade!'

Horatio has returned with two glasses on the silver tray. 'Sicilian lemons.' And then he is gone again, his ornate pumps *click-clacking* on the tiles.

Dora raises the glass to her lips, takes a sip. She grimaces – so sharp! – but it is cool and refreshing, and she is thankful for the treat. It reminds her of blue skies, summer heat, and for one painful moment the image of her mother appears in her mind's eye. A tent. Raised voices. A memory she cannot quite grasp . . .

'Careful!'

Dora looks up to see that the pithos is upon them now, Mr Coombe and his men grunting under its weight. Free of its protective sheet she glimpses the pithos' carvings through the bonds, frustrated again that she has not completed the final scene. Then the pithos passes them; Dora watches its procession into the ballroom, the shuffle and squeak of boots on polished wood. To distract herself she addresses Edward once again.

'Why did you leave?'

He blinks up from his glass. 'Sorry?'

'Why did you leave?' she asks again.

'Staffordshire?'

'Yes. Why did you come to London?'

Edward sucks in his breath. He is quiet for a full minute, and Dora regrets her forwardness.

'Edward, I'm sorry, I did not—'

'No, it's fine.' He grips his glass tighter. 'My mother died giving birth to me. When my father died the summer I turned twelve, it was decided that instead of being kept on at Sandbourne as a groom I be sent to London to learn a trade, one that would give me a better life. The bindery. Old Mr Ashmole paid for everything. A gift, he said, in honour of my father's good service.'

'And how did you like learning the trade?'

The question is innocent enough but Dora knows the moment the words leave her mouth she has asked the wrong thing – Edward has paled, the glass wobbles in his hand, the lemonade threatening to spill. Then he shakes himself, turns to her and asks, 'What does the letter say?'

'The letter . . .'

She looks down at it clasped in her free hand. She had forgotten all about it.

A small square note, elegantly sealed by a deep, rich-red disc. Dora places her glass at her feet, snaps the wax.

*Miss Blake,*

*I cannot express to you my pleasure at having found the perfect piece of jewellery to complete my costume for tomorrow's festivities. I extend my deepest thanks to you by enclosing two tickets to my soirée, for yourself and a guest. I do not approve of*

*your uncle, therefore it behoves me to request that you do not*
*choose him as your companion!*

    *You will have determined by now, my dear, that I am not a*
*woman to be disappointed. I expect your presence. To assure*
*myself of it I suggest you use this experience as an opportunity*
*to satisfy yourself, and Mr Blake, as to the safety of my*
*purchase throughout the evening.*

*Yours respectfully,*
*Lady Isabelle Latimer*

'Oh, dear.'

'What is it?'

Wordlessly Dora hands Edward the letter, just as Mr Coombe and his men quit the ballroom, ropes and pulleys in their arms. Dora looks beyond them into the room. The pithos stands – tall, regal – perfectly situated in the middle of the plinth. Dora feels a shiver run down her spine. How desolate it looks out in the open . . .

'Ah, Miss Blake!'

Lady Latimer is striding toward them from the vicinity of the staircase, dressed head to toe in a shock of magenta taffeta, wig piled up high on her head with small silk roses dotted through. Both Dora and Edward jump up from their seats.

'You received my note, I see.'

'I did, madam,' Dora says, flustered, 'and I'm very grateful. But I cannot possibly accept.'

'Tosh!' Lady Latimer waves her hand across her rouged face. 'I decide who attends my social gatherings.'

'But I have nothing to wear.'

'You have something plain and serviceable, surely?' the old woman scoffs and Dora blushes with shame, for though she does indeed own many a plain and serviceable gown, not one of them is less than five years old.

'I do, but nothing suitable for a soirée.'

'I see . . .'

It is clear Lady Latimer has not thought of this, not considered the divide between their classes as in any way a barrier to fashion, but then Edward steps forward, dips in an awkward bow.

'If it pleases, my lady, I will make sure Miss Blake has something suitable for the occasion.'

Lady Latimer looks at Edward with sharp, appraising eyes, then back at Dora.

'Your young man, I take it?'

Edward blinks, begins to stammer. 'Oh, no, madam. I mean, that is—'

Lady Latimer cuts in with a short laugh. 'Bring this one along, Miss Blake. He has a timid look about him. I do like that in a man.' She glances at Horatio who has appeared at her side. 'They are like not to be rogues then, my dear. The timid ones are malleable, easily guided to our whim. Better we woman have the upper hand in matters of the heart, don't you think?'

Dora is at a loss for a response, but then she realises there is no need of one; Lady Latimer has seen the pithos. She claps her hands in pleasure, strides toward it with almost childish excitement.

'How glorious! Yes, yes, it is perfect, utterly splendid. Horatio, you will show our guests out, won't you?'

This last is thrown over her ladyship's shoulder, and Horatio loses no time in guiding them to the door. Mr Coombe, Mr Tibb and the two lads are already on the wagon, waiting. When they reach it Mr Coombe reaches down to help her up. Dora straightens her skirts, and Edward settles in the seat beside her.

'I hope,' Edward murmurs shyly, 'you did not find me too presumptuous?'

'No,' Dora answers, shy herself, 'though I confess myself surprised. Surely you don't mean it?'

'Of course I do. Mr Coombe, would you be willing to drop us off at Piccadilly?'

'If you like,' the large man sniffs, flicking the reins. 'Makes no difference to me.'

As the cart rumbles away down the drive, Edward clears his throat, straightens his cuff.

'I am not timid,' he says.

It is more than a put-out grumble. His voice is pained in its defensiveness and Dora reaches out, gently takes his hand.

'I know you are not, Edward,' she says softly.

Edward looks away. He does not pull his hand from hers.

# CHAPTER
# TWENTY-EIGHT

Hezekiah cradles his gin against the fleshy plane of his naked chest. He is thankful for the fug alcohol affords, the way his mind fizzes and lulls, how his vision blurs a little when he turns his head. *Like that.* He takes a long sip from his glass, rests his head back against the headboard, feels the comforting solidness of carved oak.

At his side Lottie wrings out a cloth in a basin. When she started the cloth was white. Now it is stained yellow with a tinge of green-pink, and on the surface of the cloudy water, questionable gobs of *something* (Hezekiah will not let himself think on it too much) are floating. Soapsuds, he tells himself. Nothing worse than that.

It is not denial. Not precisely. He knows something is not right. But to put it into words . . . Well, that is something he does not wish to do. To say he is ill, to *say* he fears his leg has grown gangrenous, that might make it true, and he is not willing to give voice to such an unhappy truth. Not yet.

He hisses as Lottie lays the cloth over the wound, bunches the sodden bed sheet in his fist. Lottie tuts, shifts on the bed. Hezekiah glances at her swollen lip, then away again. He did not mean to hit her, but he was just so damn angry and it was done before he realised it. He had not felt so much anger since . . .

Since.

In his mind's eye Coombe's face looms before him. *There is a fine line between coincidence and fate.* Is there really something to what the oaf says? *Is* the vase cursed? Is that why he reacted as he did?

*Fool!*

Hezekiah dampens the memory down, shifts again on the bed. It creaks under his weight and Lottie adjusts her own position, folds the wet cloth in her hands.

'How do the Coombe brothers?' he asks as she wipes the cloth over the tender skin of his thigh. He tries to stop its involuntary shake. Noticing, Lottie gentles her touch.

'They do not improve, though they do not grow worse.'

'Does Matthew help you?'

'He helps turn Sam so I can wash him. He encourages Charlie to take food. There is not much else to be done.'

'And his own wound?'

Lottie hesitates. 'Matthew's wrist looks much worse than this.'

She gestures at the growing hole in Hezekiah's thigh, the foul-smelling sore that should not be a sore at all but a shallow wound, only. A wound that should have scabbed over days ago.

'It starts to turn black. I fear . . .'

She does not say what he knows she thinks, that the skin on his leg – like Coombe's arm – will soon begin to die. Hezekiah takes another long sip of gin.

'I am glad,' Lottie says now, her voice a little brighter, 'that I no longer need go there. It's as well you gave Matthew his money so he can fetch a doctor. He was desperate, yesterday. Kept telling me how he would have made things difficult for you. He still might.'

Hezekiah grunts. Another thing he does not wish to think of.

The money from Lady Latimer has more than amply paid off Coombe – the man should not bother him again – but it does not help *his* cause. The buyer he claimed to have in line does not exist;

Hezekiah wanted to salvage his prize first before approaching his associate to open sales, ensure his future, make it secure.

The idea of the vase being somewhere he cannot keep a close watch on it disturbs him. What if someone recognises it? But then, he reasons, who would? The only people who might have recognised it for what it is are either dead or far, far away from London. And there can certainly be no chance of one of Latimer's guests opening it and finding what he has sought so desperately all these long years. Not now Dora . . .

He thinks of her, thinks of what she does not own up to but what she surely, *surely* must know.

'She must have hidden it,' he mutters.

Lottie pauses in her tending.

'Hidden it?'

He did not realise he had spoken out loud. Hezekiah looks at Lottie through gin-fugged eyes.

'What was in the vase. It was there. I know it was.'

'What, Hezekiah?'

He takes a breath. He has not told her everything, only what she has needed to know. Too dangerous. Too . . .

'The damn girl has taken it. She keeps it from me. But why doesn't she *do* anything?'

Hezekiah tries to turn. The water from the basin slops over the side onto Lottie's skirts. He presses a fist to his eye, the glass to the other.

'She must be waiting,' he moans. 'She is working against me, I know it. Has got that *boy* involved. She has told him everything, he must be helping her. She's told him everything!'

How dare she? How *dare* she!

'After all I've done for her over the years. Have I not kept a roof over her head? Have I not pandered to her fanciful little hobby? Have I not secured a place for her, when the time comes to sell?'

235

'What place?'

Hezekiah pauses, bites his tongue. He takes a shaking sip of gin. 'I could have left her there, Lottie. I could have made sure . . .'

'Shush, now.'

He feels Lottie's weight lift from the bed. The glass is taken from his hand, the *tink* of decanter, the *glug* of pouring liquid. The glass is returned, is raised to his mouth.

He drinks. Drinks.

Lottie begins to sing. After a moment she resumes her strokes, runs her hand up and down his leg.

He closes his eyes, listens to her low, gravelly voice.

The gin helps to deaden the pain. All of his pain. Her touch is pleasant, a tickle. He feels a twitch in the seat of his manhood.

> *Kingdoms wide that sit in Darkness,*
> *Let them have the glorious Light,*
> *And from Eastern Coast to Western,*
> *May the Morning chase the Night.*

Lottie stops. He opens his eyes. She is peering down at his thigh.

'It seems to be drying some.'

She runs the cloth once more across the wound, feather light. His breath hitches. A moment of pain. A brief spell of pleasure.

Lottie sighs. She returns the cloth to the basin. It floats on top like a dead fish before disappearing under the water's bitty surface.

'Please,' she whispers, 'let me fetch for a doctor. I wish I could make you feel better, but I can't, I can't!'

Her words carry worry, a hint of desperation, and in that moment Hezekiah has decided.

'You can.' He takes her hand, guides it up, up, tightening his grip when Lottie tries to pull back.

'No. No. I . . .'

'*This* is what you're trained for,' Hezekiah whispers. 'You know how much pleasure you give me.' With his free hand he pulls the sheet from him, shows her. 'It will distract from my pain.'

She is hesitant still. Slowly, he places a finger on the tender cut of her lower lip, presses in.

'Remember, Lottie. I didn't take you on to be idle.'

Hezekiah watches her face waver. Triumphant, he places her hand on the hardening stub of him and groans, grips tight his glass.

# CHAPTER
# TWENTY-NINE

Cornelius cannot abide tardiness. It is something of an obsessive tic with him, and so Edward hopes that Dora will not make them wait. Certainly it is for her sake, he thinks grimly, looking across at Cornelius lounging on his cushioned seat in the carriage, rather than his.

The darker man reclines as if bored, a small pipe nestled between his long, thin fingers. A fine trail of smoke circles upward, disappears into nothing two inches from the vehicle's roof. But Cornelius, Edward knows, is not the victim of ennui. His friend is alert, uncomfortable. Though socially attuned to them Cornelius does not like large social gatherings. He would wonder why Cornelius insisted he come at all if Edward did not already know the answer – he wishes, for want of a better word, to chaperone.

Edward truly hoped his friend would change his mind about Dora once he met her, that he would see what Edward sees – an honest, respectable woman, a fellow dreamer, a girl deserving of far more than she has received – but there has been no changing his mind. Cornelius has already determined to dislike her. Why, Edward cannot fathom.

He regrets telling him that Dora asked Edward to accompany her, regrets mentioning offhand that he purchased for her a gown.

'You did what?' Cornelius demanded, breathing his disapproval deeply from his long nose.

'I gave her the means to buy a gown. There was no time to have one made. After we delivered the pithos I took her to a second-hand shop that would have something suitable. One was adjusted . . . Dora was thrilled with it,' Edward finished defensively.

'The money I give you is meant for *you*, for your pleasure, not anyone else's! Certainly not *hers*!'

'Buying it for her *does* give me pleasure,' Edward countered, watching Cornelius in dismay. 'And what else am I to spend my money on? You provide me with everything I need,' he reminded him, and the reminder had made Edward's gut twist when in that moment he realised he was, without any shred of doubt on the matter, *kept*.

Why did this not occur to him before? Why had he never tallied the fact that the money he earned at the bindery was paid out as a salary from Ashmole coffers, which in turn paid for his lodgings, the food on his table, the clothes on his back? The handouts Cornelius insisted on slipping into a coat pocket, the pages of a book, they were things his friend did not allow him to refuse. The regular delivery of paper, quills, ink, all these things Edward accepted with gratitude and until now, without thought. To Cornelius Edward has always been – and for ever will be – grateful. But since when did gratitude mean the acceptance of a cage?

The thought had left him breathless, cold, and Edward could not then keep the harshness from his voice.

'Charity, Cornelius,' he said, 'I did it for charity.'

'You did it out of guilt. Do not try to pretend otherwise.'

'No,' he snapped back, though Edward was conscious there was indeed some truth in the words. 'I did it for charity. It is what you do for me, every day,' and only then did Cornelius fall silent, a nerve jumping in his jaw.

'I think I shall come to Lady Latimer's soirée,' he eventually replied in a voice over-careful. 'It will be nothing to solicit an invitation from her. Besides, you've never been to an event such as this before. You might need me.'

The turn of tide threw Edward. For a moment they stared at each other across the tiger skin and Edward understood that there was little use in arguing; once Cornelius' mind was made up there was no chance of changing it, no worldly chance at all.

Now the carriage inches down Fleet Street. Outside, Edward can hear the raucous cacophony of London's salt, their merriment spilling from alehouse doors and broken windows, skipping along to the strains of a lively violin and laughter fugged with booze. But beneath it, like the whisper-rustle of leaves on autumn air, he hears another less comforting sound, a sound so easily ignored but with which Edward is all too familiar, can identify in an instant.

He looks out the window, searches for its source. It takes him a moment to locate beyond the crowds but then he spies it: a crying child, his naked feet and empty eyes overlooked by passing strangers, his cries a soulful hymn. The sound awakens in Edward a sense of desolation, of pain, and he feels a lump form in his throat that threatens to choke him. But as the wheels of the carriage jostle and judder across the uneven roads Edward loses sight of the child and he takes a deep breath, lets it out slowly.

He will not think of such things tonight. He will push such darkling thoughts to the back of his mind. Tonight he will think only of Dora, of the prospect of meeting William Hamilton. Think of the future, Edward reminds himself. Think only of what is to come.

Across from him Cornelius breathes on his pipe. Edward leans forward.

'Are you sure he will be there?'

Cornelius blows smoke out the window, watches as if bored a man piss against a lamp post.

'It's the height of London's season, Edward,' he says with

something of his old warmth. 'Old Latimer won't miss a chance of inviting him if she knows he's in town. She likes to be entertained.'

'Entertained?'

Cornelius turns his attention from outside, quirks a sardonic smile.

'Hamilton's wife, Emma. A chorus girl he picked up in Naples, palmed off on him by his nephew. She's younger than Sir William by some years, but it's heard she's now letting Nelson dip his nib. The scandal of it.' He picks a piece of tobacco from his tongue. 'Oh, yes, Latimer will enjoy their presence there immensely.'

The carriage picks up speed. The rumble of wheels beneath him has Edward holding on to the leather straps so tightly they pinch his palms.

Edward is relieved to find Dora waiting for them outside the shop.

On the approach Edward notes how lost she looks, how forlorn, then notices how she hugs her elbows, considers how the cold air must bite the soft flesh of her arms, and it occurs to Edward he should have purchased Dora an evening cape, tells her how sorry he is when he helps her up into the carriage and drapes a woollen blanket over her knees. As she settles into the seat beside him she waves the apology away.

'Oh, please do not worry yourself. You've been more than generous. I am most grateful.'

From the corner of his eye Edward notes the way Cornelius purses his lips, wonders if his friend means to make comment, but after a brief cursory glance at Dora he raps on the roof for them to continue, and they vault off once again into the night.

The carriage sways. Dora bumps into Edward's shoulder and he catches his breath, distracted by the smell of her lily perfume. Dora reaches out a hand to steady herself against the window frame, blushes an apology, clutches tightly at the blanket.

Then she is silent. As Edward searches for something to say he watches the way the lowlights from outside skitter across her features, the soft curve of her cheeks, the elegant line of her long neck. Without meaning to, he draws his gaze downwards. Around her neck she wears an intricate necklace of coiled loops and spiralled florets, and in its centre sits an oval stone the size of an egg. Against the pale walnut of her skin, the colour is almost grey.

'One of your creations?'

Dora glances down, lets out a shy laugh. 'Yes. Mock cannetille. One of my favourite pieces. I . . .' Edward senses her hesitance. 'I suppose it will look rather out of place where we're going, but I thought perhaps if I wore something of mine it might encourage others to ask about it.'

'And why shouldn't they?' Edward says, keen to put her at ease. 'Lady Latimer invited you, I'm sure, precisely so you might have others enquire about your work. I hope you receive many commissions tonight.'

Dora ducks her head. 'Thank you.' She pauses. Then, 'How are you this evening, Mr Ashmole? I appreciate you collecting me. I understand it must have been quite out of your way.'

For a moment Edward is not certain that Cornelius has heard her for his friend keeps his gaze firmly fixed on the view outside. But then he turns his head, chews his cheek a moment before saying, 'Edward was most insistent that we shouldn't permit you to find your own way. I could hardly argue with him since you are Lady Latimer's guest of honour.'

There is a drollness to his voice, an uncharacteristic meanness, and Edward is thankful for the dimness of the carriage that shields his embarrassment.

242

Dora glances at Edward. 'Well, I hope I didn't inconvenience you over much.'

'You didn't,' Edward says, glaring at Cornelius. Cornelius looks away, resumes the chew of his inner cheek. 'It was no inconvenience. No inconvenience at all.'

Dora nods, once.

Edward is ashamed.

The rest of the ride passes in silence, and once the carriage has succeeded in worming its way through the network of Fleet Street and circled its way back via Holborn, the journey is blessedly swift.

When they reach the vicinity of Lady Latimer's villa the roads become smoother, the air smells less of woodsmoke and rotten vegetables, the hubbub of the streets is decidedly more subdued. Still, Lady Latimer's soirée has gathered quite a crowd, and it is evident from the crush of other carriages that an easy entrance will prove unlikely. At length Cornelius suggests they alight. A heavy wind still quips the air, and the awkward party of three make their way toward the house.

Cornelius strides up in front, leaving Edward and Dora to follow in his wake. Edward offers his arm to Dora and she takes it, he thinks, gratefully.

'I must apologise for Cornelius,' he murmurs, keeping his voice low so his friend cannot hear. 'I don't understand why he acts in such a way.'

'Don't you?' Dora responds, fingers pressing into Edward's sleeve. 'I think it very obvious. He has taken a dislike to me.'

There is no use denying it.

'He has. That is true. But it is also true that I don't understand why. Truly I don't. I've never known him to act so discourteously. To a lady no less.'

'Perhaps he does not think I *am* a lady?'

'But of course you are.'

She laughs low in her throat. 'I am a mere shop girl, as he so ably pointed out. You can hardly blame him for thinking so little of me for it.'

Edward opens his mouth to respond to the contrary, to remind her that he himself is a mere 'shop boy', but then the street opens out into the square and together Edward and Dora stop and stare, struck.

When they delivered the pithos the circular green was beautifully tended but without adornment. Tonight, the square is bejewelled with flaming torches, connected with ivy garlands via stone plinths. Atop each, a gloriously coloured parrot perches within a gilt cage. There are twelve in total, and even Cornelius pauses in his saunter.

'The old madam has really outdone herself.'

'It's . . .' Edward tries to find the appropriate word. Ostentatious would certainly do, a needless extravagance to be sure, but then how could he ever purport to understand the whims of high society?

'Quite,' Cornelius throws over his shoulder, as if he has read Edward's thoughts.

A pair of heavily powdered dowagers totter past, holding desperately on to their set white wigs in the wind. Three younger women, giggling as they rush by, cling on to their cloaks. A servant battles with an umbrella, trying unsuccessfully to shield them.

Cornelius has picked up his pace once more and Edward guides Dora past the crush of carriages, must skirt by a white mare that has taken this very moment to evacuate its bowels on the cobbled street, and joins Cornelius in the queue forming to enter the villa. A pair of footmen stand either side of the ornate door, so similar in face they could as well be twins, and Edward concedes that all Lady Latimer's

244

footmen look as though they have come from the same plaster moulds.

'She keeps a very young and pretty staff, doesn't she?' he whispers to Dora.

At this Cornelius looks himself, assesses them with a perfunctory glance before tweaking the lace at his cuff.

They do not have to queue for long. Soon they are through those yawning doors and Edward's breath catches in his throat. He presses Dora's hand. It was a tactical decision on his part that they did not arrive early; he hoped to disappear into the crowd so as to avoid explicit attention but now they are here, surrounded by beautifully coiffed men and frocked ladies, Edward feels a flutter of panic, a claustrophobic crush. Cornelius steps close to Edward, touches his mouth to his ear.

'All right?' At Edward's small, hesitant nod he leans away again, says in a louder voice, 'I shall see the lay of the land. I assume you and Miss Blake will cope together without me?'

He is not looking at Edward now, but Dora. Edward can see that Cornelius does not wish to leave them alone, and this show of hostility has Edward forgetting his discomfort.

'Of course, Cornelius,' he snaps, his patience with him shot. 'I can survive without you for half an hour.'

Cornelius stares. Next to him, Dora turns her face to stare too.

'Very well.' Cornelius adjusts his cravat. 'I shall seek you out later, if you aren't otherwise engaged.'

His tone carries an undercurrent of hurt. Edward bites his lip. 'Cornelius, I . . .'

But he is already gone.

# CHAPTER THIRTY

Dora watches Edward look after his friend, considers the injured expression that had crossed Mr Ashmole's face, and a thought occurs to her. Does Edward really not know? Has he no inkling at all?

'Come,' she says gently, offering up a smile, and her companion seems to shake himself. 'Let's brave the crush together, shall we?'

They let the crowd sweep them along; the heat, the smell of honey candles and other perfumes (a hint of sweat and onions), seem to swallow them from all sides. Near every person is dressed to accommodate Lady Latimer's theme – the 'Mysterious Exotic', as she called it. Dora has never seen anything to equal it: men and women dressed as lions, Egyptian queens, tropical birds, the gorgon Medusa . . . And the interior of Lady Latimer's villa is even more ostentatious than the exterior; as they move with the buzzing crowd and pass the large sweeping staircase Dora looks about her, in awe of the sheer, magnificent scale of it. Lady Latimer has decorated the hallways with more parrots in cages perched on pillars encased in white and gold latticework; garlands of ivy and spiky grasses surround every surface; large paintings hang on each wall depicting exotic landscapes, romantic scenes. Above her a pair of colossal chandeliers glint brightly and Dora thinks of Hermes, how his little eyes would gleam.

She is so busy taking everything in that Dora treads on the

246

slippered foot of an older gentleman in maharaja garb, his glorious magenta turban shot with fine gold thread, and she calls out an apology over the din. A geisha pushes past them. As the kimono-clad woman (or is it a man?) disappears into the crowd Dora spies two pretty boys dressed as swans sitting in a darkened corner, bussing each other's necks.

'Miss Blake!'

Together, Dora and Edward turn. Coming down the grand staircase, in a blinding white toga – a crown of bronze laurel nestled in her wig – comes Lady Latimer. And around her neck . . .

Dora's breath hitches. Her peacock choker, come to life, the gold gleaming bright.

'Madam,' Dora breathes.

She dips a curtsey. Edward follows suit with a bow.

Lady Latimer beams. 'I'm delighted you could come, my dear. And your young man, too, I see. You have done well, Mr, ah . . . ?'

'Lawrence,' Edward provides.

'Well, Miss Blake, you look very well indeed.'

'Oh, I . . .'

Dora looks down at her gown. She and Edward decided that they would not attempt to dress for her ladyship's theme, that it would be more acceptable to wear something better suited to their station. Dora chose a simple dress of cream-patterned muslin, styled it only with a blue ribbon in her hair that matches the blue-grey stone of her necklace. And Edward, Dora thinks, looks very handsome in his simple suit of black sateen.

'Well, my dear, and what do you think? Are you pleased?' Her ladyship rushes on without waiting for an answer. Her cheeks are almost scarlet, with either too much rouge or wine. 'Does your design not look grand about my neck?'

She turns her shoulders in a girlish show. The thickness of the choker serves to conceal some of Lady Latimer's wrinkled décolletage, and while Dora would prefer to see her design on a younger neck she cannot deny it looks well on the old woman.

'It does indeed, my lady. I had not thought to ever see . . .' She trails off. Dora suddenly feels quite overcome. 'He made it so quickly,' she finishes lamely, and Lady Latimer laughs.

'La! Anything, my dear, can be achieved with money. Clements can work *very* quickly if he wants to.'

Edward, who has been shifting from foot to foot at her side, takes a small step forward.

'Your ladyship, forgive me, but am I to understand that William Hamilton is here?'

Dora looks at him in surprise.

'Why yes, yes, he is,' the old woman says. One of the laurel leaves quivers on its gold wire. 'He did not wish to come, I understand – his spirits are quite disturbed lately,' she adds, in a tone turned conspirator, 'but Emma wanted to and he is not a man to disappoint a woman such as *her*!' She laughs. 'You wish to be introduced?'

'I do, ma'am.' A blush rises on Edward's cheeks. 'I am an antiquity man myself.'

'Well, then, he will be thankful for the distraction. Come, I shall acquaint you.'

Lady Latimer takes off down the hall, leaving Dora and Edward to follow behind. She is light on her feet for such an elderly woman and they must struggle to keep up.

'Edward?' Dora asks, a thought turning in her head.

'Yes?'

'This man, Hamilton . . .'

'Forgive me.' Edward glances at her apologetically. 'I did not mean to commandeer the evening with talk of work, but—'

'Do you mean *Lord* Hamilton? Sir William Hamilton?'

'Yes,' he says briskly, 'the very same.'

Dora stops so suddenly Edward is forced to stop too, and he looks at her with concern.

'What is the matter?'

Dora's heart has begun to hammer in her chest. '*He* is your expert? The man you wrote to?'

Ahead, Lady Latimer has reached the ballroom. She turns, beckons them with a flick of her fingers. Reluctant, Dora starts up again. Edward follows.

'I had not imagined,' Dora says as they enter the ballroom, 'that you meant Sir William.'

'Do you mean to say you know him?'

Dora lets the question hang a moment. 'He saved my life.'

'He . . .' Edward stops again. Gapes. 'He what?'

'Emma, my darling!'

Lady Latimer's voice cuts across them. With difficulty Dora turns her attention back to their host.

*What are the odds?*

'My dear Lady Latimer.'

A tall, extremely beautiful woman dressed as a phoenix is greeting the old woman with a deep and perfectly executed curtsey.

'How splendid you look!' Lady Latimer is saying as Dora and Edward join them.

Emma Hamilton tilts her dark bejewelled head in demur.

'And where is your illustrious husband?'

'Admiring your centrepiece,' Lady Hamilton replies with a smile. 'See, madam, how he cannot detach himself from it!'

Dora turns to look, letting out the long breath she had not been aware she was holding.

The pithos – she had almost forgotten its presence here – is decked beautifully with a garland of ivy to which are attached apples and

249

pears and oranges, all intertwined with gold braiding. It stands, imposing, raised up on the large circular plinth, but now it is all cordoned off by a rope of blue and gold. At the base of the plinth are two steps . . . and on those steps a man, leaning on a cane.

He is older – much older than she remembers him – but Dora recalls all too well the aristocratic face, that inquisitive tilt of the chin, the kind eyes presently fixed on the third scene of the pithos, that of Hephaestus' transformation of clay into the first woman: Pandora.

'Why am I not surprised?' Lady Latimer exclaims, and she takes Dora's arm. 'Come, my dear, let me show you your vase, the crowning glory of tonight's celebrations!'

Dora's heart pounds. She wishes to run, she is not ready for this, but there is nothing she can do; Lady Latimer has hold of her and the feeling of inevitability crushes over her like a wave.

'Lord Hamilton! I have a gentleman here who wishes to make your acquaintance. Mr Lawrence, if you please.'

Sir William looks up; his face is creased in a deep frown but it clears on their approach. He steps down from the plinth, holds out his hand for Edward to shake.

'Mr Lawrence, how do you do.'

'Sir,' Edward is saying, almost breathless. 'It's a pleasure to finally meet you.'

'Finally?' The diplomat's eyebrows meet briefly in the middle.

'I have heard much of you. I am a scholar of antiquities, you see.'

'Are you, indeed! What is your speciality?'

Edward stands up taller. 'I don't have one, as such, sir, but I had hoped—'

Lady Latimer impatiently waves her hand. 'Oh, that's quite enough of that. You men can discuss old bones and broken crockery to your hearts' content once I'm out of earshot.' She brings Dora forward on her arm. 'Sir William, let me introduce you to my guest of honour, Miss Dora Blake, the procurer of my masterpiece which I see you admiring. Isn't it a wonder?'

The instant the old woman speaks Dora's name, Sir William's attention snaps from Edward to her. For a long painful moment he stares. Then, very gently, he takes her hand in both of his.

'Dora.' He kisses her hand, lingers over it. 'You are the very picture of your mother.'

'Sir William,' she says. Her mouth feels dry. 'I had not thought to see you again.'

'No, indeed. It has been . . . some years.'

'What is this?' Lady Latimer looks between them, enthralled. 'You mean to say you know each other?'

Sir William clears his throat. 'Miss Blake is the daughter of Elijah and Helen Blake, your ladyship. The Blakes were esteemed colleagues of mine, many years ago. Fellow antiquarians,' he explains at Lady Latimer's wide-eyed surprise.

The old woman claps her hands on a laugh. 'What a happy coincidence! There, my dear,' she says, patting Dora's arm. 'You will be entertained after all. I had worried you would be struck down with boredom. Now if you will forgive me, I ought to mingle.'

In a swirl of lavender scent Lady Latimer disappears into the crowd, and the three – Sir William, Edward and Dora – look at each other, the air between them heavy. Beside them the pithos seems to glow eerily in the golden light of the ballroom. It is Sir William who breaks the silence.

'Lady Latimer said it was you, Dora, who procured this,' he says, gesturing to the pithos. 'May I ask how?'

Dora hesitates. She and Edward share a look. There is something in Sir William's tone, a quiet sort of guardedness that puts Dora on guard herself.

'I confess that—'

'Please, sir,' Edward cuts in, sending Dora an apologetic glance. 'It is fortuitous that you are here this evening. I had sent a note to your lodgings in the hope of speaking to you about this very thing.'

Sir William is looking at Edward now with interest.

'I'm afraid I have received many notes since my return to town. With so many business matters to hand I've barely made a dent in them.'

'I understand. But . . .'

Dora watches them. In one moment she has been confronted with her past in the most unexpected way, wishes both to retreat from it and face it in equal measure and the next . . . Again, she cannot shake the feeling that there is something Edward is not telling her. The way he was so keen to speak immediately of the pithos. Not even pleasantries first . . .

She glances at it now, adorned in all its austere glory. It appears exactly as she pictured it would – a lavishly decorated ornament fit for a gathering such as this – but why is it, Dora thinks, that the pithos looks so out of place? It seemed so much more suited, somehow, to the dark of the shop's basement. Unexpectedly her fingertips begin to tingle. Dora frowns, is reminded of that first night, how she imagined that low hum in the basement, that pulse of expectation.

'Miss Blake, is it?' a voice cuts in, and Dora turns gratefully to find a young woman – this one dressed, she thinks, based on the floral garland crowning her long flowing hair, as Ophelia – at her elbow.

'Yes?'

'Oh, good!' She smiles widely, reveals a set of small pearl-like teeth. 'Lady Latimer said I should speak to you. About your jewellery designs?'

'Oh!' Dora raises a hand to her throat. 'Why yes, please, I—'

'I've been looking all over London for something unusual and have been disappointed at every turn.' The woman looks to where Dora has

252

rested her hand. 'Is that one of your own too? So lovely! I wish to commission you. The necklace you created for her ladyship, it is like nothing I have seen before.' She looks to Edward and Sir William. 'May I steal her?'

Dora turns to her companions – disinclined now to leave them when her instincts tell her something is amiss – but she is already being pulled along on Ophelia's arm and soon she is lost in a crowd of whirling skirts and fluttering fans.

Not in her most fanciful dreams did Dora expect to be the recipient of such a deluge of praise.

They came from all sides – from the young girls who had chosen Lady Latimer's soirée as their 'coming out' event, to countesses, to Lady Hamilton herself. Even a duke praised her work, enquired if her talents stretched as far as men's fripperies, and all Dora could do was smile and nod and smile and laugh and smile and . . .

She presses now her fingers to her temples, tries to find her way back to the entrance hall from the powder room to where she made an escape. It is all too much; not just the unexpected attention, the shock at seeing Sir William again, but the heat of bodies, the gaudy decorations, the blinding glow of candles, the chatter of the inebriated, the noise of the orchestra, the squawk of parrots in their gilt cages – Lady Latimer has even acquired a pair of capuchin monkeys to sit on a red cushion either side of the refreshment table, one of which let its tail dangle in the punchbowl.

Oh, but what all this could mean! Dora tries to keep her wits. Nothing may come of it, she scolds herself. But if it *did*! All she has ever wanted, finally in her grasp—

Dora stops.

Which way? Should she turn left? Or was it right? She cannot remember. She should not have accepted that glass of wine from Ophelia. Straight on? Just as she begins to panic there is the sound of boisterous laughter and in relief Dora follows it to the end of the hall, turns a corner, only to barrel right into a footman coming the other way who is fumbling at the buttons of his britches.

'Oh! I'm so sorry, I . . .'

The apology dies on her tongue, for on the heels of the footman appears Cornelius Ashmole, long fingers at his cravat. In surprise Dora takes a step back. He in turn does the same. The footman – two pink spots high on his otherwise pale, powdered cheeks – rushes past them both without a word.

For a long moment Dora and Mr Ashmole simply stare at each other. Then Mr Ashmole clears his throat.

'Miss Blake.'

'Mr Ashmole.' She stops. 'I needed some air.'

'Quite.' He lazily finishes tying the cravat. Like herself and Edward, he chose not to wear a costume. 'Are you recovered?'

'Yes, thank you. I'm—'

He cuts her off by taking her hand in his, begins to stride in the opposite direction. 'Then let's dance, Miss Blake.'

Dora cannot argue; he is sweeping her along as if she were a mere ribbon trailing behind him and all at once they are within the bright lights of the ballroom, coming up on the opening bars of an allemande.

'Sir,' she hisses, 'I do not know how.'

'Just imitate what the others do,' Mr Ashmole says tightly.

Before she can say anything else the dance has started, and Dora finds herself trying to replicate – rather poorly – the steps of her unwanted partner. She is relieved, at least, that her skirts hide her feet.

Mr Ashmole guides her around in a slow circle, clasps her arm to his.

'And how are you enjoying your first soirée, Miss Blake?'

That hint of condescension again. Dora sets her teeth.

'It is like nothing I have ever experienced, I admit.'

'I have no doubt. Go right, now.'

Mr Ashmole indicates her to follow another woman before circling back to her original position, and for a full minute they say not one word to each other. Dora watches the lady next to her – dressed in pale flamingo pink and a feathered mask to match – orchestrate an intricate series of steps that Dora cannot even hope to copy. When Mr Ashmole takes her hand again to spin her, she draws a deep breath.

'You are very protective of him.'

She does not need to name 'him'. Mr Ashmole knows all too well who she means.

'I have every right to be,' he replies, curt.

'Do you?'

He clenches his jaw. 'My business is none of yours.'

Dora tries to command patience. 'Mr Ashmole, I understand you do not like me, but you must understand that I mean no harm.'

He scoffs on a turn.

'Truly, I don't.'

Mr Ashmole glances over his shoulder. Dora tries to follow his gaze. Uneasily she notes that neither Edward nor Sir William are anywhere to be seen.

'What has Edward told you?' he asks, sharp.

Her face snaps back to his. So, they are to be frank with each other. It is, Dora thinks, a relief, and she looks at him with the most direct stare she can muster.

'He told me that you grew up together. That he was the groom's son, you the heir of an estate.'

255

'What else?'

'That when his father died your own father sent him to London to learn a trade.'

'And that's it?'

'Is there more?'

She knows there is – is instinctively positive there is – but it interests her to see what Mr Ashmole will follow with. The tempo of the music picks up then, and for a few minutes Dora is too consumed with imitating the steps of her dancing partner to continue the conversation. When the music slows and they join together once more, Mr Ashmole replies.

'My father paid for everything – the apprenticeship, Edward's board, all of it. And for years we did not see each other. I'm older than him, did he tell you that?' Dora shakes her head. 'I was sent to Oxford, went on the Grand Tour afterwards, as many boys of my station are wont.'

'And then?'

'And then I came home. Sought him out.'

'The bindery—'

'What of it?'

'Well, that's unusual, isn't it? A man of inherited fortune owning an establishment? It is not typical for idle men such as yourself to involve themselves in trade.'

'I bought it,' Mr Ashmole says darkly, 'with good reason.'

'What reason?'

Mr Ashmole raises his dark eyebrows, ignores her. 'Do you think all men of fortune are idle, Miss Blake?' he asks, taking her hand to lift her arm in time to a high note.

Dora thinks of the clients Blake's Emporium used to entertain. Of their present company. With a tilt of her head she gestures to the room.

'How many men of fortune *here* can say they keep a shop?'

The dance seems to be coming to an end; the tempo begins to ease along violin strings, and on a knee-bend Mr Ashmole sneers

'I do not "keep" a shop, Miss Blake. That's what Fingle is for.'

Dora narrows her eyes. 'Do not patronise me, sir. You know what I meant.'

'Why should it matter that I own the bindery?' he returns with a lift of his chin. 'How is my owning a shop any different to men of new money who have made their pockets fat from trade? To plantation owners, even?'

'So you liken yourself to a slaver?'

A flash of anger crosses Mr Ashmole's face then, and when Dora begins to pull away he pinches her fingers meanly.

'Damn you, no. The very idea of slavery on any level is abhorrent to me.'

Mr Ashmole places his other hand on Dora's back, guides her stiffly into a final turn, and at her dancing partner's derogatory tone Dora's patience finally snaps.

'Why do you find it necessary to challenge me at every quarter? What is it you suspect me of?'

The music stops. The dancers begin to clap. Neither Dora nor Mr Ashmole join in, and her companion releases an unamused breath.

'Very well. Edward believes you have no part in whatever your uncle is involved in. He might be right. But I do not – have not, for a very long time – go on blind faith. Until proven otherwise, Miss Blake, I shall continue to treat you as I have done. It's nothing personal,' he adds, and Dora utters a short, disbelieving laugh.

'But it is. You've made that more than clear and I heartily resent the implication. Whatever my uncle is embroiled in, I want no part of it.'

'Do you not sell forgeries openly on the shop floor?'

Dora bites her lip. 'That's different.'

'Is it?'

The dancers begin to disperse. Without ceremony Mr Ashmole walks her out of the ballroom, deposits her in a shadowed vestibule near a gold-embossed pot, the edge of a punch glass poking out from the fronds of a fern. He stares at Dora a moment before speaking again, dark eyes calculating.

'Do you honestly expect me to believe that you had no idea your uncle was involved in illegal trading? I've read Edward's notes. It simply isn't possible that your uncle was capable of hiding it from you for all these years, while you lived under the same roof.'

Dora's stomach twists at the words. She hears the truth in them, understands his suspicions. When he puts it that way it does indeed look very bad. And yet . . .

'It is the truth,' she whispers.

Her companion scoffs. 'You will forgive me if I struggle to believe you.'

'Mr Ashmole,' she says tightly, her shame ripe. 'Edward has been extremely kind to me. I . . .'

Dora trails off. Frowns.

'What notes?'

There is a split second of agonised silence. Then, as if someone has flipped a lever inside him, something shifts in Mr Ashmole's face. The hand that has kept such a stern hold of her arm since he guided her into the vestibule drops so suddenly it is as if she has burnt him. Mr Ashmole curses, begins to turn away, but Dora stands firm in his path, a fire setting flame in the pit of her chest.

# CHAPTER
# THIRTY-ONE

Sir William suggests they speak on the balcony where the crowds are thinner and where, the diplomat quips, he might actually hear himself think. Following him out, Edward thinks again of what Dora revealed.

*He saved my life.*

The wind is not as strong here. The back of the villa faces a bank of water, shielding them from the worst of it, and Edward is thankful for the cool air as it is over-hot in that ballroom and his claustrophobia (though he has tried his best to hide it from Dora) was beginning to rear itself. He feels completely out of place and utterly ridiculous. His slippers pinch his toes. There is far too much pomp. Lady Latimer's decorations – though undeniably impressive – are altogether too grandiose for his tastes. Edward prefers simplicity. Peace and quiet. It amazes him how much money rich people seem happy to waste on entertainment for one mere evening.

They skirt past two couples who have also taken the air and a group of older gentlemen dressed in togas. For one brief moment Edward sees a familiar face among them – long white beard, a pair of piercing blue eyes – and he stumbles, tries to get a better look.

'Mr Lawrence?'

Hamilton has stopped, is looking at him with an expression bordering on impatience.

'I . . .' Edward strains to see, but the man has gone. 'Forgive me, I thought . . .' He shakes his head. 'Never mind.'

'Come then,' his companion says, and Edward lets Sir William lead him to a more secluded area on the far right of the pavilion.

'So, Mr Lawrence,' Hamilton says when they are out of earshot, leaning his weight on his cane. He grips its handle, what looks to be a Grecian face carved in ivory. 'You have my undivided attention.'

The diplomat's stare is uncomfortably direct. Edward recognises that he will not stand for time-wasting pleasantries, and so he comes straight to the point.

'In my letter – which I wrote on the advice of Richard Gough – I said that I had come across a pithos. That pithos,' he adds, chucking his chin in the direction of the ballroom. 'I also said that its owner has many articles of Greek pottery which have possibly been acquired by underhand means.'

'I see.'

'I wrote requesting your advice.'

Sir William is very still. 'Am I to understand that the owner of these artefacts is Dora Blake, as Lady Latimer indicated?'

'The owner is her uncle.'

Hamilton's expression darkens. 'Do you know where *he* acquired them?'

'We do not. Though that is something I am trying to discover.' Edward thinks of the man Coombe, determines to visit his lodgings the first moment he can. 'Dora found the pithos in the shop's basement.'

'And how did it find its way here?'

'She has been using it for her jewellery designs. Lady Latimer took a liking to one of them, demanded to know where the inspiration came from.'

Sir William nods. 'Yes, her ladyship has always been a stickler for getting her own way. How did Dora's uncle take it?'

'You must ask Dora.'

Hamilton pauses. Twists the cane on its foot.

'What advice were you hoping I could give, Mr Lawrence?'

Here then, the crux of it.

'Dora gave me permission to use the pithos as a study, as a means to gain entrance into the Society of Antiquaries. She has been sketching the pithos. I meant to write its history but the problem is – understanding now that it is of questionable origin – the Society cannot possibly publish it. I hoped, as an expert on Greek antiquities, that you would take a look at it, that you might give me an understanding of the black-market and its operations.'

'Why?'

Edward hesitates. 'For a different study.'

'And does Dora know you wrote to me?'

Edward hesitates again, shuffles his feet, winces at the painful pinch of his slippers.

'She knows I asked advice about the pithos. As for the other matter . . .'

'Hmm.'

Hamilton does not deliver the admonishment Edward feels sure to be on the tip of his tongue. The admonishment he deserves.

'What do you intend to do with that knowledge?'

Heat floods Edward's cheeks. The guilt again, churning in the seat of his belly.

'I intend to publish my findings.'

'Do you plan to name her?'

'I plan to name no one.'

Sir William frowns. 'You realise there is a great danger here? The authorities will have to be taken into account. Whether or not you name Dora or her uncle . . . you understand what I mean to say?'

Edward does. He squeezes his eyes shut, snaps them open again;

black spots dance across his vision like ants. He takes a deep, calming breath.

'I care very much about Dora's welfare. Believe me, sir, I understand the dangers. But I will not allow anything to happen to her.'

He will not. He will make sure of it.

For a long moment Hamilton watches him. Then he turns, walks to the edge of the balcony – his cane a sharp *click* on the flagstones – leans on the stone balustrade and looks out into the night. Edward follows, goes to stand beside him.

Below them the water lulls quietly. Somewhere, an owl shrieks. Raucous laughter spills from the ballroom behind them on the musical strains of a cotillion.

'I have no doubt Hezekiah Blake acquired both his collection and the pithos illegally,' Sir William says finally, and Edward looks at him in surprise for he has not mentioned Hezekiah's name. 'I always knew him to be a deceitful man. As I said to Lady Latimer, I knew the Blakes many years ago. We met in Naples. Helen – Dora's mother – was an accomplished artist, and I often commissioned her to sketch for me. Hezekiah sometimes travelled with them, back then. He was good with maps.'

Hamilton seems lost deep in thought, and Edward watches the plane of his face. In the moonlight his aquiline nose, his high cheekbones – they are all even more pronounced. The scarlet ribbon on his wig flutters in the wind. Like Edward, he decided against wearing a costume.

'How is it, sir, you came to save Dora's life?'

His companion turns to face him once more. 'Tell me,' he says, ignoring the question in favour of one of his own. 'What do you know about the pithos?'

'I know – from the investigations of the Society's scientists – that it predates history. That is why, in part, I wrote to you.' Edward pauses for effect, but Sir William seems strangely unfazed by this. Edward clears his throat. 'Gough is charging them now to ascertain its geographical origin.'

Hamilton scoffs. 'I can save them the trouble.'

'Sir?'

'That pithos was dug up in the foothills of Mount Lykaion. Six months ago.'

Edward stares. 'How do you know?'

'Because, Mr Lawrence, I was the one who organised the excavation.'

'There you are,' Lady Hamilton calls from across the balcony, her tone playfully mutinous when she discovers Edward and her husband deep in conversation. Edward straightens his features, tries for a look of nonchalance he does not feel.

No indeed, Edward feels, suddenly, overwhelming tiredness. What the diplomat has told him, it is beyond any stretch of his imagination. He shares a look with Sir William, whose eyes press upon him a warning that cannot be misinterpreted.

*Not a word*, they say. *Not yet.*

'Really, William, is it necessary for you to discuss business the entire evening?' Lady Hamilton remarks when she joins them, dazzling in bronze. 'You have forced your new friend to neglect Miss Blake completely.'

'Where is she?' Edward asks and the older woman smiles at his concern, taps his shoulder playfully with her fan.

'La, just behind me with Mr Ashmole.' She turns, smiles. 'See? Here she is, safe and sound.'

And yes, there Dora is, coming through the wide ballroom doors, Cornelius at her side. Edward begins to smile at her but then he sees Dora's expression – closed, tight, frighteningly cold – and he falters.

*Something is wrong.*

'I have found them, Miss Blake,' Lady Hamilton quips on a laugh. 'Typical men! We women are quite overlooked when business is at hand. And now the evening is drawing on and Miss Blake is tired and wishes to go home. Honestly, Mr Lawrence,' she says, flicking her fan again. A stray gold feather slips from the seam. 'How could you have deserted your charge?'

'Dora,' Edward says, over-careful now, trying to look into her eyes. 'I am so sorry. I had not meant to commandeer so much of Lord Hamilton's time. Do you really wish to leave?'

'I do. I find my enjoyment of the evening has been somewhat dampened.'

Her tone is like ice. There is a sinking in the pit of Edward's stomach. He glances at Cornelius. His friend meets his gaze, a warning in his eyes that Edward cannot interpret.

'Are you sure?' Edward tries again, and Dora turns her face.

She will not look at him, he realises in dismay.

'I have already made my excuses to Lady Latimer.'

'I think I might retire as well, my dear,' Sir William adds. 'You know how much events like this exhaust me.'

Lady Hamilton clucks her tongue. 'By all means, William, if you prefer.'

Hamilton turns to Dora. 'What will happen to the pithos once the soirée is over?'

Edward watches her, heart hammering. He wants to speak with her. He needs to know what has happened. Why she smiles at Sir William and not at him . . .

'It is to be delivered back to the shop tomorrow. After that, I do not know what my uncle has planned for it.'

Only now does Dora look at him, but the second her gaze meets his it slides away again. It is enough. He sees the accusation in her eyes, the anger kept so assiduously at bay. Edward looks to Cornelius in alarm, but his friend is now staring studiously at the floor.

'I see,' Hamilton says. 'Dora, I should like to invite you and Mr Lawrence – and Mr Ashmole too, of course – to dine with us tomorrow evening. You have no objection, do you, Emma?'

'Not at all! I will welcome the chance to speak with Miss Blake in more intimate surroundings. I have the most superb creation in mind. My dear Hora—' She cuts off, blushing prettily, says to Dora instead, 'Yes, please do come. It would be our honour.'

There is a hesitation. A small nod in assent.

Sir William stamps his cane, offering up a smile. It is the first time Edward has seen him smile all evening, though it appears forced.

'It is settled then,' he says.

Lady Hamilton flicks her fan.

'Well, as you're retiring for the night, I will return to my dancing. I have such a love of dancing, you know, and I intend to have my fill of it before the evening is done. You'll be quite all right now, Miss Blake, won't you?'

Dora takes a telling breath. 'Yes, my lady. Thank you.'

'Then I wish each of you goodnight.'

And off Lady Hamilton goes, a beautiful phoenix in a swirl of fire-shot skirts.

# CHAPTER
# THIRTY-TWO

Mr Ashmole hails a carriage that sits directly outside the villa's yawning doors. Dora has been striding ahead of them, fully determined to journey back to Ludgate Street by herself, but Edward has caught up with her, reaching for her hand, and before Dora can shrug him off the carriage is upon them and she has been bundled inside.

She knows Edward and his friend were whispering fiercely to each other as they followed after her, knows that Edward understands he has been found out, and the wheels of the carriage have barely run a full circle before Dora turns on him. Her anger – so fiercely ripe – frightens her, but she cannot contain it, it is impossible to do so.

'How dare you,' she hisses as the carriage trundles away through the iron gates. 'I trusted you! I invited you into my home, offered my help, and this is how you repay me?'

'Please,' Edward tries, wringing his hands together on his lap. 'You must understand, that's not—'

'You're writing about me!'

'Now, that's not precisely what I said,' Mr Ashmole interjects, but Dora ignores him, feels her voice rising to hysteria pitch.

'You are writing about the shop, about my uncle.'

'Not in so many words. I swear, I—'

'You have told your superior at the Society about us!'

'No, Dora, I have not! I've mentioned no names, I promise you that.'

Dora can hear the plaintive in him but she does not trust it. Edward sits further forward in his seat, tries in vain to reach for her hands but she pulls them away, crushes them into the folds of her arms.

'Please,' he begs, 'you must understand. Let me explain. Dora, I couldn't possibly use the pithos as a credible study knowing that it had been sourced illegally. My reputation, the Society's reputation, it would have been compromised! But there has never been a study published about the black-market before. If you would only—'

'No, damn you,' Dora chokes out. 'I won't hear this. I can't hear it! You have broken my trust completely. What about *my* reputation? What of that? I could *hang* for this, don't you see?'

It is as if she has slapped him. Edward sits back heavily in his seat. In the darkness she cannot see his face, nor that of Mr Ashmole, and Dora is glad of it for seeing them may very well undo her completely. All that exists between them is the sound of their breathing, the thundering whistle of the wind.

'Dora . . .'

The sigh in Edward's voice is too much. Decided, she thumps her fist on the carriage roof. She cannot stay another minute with them. Not one. The carriage judders from side to side a moment before slowing, its brakes creaking over the cobbled road.

'Dora,' Edward pleads now, 'don't, you'll—'

'I'll be fine, Mr Lawrence,' she says coldly. 'I dare say I can manage well enough without you. Better, I should think.'

The carriage comes to a stop.

'Dora, I—'

'Oh, Edward, leave her,' Mr Ashmole interjects again. 'It's interesting, don't you think, that Miss Blake should make such a fuss? Perhaps she has something to hide after all.'

'For pity's sake, Cornelius,' Edward snaps, 'not now. Dora, please!'

But Dora has already stepped down from the carriage, the wind a sharp bite on her cheek. With a pointed look at them both that could freeze water, she slams the door hard behind her and turns fast away into the night.

*Dear Dora,*

*There are a great many things I wish to say to you, but I feel it best that I explain myself in person. Please know, however, that you are entirely mistaken in your beliefs. Cornelius has enlightened me as to the precise conversation which passed between you last night. I can only apologise for his behaviour and, of course, for mine. I should have told you what I was writing, and why. I have been a complete and selfish fool. I sincerely wish to set things right between us, and that upon hearing my explanation I might in turn beg your forgiveness. You must understand how much your friendship has meant to me. I sincerely hope it may continue.*

*We are due to arrive at Lord Hamilton's this evening for six o'clock. Cornelius has kindly agreed to send a carriage for you at a half past the hour of five, and I implore you to take it and join us there. The party will not be the same without you. I am sure Sir William only invited us for your sake, after all.*

*Yours,*

*Edward*

Dora sits on the edge of the stool behind the counter, her head buried deep in her hands. Above her on his perch Hermes sleeps, his own head tucked beneath his wing.

It is a quarter to ten, and she has already cleaned and aired the shop by opening the door – has purchased sprigs of lavender from the hawker who stuck her head inside – in a bid to disguise the smell of fermented booze and the subtle stench of Hezekiah's sodden bandages that have begun to filter their way through from the main house. Out here on the shop floor it is not so bad, but every now and then Dora catches an unsavoury whiff.

Behind her she hears the distant sounds of Lottie clattering in the kitchen. The slice of bread and cheese she pilfered from the larder earlier this morning are not near enough to stem her hunger. Ignoring the grumble in her belly she thinks instead of Edward, and feels a rush of rage.

How could he? To do such a thing behind her back, to risk all she has and is for the sake of his own career, is unpardonable. She did not think this possible of him. After all they have shared together . . . And yet, what does she know of Edward, really? Dora thinks back on those times she felt he held himself at a remove from her, the things he left unsaid, the shared looks between him and Mr Ashmole the day she visited them at Clevendale. Dora lifts her head from her hands. Oh, how can she have been so hideously misled?

She runs a finger over Edward's letter on the counter in front of her, and her thoughts turn to Sir William. They barely exchanged words at all. No, indeed, Edward commandeered his attention completely. What was it he spoke to Sir William about? A part of Dora is tempted not to attend the dinner at all, but she knows her absence will achieve nothing, would only serve to torture her. No, she must go. And she must, Dora decides, speak with Sir William alone.

The bell sounds behind her. She need not turn to see who it is – she can smell him already, like a cadaver in a ditch.

'You returned late.'

Hezekiah croaks the comment and Dora has no sympathy. If he insists on drinking himself into a coma then it is nothing to her.

269

'I did,' she says, not looking at him.

There is a long pause.

'You cleaned.'

'Someone had to.'

He grunts, comes full into the shop, leg dragging. Dora folds Edward's letter, slips it into the pocket of her skirts.

'And when will her ladyship –' Hezekiah says this with a sneer – 'be returning my vase?'

Dora sniffs. 'It is due this afternoon. I doubt anyone will be awake at this hour. You know what time these things run on 'til.'

'But I don't, do I?' he snaps. He is at the counter now, a beefy hand gripping the edge. '*I* was not invited!'

He slaps his other hand down onto the counter and Dora sighs, looks up at him finally. His eyes are bloodshot. A network of tiny veins pattern his nose like red thread. The gin has hit him hard.

'You would not be three hundred pounds richer if it were not for me. Uncle.' Dora adds the last word to annoy him, though he needs no incitement. Hezekiah's nostrils flair. 'An agreeable development, considering you already have a buyer lined up to take it off your hands?' Dora watches his face close up and she knows, then, he has lied about this, too. 'Isn't that what you told Lady Latimer? You should be thanking me.'

For years Dora has trodden carefully around Hezekiah; it is not that she feared him, but from the moment he took her into his care he did not treat her as a niece, showed no grief for his brother's death, and as soon as she came of an age to be useful he utilised her. That was simply the way of things; Dora grew to accept that overnight her life had changed from one of affection and warmth to isolation and coldness, and she learnt to have as little to do with her uncle as possible. But since the arrival of the pithos . . . It is as if she has woken from a stupor, as if until now there has been a veil that has shielded

270

her from feeling more than she should. It is as if she can, finally, see. Never has she missed her parents more than she misses them now.

Across the counter Hezekiah is glowering at her. His scar shines livid white on the red plane of his face. Dora can tell from the way his fingers shake that he itches to press them into the soft hollow of her neck. The thought almost pleases her.

The shop bell jangles on its coil, the moment between them broken. Dora looks up to see a tall woman enter the shop. Her pinstripe-patterned dress hints at money, her over-large bonnet at vanity. Hezekiah recognises this and approaches her with his usual salesman's preen.

'How may I help you, miss?'

'I am looking for—'

'Ah, let me guess!' Hezekiah holds up a finger, waggles it, his attempt at tradesman's flirtation. 'A piece of Renaissance furniture? Or perhaps a Rococo chair for . . .' But he trails off as the woman wrinkles her nose – she must smell him, Dora thinks – and tosses her head.

'No.' Her tone is conceit personified. 'I have no interest in anything like that. I am here to see Miss Blake.'

Hezekiah draws up short. 'Miss Blake,' he echoes.

'Yes, indeed, I—Oh, there you are!' The woman brightens as she spies Dora behind the counter. She sweeps past Hezekiah; he looks after her in dismay. 'You did say to come to this address, did you not?'

'Miss,' Hezekiah tries, simpering. 'My niece knows precious little of antiquities. You would do best to speak with me.'

'Antiquities? Good heaven, I have no use for *those*. I am here to discuss a jewellery commission. That is still possible, isn't it, Miss Blake?'

Dora releases the breath she has been holding.

Someone has come! They said they would but she had not been

sure, did not dare to hope. Dora takes up her sketchbook, slips from behind the counter.

'Yes, of course, Miss . . . Ponsenby, isn't it? Do come in and take a seat.'

'Wonderful!' The lady sweeps past Hezekiah again, ensconces herself in the green velvet armchair.

'Jewellery?'

Hezekiah almost spits the word, and as Dora goes to join her client (the word thrills her), she notes with satisfaction that his face is now puce.

'Yes, Uncle,' Dora replies, seating herself very deliberately in the chair opposite. 'Lady Latimer was very kind last night. I had such a lot of interest in my designs.'

It is unlike Dora to be spiteful but she simply cannot help herself. It serves him right, she thinks, for underestimating her.

'Did you,' Hezekiah says, tone cold.

It is not a question. His eyes are narrowed. His jaw tics.

'Oh, yes,' Miss Ponsenby enthuses, looking up haughtily at Hezekiah. 'Miss Blake produced such a beautiful piece for Lady Latimer – she was positively raving about it! I have no doubt I will not be the only one of Lady Latimer's guests to visit Miss Blake today.'

There is a moment of silence. Hezekiah clenches his fists. Then he is striding – as best he can with his injured leg – toward the door. He flings it open, sending the bell rattling loudly on its spring. It slams shut behind him and the bell swings and swings in a tinny dance. Hermes – woken by the noise – ruffles his feathers in protest. It is not until silence descends once more that Miss Ponsenby speaks.

'What a disagreeable man,' she says, then, catching herself, she reaches out to touch Dora's arm. 'But he is your uncle! Forgive me, I—'

'There is nothing to forgive, Miss Ponsenby. You are quite right in your assessment.' Dora opens the sketchbook to a blank page, poises her pencil. 'Now, then,' she smiles. 'What was it you were looking for?'

And as Miss Ponsenby enthusiastically describes a tiara, Dora begins to sketch.

Six more ladies and two gentlemen pass through the doors of Blake's Emporium to ask for a jewellery commission, and Dora's pencil cannot move fast enough across the pages to accommodate them. At one point she is interrupted by an old man with a long white beard who hovers a little too long near the forged Ming dynasty porcelain, but after asking some cursory questions as to the origin of a bowl which has a series of bulls painted in blue around its rim, he made himself scarce without purchasing it. Hezekiah would be near apoplectic if he had seen.

As for Hezekiah, he has not come back from wherever he stormed off to, not even to oversee the return of the pithos, delivered by Mr Tibb and three other of his faecal-fragrant helpers (no Mr Coombe this time, Dora notices) at three o'clock. At four, Dora draws the bolts of the shop door.

Her head is spinning with the commissions she has received. Never before has she been so busy in the shop, and on account of her own doing, too! If she could have stayed open she would have, but since Mr Ashmole's carriage is to arrive soon she must prepare. With Hermes on her shoulder Dora has just placed her foot on the bottom step of the stairs when she hears a loud shattering noise come from the kitchen. Almost immediately the noise comes again, and Dora stares at the panelled door. Porcelain. Unmistakable. Brow creasing, she rushes down the hall, pushes open the kitchen door.

It is a small space, but it does well enough for Lottie since it is only she who works in it. Dora wondered at first if the housekeeper were killing something in here – a chicken, perhaps – and there is indeed evidence of feathers, the smell of poultry in the air, but Dora is unprepared to see Lottie sitting in the middle of the floor, surrounded by broken crockery, sobbing into her hands.

'Lottie!'

Dora rushes to her side, but the housekeeper waves her off.

'Are you hurt? You—' The words catch in Dora's throat.

Lottie's face is a purple bruise, one eye partially closed.

Dora places Hermes on the floor, and he begins to peck at the blue and white shards.

'What happened?' she asks gently.

The housekeeper stares hard at her lap, takes a shuddering gulp.

'I don't suppose you'll believe me if I said I fell again.'

'You know I wouldn't,' Dora says quietly. Lottie shakes her head; a fat tear falls onto her apron.

'He was . . .' She trails off, voice trembling. She sniffs, tries again. 'He was so angry you had gone out, that you'd taken it. I tried to comfort him. That's always worked before, but this time . . .' Lottie rubs her fingers across her cheek, her irritation at being found vulnerable evidently clear.

I have done this, Dora thinks guiltily. No, she may not have made the physical blow, but if she had not attended the soirée . . .

Hermes pecks lightly now at Lottie's skirts. Dora makes to shoo him away but to her surprise Lottie stills Dora's hand.

'No,' she hiccups. 'Leave him.'

Dora blinks. Lottie keeps her hand on hers. This is the first time, it occurs to Dora, that she has ever touched her. She offers Lottie a handkerchief from her pocket. The housekeeper hesitates, takes it, then blows her nose loudly into the cotton.

'I couldn't see what I was doing,' Lottie says after a moment. 'Bumped into the table. Dropped the plates.' The housekeeper touches the handkerchief to her lip; it comes away blood-spotted. 'He never used to be like this, you know. He was my favourite customer, way back then. Long before your time.'

Dora watches her, sees the trouble it takes for Lottie to say the words.

'Why did you leave it all?'

For a long time the housekeeper does not answer. They listen to the spit of the fire, the magpie's talons against flagstone. Eventually Lottie shrugs, folds the handkerchief into a tiny square.

'He offered me a home, safety. Money of my own. Women like me . . . It's no life, missum. I'd wish it on no one. I didn't have much of a choice.'

Dora bites her lip. There are other questions she wishes to ask, but now that her tears have stopped Dora senses that Lottie is likely to keep her cards close – to push for more will not entice her to reveal them.

'I'm sorry, Lottie,' Dora says instead.

The housekeeper squints at her. 'What for?'

'This is my fault.'

'Don't talk nonsense. He's responsible for his own fists.'

'Yes, but—'

'Help me up.'

That old stoic. Lottie shifts her position; the broken plates tinker and scrape. Dora offers a hand; Lottie's fingers pinch as she holds on and Dora must put her arm around Lottie to steady her. On the floor, Hermes tilts his head.

'You must go to bed,' Dora poses. 'I'll fetch for a doctor.'

Lottie shakes off the hold Dora has on her. She will not now meet her gaze.

'I'm not ill. I don't need no doctor.'

'Please, let me fetch someone,' Dora tries again. 'Or if you won't let me fetch someone then let me stay. I can finish off here . . .'

The housekeeper manages to scoff, and her voice is harsh when she says, 'Do you even know how to cook?'

'Do you?' Dora returns sharply – instinctively defensive – but she immediately regrets the words, touches her tongue to the roof of her mouth. 'I can help, at least,' she adds, more gently. 'Your eye—'

But Lottie turns from her, ambles over to the fire, its steaming pot.

'I'm fine, missum. I don't want no help.'

There is no arguing, it seems. With one last troubled look at her, Dora retrieves Hermes and turns to go. But at the door Lottie calls Dora back.

'Yes?'

'Guinea-fowl soup for dinner. Tatties too. Curd for pudding.'

The words are said quietly, no scorn in them, and Dora recognises the gesture – the housekeeper is trying to express her thanks.

'Oh, I . . . I won't be here for dinner.'

Lottie hesitates. 'Off out again?'

Dora understands clearly the words she does not say.

'I can stay if you want me to.'

And she will, if Lottie asks. But the housekeeper is shaking her head.

'You'll be no use here. No, you'd best stay clear.' She busies herself with stirring the pot with a wooden spoon. Then, 'Where you going this time?'

'I'll be dining with Lord and Lady Hamilton tonight. I'm not sure what time I'll be back. But thank you, all the same.'

'*Lord* and *Lady*? What high circles you travel in now! Well, no matter,' she adds, over-brisk. 'It won't go to waste, I'm sure.'

Uneasily Dora watches her. Lottie's face is blotchy from tears and even from a distance, her bruised eye looks appalling. For years Dora has felt only dislike for the woman. For the way Hezekiah always favoured her over his own niece, how he always let Lottie speak down to her, her nonchalance in the upkeep of the shop, the neglect of her attic. But something has shifted . . .

'Will you be all right, Lottie?' Dora asks quietly.

Lottie's hand stills on the spoon. 'You'd best get gone, missum,' she says finally. 'Neither one of us has time for pleasantries, do we?'

# CHAPTER
# THIRTY-THREE

Before dinner Sir William invited his guests to peruse his extensive collection of antiquities in a room reserved specifically to display them. Dora – who did deign to arrive, to Edward's intense relief – has said not one word to him, has let herself be commandeered completely by Lady Hamilton rather than let Edward near her at all. Disappointed, he has had to content himself with observing her from a distance, watching Dora trace a fingertip over the curve of a marble statue of Athena, and without quite realising it he found himself so fascinated – not by the beauty of Athena, but the beauty of *her* – that he forgot to answer when Hamilton asked him a question. Then Cornelius rudely placed himself between them, commenting drily that Sir William was lucky to acquire the statue before the French did, and it is this subject that engages the small assembly now over their white wine sole.

'He has this hare-brained idea,' the diplomat says, 'that theft is not theft but merely appropriation of the spoils of war. Moreover, that France is the best place for the things that he pilfers. But Napoleon has no comprehension of their worth, what they mean to the nations he seizes them from. No appreciation. No *understanding*. They are just trinkets and baubles to him.'

He slams his fist down on the table. The cutlery clatters against the china. Lady Hamilton – a vision in deep midnight blue – presses her lips together in disapproval.

'It is all just a game to him, and we his pawns,' Hamilton continues, quite in the throes of his subject. 'The paintings he has taken! It's said he has already claimed pieces by Raphael, Correggio, Titian, da Vinci . . . it is unpardonable.'

'So is it really true,' Edward asks, 'that nowadays French commissioners can enter any building in Europe – public, private, or religious – to confiscate artistic works?'

Sir William's face twists. 'Regrettably, yes. I have it on good authority they have already seized almost three hundred antiquities from the private collection of a cardinal.'

'How can he dare?' Dora says, pausing over her fish, a little line forming between her brows, and Edward's stomach knots itself. Oh, if she would only speak to him!

'He dares, my dear,' their host replies, 'because he is answerable to no one but a God I scarce doubt he believes in.'

Cornelius sits forward, twists his fork lazily at the handle. 'Is there any danger, Sir William, of Bonaparte reaching England?'

Hamilton sighs, picks up the wine glass at his side. 'He is a formidable force to be sure. We are on the brink of invasion but I am confident in the strength of our fleet.' His eyes flick to his wife. 'We have a great man at its helm, after all.'

Across the table Lady Hamilton colours.

'If Napoleon cannot invade,' Sir William says as if has not noticed, 'then he is determined to see Britain suffer in some other way. Did you know that since he set up camp in Egypt he has damaged our trade routes to and from India?' The question is asked to the entire room and he is greeted with four cautious nods. 'Then you might also be aware that the taxes have risen because of it, and the pocketbooks of our people will suffer in turn. If Napoleon is not stopped, in a few

279

years . . . Well, we could be brought to the point of revolution. If that were to happen, Bonaparte will have won, though not in the way he anticipated.'

The notion is unsettling. Edward snaps a hair-fine bone thoughtfully between his teeth. 'How will our antiquity trade be affected, do you suppose?'

'With the trade routes disrupted it means sales are more likely to come from personal collections rather than any outside sources. And with Bonaparte having seized the majority . . .' Hamilton shakes his head. 'He's like a magpie is to shine.'

'Speaking of magpies,' Cornelius quips, as if he has grown thoroughly bored with the conversation, 'Miss Blake has one. Keeps it as a pet.'

Edward sends Cornelius a peevish look across the table. He expected his friend to show some remorse for the part he played the night before, and while Cornelius has apologised to Edward for what he deemed only 'a slip of the tongue', he has otherwise shown no regret. 'Why should I?' he demanded after Dora had so unceremoniously left them in the carriage. 'Surely this proves her guilt, does it not?'

'A pet?' Lady Hamilton is exclaiming now, clapping her hands in delight. 'How charming!'

'Dirty birds, I find,' Cornelius sniffs, tweaking his cravat. 'Just thought that would be an interesting little bit of information to share with the party.'

Dora clears her throat, very carefully places her knife and fork down beside her plate.

'They are not dirty,' she says quietly, perfectly composed, but Edward still senses her anger across the table and shifts uncomfortably in his seat. 'Hermes is very clean. Monstrous vain, actually. He'll happily spend hours preening his feathers. He is a very beautiful bird.'

'A temper though,' Edward says, teasing, in an attempt to ease the tension. He raises his hand. 'This will scar, I'm sure.'

He does not mean it. The wound is healing nicely and Dora knows it, but his effort at humour does not break the ice. Indeed, she ignores him completely.

'Nipped you, did he?' Sir William says, taking a sip from his glass.

'He was protecting Dora,' explains Edward. 'I think he thought I was going to attack her.'

'Perhaps,' Dora says quietly, 'he thought you someone you were not?'

The comment stings. Deflated, Edward lowers his fork.

'Aren't magpies awfully unlucky?' Lady Hamilton asks after a moment, broaching the awkward pause that has befallen the table. 'That rhyme of Brand's. What was it, one for sorrow, two for mirth?'

'Not at all, my dear,' Hamilton says, keeping his voice light. 'In China magpies are thought to bring good fortune, although killing one is supposed to bring the reverse. They're actually associated with happiness; in the north-east they're regarded as sacred. The Manchu dynasty that governs China uses the magpie as a symbol of its imperial rule.'

'Really?' Dora smiles then at Sir William, and Edward feels an unjustified stab of jealousy that it is directed at someone other than him. 'I didn't know.'

The diplomat raises his glass in mock salute. The air settles once more.

'Even so,' his wife says. 'To have only one. Superstition, you see. It came from somewhere, surely. Superstition alone is a worrisome power.'

'Power is in its ability to disturb us, my dear,' Hamilton replies. 'It is all in the mind. We often run ourselves ragged with imagining some greater meaning when there is none.'

'Oh, enough, I beg you!'

Cornelius wipes his mouth with his napkin, then throws it down next to his plate. He is disappointed, it seems, that whatever ploy he attempted has failed, and Edward is torn between feeling smug and wanting to hit him for his insolence.

'My dear Mr Ashmole,' Lady Hamilton laughs, 'what a grump you are. *You* brought the subject up!'

'So I did,' he says, pointedly refusing to meet Edward's eye. 'But I am easily distracted, as I'm sure you have noticed.'

'Apparently so! You remind me in many ways of King Ferdinand. He too liked to jump from subject to subject. It drove poor Maria quite to distraction.'

'You are very close to her majesty, I understand?'

Lady Hamilton beams. 'Very close, Mr Ashmole. She confided in me for many, many things.' She sends a pretty frown over the table to her husband. 'I do miss court.'

Sir William looks sage. 'You know our return was necessary, Emma. It could not be prevented any longer.'

Dora leans forward in her seat. 'Why did you return, Sir William?'

Edward clamps his mouth. He hoped, for Dora's sake . . . Beside him, Hamilton lays down his glass.

'Ah. Yes. I had not anticipated reaching the subject quite so soon. I'd hoped we might wait until after dinner. My dear,' he says, looking to his wife, 'you do not mind if I speak of the *Colossus*?'

Lady Hamilton waves her hand. 'You know I have no objection, William. I am as much in dismay at what transpired as you are. A terrible loss. Near half your collection, gone.'

A line appears between Dora's brows. 'Gone, Sir William?'

'William, please. Dora, we know each other of old, after all. And I'm afraid what I have to say does pertain to you.'

Dora blinks. 'To me?'

Inwardly Edward groans. It was agreed that Edward was not to tell Dora what they had spoken of the night before, not to even hint at it, that Sir William had wanted to disclose the information to Dora himself, but Edward worries how Dora might react to the news, especially after last night. Coming from a friend – if that is what he still is – would surely be the best course . . .

'Dora, the tale I have to tell comes in two parts,' Hamilton says. He rests his elbows either side of his plate, steeples his fingers into a pyramid. 'As you are aware, I have spent many years collecting Grecian antiquities. It has progressed so that it is now far more than a hobby—'

'More of an obsession, I should say,' his wife cuts in, and Sir William frowns at her across the table.

'Yes, an obsession, I concede.' He clears his throat. 'I have been collecting since I moved to Naples thirty-five years ago. Sixteen years ago I decided for its protection, since the situation in Naples was becoming increasingly volatile, to send part of my collection to London. It arrived safely. But last year, when Naples was recaptured by the French, I thought it prudent to ship – along with my fine art – the second half of my pottery collection back to England. Alas, it did not arrive.'

Cornelius sits back in his chair. Edward can see that, despite his objection to any discussion that shows Dora off to effect, he is enraptured.

'Emma and I followed on the next packet. I had military business to attend to here in London, but needed to wait a few days to finalise matters in Italy before setting sail after the *Colossus*. Just as well we did, I suppose, otherwise we would have been on board when the ship sank.'

'The ship sank?' Dora is wide-eyed, her plate of sole quite forgotten.

283

Hamilton looks understandably aggrieved. 'I plan to organise a salvage expedition, but I don't hold out much hope. I've since been told the ship has broken apart on the seabed and with the weather being so monstrous . . .' He shakes his head. 'I have lost everything. Or at least I thought I had. You can imagine my shock, I am sure, when I arrived at Lady Latimer's last night to find – decked out in gaudy pomp – an item that looked strikingly similar to one of the items I lost.'

Dora is very still.

'The pithos.'

'The very same.'

Finally, Dora's eyes meet Edward's across the table. Then, slowly, she pushes her plate aside, lays her hands flat on the starched tablecloth.

'I would ask, please, that you be frank with me.'

Sir William nods. 'Very well. Twelve months ago I instigated a dig in Greece. The excavation was difficult. It took six months to finally reach the room I sought. From it, we retrieved a pithos. It was very large, extremely heavy, and took five men to haul it out.'

Hamilton pauses.

'Go on,' Dora says. Her face is perfectly straight.

'We removed the dust and mud. We were meticulous in cleaning it. And we were shocked to discover there wasn't a mark on it. Perfect condition. I alone knew its worth, suspected its age. But the truth of it is, Dora, that the pithos does not truly belong to me. It never did. I had just been safeguarding it all those years. So I had it packaged, sent to Palermo, where I kept it in a warehouse until it was time to ship it to England.'

In the middle of the table, the candles flicker in their sticks. It seems everyone at the table is holding fast their breath until Dora releases hers.

'It was found in Greece.'

'Yes.'

Dora's fingers curl into her palms. Her voice is quiet, taut, when she says, 'And where, in Greece?'

For a long moment Sir William watches her. 'Mount Lykaion. Dora, I reopened your parents' dig site.'

There is silence. Edward watches her across the table, the play of emotions that switch from pain to comprehension to resignation, and Edward wants to go to her, to hold her in his arms.

Then Dora's face crumples, and she puts her head in her hands.

# CHAPTER
# THIRTY-FOUR

He dreams. He dreams of dank wet earth, a tomb of impenetrable dark, of ancient mud and stone.

He does not know where he is. He does not know who he is. He feels like himself, yet can sense a voice whispering in his skull – a breath, a sigh, a song – that does not belong to him.

Then, there is light.

He feels elation, relief. He laughs, breathes in the sweetness of air. Oh, how he has missed its caress, how he has craved its purity! But then, then . . .

Water. He has always hated it. First dirt and flotsam, then salt and brine. The endless darkness of fathoms.

He waits, again. Again. Always waiting.

He calls out. Sings his pain across the ocean, gives life to the wind. And then, as inevitable as the stars, they come.

And how easily they found him! How he retched on their greed as they hauled him free.

For days he tosses and floats, for days he feels their disease, their insatiable lust. Why, then, should he make their journey pleasant? Why not whisper fear into their hearts, pour sickness into their wounds and run the tempests wild? They know what they are, they know what they do. They know their time draws near, for he is both their salvation and their purist hell.

Water.

It is merely a passageway to somewhere else. He feels the lull of waves, hears the call of gulls, smells the familiar scent of earth caught helpless in the breeze, and he smiles in the face of the quickening.

'Hezekiah?'

He wakes to Lottie nudging his shoulder. He groans, rolls onto his back. The basement floor is cold and hard beneath him, and for a long moment he stares up at the ceiling, the rotten beams dusted liberally with grey cobwebs that hang like gauzy garlands.

'What do you do down here?' Lottie asks.

He notes the nervous lilt in her voice but he has no patience for it. He sits up, wipes a hand over his face. Despite the chill of the basement, his skin is sticky-hot.

'What time is it?'

'Past ten.'

Hezekiah frowns.

He came home at half past six – through a fug of gin he remembers checking the gilt pocketwatch he still carries everywhere with him since purchasing it – and went down to the basement to check on the vase, to see if it was safely delivered, back where it belonged. He sat down in front of it, placed his hands on its sides (warm, he had been surprised to find) and willed it to speak. Of course, he did not expect it to. He did not expect to hear a voice materialise from its earthern bowels. No, he wanted only to know, to understand why it had thwarted him so long, why it was empty, *why why why* . . .

'I must have fallen asleep,' he mutters pointlessly.

Lottie fidgets her fingers. The action irritates him.

'Are you hungry?'

287

'No.'

A beat.

'Why is this thing so important to you, Hezekiah? Why do you covet it so?'

He feels his insides coil, his anger begins to rear, and he can hear a loud hum in his head.

'Because it is mine,' he snaps.

'Is it?'

Hezekiah curls his fist. He hears Lottie take a step back toward the stairs.

'Helen didn't deserve it. I told you how calculating she was. How deceitful. She used me.'

'But Helen is dead.'

'Yes. And now it is mine.'

The humming stops. Hezekiah sighs.

'Then why don't you sell it?'

For a long moment Hezekiah is quiet. He considers. How much to tell? To tell at all? But he knows Lottie, knows she is like a bulldog with a chop that will not rest until it has been satiated.

He breathes deeply, tastes the staleness of gin. 'There's a fortune.'

Another beat. 'What fortune?'

Hezekiah gives her a sideways look. 'There is money. A lot of money. It's tied up, somewhere, in a place Elijah kept secret from me. Me!' Hezekiah exclaims on the shout of a bitter laugh. 'His own brother!' He takes another breath, clenches tighter his fists. 'There was the contents of the shop, of course; I sold it all long ago, to make sure there was nothing for her. But there was more. Far more. And I don't know where. This vase is the key.'

'I see.'

In the dim of the basement, with her standing so far away from him, he cannot read her bruised face. Does she see? Or does she disapprove? But she has held no such qualms before. The money he has made over the years, she has never once questioned it. Not when it kept a roof over her head. Not when it kept her secure.

'The vase is the key?'

He wipes a hand across his eyes, suddenly overwhelmingly tired.

'There was a note. A piece of paper written by Helen under Elijah's instruction. It stated how Dora could claim it. The fortune.'

Lottie is silent. Then, 'And the note was in that?' She points a finger at the vase. Hezekiah nods. 'What did you plan to do with it?'

'Claim it all as mine. Destroy the proof. Sell the shop.'

Hezekiah shifts on the floor, wincing at the stabbing pain in his leg, tries to ignore – though it is becoming increasingly difficult – the smell.

'Why did they not write it in the will?'

'There was no will.'

'Then how—'

'It doesn't matter,' Hezekiah says, waves his hand to stop the words building on Lottie's infernal tongue. 'The point is the note was written, it was left in that vase, and it is not there now.'

She is silent again. His leg spasms. He breathes out through the pain.

'Hezekiah.'

'What.'

'What of Dora?'

'What of her?'

'You said you had a place for her. What did you mean by that?'

Hezekiah stares unseeing in front of him.

'I went to your old bawd. She has a room for her, when I'm ready.'

He hears Lottie's intake of breath, the scratchy pull of air in her throat.

'No. You can't.'

'I can, and I will.'

'But—'

Above them, there is an almighty hammering. The bell jingles loudly on its coil, a painfully tinny screech.

Lottie turns, pulls herself up the stairs – for Hezekiah the feat takes far longer – and by the time they both have reached the shop floor, the door is trembling dangerously in its casement.

'Hang on, hang on!' Hezekiah shouts, panting as he grapples along the shelves. A faux-Wedgwood bowl falls to the floor and shatters.

'Open up, Blake! Open this door, damn you!'

Hezekiah stops short; his innards turn a sickly somersault.

*Hell's teeth, it is Coombe.*

Hezekiah swallows, raises a shaking hand.

'Lottie, don't—' But it is no use, for Lottie has already drawn the bolt across.

The door is opened only by a mere crack, but instantly Lottie is flown aside as the door is flung wide and Coombe barges through it. The man stops as his eyes adjust to the gloom, searching through it for Hezekiah. When he sees him Coombe comes forward, arms outstretched, and Hezekiah cowers, must grip the shelf for support.

Coombe has him by the collar in an instant. Behind him the shelf tips, and there is a deafening crash as the rest of the forged Wedgwood falls to the floor.

'He's dead!' Coombe is shouting, and Hezekiah smells rotting flesh. 'He's dead, he is dead, and it is *your* fault, yours!'

With each cry of 'dead' Coombe gives him a hard shake, making Hezekiah's teeth chatter in his skull. Above the hum of blood in his ears, Hezekiah thinks he can hear Lottie shrieking.

'*Who* is dead?' he gasps, and then he feels – to his utter shame – piss begin to soak through his trousers, begin to *pit-pat-pit* on the floorboards.

'Who is dead?' Coombe's eyes widen, the whites of them stark in the dark. '*Who is dead?*'

The man breaks off into a laugh that holds no humour, and he releases his quarry. Hezekiah falls, cries out as he hits the ground, for he lands on the overturned shelf, on the shards of broken pottery. Coombe is turning away, tearing frantically at his hair.

'That's just like you, isn't it, Hezekiah Blake? To not remember, or even care, selfish bastard that you are.' He looks back at him. Hezekiah sees for the first time that his face is wet with tears. 'Don't you even know his name?'

'Samuel.'

Lottie's voice. Coombe sighs.

'Yes. Samuel. The fever took him. You should have seen . . .' His voice cracks. Coombe puts his head in his hands, and for a time there is only the sound of his sobbing.

'I'm sorry,' Lottie whispers.

Coombe wipes his cheeks, gives a disjointed nod. 'I see how you might be. But *him* . . .'

Very carefully Hezekiah manages to extricate himself from the debris but he cannot stand, not just yet. He forces himself to perch nonchalantly on the edge of the shelf, tries to pinch his wet trousers – already cooling – away from the flesh of his thigh, but the too-tight material has no give; it cleaves to him like a second skin.

'I am sorry for it,' Hezekiah says now, though he does not mean it. 'But I fail to see how this is my fault.'

'You fail to see?' Coombe tweaks at the sleeve of the elbow-length suede glove he wears. 'It is you who sent me to Greece when you found out about the excavation. You who made me track that damn cursèd thing, you who bade us salvage it when it was lost—'

'I say to you once and for all that the vase is not cursed!' Despite his fear of the man, his anger begins to ripen once more. 'You superstitious fool. How can one vase be the cause of so much? It is a piece of pottery, a mere artefact, nothing more.'

Coombe is striding toward him again and Hezekiah flinches, wishes he had the power to run. The larger man tears off the glove.

'And I say to you, how can you explain this!'

Though the shop is dark, Hezekiah can see all too well the thing before him. And *thing* it is – what should have been a hand and arm is nothing more now than a blackened appendage. From the scant light from the street he sees its pustules glisten. And the smell. By God, the smell!

Hezekiah begins to gag, to turn his face away, but Coombe takes hold of his chin with his good hand and clenches it so hard that Hezekiah cries out in pain.

'Look at it, damn you! And it all came from a simple twine burn. Twine I used so I could haul your godforsaken prize up from the seabed. You tell me that your precious vase had no part in it?'

But Hezekiah is stubborn. He will not accept this. He cannot.

'The twine was yours not mine, nor did it have any connection to the vase. It could have easily been tainted with something else, some substance, something that could have infected the skin.'

Coombe is shaking his head in outrage. His nostrils flare like a bull.

'Still won't see sense, eh? Is your leg any better?'

Hezekiah clamps his mouth. With a sneer Coombe releases his jaw.

'Matthew.' Lottie has stepped forward, is wringing her hands. 'Do you believe the vase made you ill? That Sam's death, Charlie's sickness, Hezekiah's leg . . . it's all because of a pot?'

Coombe slowly puts the glove back on. 'Yes. That's exactly what I believe.'

Lottie looks as if she is about to cry. 'Hezekiah—'

'Stop,' Hezekiah snaps.

He heaves himself up. He will not stand to be spoken to like this. By a lowborn such as Matthew bloody Coombe in his own damn shop.

'I do not believe in curses. I am sorry for your brother but it is not my fault, as little as it's the fault of an ancient piece of terracotta! You are mad with grief and it makes you nonsensical.' When Coombe says nothing to this, Hezekiah feels his confidence rise, puffs up his chest. 'What's more, you have come here at an inhospitable hour. You have damaged my wares. You have frightened my housekeeper and you have more or less accused me of murder. No, I will not have it. You will leave my premises at once. At once, I say!'

There is a foreboding silence in which Coombe watches him, clenching and unclenching his good fist, and Hezekiah begins to see renewed danger in the man's eyes. In that moment, the sudden bravado that has overtaken Hezekiah begins to fall flat; he feels doubt set in, the trickle of fear slip down his spine like quicksilver.

Coombe shifts in his boots. The floorboards creak.

'You will not take responsibility?'

Hezekiah raises his chin. 'I will not.'

'Very well. You leave me no choice. Tomorrow, once I have buried my brother, I am going to the authorities. I will tell them everything. Your niece, too. Mark my words, Hezekiah Blake, you will pay for what you have done.'

'Do so, and you will sink with me.'

But Coombe is already gone, the shop door swinging on its hinges, and Hezekiah does not notice how his breathing has shallowed until he struggles to breathe at all. He thinks of Elijah, his bitch of a wife, both long dead and buried, the troublesome daughter they left behind, their fortune, *his* fortune, the note . . .

Lottie is stepping forward, hand reached out. 'Hezekiah.'

The sour smell of his own urine reaches his nostrils; something begins to snap in his mind, a series of sharp, collective cracks.

'Hezekiah—'

'Where is Dora?' he bellows, the broken pottery clattering noisily at his feet. 'I'll have it out with her now!' He pushes past Lottie, violently pulls on his leg to help him along. 'Upstairs in that hovel of hers, is she? That pit of a room!'

'She isn't here!'

The words are spoken at such a high panicked pitch it stops Hezekiah in his tracks. He turns on her.

'What?' he snaps, and Lottie blanches. Her pale bruised skin reminds him of the bulbous mantle of an octopus he saw once, washed up on a beach in Mykonos, and for the very first time in his life the woman disgusts him.

'She . . .' Lottie wrings her hands again. 'She's dining at the Hamilton's. Lord and Lady, she said.'

Silence.

*Lord Hamilton.*

A fist clenches his lungs.

'What?' he asks again, and this time he cannot control his fear.

But Lottie has fallen silent, seems to see the Devil is in him, and he flings open the apartment door so violently the bell dents the wall. He pulls himself up on the first step of the stairs.

'Where are you going?' she cries, scrambling up the treads behind him.

'To her room! She is hiding it. She knows. Which means *he* knows! I must get to it before Coombe gets to her.'

'Hezekiah, *don't!*'

But he is already on the landing, then the second, Dora's attic, and he wrenches the door open so hard he feels the wood pull on its hinges.

The room is impeccably kept for so drear a place. The magpie – that dratted disgusting bird – squawks loudly at him, an affronted rattle, but he ignores it.

Hezekiah goes straight to the wardrobe, flings its contents onto the floor. Nothing. The chest of drawers next. Each drawer he opens, rummages between the garments, flings those too to the floor. Nothing.

Where next?

From the doorway, Lottie is watching. 'Hezekiah . . .'

'For God's sake woman, leave me be. Go on, get out. Go!'

Lottie stares at him. Then, with a resigned sigh that irritates him beyond measure she disappears, and he waits for her heavy foot on the stair before continuing his search.

Hezekiah limps toward the bed, clatters to his knees, looks underneath. A carpet bag. He reaches for it, pauses only long enough to trace the embroidered H with his finger, remembering when he bought it for Helen, and in his anger he rips it. Nothing. Nothing!

The magpie screeches.

'Shut up!' he screams. 'Shut up!'

Where else? Where else would she keep it? He spots the desk under the window, smiles in relief. Of course!

He opens a drawer, his lip lifting in a sneer. Junk. Glass, wire, scraps of leather and lace. He reaches for a glass bead. Didn't he notice one of his mock-jade bracelets had gone missing a while back? He will punish her for this, too.

Hezekiah sifts through the flotsam and jetsam of useless items. Nothing! But just as he is about to turn away he notices a familiar pouch.

His coin purse! *She* took it! He reaches for the purse and opens it. No money. No note. Instead, a small tinderbox. And inside that . . .

'That conniving little bitch.'

The box is filled with wax – a wax mould, he sees on a squint – and nestled within that, a small metal key.

Hezekiah reaches for the chain around his neck, pulls it up through his shirt, looks at both keys side by side.

Identical. Hers is newer, the brass not yet marked with age. But the teeth . . .

He remembers the night of the gin.

*So. That's how.*

He drops the chain. The key bounces lightly against the cushion of his chest.

He discards the box, the duplicate key landing on the floor with a dull *chink*. Hezekiah spins on his good leg, looks manically about the room.

Where is it, then? *Where is it?*

Is he wrong? But he cannot be! Perhaps she has the note with her, perhaps she is showing it to Hamilton this very moment, perhaps—

The magpie – having been silenced by Hezekiah's screaming – lets out one long, drawn-out cry, and Hezekiah jumps. It watches him from its cage, its small black eyes judgemental, accusatory. It cocks its head. Hezekiah sets his teeth.

'Well, then.'

And as Hezekiah approaches, the bird begins to hiss.

# CHAPTER
# THIRTY-FIVE

'Oh, my dear!'

Lady Hamilton puts an arm around her shoulders but Dora barely registers the kindness.

How can this be? How did her uncle acquire it, how could he have known?

A glass of water is placed in Dora's hand and she is forced to drink.

'Forgive me,' Dora whispers when she has emptied the glass. She looks across at Sir William, at Edward, both watching her with concern. 'Please continue. I must hear it. I need to hear the rest.'

'Dora,' says Sir William, looking deeply troubled. 'There is a serious matter at hand here. I would have protected you from it if I could.'

'Tell me.' She knows her tone is hard, unforgiving. But Dora will not let this lie, not now she is on the cusp of the truth. 'Please.'

Lady Hamilton sinks back into the seat beside her. Sir William clears his throat.

'After your parents died, I monitored the dig site for years. I bought the land, you see, put overseers in place, to notify me if there was any change.'

'What do you mean, change?' Mr Ashmole interjects.

A pause.

297

'I cannot tell the rest without you understanding the history of Helen and Elijah Blake. Dora, if you would?'

She hesitates. Edward leans forward in his seat.

'If you do not feel able . . .'

He looks at her with such concerned affection that Dora must do her best not to cry.

'No. I shall explain, as best I can. I was only a child, you understand. My memory of it is hazy at best.'

She takes a breath.

'I grew up without any set home. There was the shop, of course, which my parents often left in the charge of my uncle, and I spent many a month there when they were inclined to return. But they could never stay in one place for long. They spent their lives exploring the Mediterranean, and I accompanied my parents whenever they went there. My mother was fascinated by the cultural history of her homeland. She was always reciting the Greek myths to me, always sketching them on scraps of paper she kept in her pockets. It was she who taught me how to draw.' Dora smiles, wistful. 'It was during a trip to Naples that we met Sir William.'

'I was struck by Helen's artistry,' Sir William cuts in. 'I used Johann Tischbein to sketch my pieces, but sometimes he was engaged elsewhere so I often commissioned Helen in his place.'

'Wait,' Lady Hamilton interrupts. 'I think I remember . . . One summer you had visitors, didn't you, William, and a child was with them. Miss Blake, that was you?'

'It was indeed, my dear,' Sir William returns. 'But pray, Dora, continue. Naples?'

Dora takes a breath. 'I think you might be able to explain this part better than I.'

'Very well.' Their host takes a sip of his wine, fills it again from the carafe in the middle of the table. 'We were dining on the balcony, I remember, overlooking the bay.' He looks to Dora. 'You were sitting on your mother's lap.'

Dora offers a watery smile. 'I remember.'

He inclines his head. 'I commended Helen's choice to name you Pandora. The name means "all-gifted" and I thought it quite charming. She told me she had named you after the myth. When I asked her why, she told me how the story had always fascinated her as a child.'

'And what is the story?' Lady Hamilton asks.

Over the table Edward catches Dora's eye. She understands what he asks her, though he does not speak the words aloud. *Are you all right?* his eyes say, and Dora's chest tightens. Her anger at him is not diminished but she feels numb to it right now, finds herself nodding in answer, and Sir William seems to interpret this as permission to deviate from her own history still further.

'There have been many variations of the myth over the course of history. For the purpose of tonight's explanation I shall recount the most common one.' He takes a breath. 'You must know, of course, that in Greek myth their God was Zeus. For millennia, the world was made up only of gods and demigods and mythical creatures. Although their lives were by no means harmonious it was, in many respects, a perfect world. Zeus though, dissatisfied with this so-called "perfect world" – which he considered now altogether far too boring – tasked his good friend Prometheus to create the first humans out of mud and Zeus' own spittle, and the goddess Athena animated them with her breath.

'However, all these humans were male, and they did not possess the ability to make fire which Zeus considered a skill only the gods may own. But Prometheus felt that humans were meant to evolve and create, so he stole the fire of Hephaestus, the god of blacksmiths, and bestowed it upon the humans. When he discovered Prometheus' treachery, Zeus had Hephaestus create the first human female and

299

gave her all the womanly wiles that many believe are the cause of man's downfall. This first female was named Pandora.

'But even then, Zeus' revenge was not complete. Before releasing her he gave Pandora a jar – not a box, as many believe. That error is due to a mistranslation attributed to the Dutch philosopher Erasmus. In his Latin account of the story he changed the Greek *pithos* to *pyxis* which means, literally, "box". But the point is there was a pithos, and Zeus ordered her never to open it.

'Pandora was then gifted to Prometheus' brother, Epimetheus. The two fell deeply in love and were happy for many years. But the call of the pithos would not let Pandora rest. One night, unable to sleep, she opened the lid of the jar and alas, Zeus' revenge was realised. Out came all the evils of the world from which we have never recovered: Illness, Violence, Deceit, Misery and Want. Pandora was so shocked by what she had done, that she closed the lid just before the final evil could be released. Zeus had added Hope to the pithos, to punish and torture man. He believed that Hope was often the false promise of good to come. *I* believe that it is up to interpretation whether Hope is considered Evil or Good.'

The room sits in a suspension of quiet. The air seems charged, as if the mythical tale is a living thing that has been awoken by its very narration. Sir William takes a sip of wine; the others follow suit. It is Mr Ashmole who breaks the silence.

'How does all this connect to Miss Blake?'

Sir William looks to her. 'My dear?' he prompts.

Dora takes a deep, steadying breath. Out of her few fragmented mirror shards of memory, *this* is the one that has stuck with her all these years, the one that has remained fully formed in her mind's eye. She remembers her mother's voice recalling the Pandora myth at bedtime as Dora turned the cameo over and over and over in the palm of her tiny hand. But of course it never occurred to her that the pithos she has been sketching might have been the very same one her mother spoke of, all those years before.

'My mother believed,' Dora begins, 'that the original Pandora was real. Not the woman of myth, of course, but I remember her saying – as you suggested earlier, Lady Hamilton – that suspicion, fable, it all comes from some form of truth. My mother reasoned that there may well have been someone in ancient Greece of that name, a woman of great power and beauty, likely of aristocratic lineage, and that a vase was created as homage to her. Another argument might be that she was a corrupt woman since the myth tells that Pandora released all natural evils into the world, and therefore the vase was made as some form of insult. Either way, my mother thought it probable that a vase existed, one that would have been distinct enough to carry such a legend down through the generations. But I had no idea this was what my parents were looking for during those last weeks. To me it was just another dig site, like any other I had been on over the years.'

Here, Sir William taps his glass. 'How could you know? You were only a child.' He manages a kindly smile. 'But that *is* what they were looking for. You see, Helen told me that, having researched the myth, she'd discovered Pandora had drowned in a great flood. However, legend also said that Pandora and Epimetheus had a daughter who survived it – Pyrrha. So those three names, the flood . . . Helen used them as a starting point. She spent years, apparently, scouring ancient documents – family names, settlement lists – and believed she had not only located them in historic sources but geographically, too. She traced their ancestral heritage to southern Greece, cross-referenced natural disasters, and discovered there *had* been a great flood . . . in a town at the foothills of Mount Lykaion.'

Dora pinches the bridge of her nose. 'I don't remember exactly how we all came to be in the Peloponnese, or Sir William with us. But we were, and this was one of the rare occasions my uncle

301

accompanied us. I remember very little of that day, or the days lead-ing up to it, but I do remember something was wrong. My parents and my uncle, they argued. All the time. I . . .'

Lady Hamilton squeezes her arm. 'Go on.'

Dora shuts her eyes. She pictures a deep blue sky. Cloudless, broken only by a sun too bright to look at directly. A mountain looms before her, deep green trees blanketing its slopes, their fronds full and lush. The earth beneath her feet is parched, deep cracks mapping its surface like ancient parchment, kept too long in the open air. Somewhere, in grass that has turned to straw in the heat, a cricket is singing. Dora pictures broken stone monoliths, narrow trenches held up by wooden beams. A deep hole in the ground, a dark tunnel that leads to somewhere she cannot see unless she climbs down a ladder to reach it. Around her, white tents, their seams flapping in a breeze that holds within it no air. Then the mirror shards shiver, break apart again, and Dora can no longer get a grasp on them.

'I was at the dig site the day it happened,' she hears herself say. 'It was hot. Scorching hot. That dry sort of heat that fills your lungs and makes it difficult to breathe. No one else was around. The workers were sleeping. So I remember I went to the well to fetch my parents some water. I remember I had just climbed down into the access chamber, and the earth began to collapse around me. But I knew my parents were down in the room beyond it and I tried to reach them, I cried out . . .'

She is speaking in a rush, begins to shake, her vision starts to blur, and suddenly Mr Ashmole – Mr Ashmole of all people – has taken her hand and Dora is holding it as hard as she can.

'I remember getting trapped. I couldn't cry out, I couldn't breathe at all. The next thing I knew I was waking up on a litter in the tent. Sir William had pulled me out . . .'

Dora realises she is gasping for air, that Lady Hamilton is pouring another glass of water. She drinks long and hard, and it is some minutes before she can compose herself.

'I'm so sorry, Dora.'

It is Sir William who has spoken. She looks up to find them all watching her and – embarrassed now – Dora releases Mr Ashmole's hand. His skin changes from white to pink as the blood flow returns to it.

'Forgive me,' Mr Ashmole murmurs, flexing his fingers. 'But you said there were two parts to this story.'

Edward is rising from the chair. 'Cornelius, I don't think—'

'No,' Dora says, mastering her strength. 'Mr Ashmole is right. What did you mean, Sir William, when you said that?'

Sir William sighs. 'I do not want to cause you further pain.'

*'Tell me.'*

He sighs again, wipes a hand across his face, takes one more sip of wine.

'As you know, your parents were not so deep in the collapse as we had feared. They must have tried to make their escape. Their bodies were recovered, buried. You were shipped off back to London in the care of your uncle. It was classed as a terrible accident, the kind that happens all the time in that line of work.' A deep line has begun to form between Sir William's eyebrows. 'But something just didn't sit right with me. I had surveyed the site myself. You say, Dora, you don't know why we all came to be in southern Greece. I can tell you now that Helen's theory intrigued me. I funded the dig and asked that I be part of the team to search for the pithos.

'Your parents were thrilled to accept. I'd overseen many digs and always taken an active part in them, so they knew I was no idle aristocrat. And we did it, Dora, we *found* a pithos. One that matched in every particular to the historical and geographical sources. And even more convincing, it depicted the myth of Pandora's creation. There was no reason not to assume it was the pithos we had sought. We were ecstatic. Can you imagine the historic implications? We began to make arrangements to retrieve it. But then . . .

'Dora, I am positive that site was sound. I admit it would have benefited from reinforcing but there was nothing to make me believe there was any imminent danger, so when it collapsed I suspected some sort of mischief. I had no proof, or course. And matters were of such a nature—' Sir William stops, clears his throat. 'All I could do was preserve the site. As I said I bought the land, put an overseer in place. Then, last year, I received word of a flood. The deluge washed away enough of the earth that it seemed there was a chance we could access the site again. So, I reopened the dig.'

The whole time Sir William has been speaking, Dora has felt a clamping at her heart. Somehow, she knows what he means to say next.

'My uncle . . .' she begins.

His face closes.

'Hezekiah Blake was nowhere to be found during the cave-in. He turned up only later, a bloody scratch on his face. He claimed he had been caught in the collapse, had got out another way. But the problem is there was only one way in and one way out, and Dora . . .' Sir William looks grave. 'I was there the whole time. Digging you free.'

There can be no question of staying. No earthly question at all.

She leaves Edward and Mr Ashmole in the carriage, refuses to wait for them as she pushes open the door to the shop.

The putrid smell of Hezekiah's leg and something else – something ammoniac – hits her hard as she rushes over the threshold. She stops, notes the overturned shelf, the remains of crockery scattered on the floor like refuse on the Thames.

'Uncle! *Uncle!*'

Dora wants to cry – she can feel the tears pent up behind her eyes – but her anger is surer than her grief. How could he do such a thing? If he was responsible for her parents' deaths – and an attempt on her life too, it seems – then the pithos itself must be the cause. For it to be here in London, now, after all these years . . . But *why*? With a shout she rushes across the shop floor and scrambles over the shelf. The crockery scrapes loudly on the splintered floorboards. She hears material rip.

'Dora!'

Edward's voice, but she barely registers it. She reaches the basement doors and pulls on the handles, but they do not give way. Dora looks down to see the padlock shut and secure, the chain swaying from the force of her desperate tugging.

Upstairs, then.

She turns, makes her hasty retreat to the shop floor.

'Dora,' Edward tries again, holding out his hand, but she ignores him, sweeps past both him and Mr Ashmole who stand uselessly at the counter, watching her with ill-disguised pity. Through the connecting door she goes – the bell harshly loud on its spring – up the narrow stairs, her footsteps unforgiving on the treads.

When she pounds on the door to Hezekiah's bedroom there is no answer. Angrily Dora pulls it open, finds the room as black as pitch.

'Missum . . .'

Dora spins round. In the doorway of her old bedroom stands Lottie. The housekeeper wrings her hands together, and her unbruised eye looks red and puffy, as if she has been crying.

'Where is he?'

Her voice is full – she can hear the dangerous note in it – and the housekeeper stares at Dora without making another sound.

'*Where is he?*'

305

Lottie jumps, her face crumpling. 'Gone!' she finally cries, clenching her fists under her chin. 'I don't know where.'

The noise that escapes Dora is like nothing she has heard before. She reaches for the banister, heaves against it. Spots spasm in front of her vision. Then, decided, she pulls herself up, begins to climb the stairs.

'Don't go up there, missum.'

Something in Lottie's voice. Dora stops, turns.

'Why not?'

But Lottie just shakes her head, will not answer. Cannot, it seems, and something else begins to hammer in Dora's chest, her skull. Dora turns again, runs full pelt up the stairs.

Her attic door is wide open, hanging at an angle. From the landing she can already see the mess of clothes in the middle of the floor, and the anger falls from her in one single breath. It is as if everything slows its pace, as if she walks underwater, unable to anchor herself to the ground but somehow, somehow, her feet take her into the room.

In dismay Dora looks at the detritus spread haphazardly over the floor, the open doors of the wardrobe and chest of drawers, the demolished mess of her desk. Beads and wire, all her jewellery supplies, thrown about as if they were nothing more than rubbish.

A cold breeze gently ruffles the curtain at the window and moonlight streams into the room, a beam of white pointing at the floor. She turns her head.

'No. Oh, no. *No no no . . .*'

Like a puppet pulled along on a string Dora follows the trail of black-and-white feathers scattered across the floorboards. She raises her eyes. The door of the birdcage hangs precariously off its hinges, and Dora clamps her hand to her mouth to stifle a sob.

At the bottom of the cage lies Hermes, her beautiful Hermes, his elegant neck snapped in two.

306

# PART III.

When all of this – desire and joy and pain –
Has melted and dissolved in stormy rapture
And then refreshed itself in blissful sleep,
You will revive, revive to fullest youth,
To fear, to hope and to desire once more.

JOHANN WOLFGANG VON GOETHE
*Prometheus* (1773)

# CHAPTER
# THIRTY-SIX

From the east side of the river the journey to the Horse and Dolphin usually takes only an hour but Hezekiah's leg is a hellish pain and despite the sharp frost in the February air he is sweating profusely through his cambric. Instead, the journey takes him nearly two.

The city, when the sky is dark, lives in different skin. Nose curled, Hezekiah passes down dank, filthy alleys and is surprised to find that even at this dawn hour, harsh laughter echoes from deep within them.

Everything is coated with a repellent gloom. Loose cobbles skip where he upends them with his toe, sending flicks of mud up his trousers. His heel sinks deeply into wet earth. He pulls it free with a sickening sucking noise and still, even now, when there are other more pressing matters with which to concern himself, he worries about the stain.

He tries to ignore the beggars who watch from peeling doorways, pulls his coat tighter together, reels when he sees what he thinks is a body lying at the foot of a three-storey facade. Ironic, really, considering where he has just been.

What he has just done.

Hezekiah keeps his head down. He will not think on that. No, he will think of other things, what waits for him back in the bowels of the shop.

The long-sought note sits nestled in his waistcoat pocket – close to his heart – crumpled and ripped and stained with bird shit, but he has it. He pats the pocket, thinks gleefully on what the note has revealed. The fortune under his nose, all this time! And the key to the Bramah safe – the key he keeps hidden within the globe in the dining room – will unlock it! How has he not noticed? How did he not realise? It was Helen's idea, it must have been, conniving wench that she was. She played him like a fool from the very start. But he has won. Finally, after twelve years of waiting, he has won!

He will burn the note when he is through. And Dora, Hezekiah thinks with vindictive pleasure as he steps out from Hedge Lane into St Martin's Street, will never even know. He will ship her off to the whorehouse and be done with her. She will never bother him again.

The Horse and Dolphin is a forbidding-looking tavern with dirty bricks and low-hanging eaves above the door. Loud, unruly laughter trickles into the street and the lowlight from the panelled windows shines sickly yellow on the uneven cobbles. A cluster of doxies loiter at the corner, tiredly calling for sport, and briefly Hezekiah considers it, teases a coin in his pocket.

No, he thinks. There will be time aplenty for that.

The tavern is deep and rambling, with high wooden beams, a marigold-stained ceiling. Smoke claws irritatingly at his throat and Hezekiah coughs, slips a finger into his collar to loosen the material at his neck. Nervously he licks his lips and – furtive – looks around.

There.

Hezekiah limps to a table concealed within an alcove to the left of the entrance. A greying man in shabby, genteel black rises from his seat, eyebrows lifting in surprise. The man holds out an age-spotted hand for him to shake.

'Blake,' the man greets as Hezekiah seats himself. The cushion of

Hezekiah's belly presses uncomfortably against the wooden table. 'I did not expect to see *you* here at this hour.' A pause. 'What happened to your leg?'

'I have a job for you,' Hezekiah says, ignoring the question, and the man sits back into his seat, squinting at him.

'A job for me, is it? Best watch your tone, Blake. Remember,' he says, pointing at Hezekiah's belly with his eyes, 'without me you would not be so comfortably fed.' Another pause. 'There's blood on your cuff.'

Hezekiah pushes down his coat sleeve to hide it.

'What I mean to say is that I have a prize, something really rather marvellous. Your buyers will not be disappointed.'

'Hmm.'

The man lifts a small leather book from his pocket, opens it near the back. From his other he brings a pencil and a knife. With slow, considered care he begins to sharpen the lead.

'And what is this prize? I'm afraid our clients are becoming rather bored with your Grecian pots. They're getting harder to sell. How many do you have kept in stock now? Sixty? Eighty?'

Hezekiah shifts on the hard bench. It scratches against his buttocks.

'It *is* Greek, I grant you,' he says, and his tablemate stops his cutting, a pencil shaving dropping from the knife. 'But it's nothing like you've ever seen before.'

'Convince me.'

Hezekiah takes a breath. 'What if I told you that I had acquired a large vase in immaculate condition? One that has immeasurable historical value?'

'I would say I've heard it all before.'

'But this truly is. You see, I have it on good authority the vase predates all known history.'

Not quite true, he thinks. It is Dora's claim, and what can she know? Still, what difference does it make now – its worth will always be great, no matter its true age.

The man is placing his knife very deliberately on the table. The blade glints in the half-light. He closes the book.

'It is too early to play games with me, Hezekiah Blake.'

'I do not play games with you.'

Hezekiah bites his tongue. He must be careful. Must not over-reach. To speak to a trader is to speak to a client in the shop. Think of the sale, dazzle them with show.

*Gently, gently.*

Hezekiah sits forward, tries to hide a wince as a spasm shoots up his leg. He forces a smile.

'Let me tell you a story. A story that goes back twenty years. Imagine a young man, a cartographer. Idealistic, impressionable. One day he meets an artist, an historian, a Grecian woman who thrills him with tales of ancient myth and magic.' He pauses for effect, is disappointed to see his companion frowning, a look of mock-patience on his features, but Hezekiah takes a breath. 'She was named after Helena, the most beautiful woman the Greek Empire had ever seen and she embodied the namesake like no woman he had ever known, then or since. A man would die for her. Kill for her, she was so alluring. So the man meant to prove himself, helped her in her research. He even brought in his brother to help, because the brother knew things *he* did not.' Hezekiah clenches his fist. 'Together, the three of them investigated the possibility that an artefact described in ancient legend might actually exist. Years later, after the woman rejected this poor man's suit and married the brother instead, they discover its location. An excavation is organised. An artefact is found. But then, a great tragedy. There is a cave-in. Both the woman and the man's brother are lost. More tragically, so is the artefact.'

The man remains unmoved. 'I hope there is a point to this. Daylight will soon break. I have been up all night and my bed calls.'

Hezekiah raises a finger. 'Twelve years pass in which the man waits for his chance to come again. And then, it does. He is finally reunited with the artefact. An artefact that is in perfect condition for its age. And by God, it is beautiful. Grecian carvings, intricately detailed. A pure work of ancient art, thousands of years old, brought to light once more. A living memory.'

A muscle quirks.

'Can you imagine it?' Hezekiah lets his voice lower, injects it with his soft, salesman's tease. 'A vase of such an age. Think of the historic value. Think how buyers will be competing for it. Think of the tragedy behind it, how buyers would feel knowing it was important enough to die for. A bidding war! The most aggressive bidding war the market has ever seen. Greater than anything seen at Christie's. Wouldn't that be a wondrous thing?'

As if in agreement a yell comes from the back of the tavern, followed by raucous laughter, the sound of breaking glass.

'It must be worth thousands,' Hezekiah whispers.

The trader says nothing, does nothing, except slowly twist the pencil in his hand, tipping it back and forth against his fingers. Left, right. Left, right. Oh, the bastard plays a hard game. Hezekiah's eyes water. He rubs them, longs now, too, for his bed.

'Thirty thousand pounds. At the very least.'

A tic, a twitch. Hezekiah's confidence rises. He brings it home.

'Forty per cent of the takings will go to you, of course.'

The man watches him for one long drawn-out moment, and Hezekiah is fearful he has overstepped himself, that it all sounds too improbable, too beyond the realms of reality. But then the trader cracks a smile, gifts him a gold tooth.

'Well, Mr Blake.' He opens the book once more, poises the pencil.

313

'Let me see this artefact. If it is as you say, then it seems we have an accord.'

He will celebrate. It is only right.

As Hezekiah wends his way slowly, painfully home – past Long Acre, down through the Strand – he spies a shop that seems already to be awake. A single candle shines through the window and Hezekiah raps on the glass, his eye already on the handsome leather coin purse hanging from a hook on the wall behind the counter.

He is admitted, the purse wrapped in tissue paper, and Hezekiah is just thinking about his bed, a hearty breakfast, some gin to dull the pain in his leg and then (his stomach trilling with anticipation), a full day to bask in his longed-for rewards, when the clerk states his price.

'Charge it to my account. Hezekiah Blake, of Blake's Emporium.'

The clerk blinks at him. 'Oh, no, sir,' he says. 'I'm afraid that is not possible.'

Hezekiah stares. 'What nonsense is this?'

'No nonsense, sir. We won't be offering credit any more, certainly not until your account is in order.'

'*In order?*'

'In order,' the clerk repeats. 'Cash only.'

He cannot fathom it. It is too early, he has had a trying night, he has had no sleep.

'You have had my custom for years! All the shops along this stretch of road have had my custom, and none have complained as you have.'

'You have taken, sir, many a ware, but you have not given back. Even if the taxes had not risen to prevent credit, your debts would have been called in. There has been no payment on your account for over six months.'

Hezekiah cannot help it. His anger comes upon him like a wave and before he knows it he is slamming his fist onto the glass counter; it shudders under his weight.

'Do you know who I am?' he breathes, quite unable to contain himself. 'I am an esteemed trader! I run an antiquity shop! In fact, I am due very shortly to make a prestigious sale. A *very* prestigious sale. You will be paid in full then. In the meantime—'

'In the meantime, sir,' comes the reply, 'you must wait. We have plenty of coin purses. This one will keep.'

It is unwarranted. Never before has this happened. But Hezekiah knows as he looks into the pointed face of the clerk that he will not win this argument, not today, and so he turns with as much disdain as he can muster (and as best he can on a bad leg), and leaves the shop without a backward glance.

# CHAPTER
# THIRTY-SEVEN

Edward has not crossed the Thames since he has lived in London, not since the stagecoach brought him in when he was twelve years old. Even then, he did not go near the docks, did not see the squalor there, and when he passes an old man sleeping naked (*is* he sleeping?) against an empty barrel Edward wonders if what he suffered at the hands of Carrow was not so bad after all when compared to the circumstances in which some people are forced to live.

There is a mist over the river this morning. Edward covers his mouth at the stench of decay, not altogether sure if the mist *is* the stench. Can one *see* a smell?

Edward stops to find his bearings. When Coombe instructed him how to find his loft, that he must wade through mud to get to it, Edward thought he had been joking. *Cast right, past the crates*, he remembers the large man saying. Seeing them Edward continues on, is thankful this morning's frost has gone some way to hardening the earth, but he keeps to the wooden boards – recently lain, it seems – that have been placed down on the ground.

He almost misses the stairs, and eyes the rotting wood dubiously. Will they take his weight? But then, he reasons, if they can take Coombe's immense size surely they can take his. One-handed (his other hand still covers his nose and mouth) he pulls himself up the perilous steps. At the top, he knocks on the door.

Edward frowns. No answer. He realises he is early, but after last night, after Dora . . . Not for the first time this morning he relives it, experiences the anger churn in his gut.

They followed her in. Through the apartment door, past the terrified woman who pointed up and so up they went, to the very top of the house, to the cramped attic room that had been ransacked, Dora's belongings – he had not realised how meagre they would be – spread out across the floor. And there she was, on her knees, her back to the door, and Edward left Cornelius at the threshold, approached her, hand outstretched . . .

He will never forget her face. Will never forget the tender way she cradled the dead magpie in her lap.

Shock, Cornelius had said. Dora spoke not one word when they helped her up, not one word in the carriage, not one word when – disinclined to wake Mrs Howe – they put her to bed themselves in one of Cornelius' guest bedrooms, and Edward decided then and there he would see Matthew Coombe as soon as possible.

He will make Hezekiah pay for what he has done.

Edward will make up for what *he* has done.

He knocks again. Still nothing. Edward turns to leave but something, some feeling, a premonition perhaps, makes him think better of it. He pushes the door open and, unnervingly, it gives easily.

If Edward thought the smell outside was bad, he was not prepared for this. Even through his hand he can smell it – a fetid mix he cannot even begin to describe – that has him gagging into his palm. He puts his other hand to his pocket, pulls out a handkerchief, presses this to his face instead. It helps, somewhat, but not by much.

He forces himself into the room. And it is, it transpires, a room; no

317

others leading off, only a sheet drawn across the length of it. A crate acts as a table, nearby, three rickety-looking chairs. In the corner there is a small stove and what Edward thinks to be an old bureau standing on its right, its drawers open. Nothing else. How does Coombe live like this? How can anyone?

Edward looks at the sheet. It is dirty, stained with patches of brown. He does not want to know what is behind it, does not want to see, but it is as if his feet have a mind of their own and he is crossing the room. He stands in front of the sheet, breathing deep into the handkerchief. Then, with his free hand, he moves the sheet aside.

'Jesus Christ!'

He staggers backward and, unable to keep it in, vomits violently on the floor. Edward drops the handkerchief – useless now – and takes deep heaving breaths, runs a shaking hand over his eyes.

I'm not cut out for this, he thinks, this is beyond me. *Who could have done such a thing?*

But he knows the answer. He knows all too well.

Edward swallows, grounds himself. Then, very slowly, he moves the sheet again.

Behind the sheet are three cots. On each, a man.

The nearest looks to have been dead a while. The skin is blotched yellow, the eyes are wide open, glassy, and the mouth is crusted white at the corners. The pillow beneath the man's head is stained brown. Yet, oddly, it is not this – horrific though it is – that has his stomach threatening to heave once more.

Edward forces himself to look.

If it were not for the blood-soaked pillow, he would have thought the second man was sleeping. Perhaps, Edward thinks, that's how he did it – a coward's kill. Stabbed in his sleep, in the neck. Bled through fast. Never knew a thing. But the third man . . . It is possible Coombe was also sleeping since there are no obvious signs of a struggle, but

318

the blade did not kill him outright. Maybe Hezekiah missed his mark. Maybe – but Edward will not get close enough to confirm the fact – he had to stab him three or even four times in quick succession before the knife did its job. There is no blood spatter on the wall, but the bed sheets twisted at Coombe's legs are soaked through, a rich deep scarlet. Bled out and down, then. There is a look of horror on the man's face, his eyes wide with surprise or fright or, Edward thinks grimly, both. Coombe lies with his arm – or what Edward thinks to be an arm – flung over the side of the bed, pustulated and black, like a charred beam of wood.

Edward lets the sheet fall, pinches his eyes shut, but the vision swims behind his eyelids, indefinitely imprinted. He tries to breathe, to think.

What now? Who else can he ask? What more can he do? Nothing here, that at least is certain. Unsteady he retreats, knocking over one of the chairs in his haste. Though it can hardly matter Edward bends to pick it up, and as he turns away to leave again a flash of orange catches the corner of his eye.

He pauses. Frowns.

The stove has been recently lit.

Edward approaches it cautiously, crouches down, and when he opens the soot-covered door the embers inside burn brightly for a second before fading again with a soft *spit*. Within, Edward can just make out the remains of some papers, their pages blackened, edges curled in on themselves like dried leaves.

Very carefully, he reaches in. The papers are still warm though not hot, and while some disintegrate at his touch he manages to remove a hefty bulk. Edward places them on the floor, attempts to sift through the pages. If he squints and angles his head he can just make out what looks to be shipping forecasts, tide times, lists of cargo ships.

Edward sighs, turns a page.

319

They are practically illegible. But then, some pages down the pile where the paper has not quite caught alight, his eye chances on some names: *Eagle, Rosita, Vanguard, Colossus*. Edward pauses, sucks in his breath. *Colossus!* These must be a record of Hezekiah's transactions. He shakes his head. A pity, then, no sense can be made of them. It is only when Edward begins to gather them together again that he sees something else further down the charred page. A series of letters, written in childlike cursive:

JONATIBPUD.DOK

Edward stares at it for a long moment. A cipher? Well, it can be no harder than the Shugborough one, surely. He tilts his head, reads it aloud, and as he does so his face clears, the simple meaning hitting home.

The second dock of the morning, and this one smells no better than the last.

Edward approaches the laystall, determined not to let the stink of shit put him off. A gull cries sharply across the sky and he glances up between two towering buildings with boarded-up windows, watches its arced flight path behind a chimney.

'Watch it!'

Edward catches himself just in time to swerve around a night-soil man pushing a cart – thankfully empty, though still reeking – and the man walks unceremoniously past him, up the ramp Edward is walking down. Edward mutters an apology, but it is lost over the bustle of morning traffic and he does not bother to call after him. In the last forty-eight hours he has felt so much older – the things he has heard, the things he has seen . . . He has no energy, no mind any more to care if he has upset anyone. The image of Coombe's blood-soaked body swims in his mind's eye. Was his quest for recognition really worth all this? If he had known that meeting Pandora Blake would result in so much chaos, would he have done it? Would he have listened to the old man who helped him that day in the coffee-house? A part of him is not sure.

Edward continues down the sloping ramp to the river's edge, looking for the man he saw the day he and Dora transported the pithos to Lady Latimer's. He does not see him at first amidst the crowd of labourers hauling carts of excrement onto a waiting barge, and for a moment Edward panics, wonders if he has misinterpreted Coombe's infantile scrawl, but then he sees him. The man named Tibb has removed his cap, is scratching his ear, and Edward rushes forward, his boots sinking into the gritty sand.

'Jonas Tibb?'

The man turns. He looks Edward up and down, but there is no spark of recognition.

'Mr Tibb, my name is Edward Lawrence. I was with Miss Blake and Mr Coombe when you transported a vase to Lady Latimer's the other day.'

'Ah, yes.' Tibb frowns. 'You were pushing your nose into business that wasn't your own.'

Edward bristles. 'Thing is, Mr Tibb, it *is* my business now, and yours too, I have no doubt.'

There must be something in his tone, for Tibb shoots him a wary look. He shoves his cap down on his head again, covering his ears.

'Listen, I just do what the money tells me to. It isn't my business to know more than I need to. Knowing things,' he says with a grimace, 'gets you in trouble.'

'Yes, sir,' Edward says, and gives a humourless laugh. 'That I can attest to. And Matthew Coombe too, it turns out.'

Tibb screws his eyes. 'Eh?'

Edward sighs. 'I think you know I am here to ask about Hezekiah Blake. His dealings, what you know of them.'

'I know very little. Now if you'll excuse me.'

The man makes to get by him but Edward places a hand on the flat of Tibb's chest.

'Coombe is dead.'

This stops him.

'What?'

'I found his body – and two others – in his lodgings. Not half an hour ago.'

Tibb stares. Something shifts on his face. He stamps his feet, buries his hands into his coat pockets.

'This way,' he says quietly.

The man leads him back up the ramp, past the night-soil men, done for the night, seeking their beds. Edward slows, struck by the variety of men under Tibb's employ – men of all different colours and creeds, men who by their differences have been relegated to such lowly work – and again it occurs to Edward how lucky he is. He thinks too of Fingle, his position at the bindery, what it must mean to him to have achieved the security of a stable position and the respect that so many of his fellow men are denied, and Edward swallows, feels ashamed for acting so churlishly toward him in the past.

'Mr Lawrence?'

Edward looks back to Tibb, picks up his pace. Tibb ducks down a small alley, so small Edward did not see it walking past, and shows him through a weathered door into the tiniest office Edward has ever seen. The foreman gestures to a stool, shuts the door behind him, then seats himself at another tucked behind a table no wider than the stool itself.

322

'Matthew Coombe is dead, you say? His brothers too?'

'The state of them . . .' Edward pales at the memory. 'You could hardly tell.'

Tibb grimaces. 'Do you know how?'

'The one looked like he'd been dead more than a few hours. A day, perhaps. His skin was mottled. Bloated, maybe.'

The other man nods. 'Matthew said Sam caught a fever. And Charlie? Matthew himself?'

Edward tightens his grip on the stool-edge. 'Stabbed, I think. Charlie in the neck, Matthew in the chest, multiple times from what I could see through the mess.'

Tibb closes his eyes. 'Poor bastards. But I'd be surprised if Hezekiah did it. He hasn't got the guts for something like that.'

'You'd be surprised what lengths people will go to given the right motivation.'

Tibb says nothing to this. Edward takes a breath.

'Mr Tibb, you know things. Things I need to know. It is my understanding that Hezekiah is involved in contraband trade. Matthew Coombe hinted as much. He was going to tell me. That's why I went to see him.' Again Tibb says nothing. Edward ploughs on. 'There is a chance he is involved in far worse. Aside from the death of the Coombes, of which I am convinced he is responsible, it seems Hezekiah is also responsible for the deaths of his brother and sister-in-law.'

Still Tibb says nothing. Edward begins to lose patience.

'Please, sir. A lady's life is at stake. You remember her, don't you? The girl on the cart?'

'The niece.'

'Yes. The niece. Her name is Dora.'

Tibb touches his lip with his tongue. 'Her life, you say?'

'You heard me.' A pause. 'Please, sir. Help me. Help her.'

The man sighs deeply, runs a dirty hand over his face, stares down at his lap. After a moment he says, 'You have to understand, I truly know very little. I never asked questions. I was paid not to.'

Finally. He is getting somewhere.

'Just tell me what you do know,' Edward says, as smoothly as he can.

Tibb removes his cap again, begins to twist it in his hands.

'I met Hezekiah about sixteen years ago. The shop wasn't his then, as I understand it, but he'd begun to trade in his own right. Whether his brother knew or not, I don't know.'

Edward smiles grimly. He suspects Elijah knew all too well.

'One summer he approached me. I remember it was summer, because Hezekiah commented that the stench would be the perfect cover. No one would bother to search a laystall, he said, for unregistered shipments. He said he would pay me ten pounds a year to make space for a boat and send messengers whenever one made port. I was to ask no questions, and I never did. Ten pounds is a lot of money for a man like me.'

Edward nods. It is a lot. Far more than his regular pay would give him.

Tibb clears his throat.

'But sixteen years is a long time. You recognise patterns. You hear things. He had contacts in other countries, I know that. Every month there would be a shipment. Some large, some small, but regular, all in crates so I never saw what was in them. The Coombes came on board about seven years ago. I haven't a clue where Hezekiah found them, he just told me I was to accommodate them and their boat whenever he requested, and he'd pay me an extra five pounds a year for the inconvenience.

'Every six months he would have letters arrive from Greece. Then, last year, he received a letter from Italy. Palermo. I remember at the time because he'd never had one from there before. Letters usually came from Naples, if they came from Italy at all. I also hadn't seen Matthew for a number of weeks. Then, in December, he turns up. Babbled about a shipwreck, how he'd barely escaped with his life. But soon after he was off again, Sam and Charlie with him. And Hezekiah . . .' Tibb shakes his head. 'I'd never seen him like it before. Came down to the dock near every day the week before they came back. He wanted that shipment. Was desperate for it, which I thought odd since he had instructed them to come the long way round.'

'The long way?'

Tibb nods. Twists the cap. 'It would have been faster by road after they reached the mainland from Samson. But they came the whole way by sea, a crate in tow. Matthew made some great fuss about it being cursed.'

Edward blinks. This is new.

'Cursed?'

Tibb waves the cap. 'I took no notice, of course. You should see some of the people who arrive at the docks after a sea voyage. Many haven't seen land for months. It's no wonder their wits are gone. But Hezekiah was furious. They took it away. I didn't see either of them again until the day we delivered to the Latimer place.' Tibb frowns. 'I did wonder why Matthew wasn't with us when Hezekiah employed us to collect it again. I just assumed he'd sent him off somewhere else.'

Edward is quiet, thinks a moment on all he has heard.

'Is there anything else, Mr Tibb?'

'Nothing I can recall,' the man replies. 'Like I said, I know very little. I turned a blind eye to most things, was paid well to do so. I hope I have been of some help.'

But Edward is nodding, stepping down from the stool. He holds out his hand for Tibb to shake. Hesitant, the man takes it in his own.

'You have been a great help. Thank you, Mr Tibb. You've told me all I need to know.'

As he turns to leave, Edward pauses, his conscience pulling him back.

'They're still there. The Coombe brothers. I . . .'

Tibb notes the look on Edward's face, gives a grim nod.

'I'll see to them.'

Mute, he chucks his chin in thanks. And as Edward makes his escape, the image of Matthew Coombe's blood-soaked body follows him all the way up from Puddle Dock Hill like a plague.

# CHAPTER
# THIRTY-EIGHT

She does not know where she is at first. The room is silent, dappled dark by curtains that do not quite block out the daylight. Dora shifts under the covers, her body sinking into the unfamiliar bed. She spreads her hands out on the coverlet. Velvet. Periwinkle blue. She looks about her, at the framed pictures on the walls: all Oriental, all scenic, a collection of mountains, forests, lakes, pretty floral scenes. She stares for a long moment at one depicting three white butterflies, little black dots on their wings, fluttering over tufts of ornamental grass. Then a bird trills its midday song and she remembers it all.

Desolate, she listens to the birdsong. Hermes. For so long he was her only friend. And Hezekiah has taken him from her. But why? She does not understand. Why harm him, if not for spite? He always disliked him, always mocked her love of him, her dearest dear heart. With a sob Dora buries her face into the pillow. Soft, plush, clean. Nothing like the ones from home.

*Home.*

Another blow. The realisation that Blake's Emporium – the place she has always known to be her one true constant – is no longer her home and never will be again, makes her ribcage hurt.

Of her parents, she will not think.

She lies, staring at the ceiling, for over an hour. It is only when, somewhere in the house, she hears a clock chime half past one that she begins to stir.

Dora pushes away the covers, is gratified to see she still wears her dress. No one attempted to disrobe her, then. That is something. But it is as she is pulling on her slippers over her still-stockinged feet that she realises she *must* go back. The dress she wears . . . Dora looks down at it. Creased. Dirt on its hem. The sleeve is ripped. It will not do indefinitely.

She goes to the dressing table by the window, looks at herself in its oval mirror. Her olive skin is pale, dark circles cup her eyes like smudged half-moons. Dora attempts to tuck an errant curl back into the green ribbon still pinned in her hair but it is no use. Without a brush to run through it, it will remain untamed. No, she must go back. And the sooner the better. But she will not risk setting eyes on Hezekiah, if she can help it.

*In, out, be done.*

Mr Ashmole must have heard her descent, as halfway down the stairs he steps into the hall to greet her. He has been waiting for me, Dora thinks, and when he greets her at the bottom tread she does not know what to say. He too, it seems, is as tongue-tied as she.

'How did you sleep?' he asks eventually.

'I slept,' she says. 'That is something in itself, I suppose.'

Despite it all, Dora cannot keep the dislike from her voice, the remembrance of the part he played in Edward's duplicity, and Mr Ashmole has the good grace to flush. He looks away, looks instead at the carriage clock. It now says nearly two.

'You slept deeply.'

It is a redundant thing to say. Mr Ashmole seems to know it as well, for he shifts awkwardly on the soles of his feet. The sight irritates her.

'What have you done with Hermes?'

Her tone is over-sharp, accusatory. Mr Ashmole raises his hands, palms facing her, fingers spread wide in defence.

'Mrs Howe has him in the cold store. He is . . .' Mr Ashmole appears to test the suitability of the next word, 'preserved, until you decide what you want to do with him. I can have him stuffed, if you like?'

There is a hint of the sardonic tone Dora is used to, but his attempt at humour falls flat and Dora simply stares at him.

'I wish to bury him.'

Mr Ashmole catches his ill-received quip on a short nod. 'I have a garden.'

The carriage clock ticks loudly in its casement, the turn of the cogs matching perfectly the pulse of blood in her head.

'I need to go back to the shop,' Dora says. 'To fetch my things.'

He nods again, gestures behind her. 'Your cape and gloves . . .'

She turns to find them draped over the newel cap. She reaches for them.

Mr Ashmole watches Dora pull on the gloves, tie the cape around her neck. He seems to struggle with something – she can see from the corner of her eye how he fidgets, opens his mouth, closes it, then opens it once more.

'Would you like me to come with you?' he says at last, and she does not miss a beat.

'No.' Her voice comes out sharp again. This time she does not mean it to. 'No,' Dora says again, more softly, and ignoring his attempt at gallantry she moves past him, opens the heavy door herself, steps down into the cold street.

How long she stands in front of the shop she does not know. It seems to Dora that one moment she is outside Clevendale and the next she is standing in front of Blake's Emporium's peeling facade without any memory of how she got there or how long the journey took. It is as if she is in a daze; as if her brain has registered what has happened, what her night at Sir William's revealed, but her heart is completely incapable of accepting it. She comprehends but does not feel, sees but remains blind to implication, and on understanding *that* Dora does not know how to act in the face of it.

Still. She cannot stay out here all day.

*In, out. Be done.*

Shaking herself, Dora pushes on the door. The bell jangles. She is almost relieved to find only Lottie standing in the middle of the room, a broom in her hand. They stare at each other for a long moment. Dora closes the door.

'Where is he?' she asks, and Dora sees the tremor of the housekeeper's chin which she fails to hide.

'Out, again,' Lottie says. Quiet. Hesitant. 'I'm not sure where.'

But really Dora is past caring where her uncle has disappeared off to.

'You've cleaned.'

The shelf is upright again, the broken crockery gone. The dust, too. Lottie flushes awkward pink.

'You was always at me to do it, weren't you?'

Dora stares. Lottie stares back. When Dora keeps silent the housekeeper bites her lip.

'I'm so sorry about your bir—'

'No,' Dora cuts in. 'We shall not speak of it. I don't want to hear.'

This is a lie, she admits to herself as she climbs up to the attic room. But she cannot think on it now. She must not. She means to collect her things, leave before Hezekiah returns. No, now is not the time to let emotion rule her.

It is in this frame of mind that Dora scoops up her dresses, petti-coats, chemises. The carpet bag of her mother's – Dora's mouth twists when she sees the rip – is just serviceable enough for her clothes not to fall through, but she lines the bottom with one of her older dresses anyway, folds the rest inside.

She breathes a sigh of relief when she finds her spectacles – mercifully undamaged – but pauses when she sees the coin purse, the tinderbox, and her copy of the basement key. So, Dora thinks, he found it. Then she pauses, the realisation bringing her up short.

*He found it.*

What on earth was he looking for?

'Missum?'

Dora looks up. Lottie stands at the door. Clutched in her hands is Dora's sketchbook.

'You left this beneath the counter.' The housekeeper takes a small step into the room. 'I hope you don't mind but I looked through it. They're . . .' Lottie takes a breath. 'They're very good.'

'What do you want, Lottie?' Dora says, what little patience she had quite spent. The headache that has been threatening to dig its finger-nails into her skull since her walk over has finally begun its incessant burrow. 'You've never been this nice to me. What is it? Guilt?'

'Yes.'

Dora blinks. She did not expect that. Neither, it seems, did Lottie, for she blushes deep, fumbles the sketchbook, and it falls from her hands, slams onto the floorboards.

'Why?'

But Lottie is shaking her head and Dora hurts too much to press her.

'Please yourself,' she mutters, packing the rest of her things into the bag – her mother's cameo, a hairbrush, the jewellery supplies, her designs (the mock-cannetille has a wire snapped), scissors, thread – while Lottie continues to hover at the attic's lopsided door.

331

It is when Dora finally brings herself to turn to the cage and pick up one of the soft rainbow-shot feathers on the floor that the house-keeper speaks again.

'He is selling it.'

Very gently Dora strokes the feather. She feels a lump begin to form in her throat and she puts the feather into the bag too before the lump can take shape and choke her.

'Selling it?'

'The vase.'

The pithos. The source of her misery. All of it, as it turns out.

'To whom?'

'I don't know. He had a man come this morning to see it. He's going to auction it off.'

'I see.'

But what is it to her now? As Sir William said, there is no proof. None then, and certainly none now. So what difference does it make to her if Hezekiah is finally selling it?

'I saw your drawings. In the book.' Lottie nods at it, still marooned on the floorboards. 'You . . . you haven't finished sketching it, have you?'

'No,' Dora says, faint.

'Why were you drawing it?'

Dora takes a breath. 'For my jewellery. For . . .' She stops. Her lips twist.

For Edward.

'Then if you want to finish it,' suggests the housekeeper, 'you'd best be quick about it.' When Dora finally meets her gaze, Lottie looks grave. 'You see, missum, he means to move it to an auction house next week.'

# CHAPTER
# THIRTY-NINE

He finds a letter waiting for him at his lodgings, redirected from the bindery in Tobias Fingle's tight, spidery hand, and staring down at it Edward realises he has not been in to work for days. Had he much to do? He tries to picture his little candle-filled room, the side table he uses to stack books due for finishing – cannot – and for the first time in his life Edward feels guilty about it.

The last few days have been a revelation. So many souls in this city have suffered, and continue to do so in ways he knows he cannot even begin to imagine. He thinks of Dora, the Coombe brothers, Jonas Tibb, the night-soil men shovelling shit day after day at the docks. He thinks of the child he saw from the carriage the night of the soirée, the naked man this morning. Edward is uncomfortably conscious of what liberties he has been allowed – the reasons for it, how his friendship with Cornelius has compounded them – but truth be told his torment is long done with, has been for years. There is no reason for his complacence, his resentment. Not any more. All that work, building up. Commissions left unfinished. No wonder the bindery lads despise him.

Before he opens the letter – a missive from Gough it seems, for the wax is stamped with the Society's seal – Edward writes one of his own to Fingle, promising his presence the next day. Dora, after all, has no wish to see him; she has made that perfectly clear. No matter what his future plans, no matter what happens between him and Dora, he still has commitments to uphold. A day or two without him might do them both the world of good.

He scatters sand on the ink before he seals it. Then, Edward snaps the seal of Gough's letter. As he scans the lines he gives a wry smile.

Gough's scientists confirm everything that Hamilton has already told him. The pithos originated in southern Greece, with markers suggesting the Peloponnese. It is not to be taken as foolproof accuracy – science, Gough warns, has not progressed so far as that – but it is a good indication. Will Edward please see him at his earliest convenience?

Had matters not progressed as they have, Edward would be reaching again for the coat he has not long discarded. But he has now more important things to attend to – his application to the Society has paled in significance to all he has seen and done these last few hours. Instead Edward goes to his washstand, takes his time to clean the stench and memory of London's docklands from his skin.

Sir William shows Edward into a room at the far back of the house that he is using (so he tells Edward) as his office until Lady Hamilton takes it upon herself to commandeer it in the name of redecoration. As Edward settles himself in a deep leather chair, he looks about him.

Hamilton has spared no space. The loss of half his collection on the *Colossus* does not seem to have dented the overall collection itself. With that one room in the house accommodating a small museum, and this room showcasing many of the diplomat's favourite pieces – the man in question points to a vase very similar to the Portland one he sold some years before (his deepest regret, says he) – it is clear he has been collecting extensively near half his life.

'Grecian pottery was not my preference, you know,' Edward says, accepting without hesitation the brandy Sir William offers over the leather-topped desk. While his body is clean from this morning his mind still reels from what it has seen, and though the clock has only just struck one Edward has no qualms about drinking something far stronger than tea.

'No?' Hamilton says, seating himself opposite. 'What was?'

'In truth, no particular thing. I read excessively when I was younger, anything I could get my hands on. But the idea of understanding the past through the artefacts left behind . . . It thrilled me. Still does.'

Sir William smiles. 'You have the heart of a true antiquarian, Mr Lawrence. My love of antiquities will always be for the ones of Mediterranean origin. I find the myth and mystery of it all quite enchanting.'

The conversation has steered to Edward's reason for coming altogether too swiftly. He thinks of Tibb's word – *cursed* – takes a deep sip of the brandy to calm his nerves. It sears, strong and hot, down his throat, and Edward raises his fist to cover a cough.

Hamilton chuckles. 'Sixteen forty-nine. A strong year.' He raises his own glass. 'Did you know that in ancient Greece people used brandy as both an antiseptic and an anaesthetic? There are accounts of Arab alchemists in the seventh and eighth centuries experimenting with distilling grapes and other fruits to create medicinal spirits.'

'I did not,' Edward says, voice catching in his throat. His eyes water.

'A history lesson for you, then. But you are not here for an account of distilled spirits.' Sir William's face grows serious. 'What did you discover?'

For some minutes Edward relays the events of the night before and this morning – Hermes' death, the discovery of the Coombe brothers' bodies in the loft, the papers he found in the stove, the code-like missive directing Edward to Puddle Dock. He recounts the conversation with Jonas Tibb in as much detail as possible, and Hamilton listens in silence the whole time, a long finger pressed against the bow of his mouth. When Edward concludes his account, Sir William frowns deeply before taking a long sip of his drink.

'But this Tibb said nothing about where the Coombes took these shipments when they arrived in London?'

'No, but since I found so many pieces in the shop's basement—'

Sir William shakes his head. 'The shop is by no means the only place these pieces went. Hezekiah must have been trading them somewhere else; he wouldn't risk selling them in his home. Have you not heard the expression, "Do not foul one's own nest"?'

Edward nods.

'You see, then. And you're sure Tibb said nothing else?'

'I'm afraid not. As he adamantly made clear, he was paid not to ask questions.'

'And you thought him trustworthy?'

'I believe so, yes. He seemed a simple man.'

Hamilton's eyebrows rise.

'What I mean is, simple in his needs. You should have seen the place,' Edward adds. 'He didn't want trouble. The trade he holds – as distasteful as we might find it – is a necessary one to be sure, but I can imagine it provides him with barely enough to live on. The money Hezekiah laid out would have made quite a bit of difference to him.'

And then Edward is struck with a thought. If Hezekiah is brought to task Tibb's pockets will soon grow empty, and that will all be Edward's fault.

'Then we are at an impasse,' Sir William says now. 'If we cannot find out where Hezekiah is illicitly trading or discover witnesses to his crimes, then we will struggle to prove any foul play on his behalf. A pity those papers you found were useless. What little you could discern from them is no help without the context. Impossible to interpret.' Hamilton sucks his teeth. 'What I would give to have Hezekiah in gaol. He's always been a wily bastard.'

Together, they drink. This time the brandy goes down a little easier.

'Tibb said,' Edward begins, hesitant, 'that Coombe was convinced the pithos is cursed.'

Sir William sends him a dry look over the rim of his glass. 'The essence of antiquarianism is a focus on the empirical evidence of the past. It's perhaps best encapsulated in the motto adopted by Sir Richard Hoare – we speak from facts, not theory.'

'He sounds like Gough,' Edward says.

Hamilton inclines his head. 'There are many who share their views. It does no good to dwell on such things when facts stare us in the face. We, as human beings, can invariably be split into two types: those who believe in magic, and those who do not. Can an object really have power over man? Or is it only coincidence that bad things happen around such an object?'

'I personally feel that the line between coincidence and fate is very thin,' Edward says stubbornly, and Sir William sits back in his chair.

'Please, Mr Lawrence, do not make me think less of you.'

'Did you not just say that you found myth and mystery enticing?'

'Yes, but the idea of it, nothing more. Reality is often rooted in myth. Helen, Dora's mother, did not believe in the myth of Pandora's Box but that did not mean the box itself didn't exist in some form or other, which is what she set out to prove.' Hamilton seems to see the frustration building in Edward, and the diplomat gives him a kindly smile. 'Coombe believed the pithos to be cursed. I do not. The pithos did not cause the shipwreck. Bad weather did. Nor did the pithos cause the dig site to collapse all those years before. Hezekiah did. And Hezekiah was ruled not by an ancient piece of pottery but by greed, pure and simple.'

Edward is silent a moment. 'At Lady Latimer's you said you always knew Hezekiah to be a deceitful man. Just now you said he was wily. What did you mean?'

Sir William twists his near-empty glass. 'Do you remember what Dora said last night? She said her parents and Hezekiah argued in the days leading up to their deaths. All the time, she said, and she was right. I overheard them in their tent.' Hamilton fills his glass, offers more to Edward who declines.

'Hezekiah was among the party when I met Elijah and Helen in Naples. I disliked him on sight, but I tolerated him for their sake. I understand Hezekiah sold some of the larger and more valuable pieces they found on their behalf, and they let him run the shop in Elijah's name on the occasions he and Helen went off on their own. I don't know the full details. Pride, I suspect, made Elijah reticent in his account of the situation but Helen was a little more forthcoming. She'd suspected for a while that Hezekiah had been selling some of their pieces unlawfully.

'The arguments Dora referred to were in reference to the pithos. Hezekiah knew they would get more money from it in underhand circles than they ever would if they sold it above board. You see, for centuries smuggled goods have provided a cheap alternative to expensive imports. Taxes on imported goods make many of them costly. But illegal, smuggled goods provide a solution to the problem. Brandy –' Sir William raises his glass – 'tobacco and tea prove to be popular commodities on an increasingly popular black-market. And, as we have ascertained, antiquities. Both the Government and the

338

East India Company are hugely worried about the loss of money caused by smuggling. They've calculated that three million pounds of tea a year has been smuggled over the last forty years or so, three times the amount of legal sales. If they were caught . . .' Hamilton shakes his head. 'The Blake name was at risk. To be connected with such a thing, even if Elijah and Helen were not directly responsible, could mean their execution. There was no way around that. So, you can understand why Elijah was furious. The night before they died, Elijah and Helen ordered Hezekiah home.' The diplomat looks at Edward gravely across the desk. 'As I intimated last night, Mr Lawrence, I think Hezekiah Blake killed Dora's parents. And I am pretty sure he meant to kill Dora as well.'

Edward swallows the last of his brandy, places the glass down carefully on the desk in front of him.

'Here, then, is something I don't understand.' Edward meets Sir William's grave look. 'If you know Hezekiah killed them, why didn't you report him at the time?'

A pained expression crosses Hamilton's features. He puts his own glass down before him and sighs.

'I was afraid you would ask me that. But please, I beg you not to judge me too harshly. I judge myself badly enough. I am thoroughly ashamed.'

'Sir?'

The diplomat sits back heavily in his chair. 'When I said last night that I had no proof, that is indeed true. It would have been Hezekiah's word against mine. But Hezekiah Blake is no fool and certainly did not take me for one, more's the pity. He and Dora stayed in a hotel I procured for them after the dig was closed. I visited her every day, tried to offer her consolation, returned the cameo brooch Helen had been wearing. Christ, the child was changed almost overnight. A joyful little thing she was, but understandably her grief was acute. She became so quiet, so withdrawn. Dora clung to that brooch as though it were a lifeline.'

Sir William shakes his head at the memory. Edward's chest constricts. He has seen Dora wear the cameo often, but it never occurred to him what the brooch might mean.

'How awful for her.'

'Yes.' Hamilton hesitates. 'I noticed some hostility between you and Dora last night,' he says, and Edward winces, his guilt rising once more.

'During the soirée she discovered I had been writing about the shop, her uncle's underhand trading. I tried to tell her that I'd mentioned no names but she would not hear my explanation. I wrote to her yesterday morning but she did not acknowledge my letter. So, when next we saw each other . . .'

'I see.' Sir William's lip twists in a wry sort of smile. 'You can hardly blame her anger.'

Edward has no defence, none that will sound acceptable.

'Give her time,' Hamilton says gently. 'The truth always comes out. One way or another.'

Edward drains his glass, places it down on Sir William's desk with more force than he means. He attempts a smile, gestures for the diplomat to continue. 'You said Hezekiah did not take you for a fool?'

Hamilton clears his throat. 'No. I asked Hezekiah what his plans were. Posed some not-so-subtle questions to him.'

'Such as?'

He spreads his hands. 'How did you escape? Why weren't your clothes filthy? Why does your wound look so clean-cut? His answers were always unsatisfactorily vague. Obviously Hezekiah knew I suspected him, though I never outright said the words. Indeed, what he said to me next made that perfectly clear.'

'Which was?'

Sir William wipes a hand across his jaw. 'As you are aware, I have collected many fine pieces over the years. Many of which I sold on to buyers overseas. However. There are strict laws forbidding the export of antiquities from the Kingdom of Naples. I thought perhaps, due to my close relationship with him, the King might make an exception for me. But he denied my request.' Hamilton sniffs. 'I'm afraid I did it anyway. I kept my dealings very quiet, so how Hezekiah knew this I do not know. But I suppose a crook always knows a crook, does he not?'

Edward stares at the diplomat in shock. 'You traded in contraband?'

Sir William raises his finger, sets Edward with a piercing look. 'No. No. I emphatically reject that accusation. They were mine to begin with. Money passed hands legally. Much of what I collected I donated to the British Museum. I ensured that the finest Mediterranean antiquities reached our shores to be celebrated, admired. I gave to the people. It was selfish of the King to deny such culture to the world.' Hamilton lowers his finger, allows himself a grimace. 'I am just sorry for the manner in which it was done. Exporting antiquities from Italy is a capital offence. It is illegal. I am – was – the British ambassador to the Court of Naples, and here in England I am a much-respected member of the peerage. I need not say, need I, Mr Lawrence, what that would have meant for me, if Hezekiah had done as he hinted most indelicately that he might, which was to notify the authorities.'

Edward blinks. 'So he threatened you?'

'In not so many words, yes.'

The two men are quiet. Edward is torn. It is quite something to discover a man one admires has operated on the wrong side of the law, no matter how well he justifies the fact. But, he reasons, what is done is done; what is to come is far more important now.

341

'You let Hezekiah take Dora back to London,' Edward murmurs at length, and Sir William's expression darkens.

'How could I prevent it? On her parents' deaths Hezekiah became Dora's legal guardian.'

'Your position in society—'

'Carried weight, yes, but there were too many complicated factors to overcome. It was safer to let them go.'

Edward releases his breath. 'Weren't you worried Hezekiah might still try to harm her?'

'I feared that, certainly. I even had a man of mine report back to me every now and then, especially during the first year. But when it appeared she was safe in London, still with him . . .' Hamilton shrugs. 'It's been twelve years. I even began to doubt my original suspicion that he meant Dora ill – that it had simply been coincidence she became trapped in the collapse. She had, after all, only just descended the ladder. How could Hezekiah have known that? But recent behaviour seems to indicate otherwise, doesn't it? The Coombe brothers. Dora's bird . . .' Sir William shakes his head. 'No, Mr Lawrence. I am convinced now that Hezekiah has kept her alive all this time for a reason. I just don't know what that reason is.'

# CHAPTER FORTY

Mr Ashmole has allowed Dora, much to her amazement and against her better judgement, to use the small sitting room at the front of the house for her workshop. A small bureau has been brought in from another room; her jewellery supplies now sit neatly in its drawers, her wire and ribbon and lace reels comfortably arranged on its shelves, with plenty of room for her sketchbook to open at its fullest. She runs her hands over the rosewood, smooth and shining beneath her palms, smells the fresh coat of beeswax on its polished surface. It is the nicest thing she has ever worked at. The chair (one of the silk damasks) is the most comfortable she has sat on whilst creating her designs. Nothing at all to her own tiny desk, the too-high stool. Nothing at all to the shop counter. This new set-up is vastly superior to both.

Yet.

The paper in front of her is empty. The inspiration that took hold of her the day Miss Ponsenby and her kin came through the doors of Blake's Emporium has disappeared, to be replaced with only a listlessness, a frustrating blank in the space of her mind.

She pushes her spectacles up her nose.

It is not the first time inspiration has thwarted her. Invariably all creative minds dwindle every now and then. But the one thing that would have brought her solace is buried beneath a rosebush in Mr

Ashmole's garden and so she has nothing to comfort her, nothing to ease her artistic drought.

Absently Dora turns the pages of the sketchbook, looks at her past creations. The most recent sketches are with Mr Clements – Dora notes she must return to fetch them and the money she is owed – but the others, the cannetille necklace with its glass stone (now mended and hanging around her neck), the three pairs of earrings, the bracelet in pinchbeck and garnet, the two Vauxhall brooches, the ribbon-tie necklace of agate, all the creations that came before.

She flicks to the very back. To the drawings of the pithos.

Here is the outline, the ghost-sketches of the carvings. And here, the carvings themselves. Dora studies them, and deep down she feels pride in the way she has executed the details. There had been four in total, but Dora has managed to draw only three. She thinks about what Lottie told her, that Hezekiah will soon be removing the pithos, that her chance to finish the drawings will be gone for ever.

Is that, she thinks, such a bad thing? She has taken from the pithos what she wanted. She does not need the sketches – only Edward will benefit from them now. Dora shuts her eyes. The anger she feels at his deceit is still there but it has been dampened, as if someone has placed a cool cloth on a burn.

*You are entirely mistaken in your beliefs.*

And what is it she believes? That he has used Hezekiah's history of underhand trading for a study to further his career. This, she knows to be true. But what else? What else does he mean to do? Turn her uncle in to the authorities, and she along with him?

That theory simply does not sit right with her. It goes against everything she believes about him as a person. A friend. If not for Edward she would not be here at Clevendale, safe from Hezekiah. If he meant her harm he would have done it by now. Dora sighs, closes the sketchbook. No, she owes it to Edward to finish. She made a promise, after all.

344

Besides. There is another reason.

Tiredly Dora takes off her spectacles, puts the end of one of the arms between her teeth.

Why, she wonders, has it taken so long for Hezekiah to sell the pithos? What on earth was he doing all that time in the basement? Why was he searching her room? Why kill Hermes? She does not understand. None of it makes any sense. To find out she *must* go back, and soon.

Dora jumps as the door opens and she turns in the chair, a question on her tongue. Mrs Howe – who has taken the news that Dora appears to be a houseguest for the foreseeable future with not much enthusiasm – stands at the threshold. Her eyebrows are shooting up so high that Dora fears they may reach her hairline.

'A Lady Latimer to see you, miss.'

'Oh!' Dora stands. 'Please,' she says, rather awkwardly, for she is not used to giving orders, 'do send her in.'

And in she comes in plumes of periwinkle pink and overbearing lavender scent, her footman Horatio at her side.

'Miss Blake!' the old woman exclaims, white wig quivering precariously. 'Why is it I am being sent halfway across town and back again?'

'Madam?'

Lady Latimer sends her an impatient look. 'I reach your shop, only to be told by some uncouth woman that you have instructed all customers interested in your designs to come here instead. I assume that since I find you here this is correct.' At Dora's nod the old woman breezes on. 'It is most inconvenient. Do you have any notion, miss, how busy the traffic is at this time of day?'

'I'm afraid I don't, ma'am.'

'Of course you don't.' Lady Latimer glances around the room, spies the second damask chair and makes a beeline for it. Horatio follows her immediately. When the old woman reaches the chair the footman bends, lifts a fistful of skirts in his hands. 'Down,' Lady Latimer instructs, and as she sinks into the chair Horatio releases them. The pink silk billows before settling at her feet.

Dora must hide her amusement behind her hand, and all a-sudden she feels a wave of gratitude. It is the first time she has smiled in two days.

'Well, now,' Lady Latimer says, looking about her. 'It is a charming room, I must say.' Her eyes go to the cabinet next to the bureau Dora sits at. 'What pretty globes,' the old woman remarks, nodding at them lined together side by side. She turns her attention back to Dora. 'Now tell me, miss, why I find you here?'

The excuse is already on her tongue and it is the truth, too, or a version of the truth, at least.

'I had a disagreement with my uncle, Lady Latimer. I felt it would be best if I stayed elsewhere until I can set up an establishment of my own.'

Lady Latimer waves a bejewelled hand. 'Oh, yes, you are much better off without. That crumbling establishment of his does not suit your talents at all. Everyone was quite raving about you the day after my soirée.' She frowns. 'Although there was much complaining to be had too. It seems many of my guests were sick as dogs the next morning.'

'Oh?'

'Did you not hear? It was the punch, apparently.'

'Lady Hamilton did not say.'

Lady Latimer screws her nose. 'Emma does not partake of punch. She much prefers wine. But those who did . . . well, it is just as well they fell ill the day after. Imagine what would have happened to my potted ferns, Horatio! I can't bear to think on it.'

It is wise, Dora decides in this instance, to say nothing, but she thinks of the monkey she saw with its tail dangling in the punchbowl and wonders if that had much to do with it.

346

Lady Latimer is looking about her again, her head nodding every now and then with approval which makes her ridiculous wig bounce dangerously. Horatio seems ready to catch it at any moment.

'Your Mr Lawrence keeps a fine little house.'

Dora coughs, both at the implication and description. 'Little house' is not how she would describe Clevendale, but in comparison to Lady Latimer's own home Dora supposes it must indeed appear so.

'It does not belong to Mr Lawrence, ma'am.' The old woman blinks. 'This is Mr Ashmole's home.'

A pause. 'Oh! Then you and Mr . . .'

Her ladyship's meaning is quite clear.

'Good heavens, no, my lady, not at all.' Dora hesitates. 'Mr Lawrence could not offer me his home for he lodges. Here at least there are guest rooms and Mrs Howe, the housekeeper, acts as chaperone.'

Lady Latimer looks relieved.

As if, Dora thinks wryly, she would be in any maidenly danger from Cornelius Ashmole. She shakes herself, clears her throat.

'To what do I owe the pleasure, Lady Latimer?'

'Ah, yes.' The old woman needlessly arranges her skirts. 'I'd like to commission more pieces from you. But now that I see you are unsettled in your situation I am more than happy to wait until you have re-established yourself. You have capital?' Dora hesitates, but her ladyship seems not to notice. 'Either way I would be happy to offer my patronage. I am entirely grateful to you, my dear, for making my outfit the crowning glory of my soirée, and I would be very sorry to see a woman of your talent go to waste. There have been others who have approached you for commissions, I assume?'

Dora can barely eke out a nod in the face of this news. Patronage? Can she truly mean it?

'Very good. But I shall not bother you any more today,' Lady

Latimer is saying, and she rises from her seat in a cloud of choking lavender. 'I will let you think on it, how about that?'

Dora cannot sleep. For hours it seems, she tosses and turns, her mind fluttering frantically like butterflies trapped in a bell jar.

She thinks of Lady Latimer's offer this afternoon. A part of her is thrilled, but the old woman's news is overshadowed by everything else. Dora cannot forget the loss of Hermes, the truth about—

Dora shuts her eyes, tight. She still cannot let herself think on it. Not yet.

When the clock strikes one she finally admits defeat. Dora gets up, reaches for her father's banyan which she managed to salvage from her attic room. She ties the cord around her waist and then brushes her fingers over the bobbles in the shoulder, tries to remember what it felt like when Hermes used to perch there, talons catching in the material, and Dora swallows a sob when she realises the memory has already begun to fade.

She means to go into the front room, attempt once more to sketch out a design. But when she reaches the bottom of the stairs she notices an orange glow on the tiles. Dora turns. Under the far door – the library she was shown into the first day she came here – shines a light.

Mr Ashmole is awake.

For a long moment Dora hesitates on the stair. A part of her does not wish to see him, to speak to him at all. But company – even his – must surely be a better tonic than her restless thoughts and so, grudgingly, she makes her way down the corridor.

He answers her knock at the door wearing a banyan of his own – this one distinctly more regal and modern – but it falls open at his chest. The skin is smooth, chiselled like a Grecian bust, and Dora blushes, fast averts her eyes.

'Do not concern yourself,' he says tiredly. 'You know I won't touch you. Come in,' he adds, heading back to his chair by the fire. 'Shut it behind you, will you?'

She does as he asks, follows him into the room. He gestures at the partnering chair.

'Drink?'

He holds up a decanter. Its content is the colour of amber. Whiskey or brandy, she thinks and Dora nods, wanting to feel numb. Mr Ashmole pours her a generous helping, hands it to her over the tiger rug. She sits.

'You can't sleep either?'

He rests his head on the chair back. 'I can never sleep.'

Dora takes a sip from her glass. Grimaces.

'Rum,' Mr Ashmole provides.

The fire pops. An ember falls onto the floor, glows for a split second before fading. Edward's friend stares at her.

'I am sorry about your magpie.'

A beat.

Dora nods.

Mr Ashmole turns his face, watches the flames dance in the grate. It seems at first he means for them to sit in silence but then he shifts in the chair, lets out a long breath that promises conversation.

'When I came home from the Grand Tour,' he says quietly, 'and returned to Sandbourne, I wrote to Edward at the bindery. It belonged to a tradesman named Marcus Carrow back then, a monster of a man, though I wasn't to discover that for some months.'

Dora cradles her glass.

'I wrote, every week. Never once did I receive a reply. It didn't occur to me anything was wrong. I thought . . .' Mr Ashmole rubs a

349

hand over his eyes. 'I thought he'd made new friends, had forgotten our childhood together in Staffordshire. And that made me angry. It hurt me. After all I'd done for him. I'd shared my books, my home. My life. And my father had given Edward the means to make a life for himself, a much better one, but what had Edward done? Taken what he wanted and never looked back.' A smile twists his mouth. He looks at Dora, away again. 'You have to believe that's what I thought. I'm sure it can come as no surprise that I struggled to make friends. I've been an arrogant arse all my life. I hated my time at Oxford. Resented being sent to Europe. Oh, I learnt the ways of the world, it's true. I gained a thorough education, moved in all the right circles and I commanded respect, too. I understood how to work the ranks. But I just wanted to be home. With him. And his rejection . . . it hurt like the Devil.'

Dora watches Mr Ashmole study the glass in his lap.

'When did you realise you loved him?'

He chuckles low in his throat, but it holds no amusement. 'When did you guess? The footman?'

'A little before that, actually.'

In response Mr Ashmole shakes his head, raises the glass to his lips, and Dora can see by his inability to keep it straight that he has been drinking since long before she came downstairs. He takes a sip of rum, stretches his mouth at the burn, hisses through his teeth.

'I realised when I found him. After what must have been nine months, perhaps ten, I don't remember now, I'd still had no reply to my letters and I couldn't let the matter lie. It was stubborn pride that kept me away at first, and I'll never forgive myself for that. If I'd gone after my first letter went unanswered . . .' He shakes his head again. 'In the end I went to London, sought him out. But he wasn't there. I couldn't understand it. Had Edward left? No, sir, not that I recall. Where is he then? Oh, about. About? What does that even mean?' Mr Ashmole takes another sip of rum. 'Carrow was taunting me, didn't much care that by his very vagueness he became an object for suspicion. But I saw I'd get no answer from him so I left. I rented a hovel of a room opposite the bindery and watched. I never saw Edward, but there was a man – Tobias Fingle as it transpired – who would leave the shop every morning for an hour. And I never saw him without a bruise. After a week, I caught up with him. Demanded he tell me what went on in there. It took three days to get him to speak. I remember how thin he was. It was food in the end that loosened his tongue.'

Mr Ashmole takes a very long drink from the glass. When he lowers it again, there is only an inch of rum left in it.

'It turns out the bastard beat all the lads under his care – but Edward, him being so small, he got the brunt of it. Carrow worked all of them within an inch of their lives for no pay, and rarely let them sleep let alone eat. Three boys had already died that year, so Fingle told me. He'd had to dump the bodies in the river himself. As for Edward . . . How he survived all those years I'll never know. Carrow kept him in a pitch-black wood store for days on end.'

Dora goes cold as she remembers the shadowed spot she saw that day in the bindery. She thinks of the candles in his office, Edward's hesitance to go down into the basement that first night, his fear of the dark, and she looks at Mr Ashmole in horror.

'What did you do?'

'Had the authorities come. They arrested Carrow – he swung from Tyburn the next year.'

'And Edward?'

Mr Ashmole screws his eyes. 'Got him out of the store myself. My God, you should have seen him. Emaciated, black and blue. I took him to my father's town house to recover . . . You know the rest.'

Dora could cry. *Oh, Edward . . .*

'He doesn't speak of it. It's been some years now and still he rarely mentions it. I tried to get him to, once, but he walked out on me and we didn't speak again for a week. I've never brought it up since.' Finally Mr Ashmole looks at her. 'I know Edward will never return my feelings. He will never love me as I do him. But I suppose I always hoped that maybe, one day . . . And then you came along.'

He stares at her for what feels like an endless moment, one that spins out on itself, and all his jealousy and disappointment is encapsulated into that one single look. Then he turns his face, becomes lost once more in the flames.

'Do not punish Edward for his ambition, Miss Blake.' His voice is a low murmur, a silken thread. 'He meant no harm by writing what he did. All he has ever wanted was to rise above what once was. I should not have made things awkward between you. I know what you mean to him. He's as like to cause you hurt as I would him.'

The fire cracks. Dora's stomach flips. Mr Ashmole drains his glass.

She waits to see if he will speak again. When he does not Dora rises, places her still full glass of rum down on the small table beside the chair.

'I think I shall sleep now.'

At first he does not respond, but at the door he whispers her name, so softly she is not sure at first if she imagined it, and then he says, 'He doesn't know. I don't think it's even occurred to him. He hasn't experienced enough of life to . . .' Mr Ashmole sucks in his breath. 'You won't tell?'

Dora shakes her head. 'Of course not.'

He nods.

A beat.

Dora turns to leave. Turns back again.

'I never thanked you. For taking me in. I thank you now.'

'Well.' He turns his face to look at her. 'I hardly had a choice, did I?'

Sardonic again. She thinks she likes it.

'Goodnight, Cornelius Ashmole.'

A ghost of a smile.

'Goodnight, Pandora Blake.'

# CHAPTER
# FORTY-ONE

Hezekiah stares at the key to the Bramah safe in his hand, the smooth black revolving disc at its head. He looks back at the wall, the wall that for years has been just a wall to him and nothing more.

He thought at first they must have meant a different one, and so he moved everything into the centre of the floor, ran his hand along each blank wall in turn. But there were no keyholes and besides, it made sense for it to be this one. All that missing room . . . it never occurred to him that there should have been more floor space than this, and yet it is obvious now that he thinks about it. Hezekiah curses himself he did not think about it before.

*Use the gold-and-black key*, the note said.

The Bramah key, obviously. So why is it he cannot find a bloody lock?

He presses his hand against the wall, groans deep into his chins. His leg is agony. The pain is unbearable, the smell equally so, but he will not give in to it now. He will find a way in first, secure his fortune and then, only then, will he relinquish himself to the hands of a doctor.

Hezekiah groans again. Sweat drips like a river down his back.

He must be missing something, Hezekiah thinks. In desperation he runs his hand along the uneven wall, palms scraping against the roughness. Again and again and again he does this until, panting, he changes tack. He limps to the far left side – leaning on the wall for support – and starts a slow run of it from top to bottom. He moves as slowly as he can take, bites back his anger, his frustration, his impatience, his pain until then, *then*!

Hezekiah stops, runs his hand over the spot once more. He feels for a fleeting second nothing, or rather, the absence of something. He bends to squint.

There. A small oval indent, the exact size of the disc on the Bramah key.

Hezekiah's heart soars.

He has done it! He has found it! By God, he *knew* he would win in the end!

He laughs, laughs wildly, laughs so hard that he forgets the pain in his leg and then he is fumbling for the key, laying the oval flat, pushing it in . . .

Nothing.

He tries again.

Still nothing.

Once more.

Nothing.

*Nothing nothing nothing*!

It does not work. It will not open.

Hezekiah removes the disc a final time, presses his finger against the indent, again and again and again and then, his nail catches on a ridge. He stops, leans in closer. It takes him a moment – his vision blurs before it comes into focus – but then he sees it; an image in the relief. A bearded face.

He stares at the gold Bramah key in his hand for one long, unfathomable moment, staring at the smoothness of the disc. There is no face.

There is no face.

A hum. A sigh.

Hezekiah turns around. The pithos looms. Tall, imposing yet beautiful, and in his anguish it seems to him that in the dim light it taunts him. Then with a scream he throws the key to the floor as he realises that even in death, Elijah and Helen have thwarted him once again.

# CHAPTER
# FORTY-TWO

The note from Dora's housekeeper came at midday when Edward, Cornelius and Dora were taking tea in the parlour. She had greeted Edward awkwardly, still seemed unable to meet his eye, and he was so gratified Dora had decided to acknowledge him that he had been hesitant to ruin the fragile peace between them by revealing the full import of Hezekiah's transgressions. Indeed, it was painful to watch Dora listen to them in silence, but it was altogether worrying that she did not give even the merest flinch when he divulged the gruesome manner of the Coombe brothers' deaths, and so it was almost a relief when the note arrived. *Come now*, it said, *he won't be back until tonight*, and so Dora collected together her things – binding her sketchbook with string so the pages would not fly open in the gale that had picked up its ferocious wings the night before – and Edward and Cornelius fetched their coats.

'What are you doing?' she asked as they pushed their arms down into their sleeves.

'Coming with you,' Edward replied, wrapping his scarf around his neck. 'After everything I've just said do you honestly think we would let you go alone?'

Dora paused, unsure. 'Both of you? I'd rather you didn't.'

'We're coming,' Cornelius said then, pulling up his collar. 'No arguments.'

Edward watched the play of emotions cross Dora's face, could see how she battled to come up with an excuse. But after a moment she simply nodded, so Cornelius called for the carriage and they find themselves alighting outside Blake's Emporium within the hour.

Dora's stocky housekeeper lets them in. Edward notes the cracked lip, the black eye. The bruising, he deduces by the mottled green at the edges, is a few days old. Hezekiah's handiwork, undoubtedly.

'He's gone to organise the bidding, that much I know,' the housekeeper says as she takes their coats, Dora's cape. 'He told me not to expect him home until this evening.'

Edward looks at her. 'The bidding?'

'He had the smaller items collected this morning.'

'Do you know where they were being delivered?' Edward asks, his hopes lifting. If the housekeeper knows that then they may be able to do something after all, but his hopes are dashed when Lottie shakes her head.

'He's never told me things like that. But Coombe knows. You should ask him.'

'Coombe is dead.'

Lottie covers her mouth.

Cornelius looks at the woman. 'Knew this Coombe well, did you?'

The housekeeper lowers her hands, begins to wring them in her apron.

'Not well, exactly, but well enough to care that he's dead. How?'

Dora's lip thins. 'Hezekiah, of course.'

Lottie pales, fleshy chin trembling.

'Missum, I . . . I'm so sorry. For all of it. I should have told you.'

'Told me what?' Dora's voice comes sharp, and tears begin to well in Lottie's eyes.

'He was looking for something. That night, in your room. A note. He found it in the cage.'

Something shifts in Dora's face. 'Lottie.' Her voice is pinched. 'Speak plain.'

Edward thinks the housekeeper truly does look as though she is about to cry.

'I asked him why he hadn't sold the vase. He told me that there had been something in it.'

Cornelius folds his arms. 'See? Didn't I tell you?'

Dora ignores him. 'What thing?' she presses, and Edward can see she holds herself so tightly together he is afraid she will snap.

The housekeeper takes an unsteady breath. 'He said that inside the vase there was a note. A note written by your parents, about a fortune they left you. The note would say how to claim it.'

Edward lets out his breath. 'Christ.'

Dora is standing very still, her face a perfect blank. Very quietly, so quietly they would strain to hear if they were outside, Dora says, 'And he found it? In Hermes' cage?'

Lottie nods.

'But how?'

Confusion knits her forehead. Cornelius cuts in.

'Where is this note now?'

Lottie looks to him. 'I don't know. Honest, I swear I don't.'

Dora is silent for a long and painful moment. Edward watches the pulse pound in her neck. He wants to reach out and take her hand but instinctively he knows she will not allow it, so all he can do is watch as Dora looks to him, to Cornelius, then back again to Lottie.

'Why are you telling me this? Why are you helping us?'

The housekeeper shakes her head, split lip trembling. 'I've got no good excuse for the way I treated you. I knew Hezekiah long before he met your mother. I loved him, you see. And when I saw how cut up

359

he was about Helen after she . . . I hated you because I hated her. But that was wrong of me, I know that now.'

Dora stares at the floor for a very long time. Then, finally, she exhales. 'It's all right, Lottie.'

'It is?'

Suddenly Dora looks tired. 'We'd best be getting on. Would you mind very much bringing us some tea?'

Dora sets herself down on the floor in front of the pithos, unties the sketchbook with such vigour that Cornelius and Edward share a concerned look.

'Would you like to speak of it?' Cornelius tries, but she cuts him off with a short sharp shake of her head.

'No, I wouldn't.'

Edward opens his mouth to respond.

'It is best I concentrate, if you please,' she says, pencil poised on a fresh page, and Edward reluctantly closes his mouth again.

Dora will speak when she is ready. Attempting to force her will not work, and with regret Edward watches her sketch, knows exactly what her concentration costs her. He understands all too well the need to bury pain with work.

Keep busy, it does not hurt. Keep busy – it leaves no time to think.

Cornelius has begun taking a slow turn around the pithos, and he releases a long whistle.

'It really is quite magnificent, isn't it? I didn't look at it properly before, at Latimer's.' Then he hesitates, catches sight of Dora's sketchbook. He leans over her shoulder, rests his hands on his knees.

'Edward was right,' he murmurs. 'Your drawings are quite spectacular. You are an extraordinary artist, Miss Blake.'

Dora's pencil hovers over the page. She looks up at him, blushes. 'Thank you, Mr Ashmole.'

Edward stares, notes Dora's pinked cheeks, Cornelius' admiration that shows so clearly on his handsome face.

It has not escaped Edward's notice that Cornelius' attitude toward Dora has changed. He knows there was no choice in letting Dora stay with him, that to stay with Edward would have broached the bounds of propriety altogether. Certainly, after their disagreement, such a thing would have been untenable, but since Dora has been staying with him Cornelius has been less vitriolic toward her, more – if not kind, then – accommodating, and Edward feels a flicker of jealousy.

Has something happened between them? The thought makes him breathless.

'What does this scene represent?' Cornelius asks Dora now, gesturing at the section of pithos she sketches, and Edward's stomach begins to churn.

Dora shifts her position on the floor.

'It is a depiction of Athena blessing Pandora with all the gifts Zeus felt it necessary for her to have. There are different versions of the myth – some say the gifts were given not by one goddess but many. Given by gods, too.' Dora shifts again then huffs in frustration. She moves to lie on her side to take a closer look at some of the detailing at the base. 'Apollo taught her to sing and play the lyre, Athena taught her to spin, Demeter to tend a garden. Aphrodite, apparently, taught her how to dance without moving her legs.'

'An impressive feat, I dare say.'

'Hardly possible for anyone, I would have thou—' Dora breaks off.

Cornelius frowns. 'What is it?'

361

'My God,' Dora whispers. 'Look at this.'

'What?' Edward asks.

'Come and see.'

Edward gets down on the cold floor next to her, must lie flat on his chest to see what she is pointing at.

A series of words, in Greek:

$$εδώ \; βρίσκεται \; η \; τύχη \; των \; κόσμων$$

Cornelius squats down beside them. 'What does it say?'

Dora licks her lips. *'Edó vrísketai i týchi ton kósmon.'*

'I'm sorry?'

Another beat.

'Herein lies the fate of worlds.'

There is a palpable pulse in the air.

'Dora,' Edward breathes, his jealousy forgotten.

Cornelius looks at Edward. 'Greek pottery never has writing on it. Does it?'

'It is rare,' Edward says in a rush, 'and even then never whole sentences.'

'What are you saying?' asks Dora dubiously.

Edward takes a deep breath. Could it really be?

'Has it not occurred to you that perhaps . . .' But he struggles for the words. No matter what Hamilton said, there is no arguing this.

'What?'

He tries again.

'This pithos is so old that not even Gough's scientists could date it. It depicts the story of Pandora's creation. All the things that have happened, that *are* happening –' Edward ticks them off on his fingers – 'the sinking of the *Colossus*, the illness of your uncle, the deaths of the Coombe brothers. And then there's this godawful weather to account

362

for. Even Bonaparte! The divisions in Europe, the pressures on the economy, our trade routes . . . We are on the brink of invasion, Sir William said so himself. Has it not occurred to either of you that these things have happened for a reason? That this pithos might actually be Pandora's Box itself?'

Cornelius stares at him as if he has gone mad.

'Oh, Edward, no. Have you taken complete leave of your senses? Pandora's Box is a fable! Fable is fable, a mere story told to entertain.'

'But all fanciful concepts grow from concrete reality!'

Cornelius stands up, is shaking his head. Edward implores instead to Dora.

'You conceive of it, don't you?'

Dora looks struck.

'It is mad. It can't be, it just can't. But . . .'

Cornelius folds his arms across his chest, looks down at her with ill-concealed frustration. 'Not you too? Honestly, I thought you at least had more sense.'

But Dora is biting her lip. 'If my mother taught me anything it was to always look for a factual and historical basis for myth. It is ludicrous to think the pithos was created by a god. Besides,' she adds, gesturing at the carvings circling the pithos, 'what mythical artefact would recount its own creation? It *is* mad,' Dora says, her voice strained. 'There are just so many ways to explain it all away. *Logical* explanations. And yet, Edward does have a point.' She gestures at it again, and Edward is gratified that Dora has not rejected the idea completely. 'Why does it not break, how has it survived intact all these years, why did Hermes fear it so? Animals know, they always know. What power does this thing hold?'

Cornelius is raising his hands in mock defeat. 'For pity's sake. I'm disappointed in the both of you. Of all the hare-brained, ridiculous . . .' He catches himself as the basement door opens and Lottie appears at the top with a tray. Cornelius lowers his voice. He looks between Edward and Dora, dark eyes serious. 'There will be plenty of time to argue about this later. The last thing I want is to discuss nonsensical theories. I'm sure I have far better things to do with my time.'

# CHAPTER
# FORTY-THREE

In the four days that have passed since their visit to the shop, Dora has thrown herself into finishing the sketches of the pithos. It has rained, rained so hard the guttering leaks and Mrs Howe must fetch for a man to fix it and Dora, sitting at the window seat in her new bedroom that has a pleasing view of the garden, watches the water run rivers down the glass.

She is not dressed, and so she has not gone downstairs to work. A lunch tray was left outside the door, replacing the breakfast tray from this morning, the dinner tray from the night before; all were returned to the kitchen untouched.

Three times already today Mr Ashmole has knocked on the door, and three times Dora has ignored him.

She does not want to speak yet. Is not sure she can.

Dora flexes her fingers, takes a firmer grip on her pencil. Her original compositions of the individual carvings require finer details adding, the sketch of the pithos in its entirety redrawing completely; and a further three sketches need to be drawn to demonstrate its detailing on all sides. Then, the wording. Dora bends over the sketchbook balanced on her tucked-up knees, narrowing her eyes through her spectacles as she creates the flick of the lowercase *kappa*, adds the final Greek letters to the phrase.

*Herein lies the fate of worlds.*

Dora does not know what to believe. As she said to Edward, everything that has happened has a logical explanation. The *Colossus* – any ship for that matter – is susceptible to the elements, but most especially in December. Hezekiah's wound came from a rusty nail, left untreated. The streets of London are filthy, after all; no wonder his wound became infected. Dora remembers Matthew Coombe's words the day they took the pithos to Lady Latimer's. *That damn cargo happened.* Well. His wound, too, can be accounted for in much the same way as Hezekiah's, she is sure.

What else did Edward mention?

All three Coombe brothers, dead at Hezekiah's hands. Dora grimaces. No, the pithos cannot be blamed for that. Napoleon Bonaparte? His actions are his own. So much of what is wrong in Europe can be laid at his door, and he has been threatening to invade for years. As for the weather . . . she looks out the window again. Snow, gales, biting frosts. The rain is relentless. But. It is winter; one cannot expect the conditions to be kind. Briefly Dora thinks of Lady Latimer's guests, their sickness the day after the soirée. It *could* have been the monkey. And yet . . .

Why does Dora find herself daring to believe?

For a piece of pottery to survive undamaged underground for so many thousands of years? Unprecedented. If it had not been touched by the toxicity of open air then she supposes it could be preserved beautifully. But a flood buried it in the first place – it is a miracle no damage occurred then. Even if it had survived the flood unscathed, her parents had excavated deep enough to have freed it from the earth that held it. When the cave-in happened, it should have been damaged then. And if not then, the second flood and excavation would surely have caused *some* harm? And if not then, certainly the shipwreck would have done the job, and if not *then* . . .

366

Dora shakes her head. How can all *that* be explained?

And it spoke to her . . . did it not? She heard voices. Crying. Perhaps she imagined it, all the other things too.

But Hermes, Hermes did not imagine it. Hermes felt something was wrong. He did not want to go down to the basement that first night, was uncommonly restless. She thinks of how he fled when she whispered Pandora's name. He was perfectly occupied pecking at the lid bef—

Dora lowers the pencil.

So that was it.

The note must have been in the lid, rolled up or folded so small she would not have noticed it at the time. That was why Hermes was so defensive when she went near the birdcage, why he made such a mess . . .

Dora shuts her eyes, pinches back the tears that have begun to form at the corners.

Hezekiah killed her pet bird for a scrap of paper that did not belong to him.

By the time she is washed and dressed and has eaten it is past six, the rain has paused in its onslaught, and so she goes directly to Edward's lodgings, knowing he should have returned from the bindery long before now.

His landlady – a fat woman with too many chins – directs her up to a pokey first-floor landing and Dora raps hard on the door, her sketchbook clutched close to her chest.

'Dora,' he exclaims in surprise. 'What are you . . . ?'

Edward blushes. His shirt is untucked, his cravat loose about his neck. His blonde hair is wet at the temples, and Dora sees she has disturbed him in his toilette.

'I . . .' Dora tries to compose herself. After Mr Ashmole's revelation about Edward's past she has been unsure how to act around him, how to feel. Her original anger is more now an irritable ache, and her knowing more of him . . . Well, it changes things.

'Dora?'

'I thought you should know I've finished the sketches of the pithos. For your . . .'

The words lose themselves in her throat. He seems to shake himself.

'Of course! Please, please, come in.'

He steps aside. Dora ducks her head under the lintel.

It is the first time she has seen his lodgings. The set of rooms he keeps, she notes, is not much bigger than her attic was, but it is clean and warm and serviceable, no peeling window frames, no wood-wormed beams. Dora smells the musty scent of books, a hint of candle wax. She looks about her with interest, at the bookcase tucked into the alcove next to the narrow fireplace that blazes brightly in its grate, the desk that stands at the window, spread with papers of tightly packed text.

'Forgive the mess.' Edward is darting around the room, picking up discarded stockings, shirts, shoes, and he piles them in his arms, looking deeply embarrassed and flustered. 'Would you give me one moment? I just need to . . .' and he is trailing away, retreating into a bedchamber off to the left, taking his creased garments with him.

Dora wanders over to the desk, removes the sketches of the pithos, spreads them out across its surface and as she does, one of the papers beneath is knocked aside, catching her eye. A phrase pops into focus, and she moves the rest of her drawings to take a better look.

*It is easy to hide such pieces in an establishment that has become
known only for its counterfeit wares. While deeply frowned upon,
duplicates are not uncommon in trading circles, and so authorities
are unlike to suppose that genuine articles might be hidden in
amongst the dross of a business whose complete catalogue is made
up entirely of forgeries. And that is how the black-market operates –
deception within deception – the oldest trick known to man.*

'I am so glad you came,' Edward's voice sounds behind her. 'I've
wanted to—'

He stops when he sees what she is reading. His hands fall limply
at his sides.

'So,' Dora says quietly. 'This is it.'

Edward's face has paled to porcelain.

'Yes.'

They watch each other. He makes to step forward. Dora turns her
head.

'"Genuine articles might be hidden in amongst the dross of a business whose complete catalogue is made up entirely of forgeries",' she
reads. Dora turns back to look at him, and despite her earlier thaw,
the stab of betrayal is still sharp in her chest. 'Are there other antiquity
establishments such as Blake's Emporium, then? Can you honestly
stand there and say this is *not* about me?'

She somehow manages to keep her tone calm, but the words wobble in the seat of her throat. There is a *pat-pat-pat* of water on the
windowpane, and the rain starts up once more.

Edward runs a hand across his eyes, sighs deeply.

'Are there others like Blake's? Yes, probably. Have I used your
shop as inspiration? Yes, of course I have. But I do not explicitly mention you. That shop could belong to anyone.'

Dora chokes down a bitter laugh. 'And yet, it does not.'

Edward steps forward, expression pleading.

'I promised I would help you, don't you remember? I am convinced this is the only way of doing that. This paper will secure my acceptance into the Society which means I could then employ you to sketch for me. You would be free of your uncle, the shop. The independence you crave would be yours.'

'But I don't need your help!' she cries. 'Have I not proved that? Lady Latimer's faith in me, the clients she has already sent my way. I don't need you, Edward, I never did!'

'You're right,' he says. 'I see that now. I'm sorry. But I couldn't be sure of your success, and I thou—' He cuts off, runs a hand through his hair. 'You must discover the truth from your uncle, once and for all. About his trading, your parents—'

Dora gasps, puts her hands over her ears, and Edward's voice rises in frustration. 'You can't ignore it for ever! You must confront him, Dora, you must.'

It is too much. Too much. Has Edward not seen her try to stamp down her emotions these past few days? Can he not see she is not yet ready to face them? With a groan Dora violently shakes her head, and it is only when she does so that she realises she is crying.

'No,' she bites out. 'I won't hear this. I can't hear it!'

It is as though a dam has burst in her chest. The rain pounds loudly against the windows and Dora lowers her hands, clenches them into fists at her sides. She turns around, looks everywhere but at nothing, and Edward is saying her name over and over and then he is crossing the room to reach her and she does not know what to do.

'You used me,' she chokes. 'You've used me from the beginning.'

This brings him up short.

'No. No, Dora, I did not, at least not in the way you think—'

'You and Mr Ashmole, you've been working together, haven't you? Laughing at me behind my back, all this time!'

She knows she is being irrational, that they have done no such thing, but the old anger has risen and the words will not stop, seem determined to run themselves over her tongue like knives.

'No! Dammit, no, never, never!' and Edward reaches for her, clamps her upper arms in his hands, holding her fast. 'How can you even think such a thing? After everything we have been through together! Dora, what I feel for you—'

She tries to pull away. 'What you feel for me is nothing more than—'

And then, then he is kissing her.

The shock of his mouth on hers brings her up short. As Edward's lips brush against hers she lets her own part, she tastes ale on his tongue, and then she feels herself sinking into him, the hurt and anger shifting into something else. He smells of leather, of soap, and that heady mix does something to her, sends tantalising tingles to nerve endings she does not even know she has. The hem of his shirt teases her wrist and Dora puts a hand up underneath it, runs her palm against the plane of his flat stomach, caressing the smooth skin, fascinated by the way he shivers under her touch. Moving upward her nail grazes his nipple and he sucks in his breath, kisses her harder, and she kisses him back, losing herself in the intoxicating feel of him.

'Dora, I . . .'

'Shh,' she whispers against him for she needs this – to be touched, to forget for just a little while – and she bunches the shirt in her hands, takes it up over his head, and when he is free of it he clasps her tightly to him, kisses her once more.

Edward's arm circles her waist, the other cups her cheek. Dora's hands are trapped against his chest. With nothing else to do with them she begins to stroke his skin again, lets her fingers trail upward and then, then, the texture of the skin changes. She stops. Edward's lips still on hers.

371

He does not say anything when she leans away from him to look.

A scar, deep and furrowed, spans the bottom right of his collar-bone. Dora hears Edward's breath catch in his throat as she gently maps it with the pad of her fingertip.

And in that spun darkness – with the rain cleansing London's streets clean – she kisses the puckered skin of his breast, asks him how it came to be, and he tells her, tells her it all, as night begins to chase away the dusk.

# CHAPTER
# FORTY-FOUR

Edward wakes to find Dora gone.

He stretches in the bed, feels – for the first time he can ever remember – happy. Edward luxuriates in the possibility of this for a moment, smiling deeply into the downy pillow.

Outside he can hear the sounds of the city going about its dawn business, the call of hawkers over the high wind. He listens to the roll of carriage wheels, the wet sluice of their trajectory though puddles left from the rain, but then Dora's absence wends a niggle in his stomach and he sits up, frowning into the dull morning light.

'Dora?'

Perhaps she is in the other room. He gets up, walks naked from the bedroom, pauses at the threshold when he sees the room is empty.

Where is she? He wonders briefly if she has gone back to Clevendale but somehow, *somehow*, he cannot shake the feeling that she has not gone there, that she has, in fact, done exactly what he said she should the night before.

*You must discover the truth from your uncle.*

He curses underneath his breath, rushes to pick up his clothes from the floor.

The door is locked. There is no answer when he calls. No Hezekiah, no Lottie, no Dora. For minutes Edward stands there, peering into the gloom of the shop. There is no sign of movement, no candles burn in their sconces, and Edward feels the niggle in his stomach slip its noose and knot itself into fear.

He cannot stand here all morning. What if Dora is in there and Hezekiah has harmed her? What if . . . But Edward swallows, will not entertain the thought.

Furtively he looks about him. No one will pay attention, no one will hear over the loud flow of traffic moving like a river down Ludgate Street. Quickly, before he can change his mind, Edward jabs his elbow hard into one of the door's glass panes. He winces at the break, looks about him again to see if anyone has noticed.

No one has noticed. No one has even blinked an eye.

As fast as he can he slips his hand through the empty pane, locates the rusting bolt, draws it across. He lets himself in, the bell above him jangling. Edward shuts the door.

The shop is dim. It takes a moment for Edward's eyes to adjust.

'Dora? Lottie?'

The hairs stand up on the back of his neck.

He takes a shaky breath, moves slowly into the middle of the room, looks down through the shelves to the basement doors.

And Edward stares. They are wide open, but that is not what shocks him. The floorboards . . .

'What on earth?'

He begins to move forward, then stops. Something catches in his nostril, making it twitch.

A smell. The same smell as the one at the Coombe loft.

A creak behind him. A blinding pain.

And then there is nothing.

# CHAPTER
# FORTY-FIVE

Dora clutches her reticule close, marvels at the weight of it in her hands.

She did not expect Mr Clements to be so generous, but when the jeweller opened his doors to her – she called on him so early that not even his liveried footman had arrived – he seemed quite unable to hide his shock and excitement.

'They took all of them, Miss Blake! I could scarce believe it. First thing Monday morning, in they came. You only left me with a few designs and when those had gone, they wiped my cabinets clean!' He blinked at her over the top of his spectacles. 'You're creating more, aren't you?'

Dora assured him she was, told him of the commissions already lining up, that Lady Latimer herself had offered patronage, and Mr Clements excused himself into the back room, returning with a purse the size of his fist, filled with banknotes and coins.

Outside Dora locates the pocket in her dress, drops the purse inside. The weight makes her lopsided but she does not care – the idea of being attacked for it (though the likelihood of such a thing at this time of day is exceedingly slim), makes her over-cautious.

For a long moment Dora considers her next move. She spies an empty bench in St Paul's churchyard and makes her way over to it. The seat is wet but she gathers her skirts and sits anyway.

The sky threatens rain again. How miserable this country is, Dora thinks, then conjures in her mind's eye cerulean skies, the warmth of a Mediterranean breeze, verdazurine oceans and mountains lined with Cypress trees. All the joys of her childhood, lost. Slowly Dora removes the black-and-white feather she had slipped between her sleeve and the skin of her wrist, twists the calamus between forefinger and thumb, watches wistfully how the light catches the memory of Hermes' rainbow hue.

*You can't ignore it for ever.*

Dora knows Edward is right – she cannot put it off any longer. She rises from the bench and begins to slowly walk in the direction of Blake's Emporium.

She thinks of Edward's paper. He let her read it, the sheets twisted between their naked legs. Her cheeks colour at the memory.

'You see,' he murmured, his fingers lifting a curl from her neck. He pressed his mouth to the tender skin he exposed, sending thrilling shivers across her scalp. 'Your name isn't there. Neither is his. I would never hurt you, Dora. I couldn't. It would be like hurting myself.'

And then he had kissed her, and she had pulled him close.

# CHAPTER
# FORTY-SIX

He wakes to blackness.

It is familiar, a thing he thought long behind him, yet here he is again. He thought he had mastered it, that old panic, his irrational fear of the dark, but it has already begun to rear itself and Edward starts to shake uncontrollably.

And the fear *is* irrational. He taught himself that after he became accustomed to the wood store and all its nooks and dents and scents and sounds. Reason, he thinks to himself now. You are not there, you are not at the bindery, Carrow has not locked you in. You are here.

But where is here?

Edward raises his arms, immediately cries out in pain when they hit something hard, and he tries to stem the terror that teases the length of his spine.

Try again.

Slowly he lifts a hand. It brushes against something. Paper? Is that leather? When he moves it further up his fingers hit something cold, solid. He blinks into black, runs his hand along it. A . . . shelf? He raises his hand again, feels what he thinks are the same objects, up and up. Yes, a shelf. Lots of them. Then what? In answer Edward's hand hits ceiling. His heart hammers loud in his chest.

He raises his other hand, repeats the process. Reaches out behind him. The same.

The same.

Edward sniffs, smells the sharp tang of industry, the distinct scent of oil. He slowly moves his feet, hears the sound of heel against metal.

No. Not metal.

Iron.

*My God.*

He is in the safe.

The panic comes swift then and he screams out, again and again and again, and when he has exhausted himself he strains to listen, but there is only silence and that is just too much for him to comprehend. His pulse races, he breaks out into a cold sweat and Edward pushes his skull against the hard expanse of iron in front of him, tries to breathe but cannot, and he is gasping, gasping, gasping . . .

# CHAPTER
# FORTY-SEVEN

Dora's boot splinters glass. She lifts her foot, sees the shards beneath it. Her heart begins to pound fitfully against her ribs.

Alert now Dora moves slowly, places one foot carefully in front of the other, takes great care not to make another sound. Her eyes narrow when she recognises Hezekiah's grotesque iron fish stranded on the floor. She approaches it cautiously and catches herself on an admonishing laugh. It will not move. It will not attack her. But then she squints. Dora lowers herself, rests her weight on the balls of her feet.

Blood. That is blood on the sharp curve of its fin.

Dora swallows, stands up again. She turns toward the basement. Her eyes widen.

Beyond the shelves, it is as if something has pushed through the floor from underneath. The floorboards are splintered, some ripped from their nails completely. She goes to them. Boards snapped in two, jagged edges, many rotten. Dora looks at what is beneath and sees, oddly, only stone.

There is a noise from below. The basement doors are open, and a light glows eerily beyond.

Something, she knows, is terribly terribly wrong.

Dora forces herself to cross the length of the shop, forces herself to the basement door, forces herself to lay a hand on the balustrade.

There is another sound, and this time Dora can make it out – earth rolling, the slam of metal against stone, and she braves the first step of the stairs.

The basement is flooded with light. With candles, Dora realises. In the middle of the basement floor the pithos stands regal, imposing as ever it did, but at its base are chunks of brick and mortar – some small, some large – and Dora jumps when another is flung into the room from somewhere beyond the stairs.

She begins her descent. She can hear him panting, can smell the putrid stench of his wound, and when she reaches the bottom of the steps all Dora can do is stare in dismay.

The basement floor is covered with debris. Lying on her side against the far wall is Lottie, her arms and legs bound with packing twine. When Lottie sees her she moans through the gag at her mouth, gestures wildly with her eyes for Dora to look behind her, and Dora turns.

'Dear heaven, Uncle. What have you done?'

The wall behind him is a ruin, but still whole, and Hezekiah stands – barely upright on his ailing leg – in the middle of a large mound of rubble. Clasped in Hezekiah's hands, his knuckles bloody, is a pickaxe. She smells something else on him now – gin, she thinks – and Dora realises he is covered with the stuff, that Hezekiah is dangerously drunk. He does not wear a wig, his skin is filthy, his shirt ripped and blackened. He drips with sweat, and when she meets his eyes she sees her uncle is looking at her with pure, unadulterated hatred.

'So, you've come at last.'

His voice is a sickening wheeze.

'Hezekiah,' she says, and the sound of his name on her tongue seems to shock him.

He drags his leg, moves further into the light. His eyes are bloodshot, seem to carry within them the spirit of madness. With difficulty he lifts the pickaxe, points its butt at Dora's face.

'You dare talk to me like an *equal*?' he spits. 'You are worthless! Just like your bitch of a mother. Look what Helen has brought me to!'

The pickaxe swings; Dora stumbles back, holding up her hands in defence, and she realises she must mollify him, coax him sweet if she is to have the truth.

If she is to remain unharmed.

'What did she do?' she asks. 'What did Helen do?'

'Ah, Helen,' he breathes.

Hezekiah blinks at her like a confused child and lowers the pickaxe. Its vicious point scrapes on the floor.

'I met her first, you know. I introduced them!' He cracks a bitter laugh. 'I wanted to impress her. *Showered* her with gifts, I did. But she chose Elijah in the end and like the whore she was she opened her legs to him before they even reached the altar.'

The vitriol in his voice. Dora tries not to flinch at it.

'That must have hurt.'

'It did.' He looks confused again. 'It did. How could she do that to me? After everything I did for her?'

Dora swallows, prays for calm.

'What did you do for her?'

Hezekiah's expression turns wistful, and for the briefest of moments Dora sees the ghost of the man he might have been all those years before – young, carefree. Handsome, even.

'It was me who traced the geographical history for her precious Pandora myth. But I did not understand the *ancient* history that would reconcile the evidence. Elijah, though, he was always clever in that way. And then . . .' He trails off. His eyes darken. 'I loved her. I loved her but she chose him. Do you have any idea how that made me feel? To be used like that?'

Dora shakes her head. She cannot find the words.

'Elijah thought he was being charitable, letting me manage the shop. A living, he said, in thanks for bringing them together. As if I would be thankful for that, when he had taken her from me, the only thing I ever truly wanted!' Hezekiah laughs resentfully. 'And still, they used me. *She* used me. My knowledge, my skills. But they under-estimated me, Dora. They had no idea what I was capable of. I could have made their fortunes, if they hadn't been so blind.'

The venom in his voice is enough to loose her tongue.

'Why did you kill them?' she asks quietly.

Hezekiah sneers. 'They didn't have the imagination, didn't com-prehend. Oh, what we could have done with it! The amount of money we could have made if we'd sold it *my* way!' He looks past her, at the pithos, and Dora sees he is lost in his memories, is trapped in a dream. 'I told them what I'd done back here in the shop. The sales I'd made. I thought they would be pleased, but they told me to leave. Leave! After *I* was the one who helped her discover where the bloody vase was in the first place!'

He shakes his head. Somewhere behind her, Dora thinks she hears a shout.

'I went down to the dig site, tried to reason with them, but they wouldn't have it, said that if I tried anything they would report me. Can you believe that?' Hezekiah asks, his sweating face incredulous. 'Their own flesh and blood, threatened with the hangman's noose. It was the last insult. I made a decision. If I couldn't have the vase, then neither could they.'

He looks at her once more. His expression shifts into scorn.

'It wasn't hard to find the kinks in the site; it was already weak. The land was sinking. There'd been plans to reinforce it but Elijah and Helen, they always had been impatient. Hamilton said it was sound enough, that it would keep for a while longer and it might well

383

have . . . if not for me.' His mouth twists. 'It was nothing to knock down a retaining wall, a beam here and there. I set it all up, ready. A swift kick, a swing of a hammer, that's all it would take. But I wanted to give them another chance. I wanted to make them see reason. So I went back down into the tunnels while Hamilton slept, knowing they would be working there alone. They were arguing, the vase between them, still half-buried in the earth. I hid.' Hezekiah's eyes glaze over. 'Helen knew, knew what I would do. Always sharp, that one. Hezekiah means to kill us, she had said, and what will happen to Dora then? Elijah tried to convince her to leave the dig but Helen refused, said they hadn't come all that way only to abandon the vase. And then. *Then!* They spoke of a private collection, a fortune back in London, but they did not say where it was. I watched as Helen took out a sheet of paper from her pocket. Elijah told her to write it down. Instructions. For you, Dora. A failsafe, he called it. A fortune! Hidden from me, all this time . . . I lost my temper. Flew at them. Helen pulled a knife.' Hezekiah raises a finger to the scar at his cheek.

In disgust Dora watches him run his finger down the length of it, and she swallows hard.

'Then what happened?'

Her uncle's face splits into a humourless smile. 'I snatched the paper from her and fled. It was late afternoon. We had hired locals, so the dig site was empty. *Mesimeri.* Everyone was still sleeping in their tents. No one saw me. I collapsed a wall, some beams . . . The sound was deafening. It all came down so fast.'

They watch each other. Dora takes an unsteady breath.

'How did you know there was a note in the pithos? Why claim it back, after all these years?'

Suddenly Hezekiah lets go of the pickaxe. Dora jumps as it clatters to the floor.

'I wondered at the time why they did not come after me. Why they did not try to get the paper back. If they had they would have caught me, I'm sure. But they didn't come, and in the commotion that followed I did not look at it. It was only later that evening I realised the paper was ripped, that all I had was a blank piece. And when the bodies were retrieved not far from the site entrance and no note was found . . . I understood, then, what Helen had done. As the walls collapsed around them Helen must have hidden the note in the vase, knowing Hamilton would take charge of its excavation. She knew, otherwise, the note would have been passed back to me. But what she could not have anticipated is how long it would take to reopen the dig. A failsafe, indeed.' Hezekiah dips his hand into his trouser pocket. 'Twelve years it's taken me to get the vase back. Do you have any idea how much I have suffered? Knowing that a fortune exists, but not knowing where?'

She cannot stand it any longer.

'Did you plan to kill me?' Dora asks, her voice a pained whisper.

Hezekiah cocks his head. 'Honestly? No. I didn't even realise you were down there. It's a shame Hamilton managed to dig you out but, alas, he did. And you've been an inconvenience ever since.'

'Then why keep me alive?'

Somewhere behind her, another muffled sound.

'Oh, Dora,' Hezekiah mocks. He half-turns, reaches for a candle in one of the sconces behind him. 'I've done many a damning thing in my life, but murdering a child in cold blood didn't sit well with me. Besides.' His eyes narrow. 'You had no knowledge of any of this. You would never have known that the fortune existed if not for me, now. No, there was no point in killing you. You've been useful to me in many ways, after all.' He cocks his head. 'You realise, Dora, there will be no way you can prove anything I've just said.'

Very slowly Hezekiah lifts his hand from his pocket. In it he holds a folded piece of paper, the edge ripped at the bottom. It is creased, yellow with age, but Dora knows what it is.

'The note,' she murmurs.

Hezekiah looks down at it, runs a dirty thumb across its yellowed side. '"For the care of Sir William Hamilton on behalf of our daughter, Pandora Blake,"' he reads. He unfolds the note, looks up once more. 'Tell me, Dora. What is the gold-and-black key?'

The emphasis on the last four words takes her off guard. She stares at him in confusion.

'The gold-and-black key?'

'You heard me.'

Dora shakes her head. 'I don't know. The safe is black and gold . . .'

'It isn't that. I've already tried.'

She says nothing. For a long moment Hezekiah stares at her.

'This note was meant for you. Helen says to use the gold-and-black key. She must have thought that meant something to you.'

Her heart drums heavily in her chest, she does not understand what he wants from her. She looks at Lottie tied so cruelly behind her, the looming pithos, the rubble on the floor, and in confusion Dora shakes her head.

'But it means nothing to me,' she whispers.

Again, Hezekiah stares. Then he raises his arm, holds the note out in front of him like a prayer.

'Well, then. If I can't have their fortune, neither can you. I still have the pithos, after all. Think how much money I'll make from that alone.'

Hezekiah is smiling, a smug, knowing smile that makes her stomach turn, and it takes Dora a moment to understand what he means to do. But then he is moving the candle, is touching a corner of the paper to the flame . . .

'No!'

The note catches. Hezekiah smiles widely as he watches the paper burn and begins, manically, to laugh. But then, after a moment, his laughter pitches higher, higher, and to Dora's horror she realises that Hezekiah is not laughing any more.

He is screaming.

The flames travel up his arm with unnatural speed. The fire catches to his chest, snakes down his legs. In desperation Hezekiah pulls at his shirt but his hands are engulfed in fire and he cannot find purchase. He seems to realise the futility of it, tries to run, but his wounded leg prevents him and when he collapses hard onto his knees Dora is unable to look away.

Paralysed, she watches. Hezekiah's skin has blistered, and the smell of burning flesh is so strong Dora starts to gag. The smoke begins to rise from him in plumes and as the flames lick his face Hezekiah holds a scorched and trembling hand out to her. For one spun-out second their eyes meet, but then the flames overwhelm him completely and Hezekiah screams wildly, over and over, a flailing bank of fire.

Behind her Dora hears Lottie's muffled cries. Coming to herself Dora turns from the horrific sight of him and rushes to the housekeeper, pulls down the gag.

'Missum!'

'Shush, Lottie, I know. We need to get away.'

'No,' she gasps as Dora looses the ties at her feet. 'Your young man. He's in the safe!'

Dora stares. Behind her, Hezekiah has stopped screaming. There is only the sharp spit and crack of flame, the scent of burnt flesh and smoke.

'What do you mean?'

'There's no time to explain!' Lottie cries. '*Look.*'

And Dora looks. The wooden banister has caught on fire.

'*Theé mou* . . .' Fingers shaking, Dora unties the twine at Lottie's wrists. 'The key, Lottie! Where is the key?'

'Still in the lock!'

Heart in her mouth Dora rushes to the Bramah safe, twists the key, and Edward falls out, collapsing into her arms.

'Edward, I'm sorry! I didn't know, I—'

Dora tries to take his weight but he is too heavy, she cannot manage it alone.

'Lottie!' Dora shouts over the roar of flames, but Lottie is already on Edward's other side.

'I have him,' she huffs, and between them Edward stirs.

'Dora . . .'

'Edward, wake up,' Dora urges as she and Lottie manoeuvre him past the pithos, and she is relieved to see him reach out, use the pithos itself to pull himself up.

At the basement stairs the flames threaten to set them alight but somehow – *somehow* – they manage to break free of them and up the steps they go, stumble out through the shop, and together they fall into Ludgate Street, gasping into the cool morning air.

# CHAPTER
# FORTY-EIGHT

They sit against the wall of a cobbler's and watch as six men carry Hezekiah's body out of the shop. The men buckle under the charred heft of him, and Dora turns her face into the cushion of Edward's shoulder.

He brings her knuckles to his, kissing them. With his other hand Edward touches the tender wound on the back of his head. When he lowers his hand again his fingers are crusted with blood.

'Let me see that,' Lottie murmurs beside him, and he lets her push his head forward to prod at his skull. Her touch is neither rough nor gentle – somewhere in between – but she does not hurt, and with a loud *tsk* she releases him.

'The blood makes it seem worse than it is,' she says. 'It's a small cut, will heal well enough. Might have a nasty bump for a few days.'

He manages a smile. 'Thank you, Lottie.'

Lottie hesitates. Edward looks at the housekeeper's bruised face, her split lip, the red mark the gag has left. 'Will you be all right?'

'I'll be fine, sir.' She rubs a thumb under her nose. 'I'll find somewhere. I know places to go.'

Dora lifts her head. 'No, Lottie, you can't.'

Lottie looks away. 'You needn't concern yourself with me, missum.'

389

Dora looks at Edward. He squeezes her hand, understands what she does not ask.

'You'll come to Mr Ashmole's, with us. At least for tonight,' he adds before she can object, and Lottie breathes out, long and slow.

'I'll get my things, then. If you're sure.'

'Is it really safe to go in?' Dora asks.

The men who brought Hezekiah out were the ones who had stopped the fire before it could get any further. Though it burnt the basement stairs black the fire did not destroy them, somehow did not make it past the basement doors.

'It's safe,' Edward says.

Dora and Lottie stare at each other, then the housekeeper nods, ambles across the street, disappears into the shop, and Dora looks after her, a troubled expression creasing her forehead.

'What is it?' Edward asks.

She does not answer at first.

'A miracle, don't you think, that the fire did not take the shop.'

'You know I don't believe that.'

'No,' she says, and Dora rests her head against his shoulder again.

Just then a carriage clatters past, the cobbles making its wheels rattle loudly on their springs. Edward glances up. Stares.

'Dora, did you see?'

But the carriage is already away, and Dora is yawning into her free hand.

'See what, Edward?'

'An old man. Through the window.'

Dora watches Edward stare after the carriage, touches his arm to bring him back.

'Edward, what is it?'

He hesitates. 'Do you ever remember knowing, or your parents knowing, an old man with a long white beard and blue eyes? Strikingly blue?'

Dora frowns. Something on her face tells him that this man sounds familiar to her, but then she sighs and shakes her head.

'I have never known anyone like that. Not personally, at any rate. Perhaps my parents did, but . . .' She looks at him carefully. 'You told me, when we first met, that you had spoken with a gentleman who said he knew me.'

'Yes.'

'Is that man who you mean?'

'Yes.'

'I thought as much.'

He puts his arms around her, holds her close. They sit that way for some time. Edward breathes in the scent of smoke on her hair.

'I want to know what he was trying to find,' she says quietly against his chest.

'Dora,' he tries, but she is already pulling away from him, is standing, leading him by the hand across the street, into the shop.

'I need to know, Edward.'

Inside she releases him. She turns away, walks with purpose down the shop floor and Edward follows her, past the upturned floorboards, up to the basement doors.

'Be careful,' he warns.

'It's safe,' Dora replies, stepping onto the first step. 'You said so yourself.'

Edward cannot argue with that but he keeps close behind her all the same, holds his hand out in case she takes a fall, but the stairs hold them, and at the bottom they look around.

The basement walls are completely blackened. The desk is ash and the Bramah safe – Edward shudders at the sight of it – is covered with patches of soot. But somehow the candles still burn in their sconces, and the pithos . . .

It is unmarked.

Just as Edward knew it would be.

Dora stares at it but she makes no comment, seems also to have accepted that the pithos has an uncanny ability to remain indestructible.

She turns away.

'Here, Edward,' she says, beckoning him to the ruined wall where a pickaxe lies charred against the rubble.

'Hezekiah was trying to break through. Why?'

Edward eyes the wall warily. 'Because, I suppose, there was something beyond it he wanted.'

Dora nods. 'He said he overheard my parents speak of a fortune, but that they did not say where it was. What if they hid it right under his nose?'

Edward feels the thrill of it spindle up his spine. 'A hidden room.'

'A hidden room,' she echoes. 'But he couldn't get in.'

'Why not?'

'Why not, indeed. Come on, help me.'

'Help you?'

But she is running her hands over the wall – the parts still intact at least – and suddenly he understands.

'My mother would not have made this so difficult. Hezekiah tried to break through because he did not have the means to open it the proper way.'

Edward joins her at the wall. 'So I'm looking for a lock?'

'Hmm. A lock, yes, but a standard one would have been too obvious. No, it's something else . . .'

Edward runs his fingers along the pitted wall – still warm – leaving trails in the soot. He stops. Then he begins to sweep his hand over it, tries to clear as much soot as he can and Dora watches him, her breath hitching in excitement.

'Yes,' she whispers, 'keep going,' and he does, but after a few minutes he begins to lose momentum. Surely all he is doing is moving the soot around?

But then . . .

'Edward!'

Dora is looking at a section of wall that comes level with his knees. Together they bend. Together, they see what appears to be a small oval recess in the stone.

'What is it?'

Dora reaches out a finger. Then, very slowly, she presses her fingertip into the nook, brings it away again.

There, on the pad of her finger, is the black outline of a face.

The face of a bearded man.

'Impossible,' Edward breathes.

Dora looks at him. She is smiling. It is, he thinks, the first time he has ever seen her truly smile.

'Do you know who this is?'

'The old man,' he says, as if there can be no other answer.

'Edward. It is *Zeus*!'

He blinks at her. 'I don't understand.'

'It's a key!' At his blank expression she gets to her feet. 'Look,' she says, striding over to the Bramah safe. She pulls out the key from its lock, brings it back for him to see.

'My parents had this safe installed years ago. It's fireproof and self-locking, so they knew that anything they put in there would be protected. The key to it is gold and black. Hezekiah asked me about a gold-and-black key. This key, I thought,' she says, holding it up. Edward looks at it. Gold, filigree detailing on the stem, a revolving oval jet disc. 'And I bet anything that this is the key Hezekiah tried.

But it didn't work. He tried the wrong one! He didn't realise, did he, that there were two. He must have been trying to access the chamber from above but when he saw it was sealed in stone—'

'He tried to break his way through.'

'Exactly.'

'All right,' Edward says. 'So where is this second key?'

Dora immediately turns away and disappears up the stairs.

'Where are you going?' he shouts after her. 'Be careful!'

'I found it,' she is saying from above, '*weeks* ago, when I was look-ing for some of my father's old wares! A gold-and-black key, a key I used to play with as a little girl. I didn't remember at first, I couldn't think clearly, couldn't understand what my uncle meant . . .'

He hears frantic jangling, the sounds of objects rolling across the floor, and then she reappears, almost skips down the stairs, and Edward watches her with his heart in his mouth.

'For God's sake, Dora,' Edward groans, 'be care—'

She is holding out her hand.

In her palm is a key, almost identical to the safe key clutched in her other hand. The only difference . . . He takes a deep breath.

Imprinted in the jet is the face of a bearded man.

The face of Zeus himself.

It fits perfectly.

There is a click, a series of whirrs, the heavy scrape of pulleys and weights. And then a door – large, two feet thick – slides back and then across, a deep rumble against stone.

Dora holds the candelabrum high, its candles flickering brightly.

She steps forward and Edward follows, can scarce believe what he sees.

The chamber is filled to the brim with antiquities.

There are rows upon rows of ancient pottery, urns and amphorae of all shapes and sizes, hundreds of plates decorated in red and white and black. Minoan, Mycenaean. There are marble statues, glass chalices, porcelain busts, terracotta figurines. All the riches one could dream of, kept safe just for Dora, in this one hidden room.

'Merciful heaven,' Dora whispers. Her voice cracks. 'How can this be? Is this really all mine?'

Edward shakes his head in wonderment. 'They thought of you to the very end.'

Beside him, Dora takes a deep shaking breath.

'Shall we?' he says, taking her hand.

And together, as one, they step inside.

London
June 1799

*Dear Mr Lawrence,*

    *As Director of The Society of Antiquaries, I am desired by the President, to return you their Thanks for your Communication of* A Studie of a Grecian Pithos *on Friday evening last 14th. Another paper in addition to the one initially agreed upon was not expected and though the subject matter, in parts, digresses into speculative fancy, I am pleased to inform you that this paper, as well as your most excellent accompanying paper titled* Forgeries and Black-Market Custom within the Antiquity Trade, *has been accepted, and therefore your entrance to the Society has been successful, with votes a most healthy 30 to 5, and wish to congratulate you on your election to the Society as a new and respected member of our ranks.*

    *The accompanying drawings in relation to the subject of your first paper are particularly impressive. We encourage your continued partnership with your fiancée Miss Pandora Blake for all future works, and look forward to seeing what you will contribute to the Society in the coming years. The Society think themselves much obliged to all who assist in promoting the useful purpose of advancing Science, for which they are incorporated,    and I am*

           *Sir*

        *With much Respect*
                *Your most Obedient humble Servt.*

*Somerset Place*                                *Richard Gough*
*19th June 1799*

# Blake and Lawrence
## Emporium for Respectable Antiquities

### Ludgate Street,
### London,

Purveyors of Fine Art, Furniture and Ornaments, providing a
Scholastic Sanctuary for the Learned and Curious. A small but
Finely Stocked Museum on site, with Most Impressive Centrepiece.
Binding and Finishing of Studies Available on Request.
Excavations Offered by Commission to Climates At Home and
Abroad. Bespoke Decorations available on Loan for all
Entertainment Needs.

**For the Discerning Lady and Gentleman,**

Elegant Jewellery Designs in the Manner of Antiquities, wrought
in Gold & Silver with precious Gems, Marcasite and Paste, under
the Esteemed Patronage of Lady Isabelle Latimer. Items Available
for Composition by the Honourable Clements & Co.

**Please Ring the Bell**

# AUTHOR'S NOTE

*Pandora* started off as a fleeting idea which had no link in its inception to any historic event. I knew I wanted to write a piece of fiction set in my favourite period of history, the Georgian era. I knew I wanted to have a jewellery designer as my heroine, and Hermes the magpie came to life fully formed in my mind. But I also knew I wanted to explore the myth of Pandora's Box, for no other reason than that it felt like a good idea at the time.

The notion that Pandora's Box was not, in fact, an actual box as the Dutch philosopher Erasmus claimed was food for thought, and so I set to researching what it might have been instead. Results threw up the suggestion of a jar, a vase, a pithos – ultimately, I was looking at Grecian pottery. But how to fit Grecian pottery into a novel set in Georgian London?

I have always worked best using a historical event as an anchor, and so I began to look for one which would link my initial ideas. Imagine my elation when I came across a section of a letter written by an unnamed eyewitness, featured in Volume 1 of the British periodical *Naval News*, dated December 1798. It detailed the sinking of HMS *Colossus*, a naval warship which had been carrying a large part of the diplomat William Hamilton's treasured collection of Greek pottery on board. An extract of the letter can be viewed on my website www.susanstokeschapman.com.

For Dora's knowledge of jewellery I found *Georgian Jewellery 1714–1830* by Ginny Redington and Olivia Collings invaluable. For the myth of Pandora, I am indebted to Stephen Fry's *Mythos*, and *Pandora's Box: The Changing Aspects of a Mythical Symbol* by Dora and Erwin Panofsky. For recreating Georgian London I referred extensively to *The Secret History of Georgian London* by Dan Cruickshank, *Georgian London: Into the Streets* by Lucy Inglis and *Dr Johnson's London* by Liza Picard. When writing Edward's bookbinding scenes I referred to the Guild of Theophilus and their brilliant online resources.

The Society of Antiquaries is still a thriving establishment today and *Visions of Antiquity: The Society of Antiquaries of London 1707–2007*, published directly by the Society, considerably aided my research. Other useful sources included *A History of the Society of Antiquaries* by Joan Evans, *Antiquaries: The Discovery of the Past in Eighteenth-Century Britain* by Rosemary Sweet, and the essays compiled within *London and the Emergence of a European Art Market, 1780–1820*, edited by Susanna Avery-Quash and Christian Huemer.

However, as is inevitable with historical fiction, I have taken liberties with certain facts. Edward would not have been able to make a living from writing papers for the Society alone, nor would he have been able to pay Dora for the sketches she drew for him; while the Society did employ and pay draughtsmen to produce detailed drawings of objects for publication, they did not pay its Fellows for producing papers, nor did they fund excavations until many years later. As for dating archaeological finds, eighteenth-century antiquarians would have relied on relative dating based mainly on the typology of an object, i.e. its shape, style, decoration, etc. (which is the method Edward used when cataloguing the Blake collection). Relative dating does include other techniques; the most commonly used is soil stratigraphy analysis. The first practical large-scale application of stratigraphy was by geologist William Smith in the 1790s and early 1800s, but stratigraphic excavation didn't become a standard part of archaeological study until the 1920s. It is unlikely stratigraphic analysis would have been carried out by members of the Society or their counterparts in the 1790s but because it is not impossible, I chose to apply the methods here. Further, Richard Gough only served as director of the Society of Antiquaries from 1771 to 1791. However, Gough's sentiments favouring British antiquarianism over the glorified and overdone Mediterranean were necessary for Edward's story arc and so I decided to keep Gough in place for this reason. I should also note that Hamilton and his wife Emma (along with her lover Horatio Nelson) did not return to England from Italy until 1801, but I plead creative licence by bringing their return forward to match the narrative's timeline.

A smaller liberty came in the form of Matthew Coombe's recovery of the crate from the seabed at the beginning of the novel. In the late eighteenth century, German mechanic Karl Heinrich Klingert created a device which was the first to be called a 'diving suit'. This suit consisted of a jacket and trousers made of waterproof leather, a helmet with a porthole, and a metal front. It was linked to a turret with an air reservoir, and a lantern which worked underwater. Klingert's designs, however, were never put into practice despite their detailed descriptions published in two of his books in 1797 and 1822 respectively. An account of the diving suit can be found in *Description of a Diving Machine*, an excellent publication incorporating both of Klingert's works, printed in 2002 by the Historical Diving Society.

# ACKNOWLEDGEMENTS

At least 75,000 words of this novel were written during the 2020 Covid pandemic. While this period was extremely dark for many of us, it did allow me the free time many writers crave to put pen to page and so in that sense I am thankful for those strange and often, for me, very lonely months. It taught me discipline of a different kind – I wrote differently, I researched differently, and I do wonder if *Pandora* would have become the novel it has if not for those differences. Even so, I could not have written any of it without the support of many and so I list them here, as best I'm able, though for anyone I have missed I can only apologise and blame a rather fraught and hectic mind after such a whirlwind publication journey.

Thanks to Michael Fardell at the Historical Diving Society for his insight into shipwreck salvage during the early stages of my research, and to Kate Bagnall and Dunia Garcia-Ontiveros of the Society of Antiquaries for answering my many difficult questions regarding more particular Society procedures.

My early-snippet readers William Gallagher, Mike Jennings and the members of my Leamington Writers' Group, who all helped me gauge whether to continue or not, as well as my superb betas Hayley Clarke, Heddwen Creaney, Sarah Penner and Carly Stevenson for their incredibly helpful comments on the first draft which helped me shape the second.

Thanks also to Elizabeth Macneal for being unfailingly patient and generous when I asked for advice, as well as Jonathan Davidson, Emma Boniwell and Olivia Chapman at Writing West Midlands for their continued encouragement and guidance.

To the judges of both the Lucy Cavendish Fiction Prize and the Bath Novel Award for seeing the potential in *Pandora* – I feel so grateful for the support I received and without those accolades I have no doubt Dora and Edward's story would have taken far longer to find the perfect home.

My wonderful agent Juliet Mushens, without whose unmitigated enthusiasm, sharp eye and professional verve, none of this would have even been possible. For everything you have done for me and for all you will do for me in the future you have my sincerest gratitude, and I shall continue to be overwhelmed by it all. How lucky I am to have you in my corner.

My equally wonderful editor Liz Foley, who often seemed to understand the nuances of the novel far better than I did and therefore made it far better than I could have done if left to my own devices. My thanks as well to Mikaela Pedlow and Mary Chamberlain for their eagle eyes, Suzanne Dean for designing the wonderful Georgian-styled interior artwork that suits the novel so beautifully, and the rest of the amazing team at Harvill Secker and Vintage for turning *Pandora* into a physical book with such a phenomenal marketing campaign behind it that surpassed everything I could have hoped for. Thank you also to Micaela Alcaino for creating such a stunning jacket. What a brilliant way to launch a debut into the world.

My deepest thanks go to Barry Lambe who encouraged me from the get-go and pushed me whenever I started to flag, and to Jean

Grant, a truly lovely lady whose passion for antiquities partly inspired the idea, and who I am sad to say will never be able to read the novel I dedicated to her.

Richard, always.

And finally my mum Sally, who never (ever) failed to believe.